THE RULE BREAKERS

Also by Preeti Shenoy

The Secret Wish List
The One You Cannot Have
It's All in the Planets
It Happens For a Reason
Why We Love the Way We Do
A Hundred Little Flames
The Magic Mindset
A Place Called Home

THE RULE BREAKERS

PREETI SHENOY

HarperCollins *Publishers* India

First published in 2018

This edition published in India by HarperCollins *Publishers* in 2022
4th Floor, Tower A, Building No. 10, Phase II, DLF Cyber City,
Gurugram, Haryana – 122002
www.harpercollins.co.in

4 6 8 10 9 7 5 3

P-ISBN: 978-93-5629-303-8
E-ISBN: 978-93-5629-308-3

This is a work of fiction and all characters and incidents described in this book are the product of the author's imagination. Any resemblance to actual persons, living or dead, is entirely coincidental.

Typeset in Sabon by SÜRYA, New Delhi

Printed and bound at
Thomson Press (India) Ltd

MIX
Paper from
responsible sources
FSC® C010615

This book is produced from independently certified FSC® paper
to ensure responsible forest management.

For my daughter Purvi, who lives life by her own rules.

The legal age for marriage in India is eighteen for women and twenty-one for men.

In 2001, 94 per cent of all women in the country were married by the time they were twenty-five years old. Furthermore, 44 per cent of these women got married when they were under the age of eighteen.

Excerpts from a few letters written in 1995.

I don't have the strength to fight anymore.
I don't even know when the days begin and end. These are my study holidays and I am supposed to study. But that's just not happening.
The little free time I get, I sit in front of my books—but nothing I read enters my head.
Back in Joshimath, I was a topper. I had a life.
Here, there is nothing. All I see is endless days merging into one another. I have no idea where one begins and the other ends. This is a meaningless existence.
I feel so alone.
I feel so betrayed by my own parents.
I feel trapped.
I cannot fight anymore.
I am a coward.

You are just twenty. You have a whole life ahead of you.

Part One
THE RULES

Rules and responsibilities: these are the ties that bind us. We do what we do, because of who we are. If we did otherwise, we would not be ourselves.

– Neil Gaiman,
The Sandman: Book of Dreams

Chapter 1

September 1995
Joshimath

There are two kinds of people in this world—the ones who follow the rules and the ones who do not think twice about breaking them. It is as though there is an invisible line separating the rule breakers from the rule followers. To cross over to the other side is blasphemy, a disaster of epic proportions.

But, sometimes, the lines blur. The rule followers are then thrown into a tizzy. They do not have the boundaries which keep them safe. They are unsure of what to do, and how to behave. They go through the motions of life, hoping that they haven't broken any rules. But that niggling voice in their head refuses to shut up.

For Veda, that voice was booming inside her head that morning. And the fact that her sister Vidya had caught on to it was not helping.

Veda was definitely a rule follower. Her parents would describe her as 'sweet, charming and obedient'. Their father, Rajinder, wasn't exactly a mild-tempered man. With four daughters and a son to look after, he ran his house with the precision of a military sergeant. Their pliant mother, Kamala, just went along with whatever their father decided.

Veda descended the few steps that led to the rose garden in front of her house and inhaled the cool mountain air. She could hear the wind whistling along the bare slopes. The tall deodar and fir trees stood like soldiers behind the lone house perched atop the hill. In the distance, the Garhwal range of the Himalayas glistened like a crown. Veda liked this time of the year, before Badrinath town closed in November and re-opened only in April or so.

It was then that Joshimath transformed from a sleepy mountain town to a bustling tourist centre, as it was the winter abode of the presiding deity of Badrinath. Joshimath had a rich history, as Adi Shankaracharya, an Indian philosopher and saint, had established a monastery there in the eighth century, named Jyotirmath. But Veda rarely visited that spot. To her, it was all part of ancient history. It was only when relatives from other cities came to stay with them, and they had to take them around, that Veda even thought about it. For her, Joshimath was just a small, nondescript, mountainous town, which did not afford her too many opportunities to pursue her dreams.

Veda went into their little step garden, carved out into the mountain, whenever she wanted to think. Today, she definitely had to. The voice at the back of her mind was not allowing her to focus on her course work.

From where she stood, she could see buses and cars making their way up the hill, slowly navigating the hairpin bends. They looked like toy cars and toy buses. Veda wondered where these people were coming from, how their cities looked, and what their lives were like. She had never travelled beyond Dehradun, except for one trip to Delhi when she was a child. She did not have any distinct memories of it, and she longed to visit other cities. She gazed at a lone eagle that flew high overhead and perched on a treetop.

'Dreaming of Suraj again?' Veda felt a sharp tap on her head. She turned around to see her sister Vidya grinning.

'Ouch! That hurt, *pagli*,' she said, as she rubbed her head.

'Don't change the topic. I saw him looking at you when we visited the Narsingh temple.'

'He wasn't looking at me,' Veda quickly denied it, even as she felt her cheeks turning red at the mention of Suraj's name.

'Oh, he so was! He just couldn't take his eyes off you. Look at you! Oh, good lord, you are blushing!' Vidya continued relentlessly, as she teased her sister.

'Who is blushing? Who, who? What are you talking about?' asked Vandana, as she climbed down the steps carrying a large bowl of boiled peanuts garnished with chopped onions and finely sliced green chillies.

'Nobody, nothing,' said Veda and Vidya together.

'Tell me, didi! I am not ten years old like Vaishali. I am thirteen!'

'Thirteen is not old enough,' said Vidya, as she helped herself to the peanuts.

'Didi—tell her I am old enough! Just because she is older than me by three years, it doesn't mean she has to leave me out,' Vandana turned to Veda, her eyes pleading, as she extended the peanuts to her.

'Almost four years; I will be seventeen soon,' Vidya corrected her.

Veda helped herself to a handful of peanuts and pretended to be a judge passing a sentence. 'Order, order! This court rules that the legal age for knowing all about your older sisters' conversations is fifteen.'

'So unfair! I object. I shall not give you any peanuts,' said Vandana.

'Pay in peanuts and you will attract only the monkeys,' quipped Vidya.

All three sisters laughed. Veda and Vidya glanced at each other, relieved that Vandana had not pursued it further.

The two older sisters didn't always share things with Vandana or Vaishali. As far as they were concerned, Vandana and Vaishali, and their brother Animesh who was only seven, were just babies. The two older sisters looked after the younger siblings: they supervised their homework, helped them with the difficult subjects, combed their hair, and ensured that their school uniforms were kept washed and ironed the previous day. In short, they took over most of the childcare duties from their mother.

Their mother was a frail woman, mostly because she neglected her diet and health. Giving birth to five children had taken a toll on her. She was a passive woman, showing no interest in anything, going through the motions of daily life as a matter of routine. It seemed like she had resigned from life itself. She was meek and unassertive and went along with everything that her husband said.

The sisters were soon joined by their two other siblings, Animesh and Vaishali.

'Didi, want to play badminton?' Animesh asked, as they came down the steps.

The terrain was largely hilly, but there was a small flat patch of land, about 20' x 15', which served as a makeshift playground, a badminton court, a volleyball court as well as a hopscotch ground. Their father, Rajinder, hadn't wanted to waste that land, and asked for vegetables to be planted there. But Rudra kaka, their gardener, who lived in the outhouse, had convinced him to leave it the way it was.

'*Sahib*, nothing will grow there. It's all rocky underneath. Let the children play. There is no playground anywhere nearby,' he had pointed out.

Rudra kaka tended to the menial jobs around the house, like carving out graduated terrace steps in the mountains around the house, where he planted *shalgam, seb, methi, palak*, and anything else that he could cultivate. His wife, Paro didi, worked as their house-help, assisting in all the cooking, cleaning and numerous other chores that invariably had to be done in a household with five children. They had lived in the outhouse ever since Rajinder had bought the land, many years ago. He had got it cheap, and he had constructed a modest three-bedroom house on the land. Over the years, his family had grown, but he had not expanded his house.

'This is all I can afford on my block development officer's salary. Besides, don't forget, we have four girls to marry off,' he would proclaim from time to time, whenever well-meaning relatives advised him to build another room.

'I don't feel like playing badminton right now,' said Vidya.

'I will play with you, but you will have to fetch the shuttlecock if you miss it and it tumbles down,' Veda made her terms clear.

Animesh readily agreed. His level of skill in badminton was not as high as that of Veda and Vidya, who had years of practice. If he missed returning a shot, the shuttlecock often fell to the lower level, and he had to climb down a few steep, rocky steps, go around the vegetable patch, retrieve the shuttlecock, and climb back up again, to reach the court.

Veda partnered up with Animesh against Vandana and Vaishali. Animesh would miss returning a shot every now and then, and he would uncomplainingly fetch the shuttlecock each time. After the eighth time, Vandana and Vaishali began to feel sorry for him, and they volunteered to get the shuttlecock.

When they got tired of playing badminton, the five siblings sat on the rocky steps and talked until it was time to go inside for dinner. They talked about cities, and Veda told them how she wanted to escape from Joshimath, get a job as a lecturer in a college and work in a big city.

'But you know Papa will never agree to that,' said Vidya.

'Well, you never know. He may change his mind. I intend to top the college this year too. And then I will get my lecturer to talk to him. She was encouraging me to do my Master's, and she said she would talk to Papa,' Veda said.

She had heard her parents tell the countless relatives in their circle that they were worried about getting four girls married off. Veda always brushed it aside, thinking that if she studied hard enough, her father would be proud of her and not think only about her marriage.

The praise never came. Year after year, as far back as Veda could recall, she had only received the same unenthusiastic response. He would glance cursorily at her perfect scores, say, 'Hmmm...', and then sign the report card.

Vidya, Vandana and Vaishali got the same treatment, even though their academic performance was not as good as Veda's. There were no remarks made, no praise, no applause. It was mostly indifference, and the girls learnt to make do with it. As soon as Vidya realised that neither her father nor her mother cared about her grades, she stopped trying to make an effort. Though Veda tried to instil in her the importance of performing well academically.

'What difference does it make? It does not matter to them,' Vidya shrugged.

'Does it not matter to you?' Veda asked.

'Didi! There are other things in life besides books. Everyone is not a bookworm like you. What is that book you are reading? The one about lots of sisters?'

'*Little Women* or *Pride and Prejudice*?' Veda asked.

'I don't know! What I mean is, how does it matter? What do you get for scoring good marks in the exams? Nothing!' said Vidya.

Veda did not agree. Her response to her father's indifference was to study even harder. She borrowed all the books that she could from her school and college libraries and read them back to back. She loved reading the English classics, adventure stories, romances, historical fiction—anything she could lay her hands on. Vidya, on the other hand, preferred chatting with her classmates, discussing the latest Bollywood movies, hairstyles and cosmetics.

Veda was glad that she had at least managed to get both Vaishali and Vandana interested in books. She maintained a meticulous record of what they read. Many a time, she would read to both of them, as well as to Animesh, before bedtime. She would dramatise the stories and change her voice and diction to suit the characters.

'Didi, it is so much fun when you read us these stories,' said Animesh.

'I agree. I like listening to you more than reading,' remarked Vidya, who always joined in the bedtime story sessions. At times, in the evenings, when it was too windy to play badminton, the children would enact scenes from the books that Veda read to them. Vidya would improvise, creating costumes from their mother's sarees, their own dupattas and other things lying around the house. There would be cardboard crowns that Vidya made with gold foil, the 'palace' would be recreated with sarees tied around trees, and sticks the children gathered from the mountains would become swords. They had hours of fun with their pretend games.

When the siblings put up performances, their mother, Rudra kaka and Paro didi were forced to be the audience. Animesh would create 'tickets' with pages torn from his 'rough notebook' from school—the only book he was allowed to tear out pages from—and distribute them for 'sale' before each performance. Their father stayed away from all the 'nonsense', as he termed it. His chief form of entertainment was television, and as soon as he returned from work, he would sit in front of the TV and watch sports or news till it was bedtime. Even his meal was served to him in front of the television. If Animesh or anyone else tried to join him, they would be reprimanded and sent off to study. The children quickly learnt to leave him alone. Kamala rarely got to watch television, but she never complained. She was happy to serve meals to her husband as he relaxed.

None of the girls minded that Animesh was treated differently by their parents. He was undoubtedly their favourite child. Being the baby of the family, he was pampered by his sisters as well as by their parents. While their father didn't much care about the academic performance of the girls, he monitored his son's progress at school like a hawk watching its prey. If his grades slipped, he immediately summoned Veda.

'Didn't you help your brother? What is the use of your getting high marks? You have to ultimately get married and go away. He has to earn,' her father would reprimand her.

Veda would murmur that she had done her best and that Animesh had not practised enough, even though she had assigned him work.

'You four girls—all of you have to see that he does his studies. Now, your mother is just a tenth class fail. She cannot help with his studies. You must remember that. What is the use of educating all of you? Eh?' he would ask.

'Why can't I get a job and work, Papa? Why should only Animesh have that privilege?' Veda wanted to ask. But she had been taught by her mother to never talk back to her elders, especially to her father. It was disrespectful, she was told. So she and her sisters would silently listen to her father's rants.

Later that evening, Veda read to her younger siblings and put them to bed. After the others slept, Vidya and she often talked late into the night.

'Didi, I wasn't joking about Suraj. I noticed him staring at you at the temple,' Vidya said.

The niggling voice that had been bothering Veda returned.

'Hmm. I don't know. He should be focusing on his studies, not following us around,' Veda replied. She too had noticed Suraj, who was in the same college as her. Secretly, she was flattered that he had noticed her. She was beginning to develop a crush on him. That made her uncomfortable. So she had pretended to ignore him.

'Didi—don't you feel anything for him? How can you be so immersed in your books? Tell me, don't the heroines in your books fall in love?' Vidya persisted.

'Only heroines in books and movies can afford to do all that. Come on, you know my goals, and you know our situation at home. I just want to top my college. I don't have time for all this.' Veda was resolute. She did not want to think about Suraj. If their father found out, there would be a heavy price to pay.

'Sometimes, I think you are an old woman, didi,' said Vidya.

'And what are you, then? The epitome of the follies of youth?' retorted Veda.

'What? Epitome of what? I didn't get you.'

'Read some books, improve your vocabulary, and then you will get me,' Veda snapped.

'I will tell Suraj that you secretly love him, but you are too shy to admit it. Then we will see how your bookish knowledge helps you,' retorted Vidya.

'What? Vidya! Don't do any such thing, okay? Promise me you won't? You will unnecessarily cause problems,' Veda said, terrified. Her sister was perfectly capable of doing something that crazy.

'You do like him then. Confess!' laughed Vidya.

'No, I don't!'

'Then why do you get agitated when I tease you?'

'Because it simply isn't true! And I don't want you going around spreading false tales.' Veda was angry now.

'Didi, it's just light-hearted fun. Don't get mad at me,' Vidya said.

Veda was silent.

'Alright didi, I am sorry. I won't say anything to Suraj, and I won't tease you, okay?'

'Hmm. Okay. Now go to sleep.'

The two sisters went to bed after that. But Veda couldn't help wondering if there was a grain of truth to what Vidya had said. Did she truly not know how to have fun? Was she a boring person?

Veda had a lot of questions running through her head and she fell asleep thinking about whether Vidya was right.

At college the next day, Veda could hardly focus on the lecture, which was on Milton and the neo-classical age. The lecturer had a voice that droned on pleasantly, and it was easy to lose focus, even when you were alert. Twice she caught herself getting lost in thought, and not being able to recall what the lecturer had been talking about.

'What are the three forms of appeal? Who can tell me?' the lecturer asked. Veda had no clue.

She was usually the first to raise her hand when the lecturer asked a question. Today, she found herself lowering her eyes and looking at the textbook, hoping she wouldn't be called on to answer. Fortunately for her, she wasn't. Somebody else answered the question and Veda heaved a sigh of relief.

At recess, one of her friends, Rekha, whom she usually hung out with, asked her what the matter was.

'Eh? Nothing. Nothing is the matter, why?' asked Veda.

'You seem so lost today.'

'If I ask you something, can I trust you to answer me honestly, Rekha?'

'Have I ever been anything but honest with you? Tell me,' said Rekha.

'Am I a boring person?' asked Veda, as she shifted her weight from one foot to the other, feeling awkward and self-conscious.

'Hmmmm, let me see, boring? What do you mean by boring?' Rekha asked, frowning.

Veda was disappointed that Rekha had not rushed to assuage her feelings. Couldn't Rekha just assure her that she wasn't boring? Veda saw that Rekha was thinking about the question, which meant that she probably found her boring, but was too polite to say it. Or perhaps she was wondering how to phrase it. In that instant, Veda regretted even bringing it up. But it was too late—the words were already out there.

'Umm. Nothing. Just forget I asked,' she said.

'Boring? You definitely aren't boring. I find you very interesting,' said a deep male voice behind her.

Startled, Veda turned around and found herself looking at Suraj.

He was almost six feet tall, and she had to look up to meet his gaze. His brown eyes looked straight into hers, unwavering. His dark straight hair, though neatly combed, fell across his forehead, and he was clean shaven. He looked much older than everybody else in their class. Often, his striking looks were what people first noticed about him. He had earned a reputation among the college students as a heart-throb, someone whom the ladies chased. Veda knew that he had transferred to Joshimath from Bombay, and that he was living with his grandparents. Although why anyone would leave a glamorous city like Bombay to study in a small town like Joshimath was beyond her.

Rekha smiled at him and said, 'How do you know whether she is interesting or boring? You have never even spoken to her.'

'I am speaking to her, now,' replied Suraj, his eyes not leaving Veda's.

His gaze made Veda uncomfortable. She fiddled with her dupatta, adjusting it. She took a deep breath, pulled back her shoulders, stood up straighter and looked back into his eyes.

'So? What do you want?' she asked, her tone confrontational.

She did not like that he had walked up behind them and overheard their conversation.

'I just want to have a cup of tea with you. After class, in the canteen?' he asked, his eyes hopeful.

He had a dazzling smile and he disarmed her with it. She was taken aback because she did not expect to be mollified this easily, and also because she could see that it was a genuine, sincere and 'I-want-to-get-to-know-you-better-because-you-fascinate-me' kind of a smile. Up until now, she had dismissed him as nothing more than a good-looking guy, and perhaps even a flirt. But the way he was looking at her now, almost afraid of being rejected, stirred something in her.

'Ummm, let me think about it,' she said, not wanting to agree at once.

'I will be waiting. See you there after class,' he said, as he walked away.

When he went out of earshot, Rekha pounced on her.

'Suraj has a thing for you! He has the choice of any girl he wants, and he picks the class nerd. Who would have thought! He wants to have tea with *you*. Why didn't you say yes at once?'

With that, all the insecurities that Veda had felt earlier came right back and danced around in her head.

'What do you mean "class nerd"?' she asked, glancing sideways to see if Suraj was gone, or hiding behind the pillars. Veda knew she wasn't stylish like the other girls at college. She always wore well-fitted, plain salwar kameezes, which the local tailor stitched. She never ever forgot her dupatta. The necklines were always modest, and other than mixing and matching kurtas and salwars, her style of dressing was always the same. She rarely even changed her hairstyle—she wore it in a centre parting and a ponytail—and Veda knew most people would describe her as 'plain and simple'. Now here was Rekha, adding to that, terming her the 'class nerd'. Is that what others thought of her?

'*Arey baba*, it's just an expression. Don't think so much. Just go have coffee with him. Wait till the other girls hear about this,' said Rekha.

'Rekha, please don't mention it to the others. Please...'

'Why? Why are you so scared? You will only go up a few notches in their eyes, now that you have been asked out by none other than Suraj himself.'

'Shhh! If my father comes to know of this, he is going to be furious.'

'Don't worry so much about your father! He isn't hovering around here, in an invisible form, to keep watch on you. At least in college, relax a bit, Veda, and have fun,' said Rekha.

The rest of that day, Veda was distracted, wondering what Suraj could possibly see in her. Why did he want to meet her alone? She decided that she would go, just this one time, to find out what he wanted. If he asked her out again, she would refuse.

After college got over, nudged by Rekha, Veda hesitantly made her way to the canteen. Her eyes quickly scanned the place.

Suraj was seated facing the door, so he could spot her as soon as she entered. He waved when he saw her, his eyes lighting up. She nodded in acknowledgement and made her way towards him.

'Hi, thank you for accepting my invitation,' he said. 'What will you have, other than tea? Can I get some pakoras?'

'Umm, no. Just tea is fine,' said Veda.

'*Samosas,* then? I am kind of hungry.'

'Alright, suit yourself. I am fine with anything,' she said.

It was a self-service canteen, and Veda watched Suraj walking to the counter to place the order. Her heart was beating fast. She had never been on a 'date' like this with anyone. She wished she was the kind of girl who carried eyeliner and lipstick in her purse, like some of the others in her class. Today, she had been in a rush when she had left home, and she hadn't even combed her hair properly. Her eyes were devoid of kajal too, and she was conscious that she looked plain.

He returned with two cups of piping hot tea and a plate of *samosas* that looked delicious. Suraj said that these were the best *samosas* in the whole of Chamoli District. Veda couldn't help but agree, when she bit in.

'What did you want to see me for?' she asked, between bites.

'Just wanted to get to know you better,' said Suraj.

'Eh? Is that all? I thought you had some work with me.'

'Isn't it work, getting to know you? If you ask me, it is a lot of work. I wanted to ask you out that day itself, at the temple. But I wasn't sure as you were not alone.'

'That was my younger sister. And she did notice you staring at me. She teased me about it later.'

'Oh. I am so sorry. I didn't mean to stare. Just that you were looking positively radiant in that yellow salwar kameez,' said Suraj. His voice softened when he said that.

Veda felt a warm, tingly feeling creeping up inside her. She smiled as she sipped her tea, momentarily forgetting how she looked. She had read once that most men never even noticed things like eyeliner—things that women paid great attention to. Suraj was completely at ease, and that made her somewhat comfortable.

'So, what brought you to Joshimath from Bombay?' she asked, curious to know about this handsome guy with brown eyes. Eyes that she felt she could melt into. She noticed his strong, muscular arms, and his sharp jawline, as well as his Adam's apple. She was close enough to smell him, and she liked his masculine fragrance. She noticed the rolled-up sleeves of his checked shirt, and the red sacred thread that was tied around his right wrist.

'Ah. It is Mumbai now, not Bombay anymore. It has now been renamed, you know,' he said.

'Oh, yes. I know that. But in my head, it is still Bombay. Anyway, why did you relocate from *Mumbai*?' Veda asked, stressing the word 'Mumbai'.

'Ummm...' Suraj hesitated. 'It's not a happy story that brought me here,' he said.

'What happened?' she asked, wanting to know.

'I ... I lost my parents last year,' he said, as he looked away. Veda could see it was not easy for him to talk about it. But she was shocked by this sudden revelation.

'How?' she asked, before she could stop herself. 'I mean ... If you don't want to talk about it, it's fine,' she added as an afterthought.

'No, it's not like it's a secret. They were killed in that landslide which happened last year, do you remember it?'

Veda did. It was the biggest tragedy in recent years, the landslide that had occurred on the Rishikesh—Badrinath National Highway 58. A sudden downpour had caused a bus to hurtle into the valley below, killing twelve people. Suraj said that his father as well as his mother had been among the pilgrims killed.

'Oh ... Oh, I see. I am so sorry,' said Veda.

The tragedy was the only thing everyone in Chamoli District had talked about for a long time. It had sent ripples of shock through the community. Hundreds of pilgrims had been stranded at various places because of the landslide for many days, till it was cleared up. At home, they had discussed it at length. They had talked about how lucky her uncle and aunt had been, as they were supposed to have been on that bus. They had decided at the last minute to defer their trip, as one of their children had fallen ill.

Veda hadn't personally known anyone who had lost a relative or a friend, till now.

'No, that's fine. Whatever is destined is bound to happen. I grappled with guilt for a long time. Sometimes, I still feel guilty. My mother wanted me to join them on that pilgrimage, but I had refused, saying that I would stay with my grandmother till they returned.'

Veda nodded, not knowing what to say. She would have never guessed that he had such a tragic story. Their conversation, which had been light and casual till now, had suddenly taken on a sombre turn with Suraj's revelation.

'How did you manage?' she asked, her voice low.

'I stayed with my father's brother in Mumbai for a while and attended college. I could barely focus on my studies. I lost a year. Now, they have said that they cannot keep me anymore. My cousin is getting married, and he lives with his parents. I can see it will be difficult for them. That is why I came here—to live with my grandmother and to complete my college degree,' said Suraj.

'Don't you have any siblings?' Veda asked.

'No, I am an only child. Sometimes I wish I did. What about you? Do you have siblings?'

'Yes, I have three younger sisters, and a brother.'

'Wow. Lucky you,' said Suraj.

Veda had never thought about it. Her bond with her siblings was a close-knit one that had evolved naturally, without any conscious effort. For the first time she realised how valuable it was, and how she had never felt alone as she always had her siblings and her parents around.

'If you don't mind my asking, how do you manage now? I mean, the money? Your grandmother, does she work?'

'Oh no, she doesn't. My father had life insurance. So, we have a huge amount that has come to us. My uncle helped in processing all of that. Also, since my father worked for a public-sector undertaking, and he passed away while in service, they have promised me a job as soon as I graduate. My father worked in the same company for about twenty-five years, till he died. Almost everybody knew my father. You know, apart from the life insurance, the company too paid a lump-sum, and then my father's colleagues, on their own, did a collection drive. I am financially secure,' said Suraj.

'Oh, that's a relief then,' said Veda.

'Yes, but I would rather have my parents,' said Suraj, his voice barely a whisper.

Veda felt very sad for Suraj. She wished she wasn't shy. She wanted to lean over and give him a hug. There was a sadness which clouded his eyes now as he spoke of the tragedy. She wished she could make it go away.

'Look, you will always have a friend in me,' she said.

'Thanks,' he said, as he looked away.

They chatted for a little while longer about the difference in lifestyles in Mumbai and Joshimath. Veda now found herself talking easily to Suraj. He made her feel at ease. The awkwardness she had felt when she had walked into the canteen looking for him had vanished, and it seemed as if they were old friends.

She then remembered that she had to get home and gasped when she glanced at her watch.

'I didn't realise the time, I am late,' she said, as she stood up abruptly.

'Shall I walk you home?' asked Suraj, standing up too.

'No! No. That would not be okay. My father...' she trailed off. Speaking to Suraj about how strict her father was felt like a betrayal, and she bit back the words.

'Of course, just forget I even asked,' said Suraj.

He knew that Joshimath was full of gossipmongers, and that if they walked back together, news would travel fast through the grapevine. Often, he forgot how small Joshimath was. In Mumbai, there was the anonymity of a big city. The city swallowed you up and you became one with its teeming millions. Nobody cared what you did. Here, it was not like that. Even an incident as trivial as a cow giving birth to a calf, or a street cat having kittens, could become an interesting subject of discussion.

Veda hurried back home, hastily waving goodbye to Suraj, ignoring the others in the canteen. She was certain they were whispering about her. But her goal now was to reach home as fast as possible.

On most days, Vidya joined her halfway. They met under a banyan tree that stood at the spot where the roads from Veda's college and Vidya's school converged. From here, they walked back home together.

Today, she found her waiting impatiently, glancing at her watch.

'Where were you, didi? I have been waiting for so long,' said Vidya.

'I got held up,' Veda replied, her cheeks flushed.

'Ah, I see! You met Suraj, didn't you?' Vidya asked at once.

'What? How? How did you know? Is it that obvious?' Veda was shocked at how astute her sister was.

'Didi, it isn't obvious, but I can tell. I know my didi so well,' said Vidya.

As they walked up the narrow path that wound around the steep, rocky hill, dotted with dense, green shrubs with wild blue flowers, pine cones and alder leaves, Veda narrated to Vidya all that Suraj had told her. Vidya listened in rapt attention.

'Who would have thought, didi. He looks happy. He looks so calm, that nobody would be able to guess from his demeanour that he has this whole tragedy weighing him down,' she said. Veda nodded in agreement.

Unbeknownst to them, their father Rajinder was pacing up and down the garden path outside their home, waiting for both girls to get home. He couldn't understand why they were late. His tea, which Rudra kaka had served him, remained untouched on the verandah.

The cedar and maple trees swayed in the breeze, their tall branches almost touching the bright blue skies, as fluffy white clouds floated by leisurely. A small waterfall made a bubbling sound as the girls passed it. A mongoose crossed their path.

They walked on, engrossed in their narrative of Suraj,

oblivious to the beauty of the mountains, the scenery, the chilly mountain air, the stream or anything else they passed. It was only when they reached the gate of their home and saw their father waiting outside, did they realise that something wasn't quite right. Their father never waited for them outside.

Chapter 2

September 1995
Joshimath

'Ah, there you are. What took you so long?' asked Rajinder, as he spotted the girls.

'Papa, extra class,' said Vidya, before Veda could answer. She knew her sister couldn't lie as efficiently as her. Veda's expression would be a dead giveaway that she was guilty of chatting with boys, something they were forbidden to do.

'Did both of you have extra class?' Rajinder narrowed his eyes suspiciously.

'No Papa, didi had extra class and I waited for didi,' said Vidya smoothly.

Veda shot her a grateful look.

'Why? How many times have I told you to come straight home after class? Doesn't she doesn't know the way home, that you have to escort her?'

Vidya and Veda kept quiet and looked down.

'Sorry, Papa,' said Vidya in a tiny voice, modulated to convey helplessness, respect and fear in just the right proportions. It was a voice she had learnt by trial and error, and it was guaranteed to pacify their angry father.

'Sorry, Papa,' Veda echoed, imitating her sister. But for Veda, the palpitations she felt and the nervousness she experienced at her father's displeasure, were very real. For Vidya, it was just something she orchestrated to get out of a situation, which she knew could turn unpleasant. It was a skill that she had honed over the years. She had realised that it was easiest to deal with her father that way. Any argument they put forth would only result in more reprimands. This was the best way to avoid any more scolding.

'Hmm ... okay. Anyway, go get dressed. Your mother is waiting for you. Veda, wear a saree and be ready. We are going to have visitors,' said Rajinder.

'Eh? Saree?' Veda asked.

'Go inside, your mother will explain,' said Rajinder, not wanting to engage in any more conversation. Now that both girls were here, he was relieved.

The girls rushed inside and found their mother in the kitchen with Paro didi. The delicious aromas of all kinds of savouries wafted from the kitchen. They could see that whoever was coming was important, judging by the culinary preparations that were underway.

'Ma, what is this that Papa is saying? Why should didi wear a saree?' demanded Vidya.

'We are expecting visitors, girls. Both of you go and change into some nice clothes quickly. And Veda, please wear that pink chiffon saree that you wore for your school graduation ceremony. Wear some of my jewellery too, I have laid it all out for you. Brush your hair and leave it loose. And yes, apply some make-up as well. There is a marriage proposal for you.'

'What?' asked Veda, stunned.

'You heard me. They are coming home today to see you,' said her mother, as she expertly peeled boiled potatoes.

'Who are they, Ma?' asked Veda, unable to believe what she was hearing.

'Some people who are related to the boy. Now go and get ready quickly,' her mother waved her away, as though it was a common, everyday occurrence.

Veda could not believe this was happening.

'I ... I don't want to get married, Ma. I don't want any boy to see me,' she protested meekly.

'Veda, you know what our situation is. We have four girls. And this marriage thing—it all takes time. Just because we start the process doesn't mean you are getting married. But we should start looking for boys now itself. Then, by the time you finish your college and all of that, something might click,' her mother said, a little impatiently.

'But Ma—' Veda tried to reason with her. But her mother wasn't having any of it. She just wanted Veda to hurry up and get ready. Otherwise, she would have to face her husband's anger, and she was not ready for that. She also genuinely thought this was a good opportunity that had come their way.

It was not often that a prospective groom's relatives, of their own accord, asked for a meeting to see a prospective bride. As far as Kamala was concerned, this was a godsend, and she wasn't going to throw it away.

'Look, don't argue with me,' interrupted Kamala, not letting her finish. 'Also, there is no boy coming today. It is only his relatives, who live in the neighbouring town, who are visiting us. Once they see you, they will pass on the details to the boy's parents,' she said, all in one breath.

'Ma, you know I want to study, and I want to get a job in a city. You know that is my dream,' Veda continued to protest.

'Look, beti, you have to be practical about these things. You know how things are here. Sometimes, you have to sacrifice what you want in the interests of the family. You must think about your three younger sisters. Four girls are not so easy to manage, and you know that,' Kamala reasoned with her daughter. She hadn't expected Veda to protest this much. She thought it had been made amply clear to them that they would have to get married soon. Why was Veda not being understanding about this? All she was asking her to do was to get ready and look nice.

Rajinder entered the kitchen then. He had heard the exchange between Veda and her mother.

'Look, Veda, it does not matter what you want or do not want. We don't always get what we wish for—that is life. What was the condition on which I agreed to let you attend college? Do you remember?' he asked her, now looking directly at her.

Veda hung her head.

'Yes, Papa. I remember,' she murmured.

Her father had made it clear that she would have to get married before she graduated from college. It was on that condition that he had agreed to let her do her BA. She had wanted to apply for English Literature at St. Stephen's College in Delhi. It was her cherished dream, and her excellent academic grades meant she had a good chance of getting in.

'It is a very prestigious college, Papa. Many notable people have graduated from there,' she had explained to her father.

'No, no. We cannot afford the fees. Then there will be living expenses like hostel and other things. Also, Delhi is a big city. I am not sure if it is safe. It is out of the question,' Rajinder had thundered. 'Just apply to the government college here. It's not like there are no colleges in this town.'

So Veda had applied to the college in Joshimath, and when the results came out, her name was among the top in the list of successful applicants. Veda had initially been upset. This was not the college she had wanted to go to.

'Didi, don't feel sad. Maybe after you finish your degree you can get a job? Then you can go anywhere you want,' Vidya had comforted her.

After she had joined the college, the excitement of this new life had taken over. The course itself was interesting, and being a diligent student, Veda had soon become a favourite with the teachers. She had quickly adjusted to college life, happily taking part in many extracurricular activities. She also joined a few clubs, and the first two years had flown past quickly. Occasionally, she would think about how things would have been different had she got into St. Stephen's, and had her father allowed her to go. But she was not filled with bitter regret. Life wasn't too bad.

When Rajinder had laid down the condition that Veda would have to get married before she graduated, she hadn't given much thought to it. That had just sounded like one of her father's rants about raising girls.

So now, this felt like a bolt from the blue. She had never expected this.

'Beti, they are already on their way. You cannot let us down. Go now. Wear the saree and get ready. Vidya, you too. Go and change into a nice salwar kameez,' their mother's voice was now a whiny plea.

With their father around, there was no chance of protesting any more.

Veda's heart sank on hearing her mother's words. They were already on their way, and Veda had not even been consulted or informed in advance. This was what she had dreaded all her life. She did not want to be paraded around like a display-doll for a boy's relatives. But she was too meek to protest. She also knew that if she did protest, it would make her parents look bad. She could not see any way out of it.

'Okay, Ma, I will get ready,' she said, and retreated to the safety of her room with Vidya.

She took out the pink saree that her mother wanted her to wear. She knew how to wear a saree, as she had practised it since she was sixteen. Now, she draped it expertly, adjusting the pleats as she looked into the full-length mirror.

Vidya, too, quietly got dressed, putting on a full-length skirt that she had worn for a cousin's wedding.

'I hate this,' muttered Vidya, as she applied lipstick and eyeliner, handing them over to Veda when she was done.

'I have it worse. I am the one being paraded around,' Veda sighed in agreement, as she took the eyeliner and the lipstick from Vidya. When she was done, she glanced at herself in the mirror, wishing she had looked this nice when she had met with Suraj.

'Didi, you look stunning! See how beautiful you look when you make a small effort. Why don't you dress like this every day?' Vidya asked.

Veda just pulled a face at her, lips curling into a grimace as she thought of the people who were to arrive.

The special guests arrived right on time. There were two older gentlemen and four elderly ladies, two of whom Veda had met before at various social events. She was meeting the others for the first time.

They all sat in the garden, where Rudra kaka had arranged chairs.

'Be careful, didi. Don't trip in the saree,' whispered Vidya, as Veda served them tea and the savouries that had been prepared earlier.

The mood was celebratory and the conversation flowed smoothly. Veda had been told that after she served them, she and Vidya were to go inside. They weren't allowed to sit with the guests. So they sent their younger siblings to eavesdrop.

'Didi, they are saying that they like you. They are saying they will inform the boy and get back soon,' Vandana reported back to Veda and Vidya.

Veda groaned. 'Oh, God!' she said.

'Why, didi? Isn't it a good thing if they like you?' asked Animesh.

'You *buddhu*! It is a good thing only if Veda didi likes the boy,' Vaishali answered him.

'As though she will be given a choice,' said Vidya angrily.

But there was nothing the siblings could do, other than watch helplessly.

'These aunties have no other work,' whispered Vidya. She was furious at the way things were unfolding.

They heard loud laughter and they saw their parents nodding in agreement, talking animatedly.

After the guests left, their father was in a great mood.

'Veda, the boy is earning very well. He is working in a multinational company in Pune. They are a very good family. The boy's father is a retired academician. They have their own home too, in Pune. More than anything, he is a single child. So, everything that they have will automatically go to him. I think this is an excellent match,' he said.

Vidya was standing behind their father, and she pulled a face behind his back when she heard this. Veda was terrified that her father would see what Vidya was doing.

'Did you hear me? I said I think you should say yes, if the boy likes you,' Rajinder was telling her now.

Veda nodded mutely.

A thousand things came to her head, but not a single word escaped her lips. Her father and mother were almost joyous. It seemed as if this wedding had been fixed even before she had met the prospective groom.

Later, in the privacy of their bedroom, long after everybody had gone to sleep, Vidya and Veda discussed this.

'How does any of that matter? It doesn't matter to me whether he has his own house or whether he is a single child or whether his father is an academician. I don't want this marriage,' Veda confessed.

'I know, didi. I know. But look, he hasn't even met you yet. Only these silly aunties have met you,' Vidya said.

'Yes, but if he does approve of me—then?' Veda asked.

'Didi—just look at it this way. You will have to get married soon. Why don't you at least start meeting the eligible men? It doesn't mean that it will instantly click, right? And who knows, you might like one of them?' Vidya consoled Veda.

'I don't know, Vidya. All of this is just too sudden for me. I wasn't even thinking of marriage. I just want to focus on my final year of graduation and do well in my exams. These things will distract me,' Veda said.

'Look, didi. Papa is not going to let you say no. He has made up his mind. You know how it is. Maybe he will be as good-looking as Suraj,' said Vidya, trying to lighten Veda's mood.

But it had the opposite effect.

Veda felt even more despondent.

'I am not even comparing him with anyone. I am ... just sad,' she said.

Chapter 3

September 1995
Kailash Mandir Colony, Pune

The Kailash Mandir Colony in Pune woke up slowly, like a gargantuan monster stirring from its sleep. It slowly came alive with early morning sounds—the hurried footsteps of the newspaper delivery boy as he rushed from home to home, the thud of the newspaper as it landed on the mat in front of each apartment, the milk crates with packets of milk, the flower-lady delivering garlands of chrysanthemum and jasmine to the devout households, their fragrance still lingering in the narrow corridors outside each home, the early morning joggers and walkers in their track pants and running shoes, domestic house-help arriving to clean, sweep and mop. In the apartments, the children were being prepared to leave for school. Outside, an army of school buses arrived one after the other, and were waiting to whisk the children away.

Inside one of the buildings, in a flat on the third floor, Padma Devi had been awake since five o'clock, practising her meditation and her *kriyas* for an hour. She stepped out now for her morning walk, wearing her canvas shoes, pulling her maroon button-down sweater over her saree and tying a woollen scarf around her head. Outside her building, she was greeted by two of her friends from the colony, Kanti behen and Shanta, both around her age, in their late sixties. They had been friends for the past thirty years, having moved into the colony at the same time. They had all bought modest two-bedroom apartments with their life savings, while the complex was being constructed. Since then, many office complexes had sprung up around the colony, making it a prime real estate location. The prices of land, and consequently the prices of the apartments, had quadrupled. It was almost impossible now to purchase any real estate in that area, unless you were a multi-billion-dollar corporation or a business tycoon.

Amongst the swanky new high-rises in the neighbourhood,

Kailash Mandir Colony stood out like a sore thumb, with its three-storied buildings, faded yellow exteriors that needed a facelift, mosaic-tiled flooring and narrow staircases without lifts. None of that bothered the residents, though. This was where they had lived for most of their adult lives.

'Shanta, how is your knee? Better today? That oil I sent yesterday—did it help?' asked Padma Devi as she joined her friends. The women began their daily walk around the colony. These morning walks were a combination of exercise, psychotherapy and socialising, all rolled into one. As they walked, they spoke about everything under the sun. Rarely did the three women miss their walk. They had been nicknamed 'The Trimurti Brigade' by their husbands, a moniker which they were secretly proud of.

'Yes, yes, Padma. It was excellent. My daughter massaged it in, and I sat in the sun for half an hour, like you suggested. And poof, the pain vanished,' answered Shanta, as they walked briskly.

'Ah, good. Have you got any more matches for Kanika?' asked Kanti behen.

'What to tell you, Kanti behen. So many matches, but she rejects everything. She says none of them are good enough. And now that she has quit her job and joined that social work, she hardly has time for anything,' she trailed off.

'It's okay, Shanta. It will happen when the time comes. See my son, still unmarried at twenty-eight. No interest in marriage, he says. Is marriage a hobby, that you need to have "interest"? In our times, we just got married. We didn't think much about it. But children these days, I tell you...' Padma Devi's voice reflected her disappointment in her son's stand on marriage.

'At least if we were from the same community, we could have considered getting Kanika and Bhuwan married,' said Shanta.

'Yes. It's important to marry within the community. I want only an Agarwal bride for my son. And I don't want any of these modern girls who want to work and all that. I want somebody content to be at home, and to look after the house. I think men and women have their roles. It is when one tries to take over the other's role that all problems are caused,' Padma Devi was firm.

Her comment about 'modern girls' was not lost on Shanta.

'What do you mean "modern girls", Padma? What is wrong with Kanika working? The work that she is doing helps so many people,' she asked, indignant.

Padma Devi immediately realised her folly. Not wanting to offend her friend, she said, 'Oho, *baba*—I did not mean our Kanika. I meant those girls who wear tight tops and roam around with boys shamelessly. Kanika is both a son and daughter rolled into one. You are fortunate, Shanta. You ought to be proud of her.'

Shanta, mollified by the compliment, beamed.

'I have given her marital bio-data to the Kerala Samajam. Let's hope she likes a good Nair boy soon,' said Shanta.

'I have also circulated Bhuwan's horoscope to the Agarwal brokers. I have already started shortlisting candidates. Why don't you both come over for tea today, and I will show you all the photographs?' said Padma Devi.

'Come over to my place with the photos. That way, the husbands will not get in the way,' Shanta offered. She had been widowed six years ago, and had now adjusted to a life without a spouse.

The three women then chatted about various things, including maids, the prices of vegetables, and how difficult it was to get their adult children to listen to them.

By the end of forty-five minutes, they had finished five rounds of the colony. On some days, when the topic of the discussion was very interesting, their walk stretched to an hour.

When Padma Devi let herself inside the house, she discovered that Bhuwan was still asleep.

'Didn't you wake him?' she asked her husband, who was sitting in his usual chair on the balcony, having his morning tea, which Padma Devi had made and poured into a thermos flask before she had gone on her walk.

Her husband muttered something unintelligible and disappeared behind the newspaper.

'Bhuwan, Bhuwan, wake up,' she said, barging into her son's bedroom without knocking.

'Maaa,' he said, and buried his face under the pillow.

'Why are you bleating? Are you a goat? What is "Maa"? How long will you sleep like Kumbakaran? Wake up. I have finished my walk, and now it is breakfast time. And you are still in bed?' she admonished, as she slid the curtains open. Bright sunlight streamed in, making Bhuwan squint his eyes. He got out of bed without a word and headed towards the washroom.

Bhuwan knew that his mother would not let him sleep. He had been out with a friend till late the previous night, and had drunk a little too much. He had staggered back home well past three in the morning. His head was pounding now, his throat was parched, and he just wanted to sleep a little longer, as it was the weekend. But for his mother—and for his father—the concept of weekends just did not exist. As far back as he could remember, his mother had woken up every morning at five. She made sure that everyone in the house knew that she did.

'Every morning, I wake up at 5 a.m., and I cook for all of you. Not a single day do I take off. I am the only one burdened in this house with all the housework,' she would rant every now and then, whenever things did not go her way or when she was irritated about something. It did not matter to her that the two were not related. She was ready to don the martyr's hat and paint a sorry picture of herself whenever the opportunity presented itself.

Her son and husband had developed their own coping strategies. Her husband would promptly disappear behind his newspaper, and Bhuwan would get busy with his work. It never occurred to Bhuwan or to his father to point out to Padma Devi that there was no need for her to wake up that early every morning. It was something she had decided to do all by herself. Besides, she did have a maid, Shakubai, who came in at 6.30 every morning, to assist her with all the housework. The one thing about Padma Devi was that nobody could argue with her. She had a sharp tongue and a closed mind, and once she had made up her mind about something, that was what she would believe in, and would justify completely, with the zeal of a new convert who had discovered God. Her version of reality was the ultimate truth and gospel by which everybody else had to abide. She had her own rules, and these were non-negotiable. Bhuwan had been raised within the framework of these rules, and if he flouted any of them, he discovered quickly that there would be hell to pay.

As a child, he had to have a bath as soon as he came back from school. His school bag had to be put away on his bookshelf. His school books and the homework assigned had to be neatly arranged on his desk, *before* he headed for his bath. While he bathed, Padma Devi would check his school diary to see when the work he was assigned was due. After he was fresh and clean, she would give him a snack, and then it was time for him to finish his homework. She would inspect it, and only when she was satisfied could he head outside to play.

At six in the evening he had to be back home. He had to wash his face, hands and feet. His mother would then recite prayers, specifically the *Hanuman Chalisa*, and he would have to repeat the verses after her. He was twenty-eight now, and he still followed this routine, except that his school bag had been replaced by his office laptop bag.

When Bhuwan had wanted to move to a different city for his engineering degree, his mother had refused to let him go. 'What is wrong with studying in Pune? What is the need for you to live on your own?' she had protested. Her husband had tried telling her that it might be good for Bhuwan to live on his own, away from the parents, but Padma Devi wouldn't hear of it. That was how Bhuwan had found himself doing his engineering degree, and later his MBA, in Pune, while living with his parents.

After a while, he got used to it, and after he started working, even though he was eligible for company accommodation, he chose to live with his parents. It was easier that way. He didn't have to bear the responsibility of living on his own, and besides, he didn't have the strength to fight his mother, for she was sure to raise objections if he as much as mentioned the possibility of moving out. He compromised and adjusted to minor inconveniences, such as waking up early on a Saturday.

He knew that a piping hot breakfast would be waiting when he emerged from the washroom.

'Ma, I am going out today. I'll be back only in the evening,' he said, as he joined his father at the dining table and tucked into the hot *sabudana khichdi* which Padma Devi had prepared.

'Where are you going? And with whom are you going?' Padma Devi asked, as she served him some chutney.

'Vikki, Ma. We are driving to an eco-resort on the outskirts of Pune. He has bought a new jeep and he wanted me to go with him for a drive.'

'Aaah, okay,' said Padma Devi, satisfied that her son was not going out on a date, or any such thing.

Vikram and Bhuwan had been classmates at college and, over the years, their friendship had grown. Padma Devi liked Vikram and considered him a polite young man. He had come over to their place countless times over the last few years. His father had a shop that sold automobile parts, and they had done well for themselves. Vikram wasn't very good with academics, and it was Bhuwan who had coached him throughout engineering. He had managed to scrape through the final exams, while Bhuwan had excelled. After graduating, Vikki had joined his father's business and helped out at his shop. But his passion lay in filmmaking, and he intended to join the Film and Television Institute of India soon. He just hadn't found a way to convince his father yet.

'When is he getting married?' Padma Devi asked.

'I don't know, Ma. I haven't asked him about such things.'

'Why not? He is your age. Tell him to let his parents find a nice Punjabi girl for him.'

'Alright, Ma, I will tell him,' said Bhuwan, and he looked at his father and smiled.

His father smiled back. Both men knew that Bhuwan would do no such thing. Padma Devi didn't notice the little exchange, though.

'Oh, by the way, that Sharmaji has sent photos of some nice girls. Would you like to see them, Bhuwan?'

'No, Ma. What will I do with photos? I have told you this before.'

'Are you okay with directly meeting the girls I select?'

'Yes Ma, I am okay.'

'But you will reject them after you meet them.'

'No, it's not like that. I haven't liked anyone enough so far.'

'Twenty-three girls, Bhuwan. Twenty-three. What is it that you are looking for? At least if you tell me what type of girl you want, then I can narrow in on that.'

'There is no "type", Ma. It's just that I haven't clicked with anyone so far. Anyway, I am off. I will see you later in the evening,' he said, as he excused himself from the dining table, washed his hands and walked out. Vikki had agreed to meet him outside his house. Bhuwan was looking forward to the drive, as he waited for him outside Kailash Mandir Colony.

After Bhuwan left, Padma Devi gathered the photographs of the girls that the broker had given her. Among the pile, there was one photograph that stood out. It was the one which her relatives from Joshimath had sent over. They had already met the girl and spoke highly of her. She marched towards Shanta's house with all the photos. She had already chosen a bride for her son, and since her son refused to even look at the photos, she wanted to show them to her friends.

Chapter 4

September 1995
Joshimath

Veda was shaken by what had happened at her home the previous evening. She couldn't stop thinking about it. She knew that she had to get married someday, but had not thought about it, as she had been immersed in her academics. Now, it seemed as if it was in the near future. She was filled with trepidation. She definitely did not feel ready. She recalled a conversation she had had at an older cousin's wedding. 'Look, no matter how old you are, marriage is a big step, and I don't think anyone feels ready for it. You just jump into the cold water, start swimming, and then realise that it is not as bad as you thought it would be,' the cousin had said.

'What if I don't know how to swim?' Veda had asked.

Her cousin had laughed and said, 'Well, you better learn quickly then.'

Veda wondered what the 'boy' would be like. Had those aunties who had come over spoken to the boy's relatives? What had they told him? What were his expectations? With all these thoughts running in her head, Veda could barely focus on the lectures the next day.

'What happened? Your meeting with Suraj—was it that good that you are so lost in thoughts of him?' Rekha teased her.

'Er ... uh no. It's not that,' Veda replied.

'It sure looks like it. You are so lost in dreamland,' said Rekha.

At recess, Rekha made an excuse and left as soon as she spotted Suraj walking towards them. Veda raised her eyebrows as she hadn't spotted Suraj yet. But the next moment she did, and she stood frozen at the spot as Suraj walked up to her and stood right next to her. Veda once again experienced that flutter of excitement in her belly. His very presence seemed to do that to her. When he was near her, all the thoughts in her head vanished, and all she was aware of was his presence.

Suraj greeted her with a warm smile and Veda smiled back at him.

'Hi. Shall we hang out after college today? Yesterday was fun,' he said.

Veda wished she could. She wanted to tell him that she had enjoyed herself too. But she knew that if she stayed back today, she would get into trouble at home.

'I wish I could, but I cannot stay late after college today,' she replied.

'Meet me at lunchtime then?' he asked.

'But I have my own lunch. Ma always packs lunch for me,' Veda replied, kicking herself mentally the moment she said the words. Why was she putting up these obstacles? She did *want* to hang out with him. But she had said the first thing that had come into her head. She wished she was a little more calm and composed when he was around, instead of blurting out whatever she was thinking.

Fortunately for her, Suraj was not one to give up easily.

'So what? We don't have to meet in the canteen. Let's meet on the lawns?' he asked.

She did not know what to say or do. She had genuinely begun liking him after the interaction last evening. But she knew there was no future in whatever it was that they were starting. Or whatever it was that *he* was hopeful of starting. She had to explain. She felt she owed that to him. So she agreed to meet him.

'Alright, I'll see you then,' she said.

The bell rang and Veda went back to class, trembling with excitement at the prospect of another meeting with Suraj. She did not tell Rekha or any of their friends about what had happened at her home the previous evening. She was not ready. With Suraj, she felt a closeness, even though they had interacted just once. Perhaps it was because he had shared a part of his life's tragedy with her. It was strange, but after that one meeting, she felt as if she had known him for a long time. She *understood* him, or so she thought. She was comfortable with him, and felt she had found a genuine friend in him. She wondered if she was imagining the closeness, or whether he sensed it too.

'Did he ask you out again?' Rekha whispered, as they sat down.

'Uh, huh,' Veda said, nodding.

'He likes you! Not bad. Two dates in a row!' Rekha exclaimed. The two girls sitting in front of them turned to look at them.

'Shhh! Do you want the whole world to know?' whispered Veda.

'If he had asked me, I would have shouted it out from the rooftops,' Rekha whispered back.

'Shut up!' said Veda, but she smiled. She couldn't wait for lunch break to arrive.

Veda sat with Suraj on the lawn, under the large, shady peepul tree, where many groups of students, as well as couples at various stages in their relationships, hung out. This tree was a mute witness to many love stories. Veda felt a little awkward joining Suraj there. It was like announcing their 'relationship' to the world. But there was no better place to meet.

She opened her lunchbox and offered it to him. 'Do you always eat at the canteen? Do you never get food from home?' she asked.

'I don't like to burden my grandmother, although she claims it is not a problem to prepare lunch for me. But it just means she has to wake up very early. Some days, I do carry what she makes,' he explained, as he bit into one of the methi parathas her mother had packed.

'Mmm, delicious. Your mother cooks so well! You know, my mother was a good cook too,' he remarked.

He made that statement so casually, yet Veda felt the sorrow behind it. His quiet acceptance of such a massive tragedy moved her deeply. Before she had met Suraj, she hadn't even given a second's thought to an ostensibly tiny thing like a home-cooked meal. But now, she was suddenly grateful for it. She was beginning to see the world through Suraj's eyes, and she was gaining a whole new perspective.

They chatted easily and the conversation flowed smoothly between them once again. To her delight, she discovered that Suraj was an avid reader too. He talked about his favourite books and said that he loved the works of Frederick Forsyth. She confessed that she had read only a short story collection by him. She told him about her favourite writers, and what she loved about their writing. He hadn't read anything by Daphne du Maurier, and she enjoyed speaking to him about her work.

It was only towards the end of the lunch break that she even remembered what she was there for. She had to tell him about yesterday's event at her home.

'Listen, Suraj, I don't think it's a good idea for us to meet this way anymore,' she said.

'Why?' he asked, startled. 'Is it anything I said or did?'

'No. Oh, no! Of course, not,' she rushed to assure him.

Her story came out in a torrent. She told him about her upbringing, her father's outlook, how it was her dream to study in Delhi, but that she had been forced to accept this instead. She spoke about how strict her father was, and how he thought that having four girls was a huge burden. She told him about how meek her mother was, and how she and Vidya cared for their other siblings. She told him almost everything about her life. Suraj listened carefully.

'You know, you are the first boy I have had a "date" with, if you can call it that,' she said.

'What? Oh. I did not realise that,' said Suraj, surprised.

'Why? Now that you know my background, is it so odd?' Veda asked.

'No, no. It's not odd at all. It is just that I feel a bit angry with your father right now,' he said.

'Because he doesn't allow me to date?'

'No, that's not a big deal. But this whole marriage thing...' he trailed off.

He was angry on Veda's behalf.

Veda just shrugged. She was resigned to her situation at home.

'Veda, why don't you protest? Why don't you vehemently say you don't want all this? How can you just silently agree?' he asked.

'I ... I can't Suraj. It just doesn't work that way. I can't. I am ... I am afraid of my father's wrath. Terrified,' she admitted. As she spoke, tears came unannounced. She was embarrassed and horrified. She blinked them away furiously. She was not going to cry in front of Suraj.

But he had already noticed the change of expression on her face.

'I am so sorry. I didn't mean to upset you. My parents were always open-minded and I could talk to them about anything. There were never any restrictions on me. I guess I find it hard to understand your kind of upbringing,' he said.

'I guess so. Unless you walk in my shoes, how will you know what it feels like?' she asked.

'I don't know, Veda,' he hesitated. Then he said, 'All I want is to be your friend. I hope we can be friends?'

'I guess so. Yes, yes ... I would like us to be friends,' she said, voicing her thoughts aloud. How could she refuse? All he was asking was to be friends with her.

The bell rung just then, and they had to return to class.

It was with a feeling of heaviness that Veda parted from Suraj. She had told him everything, and he now knew where he stood.

Veda couldn't sleep that night. She kept tossing and turning, thinking about Suraj. She knew she would have to squash whatever it was that she felt for him. One part of her, the logical side, told her to end it before she got hurt. But another part of her reminded her that there was nothing between them, and that they were just friends. Vidya was lying next to Veda, and she couldn't sleep either because her sister was moving around so much.

'Can't sleep, didi?' she whispered.

'Yes. Just not able to,' Veda whispered back.

'Do you want to talk?' asked Vidya.

'Outside?' Veda replied.

The two sisters crept out into the moonlight and sat on

the terraced steps. The mountains behind them were a dark mass. There were no stars at all in the sky, and it looked like the moon was fighting with the clouds to make its presence felt. The sisters, however, were oblivious to the darkness of the night. They had done this many times, when either of them was unable to sleep.

Veda had carried a thick blanket outside and she covered Vidya with it as well. They huddled together, shivering a little as the cool mountain air hit their faces.

'What happened, didi?' asked Vidya.

She instinctively knew when her sister was troubled. They had always confided in each other about everything that was on their minds.

'I met Suraj again at lunch break,' Veda said.

'Hmm. And are you worried that Papa will find out?' Vidya asked.

'Umm, I don't know. I know that I don't want to start something that I will regret later,' Veda replied.

'Come on, didi! You are acting like he kissed you and now you don't know what to do. What is wrong in talking to a boy, tell me? Is it such a big crime?' Vidya asked.

'No, Vidya. You know that Papa and Ma are proceeding with my marriage. I am just too aware of that.'

'So?'

'So, is it right to continue talking to Suraj?' Veda asked.

'Tell me something—are you hiding the fact of these marriage plans from him?'

'No, of course not. I told him today. I explained my situation to him.'

'And what did he say?'

'He said he hoped we could be friends,' Veda said.

'Then what is wrong, didi? You are not hiding things from him. You have been upfront. I think you should make the best of this. It's not as if you will continue seeing him once you are married. You should spend time with him if it makes you happy! You shouldn't be consumed by guilt over this,' Vidya said.

Veda wished she could be as certain as Vidya. Vidya was strong-willed and spoke her mind.

'I enjoy his company,' Veda admitted.

'You know what, I will cover for you any time you want to meet him,' Vidya said.

She felt that Veda deserved to have some harmless fun. She knew that her sister was looking for assurance, and she was more than happy to give it.

Over the next few weeks, Suraj and Veda met every single day during lunch break at college. They just couldn't stay away from each other. The more they spoke to each other, the more they had to talk about. They never got tired of each other's company. Veda discovered that, when she spoke to Suraj, she laughed easily. It was almost as if all the worries and stress that she felt vanished. Suraj said that he felt the same way.

'Your laughter is so infectious, Veda. I don't remember the last time I laughed like this,' he told her.

Everyone in college thought that they were a couple. It was only Suraj and Veda who knew the desperation of a friendship with an end clearly in sight. It intensified their need for each other.

One day, Suraj asked Veda if she wanted to go for a picnic.

'I know a beautiful spot near Vishnuprayag River. I used to go there with my father to fish,' he said.

'I would love to, Suraj. But what if we are caught?' Veda asked.

'How will we be caught? Meet me some place where you will not be spotted, and we can drive down,' Suraj said.

'You drive?' Veda asked, surprised.

'Of course! I have driven since I was sixteen. My father taught me. See, I even have a driving licence,' he said, as he opened his wallet and showed it to her.

She looked at it, impressed.

'How will you get a vehicle?' she asked.

'I can get a car for a day, Veda. A friend owns a travel agency. They rent out cars. I will rent one from him, and I will say I don't want a driver,' Suraj said.

'Hmm ... I am not sure, Suraj. Let me think about it,' said Veda.

'Sometimes, you shouldn't think. You should just say yes,' Suraj said, smiling.

It was hard to resist him when he looked like that. Veda smiled back at him.

'Okay, I will let you know soon,' she said.

'Soon? How soon? I can't wait for "soon". "Soon", come soon,' he said, and they both laughed.

When she spoke to Vidya about it, her sister danced around.

'Go, didi! Go. I will cover for you,' she said.

'I want to, Vidya! But how? What will I tell Ma and Papa?' she asked.

'Didi, just say it is a study tour and it is compulsory. If you don't go, they will have to write a letter of explanation. That will make them agree,' Vidya said.

When Veda asked for permission to go on the 'study tour', her palms were cold with nervousness. She was certain that her father would catch her out in her lie. But to her surprise, he was more than happy to let her go. Now that the prospective groom's relatives had approved of Veda, she was in Rajinder's good books.

'Okay, beti. If it is compulsory, then you have to go. Take some money from Ma,' said Rajinder.

Veda could not believe how easy it had been.

When she got back after spending the day with Suraj, her faced glowed with happiness. Vidya looked at her sister and smiled. She was happy that she had urged Veda to go ahead and helped plan the whole thing.

'What happened? Did you—did you guys kiss?' Vidya later asked her sister, long after everybody had slept.

'Of course not! We just sat at the spot where his father used to take him fishing. He had brought a picnic basket with food and cool drinks, and a nice mat. Oh, Vidya—I thought I would die of happiness! I can't tell you how happy I am. We just talked and talked and talked! It was wonderful,' said Veda.

'I am so happy for you, didi. You deserve all the happiness in the world,' said Vidya, as she reached out for her sister's hand and squeezed it.

Vidya wanted her sister to have as much joy as possible. She knew that once her marriage was finalised, this friendship with Suraj would have to be sacrificed.

Chapter 5

October 1995
Joshimath

Veda's closeness with Suraj continued to grow. They discovered they could meet on weekends if they came up with plausible excuses. Vidya was only too happy to cover for Veda. She went along with Veda on some days, telling their parents that they were going to the Narsingh temple. Vidya would then go to a friend's place for a couple of hours, and Veda would meet Suraj. They realised that if they trekked into the mountains, there were many isolated places where they could spend a few hours alone in each other's company. They knew that they were risking a lot, and were extremely careful while choosing their meeting spots.

'Don't you ever feel like kissing him? How is it that you guys have not even held hands?' Vidya asked Veda one day.

'Come on Veda, we are just friends. We cannot be anything more than that,' Veda asserted. Their relationship was not like most other people's, she told Vidya.

'If I were you, I would have slept with him by now,' Vidya said. Veda was shocked at that statement.

Did Vidya mean it?

'Listen, even if you have a crush on someone, don't just get into anything without knowing the guy first, okay?' said Veda.

'Didi, I was only joking. Don't be so serious about everything!' Vidya brushed away her concerns.

It was a month later that Bhuwan, his parents, and the same set of people that had visited them earlier came to Joshimath to 'officially see' Veda.

Padma Devi had shown her son Veda's matrimonial bio-data, which had been sent by her parents. 'She is a very nice girl. Shyama chachi and all of them have met the family, and they speak highly of her. They say she is pretty and very homely,' Padma Devi had told him.

Bhuwan had reluctantly agreed to meet the girl. His marriage had been a topic of conversation for a year now. When he had agreed for the 'process' to start, his mother had gone into a tizzy, arranging meetings with prospective girls. Bhuwan hadn't liked any of them and had turned all of them down. He was sure that this one would be no different. But till he agreed to meet whoever it was that his mother had now lined up, he knew she wouldn't leave him alone. She had been pestering him incessantly for the last two weeks. Fed up with her constant nagging, he had taken a few days' leave from work. They had flown from Pune to Delhi, and then driven down to Joshimath, where they checked into a hotel. They were to meet the girl's family the next morning, a task that Bhuwan was not looking forward to. He hated rejecting girl after girl. But he hadn't met a single one with whom he could have even a half-decent conversation.

He couldn't tell anything much about this girl from her matrimonial bio-data—they were all tailored to show off the girl in the best possible light. In the morning, he went through the motions, and dressed smartly for the occasion. Padma Devi smiled at him approvingly, happy that he had agreed to meet the girl.

For this visit, Veda was once again wearing a saree, a different one this time. Vidya too had to wear a saree, as her parents said that this was an important occasion. They also ensured that Vaishali, Vandana and Animesh were dressed in their finest clothes. When the entourage from Bhuwan's side arrived at their gate, Veda's parents, and a couple of aunts who had joined them for the occasion, greeted them like they were royalty.

'I am surprised Papa hasn't arranged for elephants to garland them,' quipped Vidya, as they watched their arrival from the window.

'Welcome, welcome,' Rajinder was saying, joining his palms in greeting.

Veda grimaced. 'God, I hate this,' she said.

'I know, didi. It will be over soon,' Vidya comforted her.

After the customary pleasantries were exchanged, Veda was

summoned to serve the snacks. After that, Veda and Bhuwan were told that they could speak in private.

'Go, beti. Take him to your room and you both can talk there,' said Rajinder.

'Yes, yes, please go. They will have a lot to talk about,' commented one of the aunts, and all the others laughed like it was the greatest joke in the world.

It was the most awkward thing Veda had ever experienced. She wished the earth would open up and swallow her. She did not want to meet him alone, and she had no idea what to say to him. But she had to be the dutiful daughter, so she led him to her room.

As soon as they were alone, Veda sat on the bed. She pointed to her study chair for him to sit on.

'It's lovely to meet you Veda,' he said, smiling at her. His face radiated warmth and he looked like he was genuinely happy to meet her. He had a dimple in his left cheek, and it added to his pleasant demeanour. Veda noticed his long, oval face, his one-day-old stubble, his short, wavy hair, and his perfect teeth. She decided that though he wasn't strikingly handsome, he wasn't unattractive at all. This was the first time since he had arrived that she was looking at him properly.

'Nice to meet you too,' she replied.

'So, I guess we know something about each other, at least the bits we put in our respective matrimonial bio-datas,' he said.

Veda looked puzzled.

'You must have read my matrimonial bio-data, right?' asked Bhuwan.

'What? No, I only know your name and that you work in Pune. They didn't tell me anything else about you.'

'Oh! But I know all about you. They sent me your matrimonial bio-data: your interests, hobbies, everything. Your academic performance is admirable,' he said.

'Oh! Thanks. I didn't even know they had made one for me. They never told me about it,' said Veda.

'So, let's set that right straightaway, shall we? Is there anything you would like to ask me?' Bhuwan asked.

If Bhuwan was feeling as awkward as she was, he wasn't showing it at all, Veda thought. He was acting as though this was the most natural thing in the world. Veda wondered what she should ask him and decided to start with what she thought would be a 'basic' question. She asked him what his academic qualifications were. She was impressed when he told her that he had done an MBA and was working in a multinational at the mid-management level.

Then she asked him about his hobbies. He said that he loved to trek and that he enjoyed taking photos.

He asked her what she liked to read. She told him about her favourite books.

He had, to her surprise, read Daphne du Maurier.

'Oh my God—you are the first person I have met who has read her books!' she exclaimed.

'Well, I must admit, I have read only one—*Rebecca*. And that too, because I watched the movie. It's an old movie, I think, made in 1969 or so. I watched it only because one of my closest friends, Vikki, insisted that I do. He is a filmmaker—or at least wants to be one—and he talked a lot about it.'

'Still, it's a start,' said Veda.

They talked about the differences between the book and the movie. She asked him if he had enjoyed the movie, and he replied that, to his surprise, he had, even though he had watched it just to please his friend.

Then he asked her something that she hadn't been expecting at all.

'So, ummm ... any boyfriends?' he questioned.

'What? No. No,' she replied a bit too quickly, a little outraged.

'Sorry. Just so that we are clear. Because in case you have someone, we need not, you know, proceed with this,' said Bhuwan, his tone almost apologetic.

Veda thought about Suraj. Was he her boyfriend? How could you call someone your boyfriend, just because you had spent a lot of time with him for a few weeks? They had made it clear, over and over, in their conversations, that they were just friends and nothing more. She thought about the picnics, the secret meetings, the conversations at lunch break, and all the other times they had met. They had discussed it often.

'I know, I know—we can never be anything more than friends,' Suraj had said, each time she brought it up. Veda felt she had been bringing up the topic more to assure herself, than for him. Suraj definitely was just her friend, she decided.

'No, no boyfriends,' she said, firmly this time.

'Alright then, I guess we should go out before they call for us,' he said, as he stood up.

When they emerged and stepped into the drawing room, everyone looked at them expectantly. It was as though they had to make a decision right there.

'So beta, what do you think of our Veda?' Rajinder asked.

Veda wished she could disappear. She looked down, feeling embarrassed, awkward and self-conscious. How could her father ask him such a thing? What if he did not like her?

Everyone turned to look at Bhuwan.

'Your daughter is lovely, and well ... if she likes me too, then I guess I am lucky,' he said.

Veda looked up, stunned. It had not even occurred to her that she, too, would have a choice in this matter. It had not occurred to her that *she* had to *like* the guy too. Could she refuse to marry this guy?

'Of course, she likes you! From our side, consider it final!' said Rajinder.

'Wonderful, wonderful!' said Bhuwan's father.

'So we will consult the pandit and fix an auspicious date then. Their horoscopes anyway are a perfect match,' said Padma Devi.

Veda's mother nodded. Veda did not miss the look of gratitude and overwhelming relief, mingled with joy, on both her parents' faces.

Veda had also got her answer. She simply had no choice. The decision had already been made for her.

Five days later, the date of their marriage was fixed. Padma Devi had called from Pune to say that the pandit had given them a choice of three dates. The first was within forty days, the second date was eight months later, and the third was ten months later.

Padma Devi said that she was keen on an early marriage. She was afraid that Bhuwan would change his mind, though she did not mention this.

'Why delay a good thing? I would like it as early as possible,' she said on the phone.

Rajinder was over the moon. They had demanded no dowry. They were happy to leave all the wedding arrangements to him. He agreed quickly to the earliest date.

Veda was to get married to Bhuwan in forty days.

Chapter 6

November 1995
Joshimath

Veda did not know what to do anymore. Her life felt like a runaway train hurtling at full speed to an unknown destination. It was moving faster than she could run after it.

'Forty days? Really, Ma? How?' she had asked her mother, as they stood in the kitchen.

Rajinder had announced the date of the marriage casually, like it was not a big deal, and then had left home, as he needed to start making arrangements.

'There is a lot to be done and there is no time to be wasted,' he had said, as he hurried out.

'What about my college? I am in my final year and I have to get my degree,' said Veda, her voice full of dismay.

'Veda beti, we are your parents. Don't you think we will consider what is best for you? We have thought about all that. You can complete the rest of your college in Pune,' Kamala assured her daughter.

'What? How? You mean I have to shift to Pune as soon as I get married?' Veda asked, horrified. She hadn't thought out the details of what her marriage meant, and it was all slowly sinking in now.

'*Yeh lo!* Do you not know how it is? Have you heard of any bride staying back at her parents' place after the wedding? Your new home is now in Pune. Your father-in-law has said that he can get you into one of the finest colleges there. He knows the Dean,' her mother said, as she expertly kneaded the dough for rotis.

'But … but, it will be in the middle of the academic year,' Veda said. She still couldn't believe that it would all be as simple as her mother made it sound. Her mother could not be aware of what it meant to transfer from one college to another in the final year, she thought.

'Your father has spoken to them. They said you can get your marks transferred,' her mother reassured her.

'Marks? You mean credits?'

'Yes, yes—same thing,' her mother waved her hand impatiently. 'You can get it all shifted there. They said that it is a better college too. So you see, it's all okay. Don't worry so much, Veda. You leave the worrying to us. After all, it is we who have to make the wedding arrangements.'

'Can I continue going to college then?' asked Veda.

'Yes, no point in your staying at home,' said her mother.

Veda had no idea how she would be able to focus on her studies, with the marriage looming large in the near future. Now the date was finalised too, adding certainty to it. It all felt like a surreal dream.

But she discovered to her surprise that she *was* able to concentrate. By focusing on her lectures, and pretending that nothing was going on, she was able to forget this whole marriage thing for a while.

But the moment her classes got over, or the moment the bell rang for lunch break or for recess, reality came rushing back. It made her anxious and she tried to block it out. She still hadn't told Rekha or anyone else at college about her impending wedding. That would have made it seem more real. Also, she thought that Rekha might judge her for still wanting to meet Suraj, despite being engaged to be married.

She and Suraj met at lunch, as though nothing had changed. She told him about the latest developments. She told him all about Bhuwan, the conversation they had had, and how she had felt oddly comfortable with him.

'Is it final then?' he asked, as he drew a circle on the lawn with a twig, poking hard into the ground beneath, uprooting the grass.

'Stop doing that, you will ruin the lawn,' said Veda.

'It will grow back, Veda, it is only grass,' he said, not looking up, refusing to meet her eyes.

'Are you upset?' she asked.

He did not answer.

'Suraj, I had told you that there can never be anything between us. You knew all this from the start. We shouldn't have continued meeting,' said Veda, looking away.

Though she was unhappy herself, she couldn't bear to see Suraj like this. She felt she was letting him down in some way.

'Hey, listen, there isn't anything between us. We are just friends, okay?' Suraj said.

'That's what I told myself, when Bhuwan asked me if I had a boyfriend,' Veda replied.

'That's that, then. You are right in your thinking,' said Suraj. The circles he was making in the lawn were getting deeper.

Veda was silent.

Then she took a long, deep breath and asked, 'Can we ... be in touch?'

That was when Suraj looked up.

'How?' he whispered.

'I will write to Vidya. She will give you my letters. And you can give your letters to her. She will put your letter in the envelope along with hers, and send it to me. Nobody will know then.'

Veda had thought about it all night. It was the only way she could stay in touch with Suraj.

For the first time since Veda's wedding had been fixed, Suraj smiled.

'God, you are clever,' he said. Then he added as an afterthought, 'But, why are we hiding it? What is there to hide? We are just friends, right?'

'Yes, Suraj. I don't know how the others will interpret our friendship, though. So I think it's best if we don't tell anyone,' Veda explained.

'I don't think it is right, Veda. You should tell your future husband.' Suraj couldn't bring himself to say his name.

'You think I should tell Bhuwan?' asked Veda.

'Definitely.'

'I am scared.'

'What are you scared of?'

'What if he doesn't approve? What if he says I cannot keep in touch with you?'

'Then you must not.'

'Come on, Suraj! How can you say that? Is that all that our friendship means to you?'

'You know very well it would kill me not to be in touch with you. But what is the solution?'

'Look, he doesn't own me, okay? He is marrying me. Not buying me. He is not my father, that I have to take permission. You leave that part of my life to me. I will handle it,' Veda was emphatic and spoke with a confidence she didn't feel. A moment later, she asked, 'What is the alternative, Suraj? Do you see any other way out?'

Suraj paused for a moment. Then he said, 'Just refuse, Veda. Say no to this marriage. Say you don't want to get married.'

Veda frowned, deep in thought as she considered this. On what basis could she refuse this marriage proposal? There wasn't anything going on between Suraj and her. And, there was no guarantee that any another guy that her parents chose would be better than Bhuwan. Bhuwan seemed sweet and considerate. There was no reason strong enough for her to refuse. It would also make her parents look bad, if she refused at this point, without any concrete reason.

When she spoke, she was clear. 'I can't, Suraj. All the arrangements are in progress. Papa has already spoken to a few people, and has booked a marriage hall with great difficulty. He will be made to look like a fool if I say anything now. Everybody in the community will laugh at him. It's too late. This was one of his conditions, when he let me attend college. And in any case, all the girls in my family get married early. All my cousins got married before they were twenty-one. It is the norm. I can't break it. And based on what? Based on our friendship?'

Suraj was silent again. Veda was right in all that she said. How could he be selfish and ask her to break off her engagement? What right did he have to do that?

'You know what—I am sorry. You are right. I honestly do not know why I am behaving like this. I guess it is just the thought of ... losing you,' said Suraj.

'Look, I know all this writing letters in secret makes you uncomfortable. Let me just get to know Bhuwan a little better. I will tell him, alright? Don't worry about it,' Veda assured him.

She knew she wanted to stay in touch with Suraj, and she

was willing to do anything to make it happen. The weeks she had spent with him had been beautiful. Theirs was a unique friendship, and they completely understood each other. She did not want to lose him. Veda was determined about that.

She spoke to Vidya about it. Vidya said she liked Veda's plan, and that she was more than happy to be a part of it.

'Good friends are hard to come by, didi. Why should you lose touch with him just because you are married? Are married people not allowed to have friends of the opposite sex?' Vidya asked, indignantly.

'I will speak to Bhuwan about it at some point. Let me just get to know him a little better,' Veda said.

'Yes, he seems to be a reasonable guy. And he does seem nice. Are you excited about the wedding, didi? Now that the date is so close, I am looking forward to it. I feel very bad that you have to go away, though,' said Vidya.

'I have mixed feelings now. Initially, I was horrified at the thought of marriage. But now, it is like I have accepted it. Look at it this way, Vidya—this guy, Bhuwan, seems kind and understanding. What if I refuse and the next guy they pick is worse than him?'

'True—and if you had refused this guy, it wouldn't have gone down well at all. Didi—don't worry, we will stay in touch through letters. I promise to write regularly,' said Vidya.

'You better! I am not sure whether we will be able to talk on the phone. You know how prickly Papa gets about big telephone bills, and I don't know if Bhuwan is like that too. But I will call when I can,' said Veda.

'Yes, we shall write regularly, didi,' Vidya agreed.

Now that the wedding was to happen soon, Rajinder was overjoyed, and so was her mother. Veda's father had never spoken to her with as much affection as he did in the days before the wedding. He was suddenly kind and sweet towards her. It was as though, by agreeing to the marriage, she had been elevated in his eyes. She was now the star of the house.

The last few days had flown by with the arrival of relatives, visits to the beauty parlour, the mehendi ceremony, sangeet and all the excitement of a typical Indian wedding. Veda had silently participated in it all. She wasn't too keen, but she knew that her cousins were enjoying themselves and she played along.

A week later, Veda's marriage took place with great pomp and ceremony. Rajinder walked around proudly, greeting all the guests at the venue, welcoming them. Everybody talked about the wedding for days afterwards. All the relatives said that the caterer had done a great job.

'How are you feeling, didi?' Vidya asked Veda on the day of the wedding. She was the only one who understood her sister.

'Like a lamb being led to the slaughter,' whispered Veda, decked in her bridal jewellery.

'Come on, didi, Bhuwan isn't all that bad,' said Vidya.

'Yes, I know. I will try—to love him.'

Vidya felt a sharp wave of sadness engulfing her when she heard her sister say this in a resigned manner. They were the saddest words she had ever heard.

Veda dutifully took part in all the rituals associated with the wedding, even though she found them tiresome. She did not look up at Bhuwan or meet his eyes during any of the ceremonies.

Veda had invited Suraj to the wedding. From time to time, her eyes would covertly scan the hall, searching for him. She didn't see him. She spotted some of her college mates, though. Rekha, who was dressed in a blue lehenga choli, was laughing and chattering away with their friends. It seemed like everyone was having a good time at her wedding, except for her.

Veda called for Vidya as the priest chanted the mantras. When she came close, Veda whispered, 'Is he here?'

Vidya shook her head.

He had not promised her that he would attend when she had given him the wedding invitation.

'I honestly cannot be a part of this, Veda. I wish you joy. Write to me, if you can,' he had said. She had begged him to try and attend.

It was during the *bidai* ceremony, the final conclusion to the wedding rituals, when the bride leaves the marital home, that she spotted him. Her heart leapt up with joy as their eyes met. She saw sadness in his.

She crossed the doorstep, accompanied by her parents and her relatives, and according to the custom, threw back three fistfuls of rice and coins over her head.

One of the coins landed near Suraj's feet.

Nobody noticed, as he picked it up and slipped it into the pocket of his kurta.

It was an emotional moment—the bride leaving her parental home. Even Rajinder hadn't been able to hold back his emotions and looked like he would cry when he escorted Veda to the waiting car. Veda's mother and her relatives started crying as Veda got into the car with Bhuwan, the entourage following them. The car had been decorated with flowers and looked grand, festive and splendid.

As the car drove away, Veda looked back through the rear windshield, feeling numb.

Is this all there was to a girl's life? Get married and leave the home you have known all your life? What was she getting into? Why hadn't she listened to Suraj and protested? Why didn't she have the courage to stand up for herself, and express what she wanted?

She was filled with regret at how passive she had been through all that had happened.

But it was too late now—there was no turning back.

The car made its way slowly down the mountain slopes, and with each turn it took, Veda felt her heart sink further.

She had never felt this alone in her life.

Part Two

PLAYING BY THE RULES

How dreadful … to be caught up in a game and have no idea of the rules.

– Caroline Stevermer, *Sorcery & Cecelia: or The Enchanted Chocolate Pot*

Chapter 7

December 1995
Pune

Dearest, dearest Vidya,

How are you? How are Vandu, Vaish and Ani? Are you putting them to bed each night by reading out stories like I did? Animesh was distraught when I was leaving, and as you know, I had promised him that you would read them stories after I am gone. You had agreed too. I hope you are keeping your promise? Are Ma and Papa happy? I sincerely hope they are.

It's been a fortnight here, and it is only now that I am getting the peace and quiet to settle down and start writing to you. Pune is a nice city, but it is so different from Joshimath (naturally). The flat that I am staying in is in an old building. It is a tiny, two-bedroom flat on the third floor. The good thing is that it has a fairly large balcony off the living room. I can see that some of the homes in the colony have plants on the balcony, but we don't have any. There is just cane furniture there—two chairs and a circular table. My father-in-law mostly sits on this balcony, reading his newspapers and financial magazines.

'My bedroom' (I still have not got used to calling it 'my bedroom', as the term instantly brings to mind the room that you and I used to share) is small, and does not have a balcony. When I say small, I mean very small. There is our bed, and opposite that there is a desk. We have a chest of drawers filled with God-knows-what (all old things) standing in one corner. We also have a small attached bathroom. This flat is so much smaller than our home at Joshimath. At least, over there, we could step out and feel the fresh air. Here, I feel suffocated, but I guess I will get used to it.

We have had to visit countless relatives, and go to countless temples. There have been visitors coming over all the time too, and each time I have had to wear a saree and all the wedding jewellery. I also had to dutifully serve them tea and snacks. I hate all of it, but my mother-in-law insists.

And Vidya—I know how your mind works. I know what you

desperately want to know. Yes, yes—I can read your mind! No, Bhuwan and I haven't done it yet. I told him I was nervous about it. Do you remember how much we discussed it and how Anita didi had scared us with all those *suhaag raat* stories and how much it would bleed and hurt? I told all this to Bhuwan frankly, and he sounded so relieved, can you believe it? He said, 'You know, I am as nervous as you are about all of this. I am glad you told me. Let's not hurry anything. Honestly, it is not important for me.'

So, you can see, he is quite a considerate and understanding guy. I can only imagine from all the stories Anita didi and our cousins told us that the men they got married to must have been desperate to have sex. Who knows? So, for now, I am happy to let things be this way.

I can't talk to you freely on the phone, because the phone here is in the living room. My mother-in-law is around all the time. She hardly leaves me alone. Every five minutes it is, 'Veda beti this ... Veda beti that'. It feels so odd when she calls me beti. She says I can call her Ma. It doesn't feel right. I mean, for me, it is only our mother who is Ma and no one else can take her place.

My father-in-law keeps himself busy always. When he is not looking at his financial magazines or reading the paper, he is out meeting friends who live in the same complex. They are all retired professors like him. I think they bought these apartments at the same time.

Though it is an old complex, it is comfortable and nice. There are no lifts in the building, but I don't mind that. Three floors is not too hard to climb, especially when you are used to climbing hills in Joshimath! There are a few trees around in the compound, and some plants which form the 'garden'. They need to be taken better care of.

I can hear my father in-law calling out to me. My mother-in-law has gone out to some temple with her friends. I shall come back later and finish this letter.

'Yes, Baba?' Veda said as she placed the cap on the pen, put it away and went out of the bedroom to see why her father-in-law had called out to her.

'Come, beti. Make some tea and join me here, on the balcony,' her father-in-law said.

Veda was surprised. He had never invited her to join him before. She had noticed how he rarely spoke when her mother-in-law was around. It seemed to Veda that he was frightened of her. The moment her mother-in-law went out somewhere, her father-in-law's personality transformed. He became friendlier towards her. Veda had also caught the silent understanding glances between Bhuwan and his father whenever her mother-in-law said something which they did not quite agree with. It was evident to Veda that they were humouring her. They never argued with her, but found a way to change the subject. The only person who seemed to be unaware of it was her mother-in-law.

Veda was pleased at her father-in-law's invitation. She quickly made two cups of ginger tea and joined him on the balcony.

'Sit, beti,' he said, indicating the chair opposite him. Veda sank into the cane chair and discovered that it was very comfortable. Bright winter sunlight streamed in, lighting up the balcony. Veda squinted her eyes to adjust to the brightness. She had never sat here before.

'This is lovely. You make a good cup of tea,' said her father-in-law.

Veda smiled. 'My father too loves the tea I make,' she said.

'So, how are your studies going, beti? Do you like the college?' asked her father-in-law.

'Yes, Baba, it is nice,' she said, though she hadn't yet made up her mind. Two days after she had joined, Christmas break had started. She knew he had pulled a few strings to get her in. She did not want to sound ungrateful by complaining.

'Okay, that's good,' he said. He glanced furtively around. Then he lowered his voice and said, 'Listen, beti, I want to tell you something.'

'Yes, Baba?' said Veda, curious, as she sipped her tea. She had started addressing her in-laws as Maaji and Baba. She did not know how else to address them, and this seemed the most respectful way.

'You know my wife—she is just an eighth class fail. She is not educated. She does not understand or appreciate the value of education. They lied to me at the time of marriage, saying she had done her matriculation. I found out only later. But anyway, that is all many years in the past. Why I tell you this is because I do not want you to be upset about the remarks she makes. I have noticed that you feel bad, beti. I see it on your face. Bhuwan and me—we have learnt to put up with her moods, anger and sharp words over the years. But you—you are new here. I wanted to tell you all this right at the start. But only today, have I got the chance,' he said.

'Oh,' said Veda, completely taken by surprise.

So her father-in-law had noticed the sharp remarks that her mother-in-law made. He was observant. She had never thought that he was on *her* side. Veda felt happy that she had an ally. He understood her, and he had taken the trouble to explain things to her. She found it endearing.

'Thank you, Baba—thank you for telling me this,' she said.

'Don't take anything she says to heart. She has a sharp tongue, but she has a heart of gold. Just remember that,' he said.

'Yes, Baba, I will keep that in mind,' said Veda.

I am continuing this letter, after a brief chat with my father-in-law. He seems to be a nice soul! He is very different from my mother-in-law. He told me just now that my mother-in-law has a soft side, and not to take to heart whatever she says. He has noticed how she treats me! Can you believe that? He is a sensitive man.

You know Vidya, when I was in Joshimath, I dreamt of escaping to the city. Remember how I used to long for it? But now that I am living in a city, I discover that I miss the mountains. Over there, I could step outside the house and I would be in the garden, inhaling the fabulous cold, fresh air. I never thought that I would say this, but I miss the air in Joshimath. What an odd thing to miss, right?

I have to help my mother-in-law with all the cooking. She comments all the time about anything I do. If I chop the vegetables, it is too big or too tiny. If I cook the rice, it is too hard or too soft. She sighs exasperatedly, and more than twice, she asked if our mother hadn't taught me anything. I wanted to tell her that Paro didi helps our mother in our home, but that would have antagonised her, and I don't want any friction between us at this point. So I held back my words.

My father-in-law was helpful, and he got my admission done. I attended college only for two days, and then Christmas break started. I guess I will be able to tell you more about my college once I start attending regularly.

Bhuwan says that once it reopens, he will drop me to college. He drives a Maruti 1000! He says it was always his dream to own a nice car, and since he didn't have to take a home loan, he thought he might as well take a vehicle loan. My mother-in-law is very proud of it and she drops it into conversations with all the relatives we visit.

Bhuwan opened a bank account for me here, and I have deposited all the cash that was gifted to me during the wedding. When Bhuwan and I went to open the account, my mother-in-law wanted to know if the account would be in our joint names. Bhuwan told her that it would be. But on the way to the bank, he said that he did not want any of the money that was gifted to me, and I should have it all. Bhuwan also said that he would deposit a quarter of his salary in my account every month, so that I don't have to ask him for cash. I can go to the bank and withdraw whatever amount I like. He asked me if that was enough. I said it was more than enough. I think he is being very sweet and generous. I don't have to spend on anything, as it is my mother-in-law who buys all the groceries, which Bhuwan pays for. I only need money for my auto fare, and what Bhuwan deposits for me is quite a large sum.

My mother-in-law seems to have her own gang of friends here. There's Shanta aunty and Kanti behen. They came home once, and I learnt that Shanta aunty has a daughter who is around twenty-eight. Kanti behen's (don't ask me why she is Kanti behen and not Kanti aunty—everyone here calls her Kanti behen) sons live abroad, I think.

My mother-in-law has a maid, Shakubai, who is supposed to come every morning at around 6.30. She is late on most days though, and then there is a never-ending drama. The highlight of my mother-in-law's morning seems to be the arrival of Shakubai. She is very different from Paro didi, who was (and still is) a part of our family. Here, in this house, I get the impression that Shakubai is easily replaceable. Her work too is not very good. It seems like she does it only for the money, and doesn't put her heart in it. Often, after she has finished sweeping and mopping our bedroom, and after she has left, I bring the mop out, and reach far under the bed, where she has not cleaned, and it is dusty. The first time I did that, my mother-in-law shouted at Shakubai the next day. Now I am careful to do it only when my mother-in-law is not around. I don't want Shakubai to get shouted at because of me.

Vidya—your birthday is coming soon! A very happy birthday in advance! I shall try my best to call you. But if I am not able to for some reason, I am wishing you in this letter.

I am enclosing a letter to Suraj in a sealed envelope with this letter. Please do give it to him. And please do put in his letter to me when you send me your reply.

Study hard, Vidya.

Tell me all the news. I am waiting to hear from you (okay, okay and from Suraj too!) eagerly.

Lots of love,
Your sis,
Veda

December 1995
Pune

Dear Suraj,

How are you, my friend? As promised, I am writing. Vidya will give you this letter when you meet her on the way back from college.

I can't tell you how happy I was when I saw you at my wedding. Though you missed all the main rituals, I was glad that you made it at least for the *bidai* ceremony. When I saw you, I was almost in tears. But I felt very happy seeing you there. A big thank you for coming.

Life here is very different compared to how it was in Joshimath. (Of course, it was bound to be different. But I think I am surprised by how different.)

I am the same person I was before I got married. But now, I am being made to feel like a 'married' woman. I *am* a married woman, I know. But that's not how I *feel*. I feel like the same Veda who is the eldest sister at home, who is Suraj's friend, and who is 'normal'. It's not that being married is abnormal in any way, but oh, it is so strange.

Over the past fortnight, I have visited countless relatives of Bhuwan's (the word 'husband' seems so odd). I have never visited this many of my own relatives in my entire life, at Joshimath. Everywhere I go, I have to wear all these fancy sarees and deck up in my bridal jewellery. I dislike it. But it is customary—or so my mother-in-law says.

Bhuwan is a nice guy. He leaves early for work and comes back quite late. It seems like he is quite the workaholic. His father is a sweet gentleman and he has managed to secure admission for me in one of the best colleges here. There was no problem about the transfer of credits either.

I haven't yet talked to Bhuwan about keeping in touch with you. But please do not worry about it. He seems to be a very considerate person and I am sure he will understand.

What do you do during lunch break these days? Have you resumed eating at the canteen? How are your academics going? What new books have you read?

Bhuwan told me that there is a library somewhere close by, and he said he would take me there over the weekend. But two weekends have whizzed past and we still haven't made it. I guess we will go one of these weekends, and I will get a membership there. I am looking forward to it.

How is your grandmother? What is happening at your end?

Do write back soon. Put the letter in a sealed envelope and give it to Vidya.

She will co-ordinate with you about where to meet to hand over the letter.

Eagerly waiting to hear from you.

Your friend,

Veda

Chapter 8

December 1995
Joshimath

My darling didi!!

How happy I am to hear from you. When Papa and Ma spoke to you two days ago (when your letter was in transit) I badly wanted to talk to you too. I begged them, but Papa said I couldn't, as it would be expensive. I was angry. I am glad you conveyed through Ma that your letter was on the way. That consoled me somewhat.

Every day, I have been asking postman Chandu if there is a letter from you. Today, when he handed it to me, I couldn't wait to read it.

I am replying to you immediately, didi.

I have hidden your letter to Suraj in my history textbook, in between the folds of the brown paper cover, and not between the pages of the book. Clever, right? This way, nobody will discover it. I will give it to him tomorrow.

Every single day, he waits for me at the crossing, didi, and every day he asks if I have heard from you. He was happy when I told him that a letter is on the way. We do not talk more than a sentence or two, as we do not want to be seen together. You know how Joshimath is. If word gets out about this to Papa, we are both dead.

I must say it is kind of exciting to smuggle letters. I like being in the middle of your adventure, didi.

I am reading to Vandu, Vaish and Ani every day, like you used to. But they say I am not as good as you, and that they miss you. I threatened them that if that was the case, I would stop reading to them. That shut them up. Hah!

Papa and Ma are happy. Your marriage is a huge achievement for them. Papa tells all and sundry about his daughter in Pune, who is married and happily settled. He boasts about jiju's job, and his car—it's almost like he owns the car himself! His pride is evident in his voice.

So, you and Bhuwan jiju haven't done it yet? I was worried for you, didi. I prayed at the Narsinghji temple that my didi shouldn't get hurt. Do you think I should not have prayed?

Your mother-in-law sounds like a demoness to me, didi. I did not like how she behaved at the wedding, bossing everyone around. She shouted at those poor caterers when the *pooris* took a little longer to make. From what you told me about her, I feel she annoys you a lot, but you are too polite to say it. She seems to me like the stereotypical, annoying mother-in-law they portray in television serials. Is she like that?

I think if she was a little nicer to Shakubai, then Shakubai would do a better job too.

I miss you so much, didi. Now that you are not here, Vandu has moved into our bedroom. One part of me is angry that she has moved in. It is silly, I know. But I cannot help it.

Didi, why did you leave all your favourite books here? You know what—while you were here, you kept telling me to read all the time and I did not bother. But now that you are gone, I am reading your books and liking them very much. It's funny the things the absence of someone makes you do.

Try and enjoy the city, didi. Get Bhuwan jiju to take you out on weekends. I think you will start liking it then. Joshimath is still the same old boring Joshimath. Nothing new.

Life goes on, didi.

I will post this letter as soon as Suraj gives me his reply.

I wish we could speak on the phone, didi. I am going to start pestering Ma to allow me to make a phone call to you, when Papa is not around. I hope she agrees, and I hope you are at home when I call. I think I will call you on my birthday! They cannot refuse me that one phone call. And I turn eighteen! I will officially be an adult.

Will talk to you soon, didi.

All my love,

Your sis,

Vidya

December 1995

Joshimath

Dear, dear Veda,

After a long wait, I have been rewarded with a letter from you. I would be lying if I said that I hadn't been waiting for it. Vidya will tell you how I pestered her every day. At one point, I even thought she was lying and that she didn't want to give me the letter. Or that maybe you had forgotten your promise, and I was being a fool to wait for a letter from you.

I wasn't going to attend your marriage. It was painful for me, Veda. Do not ask me why, but it was. So I stayed away, fuming and fretting. I also knew that just because I stayed away, it did not mean that the marriage wouldn't take place.

Then my dadi asked me what was wrong. I told her about your marriage, and how I think it is wrong that you are getting married so early.

My dadi laughed and said that she had got married when she was eight years old. Can you believe that? She said that my mother had been married when she was sixteen. In comparison to that, twenty is not too bad. She said that if I was a good friend to you, I should be there for you, especially if you had invited me and it meant a great deal to you. She urged me to attend, and that was how I was there at your *bidai* ceremony.

Do you know, the coins you threw back—one of them landed by my foot, and I have kept it in my wallet as my good luck charm. It is a reminder of our friendship.

By the time you receive this letter, you would have started college. I hope the lecturers there are good. I hope you settle down quickly and I hope you have fun.

I miss you and our conversations. Especially since we were so inseparable in the weeks preceding your marriage. I have gone back to what I used to do—I eat in the canteen. Rekha tries to join me. But I prefer eating alone. She told me the other day, 'Don't go around like Devdas.' That irked me. I did not like the over-familiarity.

I am reading a very interesting historical novel set in Scotland called *Waverly*. It was first published anonymously by Sir Walter

Scott. Later, it became so popular that all his subsequent works were advertised as 'By the author of *Waverly*'. I am finding it a bit of a difficult read, but it is very interesting, especially as it has a love story woven in too.

Please do join that library and start reading.

You know, I must confess that, now that you are far away, I am not bothered by whether you tell your husband about our letters or not. I like to think that (perhaps it is wrong or foolish of me) this world that we carve out through letters is ours alone. Like we have said to each other countless times—we are good friends, and there is nothing wrong in friends writing to each other, is there? I am just happy to receive your letters, and if you choose to send them through your sister, so be it.

I hope I haven't bored you with this letter by giving you more details than you asked for.

Please look after yourself, Veda.

I wish you all happiness, my friend, and I look forward to hearing from you.

And yes—wish you a very Happy New Year too!

Suraj

January 1996

Pune

Dear, dear Suraj,

Happy New Year, my friend!

I was very happy to receive your letter. What a good thing it was that we decided to send these letters hidden in Vidya's letters. My mother-in-law is a curious cat. She asked me whose letter it was, and I could honestly tell her that it was from my sister Vidya. Vidya had decorated the envelope with hand-drawn flowers and doodles and had also written her name prominently. God bless her! My mother-in-law did not bother after that.

I have started attending college after the break. It is very different from our college at Joshimath. My accent and the way I speak is different from the way people speak here. They seem to use a lot of Marathi words. I feel like an outsider. They treat me that way too. Just like how it was in our college, there are 'gangs' here too, and all the gangs were formed in the first year itself. Since I have joined in the latter half of the final year, it is difficult for me to break into any gang and be accepted. I mostly eat lunch by myself.

The lecturers back home (funny, for me, Joshimath is still 'home') are definitely better in some subjects, but in certain other subjects, the ones here are very good. But what I love about this college is the library.

Suraj, if you ever come here, you will love it too. It is massive, and is spread across two floors. There are very tall wooden shelves running from the roof to the floor. It is an old college, almost a hundred years old, built during the British era. So the architecture is Victorian. The campus is very large, compared to our college in Joshimath.

I just don't feel at home here. There are many more clubs, and many inter-collegiate festivals. But I haven't enrolled in anything. It is almost as if you must be aggressive to be noticed and included. That is something I cannot do. I am the wallflower here, always on the sidelines. I escape to the library whenever we have a free period. I am writing this letter from the library.

I feel I am leading a dichotomous life. I am struggling to come to terms with being a married woman. Nobody else in my class is married and they were shocked to discover that I was. The way the girls screamed when they discovered the fact—it was like I have a disease or something. I felt embarrassed and self-conscious as they asked me a lot of questions, till one of them (her name is Betty; what a strange name!) asked them all to leave me alone and mind their own business.

One of the boys asked me out for coffee. But before I could answer, a girl called out, 'Hey, leave her alone. She is married.' That was the end of it. I would have said yes. It would have been better than being alone. But now there is no chance of that. He has told all the other boys and they treat me with great wariness. This 'married' status is something like a protection shield, or perhaps a fence.

The historical novel you are reading sounds very interesting.

I am reading a non-fiction book right now, which is a series of essays and reflections by Marcus Aurelius. I found it in my father-in-law's small collection of books. I would have loved to discuss them with you. We would have met during lunch break and talked.

Sigh—I must be content with writing to you now.

After all, it was I who made this choice.

I hope my next letter will be a little cheerier.

That's all for now.

Your friend,

Veda

PS: I love your letters. Longer the better. And no, I do not find them boring at all. Not even the least bit.

January 1996

Pune

Dearest darling Vidya,

There is such a lot to write to you. I am happy that you managed to pester Ma and we managed to speak on your birthday, even though it was for a very brief time. I am also happy that Bhuwan wished you on your birthday. I think it was nice of him.

So, do you feel any different being eighteen? I bet you feel the same way you did when you were seventeen. Nothing much changes—except that legally you can vote, get a driver's licence and, if you are a girl, you can marry. I am sure you don't intend to do any of that soon. So it's more the thrill of boasting to your friends that you are eighteen, isn't it?

Here, the situation is such that I must take my mother-in-law's permission if I want to call you. I do not want to do that. Also, I cannot talk freely if she is around. Bhuwan isn't here most of the time. He is such a workaholic.

First, the big news. Finally, we did the deed. It was HORRIBLE, Vidya. I have no words to tell you how TERRIBLE it was. He came late from an office party a few days ago. I knew he was drunk, as he wasn't at all like his usual self, and his breath had a weird smell. He told me I am a great girl. That too is very unusual. It is the first time since we got married that he is paying me a compliment like that. It is strange, but we have zero chemistry between us. There is no physical attraction whatsoever. I feel nothing when I lie in bed next to him.

I feel awful when I think about Suraj—how excited I felt to see him, how I noticed everything about him, and above all, how attracted I was to him. So I know, feeling this way about Bhuwan, this is definitely strange. I mean—I should at least feel *something,* right? But it does not seem to bother him at all. He is very okay with having no sex. Then, that night, suddenly, he seemed to have been transformed into another person. It was as if he was trying to seduce me. He paid me compliments, said I looked beautiful, and then proceeded to undress me. I was frozen with the unexpectedness of it all, not knowing what to say or how to react. I mean—he is my husband, after all.

Oh, Vidya—I clutched the bedsheets hard as he got on top of me, fumbling with his you-know-what. He then put on a condom. It hurt like crazy. It felt like some sandpaper down there. It did not last even a few minutes. A few thrusts and it was over. I breathed then. Is this what Anita didi and the others chuckle about? I can tell you one thing, Vidya—sex is highly overrated.

After the whole act, he said he was sorry for marrying me! Then he said he was sorry for having sex! He was blabbering. I have no idea why he was being apologetic. Maybe he realised that it was painful for me. Who knows? Anyway, I was just glad it was over.

The next morning, he apologised once again, saying that he had had a bit too much to drink, and he was sorry. Then he went back to being his old self. It was as if it had never happened. After that, he has not touched me again, but he continues to be polite and nice to me.

Last weekend, we went out for the first time without his mother. What a relief it was. Up to now, we have gone only to his relatives' places, and with the full family. He took me to meet his friend Vikki. I like Vikki. He and Bhuwan have known each other for a very long time. Vikki wants to become a filmmaker. He is funny, and he makes me laugh. He is quite the opposite of Bhuwan! He is spontaneous, adventurous and great to be around. Bhuwan transforms into a different person around him, and he loosens up so much. Vikki, Bhuwan and I went to Sinhagad Fort in Vikki's new jeep. (Yes, he drives an open jeep!) It's great, as your hair flies in the wind. I enjoyed myself a lot, Vidya.

If you ever come here, we should so do the Sinhagad trek. I found it very easy, as we are used to the mountains in Joshimath. I was leading throughout, because it came so naturally to me. It took us about two hours to climb. The view was beautiful and it felt good to be in the mountains again. For a brief while, I felt at home.

'You are such a mountain goat,' Vikki said.

'And you are only a goat,' I retorted.

How Bhuwan laughed!

On top, where the fort was, there were stalls selling *kulfi*, *bhakri* (a Maharashtrian savoury) and *matka dahi*. I would have liked it better if it had been uninhabited. It felt very tame to me, but still, it was a change from visiting relatives.

My mother-in-law isn't too pleased with my attending college. I heard her complaining to her friends when they came to visit. She thought I was in my room, doing my college work. And I was. I had served them tea and pakoras and had gone into my bedroom to work. But then I wanted a bottle of water, and I overheard them as I walked to the kitchen. I heard her tell them that I don't do any housework, and all I am interested in is dressing up and going off to college. She said that she wants to be a grandmother soon, and she hopes I will give her some 'good news'. I cringed when I heard that.

Shanta aunty said that I was very young, and to let me be.

'What young? At her age, I used to fetch at least eight pots of water on my head, walking twenty-five kilometres, because we never had water in our ancestral home. It was my duty to see to all of that. Here, she cannot even manage the house. I was looking forward to retiring once my son wed. But it seems impossible, with the zero responsibility that this girl takes,' she said.

I felt sad to hear that. I don't know what responsibility she wants me to take on. She decides everything that has to be cooked. I do whatever she tells me to. What more does she want from me?

Vidya, I hardly find time for studies here. My mother-in-law keeps me on my toes all the time. I tried raising this with Bhuwan.

'I wish I could do something about this. She has these set ideas in her head about how a daughter-in-law should be. The thing is, one can never win an argument with my mother. Just humour her for now, Veda. We will see what we can do about it,' he said.

I am sorry for rambling on and on about my married life. But I feel you are the only person I can open up and pour my heart to.

Do not fall into this same trap that I have fallen into, Vidya.

Please study hard and start working. Marriage sucks.

I am happy that you are reading to Vandu, Vaish and Ani. Please convey my love to them. Tell them I am longing to see them, and I miss them very much. Tell them to study hard.

Please reply soon, Vidya.

Lots of love and a big hug,

Your sister,

Veda

Chapter 9

February 1996
Pune

Dearest, darling Vidya,
Please forgive me for not writing earlier. I am still in a state of shock. I haven't recovered, even though it has been twenty-two days. I did not know whether to be happy or sad when I saw Ma and Papa here. I was so upset that the first time they came to this house was because of a death.

He was such a gentle soul. He was highly respected too. There were many academics who came to pay their last respects. All the neighbours and people who live in this residential complex came too. Bhuwan is in a state of shock. My mother-in-law is being very stoic. She single-handedly took charge of everything and Bhuwan just followed her orders.

Oh, Vidya—seeing death this close has left me shaken to the very core. What if something like this happens to Papa?

I shudder to think of it.

Everyone says my father-in-law is fortunate that he passed away in his sleep. They say things like, 'God came down from heaven and carried him away in his chariot.' I don't know, Vidya; I think death is always devastating. It leaves behind fragments for others to collect. Shards that tear your insides.

I barely knew my father-in-law. Yet, I recall so fondly the one conversation we had on the balcony that day. I can't but help wonder (selfishly perhaps), that if he hadn't had that lovely conversation with me, would I have felt his death this deeply? He had told me to be forgiving towards my mother-in-law, and that she was uneducated. He had told me to bear with her and that she has a heart of gold.

I am yet to see that gold.

Vidya—do you know, my mother-in-law openly told all the relatives who visited that I had brought bad luck to the family? I felt miserable and sad when I heard those words. She did not bother that Ma and Papa were visiting. She carried on lamenting loudly about this to all who came. My heart sank when I saw Papa hanging his head in shame, and Ma being so apologetic. I felt worthless and helpless.

Why, Vidya, why? Why did they have to shoulder this blame that my mother-in-law has chosen to place on me?

What made it worse was that Bhuwan remained silent. I hoped that he would defend me. I wanted him to tell his mother to shut up. Instead, he stood silently, holding her, comforting her.

I am glad Ma and Papa left as soon as the body was taken for cremation.

Vikki was very comforting towards me. He was present throughout. I think Bhuwan is fortunate to have him as a friend. He took me inside and told me to ignore whatever my mother-in-law was saying.

'People say all kinds of things when they are extremely upset. I'm she doesn't mean any of it,' he said.

I believed him for a while.

But the way she behaves towards me has totally changed. She wasn't friendly to begin with. But now she has become unbearably oppressive.

If she sees me, she turns the other way. She doesn't look at my face. She pretends I do not exist. It hurts me, Vidya, and I think she knows it. I hate myself because I find that I am doing things to earn her approval. For instance, I did all the cooking yesterday. She did not help at all. She said she was feeling very upset and was going to visit Shanta aunty. When she came back and saw that I had finished cooking everything, she did not even utter a single word. When I served her the meal, she said it was too bland, and that the masalas I had used were all wrong. There was no need for her to make that comment. But I cannot do anything right in her eyes.

I am now beginning to feel that maybe it is all my fault. Maybe I have been unlucky for this family. Look at the timing of his death. It's not even three months since we got married, and already they have had a tragedy. Do you remember what Renu maasi used to say—that a new bride is Lakshmi Devi incarnate and she brings luck to the family. How can this be when I have brought them only ill luck?

I am such a coward, Vidya. I should stand up to her and tell her to not ignore me like this. I feel insignificant when she does that. But I am terrified. I am unable to speak up. That has always been my problem. Back home, I had you to speak up for me. Here, I feel all alone. I bitterly regret getting married. I should have had the courage, Vidya. I should have spoken my mind to Papa. I don't blame anyone but myself. I wish I was stronger.

I asked Bhuwan to speak to my mother-in-law about how she is behaving. He says it is best to let her be for a few days at least. He says she is grieving and she is very upset. He doesn't want to do anything to upset her further. I get the feeling that he too blames me, although he has not said anything to that effect. But the vibe I get from him is of aloofness. He hardly converses with me. Any effort from my side to make conversation is met with polite, studied replies. There is no real and open interaction. Perhaps he is grieving too and misses his father. I want to talk to him, but he seems to have shut me out.

I did very badly in my mock exams because of all this. I could barely touch my books.

I hope you are studying hard, and I hope you do well in your board exams. They are just around the corner now.

Write back to me, when time permits, and I understand if you take a while to reply.

Exams are important after all.

All my love,

Your sister,

Veda

'When the proper things are not followed or done, there is always a price to pay,' said Padma Devi to nobody in particular.

Veda and she were in the kitchen, cooking. Veda winced when she heard those words. She did not know what her mother-in-law was implying, but she knew the words were directed at her. She said nothing in response and continued to chop the vegetables, her head bowed.

Bhuwan was reading the morning newspaper. He had started sitting in the balcony, in the same chair his father used to occupy. He missed his father terribly. The images of the funeral pyre and the hundreds of rituals—or so they seemed to him—that he had performed, still played in his head. His father's death had been a shock and he was still coming to terms with it. He did not know what to do with this new feeling of heaviness in his heart, which seemed to have found its way inside and had set like concrete.

Looking back, he thought about how frail his father had become over the past few months. In retrospect, he understood that his health had been deteriorating. But since his father had never complained, and since he had no ailments, they had never paid much attention to it. Bhuwan wondered if his father's death could have been prevented, had they insisted on regular medical check-ups. It was too late now, yet these thoughts kept churning in his head.

'Nobody listens to me,' said Padma Devi, a little louder this time, as she forcefully yanked a large steel vessel from a lower shelf in the kitchen. The loud clang of the steel as it hit the other vessels startled Bhuwan, forcing him to snap out of his thoughts.

'Eh? Sorry, Ma, I didn't hear you,' he said.

'How will you hear? This *kalmuhi* here has brainwashed you. You don't even have time for your mother anymore,' said Padma Devi.

Veda felt as if she had been slapped. Had she really said that? Had she just called her a *kalmuhi*?

This was an open insult. So far, Veda had silently borne the brunt of Padma Devi's behaviour and indirect abuse. But this was unbearable. Veda opened her mouth to protest. No words came out, though. Years of conditioning took over. Veda bit back the words that rose to her lips, swallowed them, not allowing them to escape. She kept mum, waiting for Bhuwan to say something.

But Bhuwan just muttered a few incomprehensible words that had a very vague resemblance to a half-hearted objection, after which he continued to read the paper.

'What? What did you say?' asked Padma Devi, ready to pounce on him.

'Nothing, Ma,' said Bhuwan.

Satisfied, Padma Devi continued her rant and directed it at Veda.

'All these happenings—it is because you aren't having a bath in the morning and you are not lighting the lamp. You know the rituals, don't you? In your house, don't they do the pooja?'

'We do,' said Veda, trying to keep her voice steady.

'Then? You know that it has to be done. Not once since you stepped into this house have you done the pooja. No wonder we got cursed. You'd better wake up at 5.30 a.m. from tomorrow. I will wake you when I get up. I don't want you lazing in bed. Have a shower and perform the pooja. Is that clear?' Padma Devi glowered.

Veda mentally pictured herself waking up at 5.30. It would be impossible. Since she had not done too well in her mock exams, she was determined to put in extra effort in her academics. She had discovered that the best time to start studying was after everyone went to bed. So she stayed up till 3 a.m. on most nights. Now her mother-in-law had just announced this new rule of waking up at 5.30. How would she manage on two-and-a-half hours of sleep? Besides, she had no idea how to perform any of the rituals. At home, it was always her mother who said the mantras and performed the *arati*. Her role, and that of her siblings, had always been that of silent bystanders.

'I ... I'm sleeping quite late these days, Maaji. To study for my exams,' Veda mustered all her courage and spoke up.

'What?' demanded Padma Devi, irritated that Veda had dared to talk back.

'I ... I will not be able to wake up that early. I have to study for my exams,' Veda stammered.

Padma Devi turned away. Her eyes blazed with anger and she gritted her teeth. Her posture reminded Veda of a bull bracing for a fight.

Veda's heart thudded faster. She was frightened of her mother-in-law's temper. Each time she raised her voice, Veda just wanted to disappear. There was something about Padma Devi that was unnerving. Veda simply couldn't stand up to her wrath.

Padma Devi snorted in derision and walked up to Bhuwan.

'Did you hear what your wife said? Eh? She says she won't be able to wake up early and do the pooja. Do you know, it is the woman of the house who must do the rituals? Is it such a big thing I am asking? It is for the good of this house, is it not? It is not for myself. I am telling you, all these things happen when you break tradition,' Padma Devi ranted.

'Yes, Ma. We will do it,' Bhuwan told his mother in a placatory tone.

Veda turned away. She couldn't believe that her husband had just agreed to this unreasonable request. Surely, he could see how much her studies meant to her? Why wasn't he speaking up?

Later that night, as they retired to bed, Veda confronted Bhuwan.

'Why do you just agree to anything she says?' she asked him.

'She is in mourning, Veda, can't you see? She misses Baba very much.'

'I know, Bhuwan. But how is it that you cannot see how hard it is for me?'

'Sleep later, *na*? Do whatever pooja she wants you to do. Can't you sleep for a bit after coming back from college?

'Bhuwan, don't you know your mother? She will not let me sleep. In her book, sleep is a crime. She doesn't ever take a nap, have you noticed?' said Veda. The frustration in her voice was rising.

'Alright, I will explain to her,' said Bhuwan. Then he turned around and went to sleep.

Veda lay awake for a long time. She thought about her life in Joshimath and how she would never have been in this situation had she spoken up boldly. But she just could not imagine taking a stance, opposing her parents. She hated herself for being so passive. She hated herself for trying to please her mother-in-law. She hated Bhuwan for not standing up for her. She was filled with self-loathing and regret.

What had her life turned into? All she was doing was cooking and housework, with only Padma Devi for company. Bhuwan came home late on most days. Sure, she attended college, but she had no friends there. Back home in Joshimath, she'd had her sisters, her friends and her academics. Here, even that—academics—was slowly slipping from her hands. She had prided herself on being an outstanding student, but now, she barely had the time to even glance at her books.

Veda felt that her dreams were dying a slow death. With each passing day, she felt as if she was fading into oblivion. She was finding marriage and all the responsibilities that came with it a gigantic burden to bear. She felt stifled, imprisoned, suppressed. She saw no escape. It was a prison she had willingly walked into. Now she was trapped.

She sobbed into her pillow, feeling miserable and sorry for herself.

Bhuwan did not even realise she was crying; he slept on peacefully.

Veda continued to sob, and when she exhausted her tears, she fell into a slumber, eyes swollen and red from crying.

Chapter 10

February 1996

Pune

Dear, dear Suraj,

How are you, my friend? I hope you are doing well.

Me—I am not doing so good. You must have heard from Vidya about the sudden death of my father-in-law. Because of that, I did badly in my mock exams. Granted, it is only the college internal exams. These marks do not get counted in the final year mark sheet. But still, it is disheartening.

I haven't yet recovered from the suddenness of all of this.

I can only imagine how much more intense your pain must have been when you lost both your parents. Here, it is a person I have hardly known for a couple of months, yet I feel this bad. How did you cope, Suraj? How? I can't even begin to fathom the burden you carry. My heart goes out to you, my friend. I wish I could lessen your pain in some way. It's only now that I am even beginning to comprehend a bit of what it must have been like for you.

Here, I am having a little trouble with my mother-in-law, henceforth referred to as MIL. My MIL thinks I am to blame for my father-in-law's death. I wish Bhuwan would stand up for me. He doesn't. I kind of feel alone.

I am beginning to think that I have brought bad luck to this family.

Anyway—enough of my married-woman troubles now. Let us talk about you.

How is your grandmother? Have you finished reading *Waverly*? Did you start any other book? How are the preparations for your final exams going? What do you plan to do after your degree? Will you take up your father's job, which you said you are eligible for? Or do you plan to study further?

Write back soon, Suraj.

I so eagerly await your letters, and Vidya's too. I feel they are my lifeline.

Your friend,

Veda

February 1996
Joshimath

Dearest, dearest Veda didi,
How are you?

You have no idea how worried your letter made me. Forgive me, didi, but I showed it to Suraj. It doesn't sound like you at all, didi.

Firstly didi—get this clear: YOU ARE NOT TO BLAME YOURSELF for your father-in-law's death. It happened as it was fated to happen. How can you blame yourself?

Secondly—whatever you wrote in that letter, it sounded like you have given up the fight. I do not know in what state of mind you were when you wrote that letter, but it didn't sound good at all. You are just twenty. You have a whole life ahead of you.

When I asked Suraj about your letter to him, he said you seemed a little sad, but otherwise you sounded okay. That got me even more worried. I had to know what you had written to him. I am so sorry, didi—I made him show me the letter. He was hesitant, initially. But I told him that if he didn't do it, I wouldn't help him in getting any more letters across to you. I arm-twisted him into doing what I wanted. You know how determined I can be, when I want to get my way.

But didi, I did it only because I was worried about you. I noticed that you haven't painted such a dreary picture in the letter to him. I knew immediately that you were putting up a brave front for him. That was when I decided to show Suraj the letter you wrote me.

Didi, Suraj too was worried, after he read your letter to me. He said I should straightaway tell our parents about it. I told him that it would be of no use. I know what Papa and Ma will say. They will say that it is now your new home and you have to adjust.

In fact, I had told Ma the gist of your letter. She said that every married woman has to learn to deal with her mother-in-law, and that is apparently a part of being grown up. She went into great detail about how her own mother-in-law was unfair to her, and how she adjusted and put up with it.

I seriously think you should stand up to your mother-in-law. Do not take any nonsense that she dishes out. Some people understand boundaries only if you show them where they stand. You haven't set any boundaries. That is the reason she is trampling all over you.

I know we have been raised to respect our elders. But what if the elders are clearly in the wrong and are being unfair? Should we still respect them unquestioningly? I don't think so.

Didi—stop blaming yourself over this. I think you need a break, away from that house. Why don't you visit us for a few days?

Please talk to your mother-in-law and tell her you want to come here.

I am studying hard for my exams. I have solved lots of practice papers and I hope to do well.

Write back soon, didi.

With all my love,

Your sister,

Vidya

February 1996

Joshimath

Dear, dear Veda,

I am so sorry to hear about how you are feeling and even more sorry to see how hard you are taking all of this. Forgive me, Veda, for showing your letter to Vidya. I read your letter to her, as well. In my defence, she insisted I read it.

Look, it is NOT YOUR FAULT that your father-in-law died. Please STOP thinking it is.

Also, Veda, you can always confide in me. You don't have to hide your problems from me. We used to talk about everything so frankly—have you forgotten? We made a pact of friendship and I am here for you, my friend.

Why don't you stay back after college and study in the library? Come home late, if your mother-in-law is not letting you study at home. Carve your own path, Veda.

I am still reading *Waverly*. I couldn't find the time to complete it, as exam preparations got in the way. I also had some paperwork related to my parents' death, which I had to submit to the company my father worked for.

I think I will take up the job that they are offering, after graduation. They say I can start from June. I do not even have to wait for the final year results to be declared. My plan is to work for two or three years. Once I get work experience, I can take a sabbatical and do an MBA.

I have spoken to Yagnik uncle, who is still with the company. He was my father's friend and colleague. It is he who is my mentor and my guide. He too felt this would be a good idea.

Life is tough. But we can be tougher.

I am here for you any time you want to unburden yourself. Please feel free to use my shoulders.

Study hard. Focus on just that and forget all of this.

Write back soon.

Your friend,

Suraj

Chapter 11

February 1996
Kailash Mandir Colony, Pune

Veda read Suraj's letter many times over the next few days. The words 'carve your own path' stayed with her. He had written it with a black sketch pen and had also underlined it. She found herself doodling those words in her notebook while in college, when the lecturer droned on about a topic she had already understood. Suraj was so right. She would *have* to do something about this. She wondered why she hadn't thought of it herself. She could stay back after classes and study in the library. It was open till 6.30 in the evening, closing only when the administrative offices did.

Veda decided to stay back that very day. It felt odd to not leave at her usual time of 3.30, but she was determined to study. She headed straight to the library, found a silent corner, and opened up a book. She discovered that she could concentrate on her work much better in the library, than she could at home. At home, there was the constant presence of Padma Devi. She did not know when she would be summoned, and she was constantly on pins and needles. Here, she was completely relaxed. For the first time in many months—since she had got married, really—she felt completely at ease.

It was three hours later that she looked up, that too, only when one of the library staff gently approached her and told her it was closing time.

'Oh, right. Thanks, I am just leaving,' she said, as she packed up. Veda was pleased. In the three hours that she had spent there, she had managed to do more work than she had done in an entire week at home. Studying in the library was an efficient method and it was very productive too. She wished she could call Suraj and tell him this.

When she got home, however, she did not feel so good anymore. Any joy at her accomplishment quickly evaporated when she discovered that she had to face Padma Devi's wrath.

As she approached the flat, she noticed that the door was ajar. Padma Devi was pacing up and down in the drawing room. She looked up when she heard Veda enter.

She glared at Veda, with her hands on her hips. Her eyes narrowed.

'Where have you been? College gets over at 3.30, does it not? I have been waiting the whole time here for you.'

Veda could not speak. She could feel her heart in her throat. The one thing that terrified her was someone's anger. She just couldn't think or process anything when someone was angry with her, and she was the target of their ire. Her mind shut down. She had no control over her body, and the reactions were physical. Her palms went cold. Her heartbeat intensified and she almost froze in terror. It was involuntary. Each step she took needed a massive effort.

When she attempted to enter the house, Padma Devi blocked her way.

'Didn't you hear me? I asked you where you were.'

Veda knew there was no escape. She wasn't going to get away that easily. She had to answer.

'I ... I was in the library ... Studying...' she managed to get the words out, her voice strained and small.

'Hah! Studying. Why can't you study at home?'

'I ... It ... It's just that I had to refer to some books and they don't let us borrow those books,' said Veda, quickly improvising on the spot, the words tumbling out in fright.

Padma Devi couldn't refute that.

'Hmmm...' she said, as she stepped aside. 'Don't be late tomorrow onwards. Come home on time.'

Veda exhaled. She had not even realised that she had been holding her breath. She entered the house, a wave of relief washing over her. It was a small triumph, she thought. She decided that she would speak to Bhuwan about it and she would continue to study in the library. She would tell him how imperative it was for her to stay back to study. He simply would have to speak to his mother about it. She did not get the same kind of focus at home, that she got in the library.

That night, Bhuwan came home late. Veda had noticed

that he had been coming home very late, well past midnight, the last few days. Despite her best efforts to stay up and wait for him so that she could talk to him, Veda was fast asleep when he entered their bedroom. She did not even stir when he crawled into bed and settled down, his back facing her. There was no exchange of tenderness or affection between them. They did not cuddle or hold each other like most newlywed young couples would.

To Veda, it came as a relief that her husband was not the kind who was big on physical demonstrations of his love. She would have felt claustrophobic if he had insisted on hugging her through the night. She had heard stories from her married cousins, about how their husbands insisted on putting an arm or even a leg across their partners the whole night, and how they had now got so used to it that sleeping any other way was unimaginable. To Veda, it sounded suffocating, and she was comfortable that she and Bhuwan thought the same way about it. They were more like roommates sharing a bed, and Veda liked it that way.

The next morning, Veda raised the topic with him when they were on the way to her college.

'The only place I can study is the library. But your mother seems to be kind of upset about my staying back after college,' Veda told him.

'Why do you say that? Did she forbid you from staying back?' he asked.

'No ... but she didn't seem too pleased about it. She was angry.'

'She is just mourning. I think we all have to find our ways of dealing with grief. Perhaps having you around comforts her?' Bhuwan reasoned.

'But my exams are around the corner, Bhuwan. If I don't study, I will not do well.'

'I know, Veda. I know. But right now, it would be impossible to talk to her. She is in no mood to listen.'

'What do I do then?'

'Let's see Veda, we will find a way. In any case, she hasn't directly told you anything, right?' he asked.

'She said I cannot be late again. Bhuwan, I try so hard to please her. And in doing that, my academic performance is suffering. I am finding it hard too, you know.'

'I am so sorry about my mother, Veda. And thank you so much for being such an understanding daughter-in-law. I will see what I can do,' he said.

Veda kept quiet. Though he had thanked her, she could see that he was being non-committal. She hadn't got the kind of support she expected from him.

Veda was hurt that Bhuwan had not instantly jumped to her rescue and that he was not looking at it from her point of view. But this wasn't even a battle of her versus her mother-in-law. All she wanted was a few hours in a day, to stay back and study.

'Just humour her for a few days, Veda. She is not very pleasant if you don't do what she wants,' Bhuwan said after a while.

Veda considered this for a few minutes as they drove through the Pune traffic in silence.

'Have you never disobeyed her?' Veda asked.

'What?' asked Bhuwan. He was lost in his own thoughts.

'Your mother. Have you never disobeyed her?'

'Oh. No, of course not! Why would I do that? She has done so much for me. She means well, Veda. Just win her over, and you will see,' he said.

That evening, after her classes were over, Veda looked at the exam timetable and was daunted by the amount of studying that she would have to do. There was so much to be done and not enough time. She thought about her conversation with Bhuwan that morning. If she wanted to study, she had to take matters into her own hands. She had no choice.

So Veda stayed back in the library that day too, till it closed. She left only when the attendant told her it was closing time. She braced herself, telling herself that, today, she was prepared to face Padma Devi's anger. She had got a good deal of studying done, and that made it worth whatever she would have to face, in her opinion.

However, when she reached home, all the courage that she had felt earlier in the library, evaporated. The closer she got home, the more her anxiety grew. Her heart began beating faster and faster as she neared home.

Padma Devi was waiting at the doorway for her. Veda froze when she saw her expression. She looked manic. She had a menacing, restless energy about her.

'Where were you?' asked Padma Devi, her voice steely.

'Maaji, I told you yesterday. At the library, studying,' replied Veda. The quiver in her voice betrayed her nervousness.

'AND WHAT DID I TELL YOU ABOUT COMING LATE?' thundered Padma Devi. Her voice exploded in Veda's ears. Veda almost jumped. She wasn't expecting her to yell.

'How DARE YOU disobey ME?' she continued.

Veda stood there, speechless, rooted to the spot.

Padma Devi was glaring at her now, the full fury of her wrath directed at Veda. All Veda could see was her stocky frame, her tense shoulders, her angry eyes and flaring nostrils

Veda's hands started shaking. Her heart began to beat in her ears now. Her palms were cold and clammy, and she balled her fingers into tight fists. She felt breathless, like someone was strangling her. This was the same feeling she used to have when she faced her father's wrath, back in Joshimath. It made her feel small and insignificant. She looked at Padma Devi with frightened eyes.

Padma Devi came towards Veda and grabbed the bag that she carried to college.

She opened it and started flinging the books out into the corridor.

'Don't think I don't know what you are up to,' she yelled.

Veda stood there, staring in disbelief. She was aghast. She had never faced anything like this before. Her books went flying in all directions. The pages of one of her books tore and fluttered in the corridor.

To Veda, they felt like blows. Her books were things that she treasured, and she could not bear to see them handled this way.

She bent to pick them up.

Padma Devi grabbed her hair in her fist.

Veda froze in fear. Her hands flew to her head to protect her hair. Pain jolted through her scalp as Padma Devi twisted the hair and shook Veda's head.

'DON'T YOU DARE DISOBEY ME—DO YOU HEAR?' she yelled.

Veda could not even nod. Moving her head caused even more pain.

'THIS IS NOT YOUR MOTHER'S HOUSE WHERE YOU CAN DO AS YOU LIKE!' she shouted, and gave Veda's head a violent shake. Then she released her.

Veda was sobbing openly now.

She couldn't believe what had just happened. She had never seen this violent side of her mother-in-law. Padma Devi had transformed into some kind of raging demon.

'And don't show me your crocodile tears. They do not melt anybody. Gather your books and get inside now. If you are late tomorrow, you need not enter the house,' said Padma Devi, as she walked inside.

Veda sniffled as she picked up her books. She could barely see through the tears that clouded her eyes. Her eyes stung. Her face was pale, drained of all colour. She couldn't think. Her pulse was still beating in her ears, blocking out all other sounds. The tightness in her throat felt like a noose around her neck. Her breath was coming out in ragged, shallow gasps as she struggled to focus on the scattered books.

Not even her father had treated her this way. She massaged her scalp where Padma Devi had grabbed her hair.

'COME INSIDE NOW INSTEAD OF DAWDLING THERE,' shouted Padma Devi from inside.

Veda felt as though the voice was amplified and was coming at her through a hundred loudspeakers. She couldn't bear it. Veda had never been this humiliated in her life. She was in shock. How could her mother-in-law do this? She was quivering with fright.

It took a humongous effort to pick up all her books. She tried to stop sobbing. But the tears kept flowing.

'Now stop crying and go and make some tea for me,' said Padma Devi, as soon as Veda entered the house.

Veda didn't want her to start yelling again. Her hands still shaking, she made the tea and served her mother-in-law.

Padma Devi barely glanced at Veda as she took the cup of tea from her hand and continued to watch TV.

As Veda turned to go, she said, 'My feet are hurting. Press them while I finish my tea.'

She hauled up her saree to her knees and stretched out her feet in front of Veda. It was not a request. It was an order.

Veda's cheeks burned as she set the tray aside and settled down by her mother-in-law's feet. She was filled with self-loathing as she started massaging Padma Devi's feet. She thought of the countless times that she had pressed her mother's feet. But that was different. That was an act of love. Veda was more than happy to do that for her mother. Padma Devi's plump, fleshy legs felt very different from her mother's thin ones.

'Little more pressure,' said Padma Devi, as she sighed and leaned back.

Veda quietly obliged, not knowing how to refuse.

She did not look up at all and Padma Devi did not say a word either.

After about twenty minutes, Padma Devi grunted, indicating that it was enough, and just like that, Veda was dismissed. Veda had never felt so humiliated in her whole life.

She went to her room, threw herself on the bed, and started sobbing into the pillow. She cried for about twenty minutes, and then got up, washed her face and sat at her desk, acutely aware of each second that passed. She did not know when Padma Devi would next summon her. She tried to focus on her books, but all that came to her mind was Padma Devi's angry face.

'How could she? How could she?' were the only thoughts that ran inside her head, on a loop.

Her dignity had been torn to shreds. Padma Devi simply did not care about her feelings. Padma Devi was a bully. There was no doubt about that.

What terrified Veda was the slow realisation that she simply did not have it in her to stand up to the bullying. She was a gutless wimp with no backbone at all.

She thought of Suraj's letter, and now the words 'carve your own path' seemed to leap out of the page, taunting her, mocking her and laughing at her.

Chapter 12

March 1996
Pune

Dearest, dearest Vidya,
I am sorry for the long delay from my end.

I haven't been able to write earlier as I feel like a prisoner here. Things are terrible at my end, Vidya. Just terrible. I am writing to you from college, as I have come here to collect my hall tickets for my exams. I am quickly writing this to you before heading back home. I don't feel comfortable writing to you from my home anymore. That is how bad the situation is.

I am not permitted to study at the library in my college. I have to go straight home after college ends. My mother-in-law keeps track of when I return. Once I get home, my 'housewifely duties' start. I have to cut vegetables, knead the dough for rotis, make the *dal*, salad, all of it. I have to press her feet, make tea for her, and do everything else that she sets out for me.

I am not able to study anymore, Vidya. As a result, my coursework is suffering and I am lagging behind. I haven't turned in assignments, and I failed in almost all the papers in the mock exams. These are taken seriously in this college and are a good indicator of how you will perform in your finals.

The lecturer called me aside and told me to focus on my studies. She asked if I was facing any problem. She said she had seen the marks from my previous papers, the exams I gave at Joshimath, and said that my performance has fallen steeply.

How could I tell her about my MIL? I just kept quiet.

I tried speaking to Bhuwan about it. I tried to tell him to discuss this with his mother. But he seems helpless. He says he will talk to her when the time is right.

Do you know what she did a few weeks ago, Vidya? She yanked my hair and threw my books because I was late coming back home. I was shaking with fright.

I haven't ever been late after that. And I haven't told Bhuwan. He might think that I am making up stories about his mother.

You know, Vidya, this feels like a bad soap opera, with an evil mother-in-law. But this is now my reality. This is my life, I am describing. I live this reality every single day. I am carrying out all the tasks that she asks me to, like a slave. I am crying as I write this. My tears just fell on this paper, and that's why the ink is blotted.

I know what you are thinking Vidya. I know what you will say too—that I should stand up for myself. You said that to me in your previous letter too.

I don't know, Vidya. I simply am not able to.

She frightens me, Vidya. I am a coward.

I feel trapped here.

I know now that my MIL would never be comfortable with my taking up a job or even studying further. I told Bhuwan that my dream has always been to start working, and I would very much like to study further. Bhuwan was surprised to hear that. He thought I had no career plans. He said that, at the time of marriage, all they had agreed to from their side was that I would complete my graduation. He said the question of my post-graduation had never come up. Papa had assured them that I had no ambitions whatsoever, and I would be happy to be a housewife.

Can you believe that, Vidya? I feel so betrayed by my own parents.

I understand that they were eager to see me married. But how could they blatantly lie?

The one thing that mattered to me was my academics. Now that, too, is being taken away from me.

Just a few months back, I was a topper in college, and I had dreams, plans, hopes.

Now I am just a housewife, making rotis, tea and pressing my mother-in-law's feet. She treats me like a slave. What is worse is that I am letting it happen.

I don't even know when the days begin and end. These are my study holidays and I am supposed to be studying. But that's just not happening. The little free time I get, I sit in front of my books—but nothing I read enters my head. I am on tenterhooks, not knowing when I will next be summoned by my MIL.

Bhuwan just does not get it.

'It's not like she keeps you busy 24x7, right? Then why don't you study?' he asks. I am unable to make him understand how it affects me psychologically.

I wish I was not a coward, Vidya.

I wish I could just walk out of this marriage.

But even if I do, where will I go? It's not like Papa or Ma are going to allow me to come back.

I managed to speak to Ma the other day, when my mother-in-law had gone out with her friends. I sneaked a call in. You were at college. I told her all that was happening here. Can you believe what she said? She asked me to adjust. She said it was not as if Bhuwan was drinking and beating me up, or that he was a womaniser. She said that mother-in-law problems are common in the early stages of marriage, and that things will settle down.

It is unbelievable that my own parents have turned their backs on me.

I feel so alone, Vidya.

I am sorry this letter has been nothing but a long rant.

I miss Vandu, Vaish and Ani. I miss the cool mountain air of Joshimath.

All of that seems like another world now.

Write back soon, Vidya.

Your letters are my lifeline.

Literally they are.

I love you, my darling sister. Your exams must be going on now. Do well.

Hugs and kisses,

Veda

March 1996

Pune

Dear Suraj,

How are you? Hope things are all good at your end?

I apologise for the long delay from my side.

Things are not so good here.

I did try to 'carve my own path', like you suggested. It backfired badly. I just finished writing a long letter, mostly comprising a rant about my current life, to Vidya.

I feel trapped, Suraj. I don't have the time to study anymore. My grades have slipped badly. I am not permitted to stay back after college and study in the library. Once I come home, I have a lot of tasks.

I get a little free time when my mother-in-law goes to the temple or for her walk or elsewhere. But when she is at home, I am unable to focus on my books.

I don't know what to do.

I wondered for a while if I am being caught in a circle of self-pity. I tried to look at the bright side. I have food to eat, I have a roof over my head, etc., which thousands of people don't.

But I had all these things before I left Joshimath too. And there I had you, and I had Vidya.

Here I have only your letters.

I know I sound pathetic—but I wait for your letters.

They are the only bright things in my life now.

I am sorry, I am keeping this very short because I have to head back home. I am writing in a hurry from college. (I came here to collect my hall tickets.)

Good luck for your exams.

Write back soon.

Your friend forever,

Veda

April 1996

Joshimath

Dearest Veda didi,

I am shocked. Completely shocked.

I don't even know where to begin, and what to tell you. The person writing those letters doesn't sound like my didi at all. This letter is worse than your last one.

Why do you see yourself as a coward? Why are you getting scared of your MIL? She sounds worse than the one that appears in the TV serial. But you don't have to let that frighten you. You can speak up and stand up to her. Be bold.

Didi—why are you allowing this to happen to you?

Why aren't you walking out of your marriage? What are you afraid of?

I think I will tell Ma and Papa what is going on. Please let me know and I shall speak to them.

I am sending this letter by Speed Post so that it reaches you soon. I am keeping this letter very short.

I am with you, didi. Together, we will find a way.

All my love,

Vidya

PS: 1. I am not waiting for Suraj's reply, because I want this letter to reach you fast. Suraj said that he would give me his letter in a few days, and I shall send that letter to you separately.

2. I did well in all my exams and am expecting good grades.

May 1996

Pune

Dearest, dearest Vidya,

I spoke to Ma again, before I got your letter. Papa too came on the line. I called them when my MIL had gone to the temple. Speaking to them was of no use. They said they would get a bad name if I came back there. They said that word will spread that they haven't raised their daughters properly, and that it will affect your marriage prospects.

They told me not to be selfish. They said to give it a few years, and everything would be fine.

When I reminded Ma that I wanted to study further, and that I wasn't getting time because of my MIL, Ma said that once a girl got married, her first responsibility was towards her family. She shouldn't be selfish.

She spoke of her own life, when she got married to Papa and then gave up studies. She said that I was lucky that they were okay with my going to college, and that I was being allowed to take the final exams at all.

She asked me who would look after my child if I went to work. She asked if I had spoken to my MIL and husband about it.

I haven't even thought of a child, Vidya. Like I told you, there is no sex life as such between Bhuwan and me. How could I tell all this to Ma? I just kept quiet.

So, at present, walking out on my marriage is not an option for me.

My final exams are going on, and I have hardly studied. I have a few days off to study in between papers, but I am finding it very hard to focus.

I haven't written to Suraj even though you sent me his letter, and I got it a few days back, after I got yours. The thing is, I feel I do not know what to write any more, other than my MIL troubles.

Right now, all of this is looming large over my head, and there seems to be no solution in sight.

I am continuing this letter after a gap of many days. I couldn't finish it earlier.

I am done with my exams. I did very badly. I have never been this ill-prepared for exams in my life.

I tried to remember what the lecturers had said in class. And that was about it.

I had not gone through notes in detail, nor read the textbooks before the exams, because of the MIL situation. As a result, a lot of what I wrote in my papers was fluff. There was no substance to it at all.

My days here are spent cooking and cleaning. It is nothing great. It is a routine life.

As long as I follow all the rules laid down by my MIL, I am okay. She doesn't get angry. If I dare break any of her 'rules', she gets nasty.

I wake up early, wash my hair, have a bath, do the pooja and do everything else that pleases her.

I haven't given her cause for complaint so far.

On the weekend, after my exams got over, I asked Bhuwan if

we could go out. He looked surprised, as though I was asking him to take me to Mount Everest!

We did go out—but guess what, my MIL came with us.

I would have liked to go out alone with Bhuwan; I was longing for it. But no—she ruined that too. He said later that it was not fair to leave her alone at home.

I don't see why! She does get to go out with her friends—Shanta aunty and Kanti behen. It is only me, who doesn't get to go anywhere.

How did you do in your exams? I hope you did well?

Did you help Vandu, Vaish and Ani to study?

Please tell them I miss them.

Convey my regards to Rudra kaka and Paro didi too.

I spoke to Ma and Papa again on the phone. Why do they always call up when you are in college? I asked Ma why she doesn't ever let Vandu, Vaish or any of you speak to me on the phone. I did not realise that Papa was listening on the extension. He said the phone is only for important things, and that STD calls are costly. He said they don't have money to waste for idle chit-chat. What could I say after that?

How is Suraj doing? I haven't replied to his letter yet. I guess he will not write to me till I reply to his last one. In his letter, he had mentioned that he was shocked by my mother-in-law's behaviour and, like you, he also did not understand why I was not standing up to her. He said he was sorry that his advice had backfired and asked me not to lose hope.

Take care, Vidya. What do you plan to do in the summer vacation? Are you going to take the tailoring classes that I had taken in my long holidays, just before I joined college? Do something useful. Do not waste your holidays. Equip yourself with some skillsets.

All my love,
Your sister,
Veda

May 1996

Joshimath

Dear, dear Veda,

Forgive me for not writing sooner.

I must confess that, initially, I thought I would wait for your letter. I kept waiting, hoping to hear from you. When I didn't, I wondered if maybe you no longer wanted to be in touch with me. But Vidya told me that you had asked about me, and that you wondered if I would write only if you did, so I decided to jot down a letter to you immediately.

I am not going to give you advice anymore, Veda. I feel bad that things got worse for you after you acted on my suggestion.

I think each of us knows our own situation best. Anybody else's advice will not be appropriate, as they don't know exactly what is going on.

Now that I have finished my exams, I have a lot of time on my hands. My father's friend, Yagnik uncle (I think I have told you about him), wants me to join the company and start working immediately. He says there are two advantages to it:

1. I will have a better understanding of the MBA course and get preference during admissions if I have work experience.

2. The company has a provision under which they will allow me to go on sabbatical, and pay my fees for the MBA, provided I give an undertaking that, once I finish my course, I will come back and work with them for three years.

I discussed it with my uncle in Mumbai, and he too feels that it is a good decision.

My flat in Mumbai has been lying locked up. I am also missing that city. After all, that is where I grew up and studied.

Try to be cheerful! Try and read a lot. When my parents died, it was books that were my sole support, and helped me get through a difficult time. Above all, do not lose hope.

Do you want me to send you books?

Take care, my friend,

Suraj

Chapter 13

July 1996
Kailash Mandir Colony, Pune

Veda craned her neck and stood on tip-toes for a glimpse of the noticeboard in the college corridor. A large group of students were already gathered around it. There were at least a hundred of them, each one trying to read their results and see how they had fared.

The faces of some fell as they spotted their roll number and the result displayed next to it. Some were elated as they had done much better than they had hoped. As each student spotted their result, they left the group, and immediately a sea of other students surged forward, occupying the space. Veda was at the edge of the group, and as each student left, she found herself being propelled forward involuntarily by the people behind her. At last she reached the front, and she ran her finger down the glass, trying to find her roll number. Her finger stopped when she found it. Her heart almost stopped too, when she spotted what was written next to her roll number.

The word FAILED leapt up at her. Her eyes filled with tears and she blinked them back. She had hoped to get through because of her strong language skills, and the fact that she had paid attention to the lectures. But the questions asked had been very different from the ones she had been expecting. She knew she had done badly, but she had never thought that failing the exam would be a possibility.

Veda turned away from the noticeboard with her shoulders drooping and a heaviness in her heart.

FAILED. FAILED. FAILED. The words in red, grew inside her head and assumed the shape of giant letters. The letters then melted and seemed to fill every part of her body. Nobody had noticed her, and nobody cared about her results. They were all far too occupied with their own results. But Veda imagined everybody staring at her and pointing fingers at her. She didn't look at anybody. She hung her head and stared at the ground.

Her cheeks burned with shame, as she made her way out of the college. In a way, she was glad she had no friends in this college. Being the only married person, and the fact that she had joined college only in the third year, she was a bit of an outcast and nobody paid any attention to her.

When she was in the auto-rickshaw heading home, the tears flowed freely and she sobbed, her breath coming in harsh sniffs and jerks. The auto-driver, an elderly man, looked at her in the rear-view mirror and asked, 'Beti—bad result?'

Veda was crying so hard she could not reply. The tightness in her chest threatened to explode. She nodded, sobbing even more.

'Don't worry. Try supplementary exams,' said the auto-driver in English.

Veda wanted to tell him that she was a topper. She had never ever failed an exam. Not in her twenty years. She had always excelled in academics. How was it possible for her to *fail*?

What would she now do?

When he dropped her off, she thanked him and apologised for crying.

'You should never hold back the tears. Let it flow; you will feel better,' he said, this time speaking in Hindi.

Veda thanked him, wiped her tears and headed home.

But when she reached the apartment, to her surprise, there was a lock on the door.

Veda frowned. She didn't know what to do. Her mother-in-law was always at home when Veda returned from college. She never went anywhere on her own. This was puzzling.

She waited for around fifteen minutes outside the house, getting restless by the minute. She kept glancing at her watch. Where was her mother-in-law? Should she contact Bhuwan? Where would she call from? She kept peering down the stairwell, to see if she could spot her returning from wherever she had gone, but Padma Devi did not appear. Veda hoped her mother-in-law would return soon. It was almost 1 p.m., and she had not eaten anything since the previous night. She had been so nervous about the results that she had skipped breakfast.

After twenty-five minutes of waiting, she felt faint. She sat down in front of the house for about ten more minutes. At this rate, she would pass out on the doorstep, she thought. Her throat felt terribly parched. Then it occurred to her that she could go to Shanta aunty's house and call up Bhuwan.

She went to the first floor of the next block and rang the bell.

She waited for a few seconds and the door sprang open.

She almost screamed in fright when she saw a masked face with only the eyes visible. The rest of the face was covered in a green, gooey mess.

'Oh, God!' she exclaimed, her hands flying to her chest.

'Ha, ha! I am so sorry. I wasn't expecting anyone. I must look a sight!' said Kanika.

Veda exhaled slowly.

'No. I am sorry. But God, what a fright I got,' she said.

Kanika laughed. Veda barely managed a smile.

'I am Veda. I live in the next block. Shanta aunty and my mother-in-law are friends.'

'Bhuwan's wife! Yes, of course. I met you when your father-in-law passed away. But there were so many people around, I'm sure you don't remember me,' said Kanika.

'You're right—I am so sorry, I can't recall,' she confessed.

'No worries at all! We have never been properly introduced. My mother and I were supposed to come to Joshimath to attend your wedding. But she fell ill, and we cancelled the tickets. I kept meaning to come and meet you, but then there was always work, and also, uncle passed away. Oh—please do come in!' said Kanika, as she gestured for Veda to come inside.

Veda stepped into the house. Kanika's home was very different from her mother-in-law's. The interiors of the house made her forget her problems temporarily.

This home was done up in clean modern lines. A tall bamboo plant stood in a corner. The seating was low, and in dark grey tones. It contrasted with the bright red and green cushions that looked comfortable enough to sink into. The effect was dramatic. A large abstract painting with vivid splashes of crimson dominated a wall. It was minimalistic, modern and, in short, everything that Veda would have liked her living space to be.

'This is so beautiful,' said Veda, as she looked around.

'That's sweet of you. Thank you!' Kanika replied, pleased by the compliment. 'I threw out all my parents' furniture and redecorated the place.'

'Didn't they mind?'

'Oh, I lost my father a few years back. Mum was devastated and so was I. I convinced her that this project would be a way of healing. It helped us both through a difficult time.'

'Oh, I am sorry,' said Veda.

'No, it's fine. It's been many years now. I am okay to talk about it. What will you have? Can I get you some tea or coffee or lime juice? Or do you want something stronger?' grinned Kanika.

'Oh no, thank you. No, I don't drink.'

'What? You don't drink tea or coffee?'

'No, that I do. I meant alcohol. Could I have some water please?'

'Sure! I will get it,' said Kanika, as she headed towards the kitchen.

When she came back with the glass of water, Veda accepted it gratefully and drank it all in one gulp.

'More?' asked Kanika. Veda shook her head as she placed the glass back on a side table.

'How old are you Veda, if you don't mind me asking? You look so terribly young,' said Kanika.

'No, I don't mind at all. I am twenty. I will be twenty-one soon.'

'What?! No way!'

Veda smiled in response. Kanika could see sadness behind that smile. She had seen far too many smiles like this on the faces of the children at Sankalp, the unique 'bridge school' where she now worked. She was all too familiar with people who made peace with their circumstances, people who swallowed and bore bravely whatever life threw at them.

'You go to college, right?' Kanika asked.

Veda nodded. 'Just finished my final year—and I failed my exams,' she said, before she could stop herself.

'What?' asked Kanika, taken aback by the sudden confession. Then she laughed, thinking that Veda was joking.

'I wasn't joking. I just got my results. I ... I failed,' said Veda, staring at the carpet, her eyes brimming with tears.

It was only then that Kanika realised how upset Veda was.

'Oh! Listen, failing in exams isn't the end of the world! Exams aren't everything,' Kanika consoled her.

Veda nodded dully. Exams *were* everything for her. Her entire life, she had excelled only in one thing—that was her academics.

'I am sorry that I have just turned up here and am blurting out all my problems,' said Veda, blinking back her tears. She didn't want to cry in front of a person she was meeting for the first time.

'Don't worry about it. You are most welcome here. Let me get you some tea. Tea always makes you feel better, like the Brits say. Now don't say no,' said Kanika, before Veda could protest.

Kanika hummed a little tune as she brewed the tea. Veda found herself thinking about how cheerful Kanika was, and how she had an air of calmness about her. Kanika lowered the flame on the stove and said, 'Let me go and wash this gooey stuff off my face. I have had it on long enough.'

When she emerged from the bathroom, her complexion was glowing, radiant and almost flawless. Veda noticed that she had a very pleasant face with large eyes. Her expression was almost angelic. She was slightly plump and she carried herself very well. Her hair was piled up loosely on top of her head, and she now shook it free. Her shiny hair now framed her oval face, softening it further.

'What? Do I still look a mess?' asked Kanika, as she noticed Veda looking at her.

'Oh, no. No. Sorry if I was staring. You are so pretty,' said Veda.

'Ah, thanks,' Kanika rewarded Veda with a dazzling smile.

She strained the tea into two cups and placed them on a tray. She took out a plate and set out some dry *kachoris* and *samosas* on it. She emerged from the kitchen carrying the tray and placed it in front of Veda.

By now Veda's hunger was raging, burning up her tummy.

'Thanks for this. I haven't had my lunch and I am starving,' said Veda, as she gratefully dug in.

'Shall I make you some sandwiches then?' offered Kanika.

'No, no, this is fine,' answered Veda, in between bites. Then it occurred to her that she was yet to explain to Kanika why she had suddenly turned up like this, at her doorstep.

'I came back from college and found the door locked. I have no idea where my mother-in-law is. That's why I came here, to ask if I could make a phone call to Bhuwan. I don't have the key you see, and I am stuck outside.'

'Oh! It's strange that your mother-in-law didn't tell you. They have all gone together for that Carnatic music concert at Aundh. They will be back only late at night. My mother had some donor passes and she invited Padma aunty and Kanti behen,' said Kanika.

'I see,' said Veda, trying to hide her bewilderment.

Veda wondered why her mother-in-law had not told her. Was this her way of 'punishing her', for staying back late in college to get her results? Was she sending a subtle message to her to be on time or had she genuinely forgotten? Veda wasn't sure.

But now it looked like she had no choice but to stay with Kanika till her mother-in-law or Bhuwan got home.

'You can stay here till they get back or till Bhuwan gets back. I don't mind at all,' said Kanika, as though reading Veda's mind.

'Oh, thank you,' said Veda, as she leaned back on the giant cushions.

The cushions were incredibly soft and very large. She could feel herself sinking into them.

'Ummm, this is so comfortable,' she said.

'I know, right? It took a lot to convince my mother. She didn't want low seating. She said it would be hard to get up, at her age. I told her we could use it as an overnight bed, and then I got that special rocking chair for her,' said Kanika, pointing to a compact rosewood rocking chair with slatted bars that stood in one corner of the room. It was placed on a multi-coloured, soft, furry rug with a large chequered pattern. Next to it, stood a square side table. A large potted plant was placed beside the table. The effect was cosy, warm and delectable. It made Veda want to immediately jump into the chair with her steaming mug of tea.

'I love this house! You have done it up so well. I know I am repeating myself, but I can't help it. I feel like I have walked into the pages of a magazine,' said Veda.

'Thank you. I can help you do up your house, if you like. I love doing up spaces,' said Kanika.

'I wish,' sighed Veda. 'But my mother-in-law has her own ideas of what the place should look like.'

'But it's your house too. Just tell her you are making some changes and go ahead,' Kanika asserted.

'Maybe sometime,' Veda said sadly.

Kanika could sense that Veda was deeply unhappy. She was so young, too. She wondered how Veda felt about the age difference between her and her husband.

'Doesn't the age difference between you and Bhuwan bother you? Bhuwan is the same age as me! We grew up together,' Kanika said, as she sipped her tea. 'I hope you don't think I am being nosy. Just feel free to ask me to shut up,' she added.

'He is twenty-eight,' said Veda. 'You know, initially it did bother me. But my parents said that it was more important that we get along well, and not to focus on the age difference. And now, it doesn't bother me anymore.' Veda looked away as she set her cup of tea down on the tray.

'That's good, then. And yes, if wavelengths match, I guess the age difference does not matter,' Kanika said.

'What about you? Are you married?' asked Veda.

Kanika was easy to talk to. Her easy-going manner and the way she was so sincere and honest about everything made Veda want to talk to her.

Kanika chuckled as she helped herself to a *kachori*. 'Oh, my mother brings it up all the time. I haven't found the right person yet. I have had three relationships—nothing worked out,' she said, shrugging.

Veda nodded. At least Kanika had got a chance to explore

what she wanted. She was free to choose her own partner. But she didn't say this to Kanika. She kept her thoughts to herself.

Veda couldn't help admiring how sophisticated Kanika was. She found herself thinking that, in comparison to Kanika, she herself was awfully naive. Kanika had an air of tranquillity about her and it came naturally. Veda could see that there was absolutely no pretence in Kanika, and she liked that.

'So, are you going to give the exams again? What do you plan to do next?' asked Kanika.

'I … I don't know,' said Veda. She felt utterly lost. But she did not want to discuss this with Kanika. She had just met her.

So she changed the topic.

'Tell me, what do you do?' she asked Kanika.

Kanika told her all about Sankalp. She talked about how she had quit her previous job, and how she found her work meaningful now. She talked about the difference that their work was making in the lives of so many underprivileged children at the 'bridge school', where she was a teacher.

'The children attend classes for two hours with us, after which they go to their regular schools. You know, we badly need volunteers and resources. These children are first-generation learners and don't have access to teachers like us,' Kanika explained. 'Would you like to volunteer at Sankalp? We could do with some good, dedicated volunteers,' she said.

'What does a volunteer have to do?' Veda asked.

'The volunteer works as a teacher's assistant first, and then they can teach. We focus on teaching the kids English and maths, which is what will help them get ahead. We do a lot. You should meet these children, Veda. You will see how silly and small all our problems seem then,' Kanika said.

'I would like to see this place,' Veda said.

It was the first time she was hearing of something like this. At Joshimath, she had never been exposed to the underprivileged or to children from a slum. She had never seen stark contrasts in lifestyles.

'You can come with me on the weekend, if you like. I am taking a colleague of mine on a tour of where the kids live. It is less than a kilometre from here, but it is a different world.

Come along, Veda. And then, if you like, you can perhaps volunteer with us, if you believe in the cause,' Kanika said.

Veda said that she would. For the first time since she had got married, she found that she was looking forward to something.

She and Kanika spent the rest of the time talking. The more Veda chatted with Kanika, the lighter she felt. Kanika made everything sound so simple and easy.

Kanika had shown Veda that there was a big world out there to explore. Veda was taking baby steps towards it. While speaking to Kanika, Veda forgot all about her problems.

At last, her mother-in-law returned and Veda went back home. She had enjoyed her time with Kanika and she felt that she had made a friend in her. She looked forward to the tour on the weekend.

There was only one problem though—she would have to first take permission from her mother-in-law.

Chapter 14

July 1996
Sitawadi, Pune

Shakubai tried to turn on her side, lying on the straw mat spread on the floor of the tiny 10' x 10' inner room. She grimaced in pain. One of her eyes was so swollen that it was only a slit, and she could barely open it. She could feel a vein throbbing in the other one. Her head ached. Her throat was dry and every muscle in her lean body hurt. She gazed at the tiny alarm clock which stood on the cuddapah stone platform in the corner of the room, which functioned as the kitchen. It was already 6.45 a.m. She was late. She cursed. Padma madam would be furious. This was the third time this month that she would be late. Padma Devi's sharp tongue and quick temper and the threats she constantly made that she would dismiss her if she was late, worried her. Her mind quickly conjured up the images of Komal madam and Indira madam, her two other employers whose houses she cleaned, and she could picture their angry frowns of disapproval. She sighed.

Ignoring her swollen eye, she examined her arms. The fresh bruises were an angry, purplish red. She winced as she tried to sit up, supporting herself on her arm. Pain shot up through her like a bolt of electricity. Struggling, she gave up and collapsed.

'Kajol ... Kajol...' she called out feebly to her daughter, who was asleep in the outer room. Kajol's room was even tinier than the room that she and her husband occupied. Kajol slept on a single bed which had been discarded by one of the homes where Shakubai worked as a maid. She had brought it home, had it repaired and managed to buy a mattress for it. Once the bed was placed, there was hardly any room for anything else. There was a window right next to the bed. Kajol would sit on the bed and use the window sill as a table whenever she had to do her homework. Their home was a two-room structure and it was one of the better homes in Sitawadi, as it had a proper cement roof, unlike the other houses that had only asbestos sheets for roofs. None of the homes had running water or attached toilets. A cluster of four or five homes shared a bathroom and a toilet. The families that used it took turns cleaning it.

'Kajol, Kajol.' The cries were a little louder this time.

Kajol jumped out of bed and rushed to her mother's side.

'Aayi, are you okay?' she asked.

'Yes, Kajol. I am fine. Can you—?'

'Yes, Aayi. I will make tea,' said Kajol, as she took out an aluminium vessel and filled it with some water, which she poured out from a plastic container beneath the platform. Then she lit the stove and placed the vessel on it.

Last night had been particularly bad, much worse than the countless other such nights that she and her mother had endured over the years. Kajol knew better than to argue with her father Rajaram when he came home drunk. It happened every few days, mostly on Fridays. The pattern was the same. Her father worked as a cleaner in one of the new offices in the mammoth, glittering glass and concrete structures that housed several multinational companies. They had sprung up a few years ago, very close to Kailash Mandir Colony, instantly creating a lot of blue-collared job opportunities—security guards, drivers, cleaners, peons—for all those who lived in the vicinity. Rajaram wasn't directly employed by the company, though. He was bound to the contractor who had got the maintenance contract. His work started at 6 a.m., as he had to be there before the employees came in for the first shift at 7.30. He had got the job as he lived just a stone's throw away from the offices. He got paid every Friday, and his behaviour was predictable. He would blow up all his earnings on alcohol at the neighbourhood 'wine shop', which was a dingy, dark store that sold all kinds of *daaru*, and where the men of the neighbourhood congregated daily. After he could drink no more, or after his money was exhausted, whichever came first, he would stagger home and demand his meal. If the vegetable cooked was not to his liking—and he had a complaint every time: not enough spice, not enough salt, not fresh enough—or if there was no chicken or fish cooked, then he would hurl the plate and yell at Shakubai.

'What use is it for us to work like this if you can't even provide a proper meal, woman? Is this why we left our property in Ambegaon? To slog like servants in the city? Do you know I wash toilets? I clean the shit of those office-goers. All for what?' he would shout, taking out all his frustrations on her. He was obscure at his workplace, just a cleaner. He disliked his job and was full of resentment towards all the people who worked there. He especially hated the foreigners. Since most of the companies in the office complexes were American and British, there were a large number of white people. He detested them even more than he detested the Indians who worked there. When he finished work and got back home, he was the king and he made it clear, over and over.

Shakubai often felt like reminding him of the times when they had starved in the village, when the crops had failed. She wanted to ask him whether he remembered how hard they had toiled in the fields, ploughing land, sowing, tilling, from dawn to dusk, labouring in the scorching sun, and yet, had never made enough money. Little Kajol would often go to bed hungry. It was then that they had decided to migrate to Pune. They were so much better off here than in the village. And, she cleaned toilets too, apart from doing the dirty dishes at the homes she worked in. One had to do whatever it took to survive.

But she never spoke up. It was futile even trying to bring all this up, as he was a bitter, angry man even when he was sober. He felt the world owed him more. When he was drunk, the monster that he managed to suppress during the day, got loose. He would hurl things, shout, curse and abuse till he passed out.

Over the years, Kajol had watched her mother trying her best to ignore his behaviour. But that would always enrage him further. He would often demand money from her. She would refuse. He would then yank her hair, twist her arm and bully her.

Last night, he had dragged her into the other room, and they had bolted the door. Kajol lay quietly in bed, listening to her mother's cries. When she could not bear it any longer, she had covered her head with a pillow and had gone to sleep.

She detested her father. She had got used to the filthy language he used and the things that he said when he was drunk. He had no control over his rage, his words or his actions. Kajol had accepted this a long time ago, and had learnt to work her way around it. She did feel bad for her Aayi, but she did not shake in fright anymore, like she had when she was younger.

When Kajol was eight, he had yelled at her mother saying, 'No money? No money? Why don't you whore out that girl of yours and then get some money?'

That was the only time Kajol had seen her mother shout back.

'*Bhadwa*. You scum of the earth. You touch her and I will kill you!' she had shouted, as Kajol had cowered in fright, hiding under the kitchen platform. Her mother had got a beating for that. She had watched as her father violently kicked her over and over, till she lost consciousness. Kajol had not moved the entire night, and had fallen asleep there.

The next morning, she had nursed her mother's wounds. She had asked her, 'Why don't you leave Baba?'

At eight, Kajol was worldly-wise. She already knew how to make tea, boil rice, cook a curry and make rotis. She would also look after the neighbour's baby, cradling him expertly on her hip while she did the household chores, as she had seen numerous others in her locality do.

'It's not so easy, Kajol. You will understand when you grow up. I want you to ignore all this and study, so you do not suffer the same fate as me,' her mother had said.

If there was one thing that Shakubai had drilled into Kajol's head, it was the importance of education.

'Don't let this affect you. You must study. Study hard. That's your only escape from this hellhole.'

Over and over, her mother had said that to Kajol.

Kajol wanted to make her mother happy. Shakubai's eyes shone with pride when Kajol came home with report cards with perfect scores, year after year. Her teachers at the local government school praised Kajol. Kajol knew she was the one bright spot in her mother's dreary life. Her mother often told her so. She had given birth to two sons before Kajol, and they had died in infancy. Shakubai was grateful for Kajol. Rajaram, her husband, did not bother much about Kajol's grades. He still mourned the sons he had lost, and in his eyes, a girl child was inferior to a boy. Shakubai did not pay any attention to Rajaram's opinion and she vowed to do everything she could to ensure that Kajol succeeded in life.

'Kajol is a smart girl. Why don't you think of transferring her to an English-medium school?' her teachers at the local government school had asked Shakubai. Rajaram never bothered to come and meet the teachers.

Shakubai had pleaded with the women she worked for, till one of them had taken pity on her and had presented Kajol's case to the local Rotary Club where she was a member. The ladies met every fortnight for high tea and local gossip. They also chose 'deserving cases' to work on, and Kajol's education, it was agreed, fell under the 'deserving case' category.

'These bright children from the slums should be given a chance, and we can make it happen,' said Mrs Parikh, as she had a spoonful of the Belgian chocolate mousse.

That was how Kajol found herself suddenly transferred to an English-medium school in Class 7. She had initially struggled to cope. But being diligent and hardworking, she had devoured all the books in the library, pestered her teachers, and had easily caught up, soon becoming one of the popular students at school.

Seeing Kajol's success, the Rotary Club had adopted the girl's locality, and now, around fifteen children from there went to the same school. The club had tied up with the school, and improved the infrastructure and the facilities. Though it was not on par with the schools that the children of the club members attended, it was still better than the local government schools.

Kajol handed her mother the tea and helped her sit up. Shakubai leaned back against the wall, gratefully sipping the tea.

'Beta, can you go to Padma madam's house just for today and do the vessels?'

'Aayi, if I do that, you know they won't let me go. They will make me do the rest of the work too. They won't let me go after doing just the vessels.'

Shakubai sighed. Kajol was right, and it was unfair to burden her.

She was in Class 10—a crucial year. If Kajol obliged, Shakubai knew she would miss her class at Sankalp.

Sankalp was a happy place and Shakubai knew how much Kajol loved going there. But, on the other hand, if she did not send word to Padma madam and the other two, she was in danger of losing her jobs. She had been warned not to take leave. She would have to go.

She struggled and stood up with great difficulty.

'Alright, I will go,' she said.

Kajol looked at her mother. She was hobbling in pain.

'Aayi—how will you go alone? You can barely walk. I will go with you.'

'Won't you miss your class? Go there, beta—that is more important.'

Kajol was torn. She wanted to speed off to Sankalp. To escape all this.

The classes at Sankalp were run in the basement of an office building. It had been originally intended as a parking lot, but the plans had changed, and the company had donated it to Sankalp. There were no chairs there. Instead, the children sat on colourful mats laid out on the floor. The space was decorated with drawings and little crafts that the children had made, which were suspended from ropes that were tied across the pillars, creating a hanging border, demarcating the area where the activities happened. The basement was open on all four sides, and bright sunlight flooded in. It was surrounded by greenery, as there was a landscaped garden all around the office building. At Sankalp, Kajol forgot her dreary home and its harsh realities for a few hours. She loved her didi at Sankalp; she taught her many things and made learning fun. Kajol remembered that the one thing her didi had always emphasised was that duty to family came first. Didi had spoken many times about having respect for and being polite to one's parents.

Kajol noticed that her mother was in acute pain. She made up her mind that instant.

'No, Aayi. I will go with you,' she said, determined to help her mother.

Shakubai reluctantly agreed.

'Let me just go tell Sanju to inform the didi at Sankalp,' she said.

Shakubai nodded.

Kajol stepped outside and went to the door of the next house.

'Sanju, Sanju,' she shouted.

'He is taking a bath,' said his stepmother, from inside.

Kajol walked towards the bathrooms. Sharan was waiting outside for his turn.

'Oye, Kajol. Homework *kiya*?' asked Sharan.

'English Sharan, English,' said Kajol, imitating Kanika didi.

Sharan pulled a face at Kajol.

At that instant, Sanju emerged from the bathroom, a towel wrapped around his waist. Kajol shyly looked away. They had grown up together, and now, at sixteen, Sanju was beginning to sprout a moustache. His limbs were long and he had suddenly shot up in height. He was now copying the mannerisms of the men around him. He flicked back his wet hair and struck a pose like a Bollywood actor.

'Kajol, *meri jaaaan*,' he drawled. His voice was gravelly, not yet a man's voice, but not a child's voice either.

'Oye *mere* hero,' said Sharan, and whistled.

Kajol blushed. She hated it when that happened. This was Sanju, her childhood buddy, her friend. There was no need to blush just because he was acting cocky now, she told herself. She recovered quickly and said, 'Shut up, shameless! Go and wear your clothes. And tell didi I won't be coming to Sankalp today.'

Before he could say anything, Kajol turned and hurried towards her house.

'Wait. Why? Why aren't you coming?' Sanju called after her.

'I have to help my mother. Baba beat her up again,' she said, as she walked away, leaving the two boys staring.

A few minutes later, Shakubai, assisted by Kajol, emerged from the house and started walking slowly towards Kailash Mandir Colony.

Chapter 15

July 1996
Kailash Mandir Colony, Pune

'Veda ... Veda. Did you hear me? Looks like Shakubai isn't coming,' Padma Devi's voice rose as she walked into Veda and Bhuwan's bedroom.

Veda had woken up early in the morning, finished her bath, and had performed the pooja, so that Padma Devi would have no cause for complaint. She had also made tea for herself as well as Bhuwan. She had served him his tea, and had just sat down to have hers. That was when Padma Devi had walked in.

'Ma, yes, we heard you. And I think the whole building would have heard you as well,' said Bhuwan, as he sipped his tea.

'Tell your wife to get up and get going. Look at her—sitting there like a queen sipping her tea. The sun has risen long back.'

'Ma, leave her alone. She even wakes up early these days, does that pooja and does everything you—'

'Shut up, Bhuwan,' Padma Devi cut him short. 'What do you know about how much work there is? It's not as though you do anything!' Padma Devi's rant continued as she walked in and opened the curtains. Bright sunlight streamed in.

Veda listened to all this, quickly taking large gulps of her tea, almost scalding her tongue in the process. If she didn't get up from the bed and head towards the kitchen immediately, she knew her mother-in-law would continue her tirade. Veda had discovered over the past few weeks that, in her mother-in-law's books, sitting still even for a few minutes was a crime. The old lady herself was rarely idle, busying herself with many activities till it was time for her to watch television in the evening. That was the only time she allowed herself a break.

'Veda, hurry up and make *poha* for breakfast. I have kept all the ingredients on the kitchen counter,' Padma Devi ordered.

Veda hated the fact that there was no privacy for them, even in their own bedroom. Her mother-in-law walked in whenever she liked.

'Why can't we lock the door?' she had asked Bhuwan in the first week of their marriage, when her mother-in-law had stormed into their bedroom without even a knock.

'Come on, Veda, it's a small thing. Ma will get offended. Besides, my parents are old. If they need anything, how will we even hear them over the din of the fan?' Bhuwan had asked.

'What can they possibly need in the middle of the night? If they knock on the door, won't we wake up?'

Bhuwan had then gone into a lengthy explanation of how one of his distant aunts had passed away in the middle of the night, and how her son and daughter-in-law had been completely unaware of the fact till 8 o'clock the next morning. All the relatives had gossiped about how callous and uncaring the son and daughter-in-law were. Even though there were chances that she had passed away peacefully in her sleep, the niggling doubts in people's minds, that perhaps she had called out to her son in her final moments and her cries had gone unanswered, were what prevailed in family discussions. This incident had left a mark on Bhuwan, who was only fourteen at that time, and ever since, he would never lock his room door while he slept. Even as an adolescent, after he masturbated, the last thing he would do was crawl out of bed, unlock the door, leave it slightly ajar, and then creep back into bed. That was how it had always been, and his new bride wasn't going to change that.

Veda had given up after trying a couple of times to get him to lock the door. Besides, it wasn't as if they had a sex life anyway.

Veda quickly drained the last sips of the tea and followed her mother-in-law into the kitchen.

The doorbell rang, and Padma Devi answered it.

'Ooooh—so now you have decided to come?' Veda heard her exclaim.

'Sorry, madam. I am slightly late,' said Shakubai, as she walked in with Kajol.

Veda glanced at the young girl with Shakubai. The girl did not look at Veda. She marched to the sink and began doing the dishes. Veda noticed that the girl was dressed in a clean and neatly ironed school uniform. She washed the vessels expertly, barely glancing up, completely immersed in the task at hand.

'What class is your daughter in, Shakubai?' Veda asked.

'She is in Class 10, didi,' said Shakubai, as she took out the broom and entered the bedroom to start sweeping the house.

It was when she started sweeping the hall that Veda noticed her swollen eye, the bruises on her arms, and her face contorted in pain as she worked slowly, with laboured, deliberate movements.

Veda knew at once that she must have got a solid beating. Veda had seen Shakubai with such bruises earlier, as she hurriedly left for college, but had never got a chance to chat with her. These days, since she was always at home, she had all the time in the world to spare.

'Does your husband beat you?' Veda asked, a little taken aback by how severe the bruises looked this time.

Shakubai nodded and continued to sweep.

By Shakubai's nonchalant attitude, it appeared that her husband beat her regularly. This was the first time Veda had seen someone this badly hurt, up close.

'Shakubai, God—look at you. How can you even work? Please take an off today. I will do the sweeping,' Veda found herself saying.

Shakubai just shook her head and put a finger to her lips, gesturing to Veda's mother-in-law. Padma Devi was on the balcony, reading the paper. Veda nodded. Shakubai was terrified of losing her job, a threat that Padma Devi made every now and then.

'Think carefully before you take another day off. We don't pay you for your leave, and there are enough maids available who will take up your job if you don't want to work,' Padma Devi would remind her.

Shakubai pretended that the conversation between her and Veda had never occurred. She continued to sweep the floors. Veda looked at the young girl washing the dishes, as she herself began chopping the onions for the *poha*.

Kajol noticed Veda watching her.

'Good morning, didi. My name is Kajol. I came to help my mother just for today,' said the girl in perfect English.

Veda was surprised.

'Good morning, Kajol. You speak English so well!' she remarked.

'Yes, didi. I go to Sankalp before I attend school. We have to speak only in English there. Didis don't know Marathi,' said Kajol.

'Sankalp? Oh, you go there?' Veda asked. She was pleasantly surprised to meet a student from there.

Kajol mistook Veda's surprise for ignorance.

'It's a centre, didi. We go before school. It is very nice. It is full of didis and bhaiyas like you,' Kajol explained.

Veda was amused by Kajol's explanation.

'Like me?' she smiled.

'Yes, didi. Sankalp has many teachers. We call them didis and bhaiyas. They are not like our school teachers. These teachers don't beat us. And they make class a lot of fun,' said Kajol chattily.

Veda was curious.

'Really? You like Sankalp that much?'

'Yes, didi. We do so many things there. All nice things. Fun things,' said Kajol, as she continued to scrub the vessels.

Veda finished making the *poha* and served her mother-in-law and Bhuwan. She wasn't invited to eat with them. When she was attending college, she and Bhuwan always ate together. But these days, Padma Devi seemed to have changed the rules.

'Listen, you serve us first, and you can eat later. Today, let me finish, as I have to leave with my son,' she had said one day, and somehow that had become the practice every morning since then.

Padma Devi remarked that the lime Veda had squeezed in was not enough, and that it was too bland.

'Next time add a little more chillies and squeeze a little more lime. This doesn't taste like *poha* at all. Don't you make it at home?' she asked.

'Yes, but at home, we have a cook,' Veda found herself answering. She instantly knew that it was the wrong thing to say. She had now set off her mother-in-law. Veda hadn't intended to say anything, but the words had slipped out.

Padma Devi did not miss the opportunity handed to her on a platter. She seized it like a hawk zeroing in on its prey.

'No wonder you can't cook. Girls should be taught how to cook. Parents spoil their daughters, if you ask me,' said Padma Devi.

Veda bristled at the insult. She looked at Bhuwan. But he was engrossed in eating the *poha*, pretending not to hear. He had heard every word, but he did not consider such trivial things important enough to argue about.

They finished the meal in silence.

'Okay, please eat now. I don't want you fainting,' said Padma Devi to Veda. Veda felt awkward to sit alone at the dining table and eat her meal.

'Bhuwan beta, let's go. And Veda, please handle the cooking for the afternoon. I think you can take care of that. I will be back for lunch,' said Padma Devi, as she left with Bhuwan.

Veda heaved a sigh of relief as she stood on the balcony and watched them leave. Then she made herself comfortable in one of the armchairs and read the newspapers for a little while. It was a rare thing for her, to be alone this way. She got very little unhindered alone time, and she loved making complete use of it. She stretched her arms and looked at the parrots on the mango trees outside Kailash Mandir Colony. How free those birds were.

Then she remembered that she had to cook. She knew that her mother-in-law would be very angry if food was not ready when she returned. She rushed to the kitchen. She had always been given precise instructions on what to cook and she usually made *rotis*. She had no idea what quantities of rice to use. She couldn't decide on the menu either. She stood in the kitchen, staring helplessly at the large plastic container that her mother-in-law used to store rice.

Kajol noticed the confusion on her face.

'Didi, do you need help with the cooking?' she asked Veda.

'Yes, Kajol. I would very much like that. Thank you. Do you know how to cook?' asked Veda.

'Of course, didi, I have been cooking since I was eight.'

'And how old are you now?'

'Sixteen, didi. This year, I will give my Class 10 exam. When I came from the village to the city, I lost a year. Otherwise, by now, I would be in Class 11.' Kajol was evidently used to people asking her this question, and she explained even before Veda had a chance to say anything.

'Oh, alright. Where I come from, a lot of people are sixteen when they finish their Class 10. In fact my younger sister is eighteen, but she has just finished her Class 12. She is December-born, you see,' said Veda.

Kajol felt happy to hear that.

'Where are you from, didi?' she asked.

'Joshimath.'

'Where is that, didi?'

'In the foothills of the Himalayas,' said Veda.

Kajol's eyes widened in surprise. '*Wah* didi, very cold place no?' she asked.

'Yes, it snows in winter there,' smiled Veda.

'Didi, you are so lucky! I have never seen snow. Only in pictures I have seen,' said Kajol.

Suddenly, she broke into a song—'*Zara sa jhoom loon mein, na re baba na.*' She twirled around, holding a ladle in her hand.

Then she and Veda burst out laughing.

'Didi, have you seen the picture? It released last year, in October. *Dilwale Dulhaniya le Jayenge*. Shah Rukh Khan acted in it, didi. He is a superstar,' said Kajol.

'I know Shah Rukh Khan,' said Veda, and she smiled at how Kajol was describing the songs and the movie with enthusiasm, her eyes shining as she spoke.

'In that picture, the heroine's name is the same as my name—Kajol,' continued Kajol, as she wiped the vessels she had washed and put them away.

'Oh, I see,' said Veda.

'Yes, didi. You can see. Tell bhaiya to take you,' said Kajol.

'No, no, Kajol. "I see" means "I understand". It does not mean I want to see the movie. And we say "movie". We don't say "picture", alright?' said Veda, gently correcting Kajol's English. She did not even think about it. It came naturally to her. Kajol reminded Veda of her younger siblings back home.

'Yes, didi. I will remember. Now let me help you with the cooking,' said Kajol.

She asked Veda how many people she wanted to cook for. Then Kajol measured the correct amount of rice.

'Didi, one cup raw rice gives three cups of cooked rice,' said Kajol.

Veda nodded.

'Don't you have to go to school?' Veda asked.

'Today, I am missing Sankalp. I told Sanju to tell Kanika didi. You know Kanika didi?' she asked.

'Yes, we just met,' Veda nodded.

'She stays here only, in the next building,' said Kajol.

'I know, Kajol. I met her,' Veda smiled.

'She is very nice. Very beautiful, didi. Just like you. But you are more beautiful,' said Kajol.

Veda smiled at Kajol's disjointed language as well as her descriptions. She loved her enthusiasm.

'I think we are all beautiful in our own ways,' said Veda. But she wasn't sure if Kajol understood what she meant.

Veda and Kajol then got busy cooking. Shakubai had finished sweeping and mopping the house by then. She joined them in the kitchen.

Between the three women, they managed to make rice, a simple dal, a salad and a vegetable in no time. Veda was very proud as she laid the table and waited for her mother-in-law to arrive.

'Thank you so much, Kajol,' said Veda.

'Okay, didi. Bye, didi,' said Kajol, as she left with Shakubai.

After they left, Veda became even more curious about Sankalp. What a well-mannered girl Kajol was, and so pleasant and cheerful. She wondered what the other children in Sankalp were like. The more she thought about it, the more certain she was that she wanted to volunteer with the organisation.

But how could she get what she wanted? She knew she couldn't talk to her mother-in-law directly.

There was only one way she could do it. She wasn't sure if it would work, but she was definitely going to try.

Chapter 16

July 1996
Kailash Mandir Colony, Pune

'Bhuwan, Bhuwan,' Veda whispered into her husband's ears.

It was only 5 o'clock, and it was still dark, the sun not having risen yet.

'Ummm,' he muttered sleepily as he turned towards her.

'Do you want tea?' asked Veda, taking advantage of his sleepiness.

'Uh, huh,' he muttered.

Veda got out of bed. She had now got used to the routine of waking up early, having a bath and then lighting the lamp as insisted upon by her mother-in-law.

She hurried to the kitchen, made two strong cups of tea, and came back to the bedroom with them.

'Wake up, here's your tea,' she said, nudging Bhuwan with her knee as she sat back, leaned against the headboard and sipped her tea.

'What time is it?' he muttered, his eyes still shut.

'Wake up, Bhuwan. I made tea for you. I asked you if you wanted tea, didn't I? Look, it will go cold if you don't have it now.'

Bhuwan sat up, his eyes groggy with sleep, and took the cup of tea from Veda's hand. Then he glanced at the clock.

'God—it is not even 5.30, Veda. Why wake me up so early?' he grumbled.

'Bhuwan, for so many weeks now, I have woken up at 5.30, had a shower and then performed the pooja. I did it uncomplainingly because you asked me to adjust. I have woken you up early just one time, and you grumble?' Veda said.

Her words had the desired effect.

'Okay, okay. Sorry. Now I am awake. Tell me, what did you wake me up for?' asked Bhuwan as he sat up, leaned against the headboard and took a sip of tea.

'No specific reason. We hardly talk as you come back late

from office. So I just thought we would have a conversation,' said Veda. She did not directly want to bring up the topic of her going with Kanika.

Bhuwan considered what she had said for a few seconds as he sipped his tea. Veda was right. They hardly spoke these days. With the second sip of tea, his brain was jolted awake.

'Aah, alright then,' he said. He tried to think of something they could converse about. Then he asked, 'How did your results go? You were supposed to have collected them by now?'

'I ... I failed,' Veda replied. Her stomach knotted up as she said the words. After her meeting with Kanika and her interaction with Kajol, she had been temporarily distracted. But now it all came back to her in sharp focus, stinging her.

'What?' asked Bhuwan. 'That's impossible. You topped the college in Joshimath, didn't you? What happened here, Veda?' he asked.

He was genuinely concerned. He knew that he had not been paying attention to how her studies were progressing, and that he had drowned himself in work the last few months. His father's death had hit him badly, and he found some solace from the pain only when he worked. He had turned into a workaholic, ignoring everything around him.

But now, when he looked at Veda's distraught face, something inside him melted. Her sorrow was evident. How could he have been so callous about her feelings? As it is, the poor girl was going through an ordeal with his mother. He could see that clearly now.

A lump formed in Veda's throat when she heard the concern in Bhuwan's voice. He had asked what had happened. There was so much that had happened. Where was she to begin?

Veda took a deep breath. Then she said, 'It was all so difficult, Bhuwan. There was no time to study. I thought I could pull it off with the notes I had been making in class. But I couldn't. It was simply not enough. I have been doing everything your mother wants and I have been looking after her, taking care of all her needs.'

Veda took care to ensure she did not complain about her mother-in-law. She knew that she had to handle this tactfully. If she complained, he would probably make a placatory comment and then tell her that his mother was in mourning.

'I know. I am so grateful to you for that, Veda. I want you to know that I appreciate it,' he said.

Veda nodded, sipping her tea. Her eyes brimmed with tears now. She hated it. She did not want to feel sorry for herself. She did not want to start crying again. She thought she was over it. She thought she had made peace with the failure. But Bhuwan's kindness had unleashed the flood of tears that she had managed to suppress.

'Veda. I am so sorry. I have been very preoccupied,' he said in a gentle voice.

Veda sniffed, wiping away her tears.

'Can't you give the supplementary exams? You should apply for them. Since you are feeling so bad about failing, you should not give up. You should give it another try,' he said.

'For what? It's not like your mother will be pleased about me studying further.'

'Not for her, Veda. For yourself.'

'I seem to have lost all motivation, Bhuwan. I once dreamt of studying for my Master's and then applying for a job. I always wanted to be a college lecturer. Back home in Joshimath, we had a professor who studied in the same college I attended. He went to Delhi for his post-graduation and later did his doctorate. He came back to teach in that same college. I foolishly hoped I could do that too.'

'Ummmm…' said Bhuwan. 'But your parents said that you did not want to study further. I think that's what my mother liked the most about you.'

'They lied. They just wanted to see me married,' said Veda, her voice drained of all emotion. She had initially struggled to accept the betrayal and had now done so, through her letters to Vidya and Suraj.

'Mmmm,' muttered Bhuwan, his brows furrowed. 'The past is past, Veda. Let's just leave it and look towards the future. What do you want to do, going ahead?' he asked.

'I am not sure. I want to think about it, Bhuwan. This has come as a shock to me. The enormity of it is just sinking in. I had not even considered giving the supplementary exams till you suggested it,' Veda said.

'I think you should. You can go to the college library and study if you are not able to study at home.'

'But what about your mother?' asked Veda.

'There's a certain way in which you have to present things to her to get her to agree to what you want. If you ask outright, she will refuse. I know how to handle her,' said Bhuwan.

'In that case, can you please get her to agree to another thing? Kanika works with an NGO, and she is taking a colleague to see the homes of the children she teaches. She asked me to come along. I was wondering how to get Maaji's permission,' said Veda.

'Oh, so you met Kanika? When?' asked Bhuwan.

'The day before yesterday. The day I got my results. I was locked out when I came back from college after looking up my results. So I waited in her house till Maaji returned.'

'Oh, I see. Kanika is doing some remarkable work.'

'You know about it?'

'Of course, I do. My company was one of the sponsors at an event they organised last year. It was an art fair. You should have seen the products those kids came up with. Do you know, our corporate calendar for this year was designed by the students of Sankalp. It has all their artwork on it. We also bought a lot of greeting cards, which the students designed. They are a talented bunch, and Kanika is doing a good job. I am glad you met her,' said Bhuwan.

'She seems to be a nice person,' said Veda.

'Oh, she is. We have practically grown up together. She and I used to be good friends. Or enemies. We used to fight, but we were also inseparable. I once poured a bottle of Coca-Cola on her head,' laughed Bhuwan.

'What?! Why?' Veda was surprised.

She had never seen that side of Bhuwan. To her, he was always the serious professional, with no time for frivolity or fun.

'This was when we were eight or nine. I did it because she dared me to.'

'Then what happened?'

'She went crying to my mother! I got a proper scolding. If that wasn't enough, she went and cried to Shanta aunty too. Shanta aunty just laughed and told her to go and wash her hair.'

Veda smiled.

'Kanika was suggesting that I volunteer at her NGO,' said Veda. Now that she knew Bhuwan was supportive of Kanika's venture, Veda felt she could confide in him.

'Do you want to? It is extremely tough. The poverty-stricken areas that these children come from are among the lowest economic strata of society. Their realities are very different from ours. Volunteering to teach them isn't easy at all.'

'I don't know, Bhuwan. But I want to see for myself.'

Bhuwan scratched his jaw as he considered it.

Finally, he said, 'I think that's a good idea.'

'So, will you convince your mother, then?' asked Veda.

Bhuwan became thoughtful once again. He would have to do this tactfully.

'I'll tell you what—this Thursday, Ma has invited her friends over for a musical evening. She wanted me to set up the music system with speakers in the drawing room. She wants to play Carnatic bhajans and has been pestering me to get the cassettes. I will bring up the topic then. Wait and see, you will be able to go with Kanika. I will ensure it,' promised Bhuwan.

Veda was glad that she had woken him up early and had managed to get what she wanted. This was the first real conversation that they had had in ages. He seemed genuinely concerned about her well-being and she felt happy about that.

On Thursday, Bhuwan returned a little early from work to set up the music system for his mother. He would leave soon after the musical evening started. He said that he and Vikki planned to go and see a plot of land that Vikki's father wanted to buy.

Padma Devi was excited about the evening. She and Veda had prepared snacks and juice to serve the ladies. She had carefully supervised Shakubai's work that morning. She had also told Veda to dust and polish all the furniture, as well as vacuum the carpet. She had taken out a brass statue of

Nataraja and told Veda to polish it with Brasso. Veda's hands hurt from all the scrubbing but she did it uncomplainingly. She knew there was no point in protesting. Veda had also filled a large silver bowl with water and placed rose petals in it. She placed a lamp next to it, which she lit.

'Maaji, is this okay?' she asked.

To her surprise, Padma Devi approved. This was the closest she had come to praise.

When Shanta aunty, Kanti behen and a couple of other ladies that Padma Devi had invited arrived, Veda served them cold lemonade. They looked at the preparations that had been made for the evening and praised the ambience. Padma Devi beamed and basked in their approval.

After a few minutes, Kanika popped in.

'Come in, come in, Kanika beti. How nice that you decided to join us. You are visiting me like this after so many months,' said Padma Devi, welcoming her.

'Yes, Aunty. So sorry, I have been caught up in work,' said Kanika, as she walked in and took her seat.

Veda was surprised. Kanika looked at her and winked. Then she smiled at Bhuwan.

Bhuwan smiled back. Everything was going as per their plan.

The ladies in the room were conversing about their children now. One was taking about her daughter who had got into IIT. Another was talking about her son doing a course in public relations.

'Yes, yes. It is good. Children should be allowed to study what they want,' said Padma Devi.

'Absolutely. Initially, when Kanika quit her corporate job, I was sceptical. Why do you want to leave such a well-paying job, I asked her. But then she explained to me. She is helping thousands of children who do not have a chance otherwise. And now I am quite proud of the work she is doing,' said Shanta.

'It is very good, beti. We should always help the less privileged. Very good,' said Padma Devi.

Kanika did not miss the opportunity that had opened up.

'Aunty, I was just thinking that Veda should come

and work with me at Sankalp. We are badly in need of volunteers.'

'Oh, is it? I think you should take Veda and show her all the work you do,' chimed in Bhuwan before Padma Devi could respond.

'Yes, yes. I would love to do that. Veda, would you like to come and work with me at Sankalp?' asked Kanika.

Veda couldn't believe what had just happened.

'Ummm ... ahhh,' she stammered, trying to speak. She wanted to jump up and say yes. But she also did not want to seem too eager, in case Padma Devi pounced on her later.

'Nothing to think about, Veda. I think you should give it a try. Now that your exams are over, you have time, isn't it?' said Bhuwan, his eyes twinkling.

'Yes. Yes, I will come with you to Sankalp and see and understand what it's all about,' Veda managed to say.

'Good, that's fixed then. If you like it, you can straightaway join us,' Kanika said. She turned to Padma Devi. 'Aunty, I will come this Saturday and take Veda with me.'

Padma Devi couldn't say anything. It had happened too quickly.

Veda wanted to hug and kiss Bhuwan and Kanika. She was so excited and happy.

Instead, she kept her eyes downcast, and served the snacks to the ladies, who were now talking about the music that would be played that evening.

When the musical evening started, Bhuwan slipped away. Kanika got a moment alone with Veda.

'See? There's always a way around these things. Bhuwan and I used to be partners in crime for a lot more such things when we were kids. He spoke to me and I couldn't refuse,' she said.

'Thank you!' said Veda, squeezing Kanika's hand in gratitude. She couldn't wait for Saturday to arrive.

Part Three

BENDING THE RULES

Some rules are nothing but old habits that people are afraid to change.

– Therese Anne Fowler, *Souvenir*

Chapter 17

July 1996

Sitawadi, Pune

Kanika and Veda stood outside the Sitawadi area, near the massive light-yellow cement arch that marked the entrance, waiting for Kanika's colleague.

'I would have never thought in a million years that you and Bhuwan would manage to pull that one over my mother-in-law,' Veda said, smiling.

'Oh, we both always conspired to get Padma aunty to agree to things when we were kids. One time, when Bhuwan wanted to go on a class trip and Padma aunty was reluctant to let him, I got my mother to talk to the class teacher who then "accidentally" bumped into them on their morning walk. She talked about how all the students were coming, and what a good opportunity it was. My mother added her two bits about how delighted she was that I was going on the class trip. Then everyone looked expectantly at Padma aunty, and she had to agree,' said Kanika.

Veda smiled.

'There are so many stories like that, involving Bhuwan and me. I covered for him when he went out drinking. He covered for me when I wanted to spend the night with my boyfriends, now my ex-boyfriends,' said Kanika, as she pulled a face.

Veda was taken aback at how nonchalant Kanika was, in admitting to having had sex with her former boyfriends. Did she trust Veda so much, or was it not a big deal to Kanika, Veda wondered.

'Don't you feel guilty about these ... err ... relationships you have had?' Veda asked.

'Guilty? No. I don't feel guilty at all. I have thought about how society makes such a big deal of premarital sex. I think if you take precautions, it is perfectly okay. Humans are biologically not made to be monogamous. If you ask me, marriage disrupts the natural order of things,' Kanika said.

Veda was uncomfortable discussing this subject with Kanika. Kanika was being so forthright and open about it. She wished now that she hadn't brought it up. So she changed the topic.

'I never knew that side of Bhuwan,' said Veda.

'He keeps it well-hidden. He has changed in the last couple of years. I do believe Padma aunty is to blame for that. She can be such a nag. Between you and me, he got married just to please Padma aunty. I hope you don't mind my being honest with you about all this.'

'I appreciate your being honest. And you know what, Kanika—I too got married just to please my parents,' said Veda.

'I suspected as much. I don't know why parents can't just let their children be. My mother keeps trying to match-make for me. But she also knows I will not be happy unless I make my own choice. She is still hopeful, though,' Kanika said, shrugging.

'I wonder where your colleague is,' Veda said, glancing at her watch.

'I think he will be on time. He is British, after all. By the way, his name is Ronald,' said Kanika. She added that they had only corresponded via letters, and this was the first time they were meeting.

Veda nodded. She had never interacted with a foreigner before. She had only seen a few from a distance back in Joshimath. Foreign tourists travelling to Haridwar sometimes stayed in Joshimath. She was curious to see what Ronald would be like. She was also keen to see the world that lay so close to her own home—a world she had no knowledge of.

The arch was the most prominent landmark in this large slum settlement spread over three acres. It was only a few hundred metres from Kailash Mandir Colony, and within the radius of a kilometre from the office buildings. Kanika wondered if meeting Ronald here for the first time was a good idea. Perhaps she should have suggested that they all meet over a cup of coffee, before giving him a tour of the slum settlements. But it was he who had insisted on it. He wanted to film it, and he said it would be best if he met her here.

'Oh, we will have plenty of time for coffee later. I think I will need it afterwards,' he had said in his British accent. Kanika had to listen carefully over the phone to understand what he was saying. Though she was fluent in English, she discovered that the way he spoke was very different from how Indians spoke the language.

'I hope his taxi driver is able to locate the place. I spoke to the driver and gave him instructions before he left the hotel,' said Kanika.

'I guess if he has the address, he will find it,' Veda replied.

The sun was beating down hard. Veda squinted her eyes. She wished she owned a pair of sunglasses, like Kanika. In Joshimath, she had never felt the need for it, and so she had not bought a pair. In any case, her father saw all such expenses as frivolous.

As they stood waiting, a boy who looked about twelve or thirteen recognised Kanika.

'Kanika didi! Good morning,' he greeted her, his eyes shining bright.

'*Kisi ke liye wait kar rahe ho, didi?*' he asked, as he rolled a dismantled cycle wheel around expertly, steering it with a little wooden baton.

'Umm, Sharan. English please. You know the rule,' said Kanika, when she turned around and saw who had greeted her.

'But didi, we … not in Sankalp. Not in class,' said Sharan.

'Yes, but when you speak to me, you have to speak only in English. You know the Sankalp rule,' said Kanika.

'Yes didi, sorry didi,' said Sharan, as he frowned, trying to frame the sentence in English in his head.

'You wait for who, didi? And who is this?' he asked hesitatingly.

'This is my friend, Veda. We are waiting for another friend of mine. He is going to film your area. Do you remember, I told you about Ronald, yesterday?'

'Yes, Kanika didi, I remember. Hello, Veda didi, Good morning,' said the boy, addressing Veda.

'Hello, Sharan,' said Veda, pleasantly surprised. She liked the boy already. He had a naughty face and an impish smile. He reminded her of Animesh.

'Sharan is in Kajol's class, Veda,' Kanika said.

Veda was surprised, because Sharan looked so much younger. Then she realised that it was probably malnutrition.

They spotted Ronald's car just then. Kanika waved her arms to catch the driver's attention. The car came to a halt.

Ronald stepped out. He was about five foot ten, only an inch taller than Kanika. Kanika knew that he was thirty-one, but he looked much younger. He had a boyish face and was clean-shaven. His brown hair was cut short, and he wore a full-sleeved, deep grey shirt, dark trousers and a green tie. His leather shoes were so polished that Kanika could see her reflection in them. She was surprised to see his formal attire.

'Hello, Kanika. I hope I haven't kept you waiting too long,' he said, as he offered his hand. He pronounced her name as Can-ikk-a.

'Hi, Ronald. You haven't kept us waiting at all. We just got here,' said Kanika, as she extended her arm and shook his hand. It was a firm handshake.

'Ronald, this is my friend Veda,' said Kanika.

'Hello, Ve-dah,' he said.

Veda shook hands with him.

Both Veda and Kanika smiled at how he had pronounced their names. Kanika discovered that his accent was a bit easier to understand in person.

Kanika liked him instantly. The green in his eyes matched his tie.

'This, here, is Sharan. He is one of the students,' said Kanika, as she introduced Sharan.

'Good morning, bhaiya,' said Sharan, as he stared at Ronald, his eyes popping out.

'And Sharan, why didn't you go to school today?' asked Kanika.

'No school, didi. *Chutti* ... er ... holiday.'

'Why?' asked Kanika.

'Festival didi. Big festival. Inside. Pooja,' said Sharan, extending both his arms, trying to convey the largeness of the festival with his limited vocabulary of English words.

'Ah, I see,' said Kanika.

Sharan studied Ronald's face. They had never had a 'foreign bhaiya' in Sankalp before. Though there were a few didis and bhaiyas who taught them, they were all Indian. This was the first time in his life that Sharan was interacting with a foreigner. He suddenly felt shy.

'Okay, bye didis, bye bhaiya,' he said, as he sped off, rolling his bicycle tyre in front of him.

'Gosh. Look at that! How does he do that?' Ron asked.

'Do what?' Kanika frowned.

'You know, that bicycle wheel he rolled. How does he move it forward without any support?'

'Oh, that! They are all experts with many unusual toys like these. Why, don't you have this in England?' she asked, with an amused expression.

'This? No. Good lord, no. I have never seen anything like this,' he said. He did not realise that she was teasing him.

'Ah, wait till we begin the tour of the settlement. And, by the way, welcome to India! How are you liking it so far?'

'Oh, it's been lovely. Mumbai was … um … crowded. But it was fascinating. The drive here was very pleasant.'

'Oh, that's good to hear. Did you sleep well? Have you rested enough?'

'Yes, I did. Thank you for asking. I slept like a baby last night. It's been a week now, in India, and I think I am getting used to it,' said Ronald.

Veda was a little awestruck by Ronald. She was tongue-tied in his presence and did not know what to say. Fortunately for her, Kanika was keeping the conversation going. Veda just had to tag along with them.

'Look, Ronald, this might be … er … a little difficult for you? If you like, we can do this after you have met the children at class tomorrow,' said Kanika. She wasn't sure how Ronald would manage to walk through the slum settlement in his spotless, shiny shoes and his formal clothes. It looked like he was dressed for a board meeting. But she did not know him well enough to tell him directly that his sartorial choice wasn't suitable for a venture such as this. He would discover that soon enough.

'Better to get this out of the way. I have to send them these films. I have my camcorder right here. Let's see—new tape ... yes, I have it,' he said, as he took out a small cassette and inserted it into his camcorder. 'As I mentioned in my letter, the Carman Foundation members want to see the actual living conditions of these children. They are happy to support Sankalp, but they have sent me here to make accurate reports. I think it's important for them to see where their money is going, and how Sankalp is helping. All the donations come from individual members you see, and none of them have travelled to India,' explained Ronald.

'Sure, I understand. You will see in the classrooms what a huge difference Sankalp is making in the lives of these children,' said Kanika, as she led the way.

Ronald switched on his camcorder and began to film. The 'street' itself was no more than eight-feet wide. Tiny hutments with asbestos sheets as roofs stood next to each other. None of the houses had windows. Instead, there was a single door that opened out onto the street. Clothes were hung out to dry outside the homes, on clotheslines that clung to the dusty walls. A woman stood outside a hutment with three large buckets, bending over and washing vessels. The dirty water flowed down the street, mixing with the mud, making a pile of slush as it flowed.

'Oh,' said Ronald, as he stepped into it, his shoes making a squelching sound. The slushy mud splattered, causing deep brown spots to appear on his dark trousers. Veda and Kanika smartly avoided it, hopping around it, treading gingerly. People glanced at Veda, Kanika and Ronald curiously, but did not stop whatever they were doing.

'Does Kajol live here?' Veda asked Kanika.

'Yes, but I am not sure if this is her street. There are at least eighteen or twenty streets like this one,' replied Kanika.

But Veda kept a lookout for Kajol.

Inside the hutments, it was dark. In one, Ronald saw a stove on the floor and a woman sitting next to it, cooking. The smell of whatever she was making mingled with the slightly rancid stench outside, assaulting his nostrils. A little toddler in an oversized muddy T-shirt, unsupervised by anybody, crossed the street, coughing loudly. Ronald found himself inadvertently holding his breath as he waited for the toddler to pass.

Women stood around in multi-coloured polyester nightgowns and talked to each other over the din of the ongoing construction. Firewood lay piled up to one side. Scooters and cycles stood scattered, parked randomly through the lane. If Ronald was surprised, he certainly did not show it. His face betrayed no emotion as he walked on behind Kanika, filming it all, his camera pausing every now and then, focusing on the children in particular, who walked, played and talked, oblivious to their surroundings. Veda trailed behind Ronald, the three of them making a strange entourage, but the residents of Sitawadi were too engrossed in their daily life to pay any attention to them, other than giving them a few cursory, curious glances. The older girls were sitting outside their homes, washing vessels or clothes. The boys were in groups, roaming around or playing. Some of the boys were playing with a top, which they took turns to spin on the ground. Garbage was piled up everywhere. There were goats tethered outside a few homes, and some children were feeding them.

A vegetable vendor pushed his cart though this street, shouting out the price of his wares. As they walked on, Ronald noticed that some of the homes didn't even have cement walls. Instead, they were made of asbestos sheets. Stray dogs lazed around. There was an open sewage system through which dirty water flowed.

The street opened out to a slightly wider area which had tiny shops that sold everything from *paan* to provisions to cigarettes. In the middle of this area stood a massive peepul tree, around which a circular platform was constructed. A few men sat on this, playing cards. Next to them were glasses of alcohol and a bottle that was half-empty.

Kanika kept a watch out for Sankalp students, but she couldn't spot any.

After they had finished walking through the lane, she asked Ronald, 'Do you want to film some more?'

'I think this will do for now,' he said.

Kanika nodded. 'Yes, it is a bit too much, isn't it? What about you Veda, are you okay?' she asked.

Veda nodded.

Ronald was silent. Then he said, 'I am just shocked. I had read about the poverty in India, and even seen pictures. But this is beyond words. I feel deeply saddened to witness first-hand their deplorable living conditions.'

Veda was a little shaken too. She had never been inside such a settlement. Though she had seen some poverty in the Garhwal mountains, she had never experienced such squalor, and such terrible living conditions.

'Yes, I feel sad too,' said Veda, agreeing with Ronald.

'Yes, Ronald and Veda. All our students at Sankalp come from such homes. So you can imagine what a challenge it is for them. Life has dealt them the unluckiest cards. I think people like you and me, together, we can make a difference. This is why we first give a tour of this place to anyone who wants to be associated with Sankalp. This way, they are fully aware of the backgrounds of the children, and it translates to more empathy and understanding in the classrooms.'

'Yes, I get it. That's what the Carman Foundation wants to do—make a difference in the lives of these children. This film will help the members back home get the correct picture.'

'Shall we go back then?' asked Kanika.

Veda and Ronald nodded.

'One more thing—you can call me Ron. Ronald sounds a tad too formal. Whenever I got into trouble at school, that is how the teachers addressed me. "Ronald Wilson", they would start, and I knew I was in trouble,' he said, and smiled.

'Were you a naughty child?' Kanika asked.

'Oh, the usual things that boys do at that age,' said Ron, dismissively.

Kanika asked them if they wanted to take an auto, or whether they preferred to walk back down the street.

Ron wanted to know if there was any way out, without having to walk back through the slum. So Kanika led them to a path around the slum.

In the initial days of setting up Sankalp—which was run

by an NGO with an army of volunteers—nobody in this settlement had understood the concept, or the need, for such a thing. When Kanika and the social workers had visited the locality to urge the residents to send their children to Sankalp for two hours before the children attended their regular school, nobody was interested.

'Sankalp is not like your regular school. We will be working closely with your children to teach them English and maths. And it is free,' the social workers had explained.

The ladies were hesitant.

'Who will do the morning chores? We go to work. Someone has to be there to take care of the household.'

'What use is this "free school"? They are going to regular school anyway.'

'It's an utter waste of time if you are going to be teaching the same things their school anyway teaches.'

These were the arguments they made. They could only see that sending their children to this 'free school'—in addition to their regular school—would interfere with the daily tasks that most of the children in the settlement performed. Clothes had to be washed, little babies had to be fed, and food had to be cooked. If the girls went off early in the morning, the women would have to work even harder, waking up an hour earlier.

The social workers had then explained to the women about Sankalp. It was not like the schools that their children attended, where the teachers were over-burdened, they said. Those regular schools were not very effective when it came to academic performance. The pass percentage of the students enrolled at Sankalp was 93 per cent, compared to the state average of 54 per cent. Sankalp was running successfully in many other Indian cities, and they told the women how fortunate they were that their locality had been chosen for a branch. Many Sankalp children had been accepted in mainstream colleges. Even though some of the children in the slum settlement went to English-medium schools, none of them could converse in English, and that was what Sankalp taught them. Once they were proficient in English, a lot more doors opened and they would get higher paying jobs. All of this was explained in Marathi by the social workers to the group of women and a few men. They had been enticed to attend the meeting with an offer of free *samosas* and tea.

The social workers had then brought in a couple of children who had graduated from Sankalp and gone on to make a success of their lives. These teenagers had narrated their experiences and talked about the ways in which Sankalp had transformed their lives. The prospect of better employment opportunities was what had convinced the women, and they agreed to send their children to Sankalp.

Kanika explained all this to Ron and Veda as they made their way back to the office complex. Ron knew a part of the story, as the Carman Foundation had investigated the organisation in detail before agreeing to give them a grant. However, he listened politely, as he found the bit about having to convince the women to send their children to Sankalp interesting.

For Veda, it was all new, and she listened with rapt attention. She felt like a child who had discovered a closed door in the house she had grown up in. Now, suddenly, the door had opened, and she had got a glimpse into the fascinating and difficult world it contained.

Chapter 18

July 1996
Sankalp, Pune

When they reached the office complex, Kanika took them to the part of the building that housed the food joints. This area had many restaurants, and it was where most of the office-goers hung out. She indicated a coffee shop which had a large striped canopy that opened out onto the inner quadrangle, providing shade. The wrought iron chairs and tables under the canopy, as well as the many potted plants with brightly coloured tiny flowers, added to the relaxed, casual, European ambience.

'This a nice place,' said Ron.

'Yes, it is. Their coffee is good too. Shall we sit there?' Kanika asked, pointing to a comfortable looking sofa, which was inside the coffee shop.

'Yes, let's do that. I will join in you a bit. I have to go to the washroom,' said Ron, as he excused himself.

Veda had never seen such a nicely decorated coffee shop anywhere in Joshimath or Pune. She looked around with approval and thought about how she and Bhuwan had never ever gone out all by themselves for a nice meal or even for a cup of coffee.

'So, do you come here often?' she asked Kanika.

'Almost never. I am always busy with the students of Sankalp. It is only when we have visitors like Ron, that I get a chance to come here,' said Kanika.

When Ron emerged from the washroom, Veda saw that he had lost the tie. His sleeves were rolled up, and his shoes were spotless again.

Kanika smiled at him as he joined them. 'So, you cleaned up?'

'Yes, oh yes; I couldn't possibly walk around in those shoes. They were filthy,' he said, scrunching up his nose.

Veda smiled.

Over coffee, Kanika asked Ron about himself. They learnt

that he was from Birmingham. His mother's main job was as an administrative assistant at a private firm. His father had abandoned them shortly after Ron's birth. He had an older brother and an older sister. His mother had later taken up a second job at a large retail store. Since she worked two jobs and was a single mother, she had applied to the council for financial aid. The council had contributed towards the education of the three children, as they were academically bright. They had been sent to boarding schools at a very young age. Soon after Ron had finished college, he had joined the Carman Charity Foundation. One of the founders of Sankalp knew a board member of the foundation, which was how they had learned of Sankalp's work and decided to give them a grant. But now they wanted a progress report, and Ron had jumped at the opportunity to travel to India.

Ron asked Kanika about herself.

'Oh, I have lived in Pune all my life. I finished college, and I joined a corporate at twenty-two. After working for five years, I was burnt out. I had travelled so much, working with companies to deliver their requirements. But honestly, it did nothing for me. I had made quite a bit of money. So I quit, and now here I am,' said Kanika.

'And what about you, Veda?' asked Ron.

This was the first time he had addressed her directly. Veda found him looking right into her eyes, and she was startled by the colour of his. They seemed to bore into her very soul.

'Uhhh ... I am married, and I moved to Pune from Joshimath, where I grew up. I just finished the final year of my college,' she said. She did not want to tell him that she had failed in her exams. She thought that detail was not necessary. She also did not trust herself to bring up the topic without her eyes brimming over with tears.

But Ron was not even thinking about her academics.

'Oh! How wonderful that you have found that special someone you want to share the rest of your life with,' he said, smiling.

Veda wanted to tell him that it wasn't the way he was imagining it. She did not see Bhuwan as her 'special someone'.

As far as she was concerned, he was just her husband, a man chosen by her parents. Yes, she was married to him, but she didn't share too many things with him. Wasn't a 'special someone' a soulmate? The one you discussed things with, the one you looked forward to meeting at the end of the day, the one in whose arms everything felt right? At least that was what the books she read had told her.

Veda did not think that someone from the Western world would be able to comprehend the complexities of Indian society, and its family-centric culture, where you obeyed your parents unquestioningly.

She didn't say any of this to Ron though, nor did she see any point in explaining things. So she said nothing.

But Kanika and Ron were both looking at her, waiting for her to respond.

'Umm … Yes … I guess,' she said finally.

Kanika laughed.

'I guess?' she said, imitating Veda's hesitant tone.

Veda found her cheeks turning red, like she had been caught out in a lie.

'I suppose I mean yes,' said Veda, haltingly. Kanika could see that she was squirming and did not want to talk about it.

'Okay, okay, I was just teasing,' said Kanika, instantly regretting making Veda uncomfortable. *The poor girl has too much going on already, without having to deal with my teasing as well,* she thought.

There was a moment of awkward silence. Ron sensed it and he asked a question about Sankalp. Kanika jumped in to answer, and with that, the tension dissipated, and the moment passed.

Once they'd had their coffee, Kanika asked Ron and Veda if they would like to see the classrooms out of which Sankalp operated.

Ron said he would very much like that. Veda too was keen on seeing them.

Kanika led both of them to the basement of the office complex where the classrooms were located.

Once they descended the stairs, they were directly in the 'classrooms'.

Ron and Veda looked a little puzzled. These were open spaces without any walls. There were pillars at equal intervals to support the structure. This looked like some parking lot, sans vehicles. Where were the 'rooms'?

'Which way now?' Ron asked.

'Here! We are right here, in the classrooms,' smiled Kanika.

'What?'

Ron had not expected it to be this rudimentary.

'Yes, do you see those tables there?' Kanika pointed to one end of the large, open basement.

Veda and Ron looked in the direction that she was pointing. Stacked behind a pillar were two rickety wooden tables and two chairs.

'That's it,' said Kanika. 'We have two more tables and chairs like this one and that is the second classroom,' she said, pointing a little further.

'Oh—but where are the benches and desks? Where do the children sit?' Veda asked.

'They sit here on the floor! We have mats for them,' said Kanika, as she walked towards the table. Behind the pillar stood two old steel almirahs, side by side. She opened one of them and took out several colourful straw and cloth mats.

'See these? We spread them out and this is where they sit,' she said.

'Where are all the children now?' Ron asked.

'Today, there is a festival in the wadi, where they live. So none of them will attend class. Today is an off for them,' said Kanika.

'Oh, yes! Choo—tea,' said Ron, as he had heard Sharan saying earlier.

Veda and Kanika both looked puzzled for a moment and then laughed as they realised that the word he was trying to say was 'chutti'.

'Not bad! You have already picked up Hindi, I am impressed,' said Kanika.

Ron pretended to bow.

'Shall we go back and meet the rest of the team, Ron? You can join us in the classrooms tomorrow for observation, if you like,' said Kanika.

'Yes, that sounds perfect,' said Ron.

'So, now that you have seen Sankalp, do you think you would like to join us as a volunteer, Veda?' Kanika asked.

Veda thought about the options she had. She could refuse to be a volunteer, in which case she would have to stay at home with her mother-in-law all day and become her slave again. The endless days would stretch out in front of her, as she did not have college to attend anymore. She would go insane with boredom.

On the other hand, if she joined Sankalp, she could interact with so many people. She had liked Kajol and had been impressed by her. Her earlier meeting with Sharan too had impressed her. These children were pragmatic and accepted the cards that life had dealt them. She wanted to work with them and get to know them.

She did not hesitate when she replied. 'I would very much like to volunteer, Kanika. Are there ... er ... any minimum educational qualifications to join as a volunteer?' she asked, unsure about that detail.

'All we need is for you to be proficient in basic maths and English. You also need a positive attitude. You can volunteer in three areas—fundraising, teaching or admin. Which one would you prefer?'

Veda did not hesitate about that either. She definitely wanted to interact with the children.

'Teaching,' she said.

'Oh, one more thing. You have to commit to be a volunteer for a minimum period of six months. The reason is that Sankalp invests a lot in the training programme. We use our resources to train people well, and we want only serious and committed people. Are you good with that?'

Veda was more than happy to agree.

'Let's go to the admin office and get the paperwork out of the way then. And Ron, you can meet the others there. I shall introduce you,' said Kanika, as she led them to the fifth floor.

The administration department was a small space in a corporate office that was a sponsor of Sankalp. They had given a cabin to the volunteers of Sankalp within their office premises, and this was where the non-teaching staff operated from. They were a team of four people—three women and a man.

'This is Aparna, she heads the team here. So, she is the boss lady,' said Kanika, as she introduced Ron and Veda.

Aparna was short, slim and very business-like in her manner. She wore glasses and her grey hair was cut very short. She wore a fitted kurti and knee length shorts. Her sartorial choice was unusual, but she managed to look smart. She looked slightly hassled and annoyed, and gave the impression that Kanika had interrupted something important.

'So you decide who stays here and who goes?' quipped Ron.

'Yes, I do,' said Aparna. She did not smile.

'I want to thank the members of the Carman Foundation for supporting our cause. Do convey my regards and deep gratitude to them,' she told Ron.

Ron replied that it was a pleasure and he would do that.

Then Aparna addressed Veda.

'Are you considering volunteering here?' she asked.

'Yes, ma'am, I am,' said Veda. She did not know why she had addressed Aparna as 'ma'am'. Perhaps it was because she reminded Veda of her headmistress, and she exuded authority.

'Good. We need volunteers. Has Kanika explained the rules to you?' she asked.

'Yes, Aparna, I have told her,' said Kanika, and she looked at Veda pointedly, as though to tell her not to be intimidated by Aparna, and that she did not have to call her 'ma'am'.

'Any experience teaching kids?' asked Aparna.

Veda thought of the countless times she and Vidya had tutored their younger siblings. She had read to them, supervised their homework and coached them.

'Yes, I have tutored children,' she found herself saying, quickly dispensing with addressing Aparna as 'ma'am'.

'Alright. The training session for new volunteers starts on Monday, and it goes on till Wednesday. Does that suit you?' she asked Veda.

'Uh, yes, yes. I am fine with that,' said Veda.

'Alright. You will first start out as a teacher's assistant. At the end of six weeks, or maybe even earlier, based on your performance, you could be offered a teaching position. Our teaching positions are full-time, and they are paid. As a volunteer, you will not be paid. Are you okay with that?' Aparna asked.

'Yes, I am good with that,' said Veda. This was even better than she had hoped. There was a chance for her to get a paying job!

'Good. You can fill up the forms then. Himanshu, please help her,' said Aparna, addressing the young man sitting in a corner, buried in a pile of paperwork.

'Sure. Please fill these. And we will need two passport sized photos too,' he said, handing Veda the forms.

Veda took them from him and thanked him.

As she, Kanika and Ron exited the building, Veda stowed the forms carefully in her handbag. She was excited at the prospect of starting to teach at Sankalp.

'Veda, it's wonderful that you have decided to join us. I am looking forward to working with you,' Kanika said.

'Me too,' said Veda.

Kanika would never get how *much* this opportunity meant to Veda. It had come to her at a time when she was feeling despondent and lost. She felt that the universe was conspiring and shining light on a path that she would have never considered, had she not failed her exams.

Veda's twenty-first birthday was in two days. She couldn't help reflect that this was probably the best birthday gift that life had handed to her. She couldn't wait for the training sessions to start, so that she could start teaching Kajol and the other children.

Chapter 19

August 1996
Pune

Dear Vidya,
It has been a while since we wrote to each other. I am sorry for the delay from my side. It was wonderful that we got to speak on my birthday. I felt happy talking to you. Bhuwan took me out for dinner that evening. Vikki joined us, and so did my MIL. But since Vikki was around, it was fun. We went to an upmarket restaurant in Koregaon Park, and got back home at around 11.30. Bhuwan gifted me a silver pendant, which I liked. I shall show it to you, when we meet next.

First things first—even though I told you this on the phone, I must mention it here again: I am very happy to hear that you did well in your Class 12 exams, and that you are looking forward to joining college. Congratulations, my dear sister! Well done.

There has been a lot happening at my end, as you probably know from Ma and Papa. I did tell them the news from my side on the phone, but you how it is—I can never speak freely on the phone. So I am writing to you, in detail.

Let me get the not-so-good things out of the way first. As you probably know, I failed my final year exams. (I did not mention this to you when we spoke on the phone, as I didn't want to talk about it on my birthday.) I took it very badly for the first week or so. I couldn't talk about it without crying. But you know what they say, right? When God closes one door, he opens another. It may be a cliché, Vidya, but I can vouch that it is true. In my case, the 'other door' came in the form of Kanika.

Kanika is Shanta aunty's daughter, and she is my new friend. I don't remember if I mentioned her in my previous letters to you. If I haven't, it is because I barely knew her till last month. I met her fortuitously on the day I got my exam results, as my MIL 'forgot' to tell me that she would be going out, and I ended up spending most of the day with Kanika.

Kanika is a fun, feisty person. I wish I had some of her qualities.

She and Bhuwan grew up together. She works at an NGO called Sankalp. I am enclosing a brochure for you about the organisation with this letter. Once you read it, you will understand the kind of work they do, their mission, and most importantly, their impact. Sankalp now has branches in five cities in India, and they are rapidly expanding.

I am so proud to be a part of this organisation, Vidya. Yes, I am volunteering at Sankalp! How wonderful it sounds, to be writing that! To be a part of something greater than you is an astounding feeling. And it is an incredible feeling to 'belong' somewhere.

Right now, I am volunteering as a teacher's assistant. I asked if I could assist Kanika, and she was only too happy to take me on, as her previous assistant recently moved abroad after her husband got a job there.

Before I joined, I had to attend a training programme for three days, during which we were told all about the Sankalp mission, what was expected of us, how to teach, what to do, what not to do, etc. We also had role play and mock classroom scenarios. One of the things we were told is never to invite the students home, or to form a connection with the students outside the classroom. We were told that many of the students are emotionally needy. Some of them have never been shown love, care or tenderness. Hence, they tend to cling to you emotionally.

'Remember, we are teaching them to fly. So do not be their crutch. Be their wings,' is what our main training co-ordinator told us over and over. I thought they were powerful words, Vidya.

It made me think about how Ma and Papa have raised us. I don't think we were ever given 'wings'. I believe now that my wings were clipped even before I learnt to fly. And I think 'marriage' was the crutch they gave me. I am sure they do not think that way. They think that marriage is my 'safety net'. But after coming to Sankalp, the way I look at things has changed so much. This has been such an eye-opener, Vidya. It is the best thing that has happened to me.

We (Kanika and I) have around twenty students in our class, and they are in the fifteen to seventeen age group. They will be appearing for their Class 10 examinations this year. Some of them are older than the others, as they have lost an academic year due to various reasons. This is the senior-most class at Sankalp, and since it is the graduating class, the activities and everything we do is monitored closely by the head office. We have class goals, term plans, teaching plans, art activities, sports activities and everything else needed to develop the students' all-round skills. The activities are charted out well in advance and we have to submit them and get approval.

Let me tell you about some of the students in my class. (I feel so proud to say, 'MY class'!)

First, there is Kajol. Her mother is Shakubai, who works in our home as the house-help. Kajol is bright, extremely bright. She is diligent in her work. Her aim is to get a distinction in her Class 10 exams. Vidya—she reminds me of myself! She does all her homework, she is always well-behaved, she grasps things easily, and you have to show her anything only once or tell her something just once and you can be sure she will follow it. In short, she is a teacher's dream. Her father works as a cleaner in an office complex and he beats up Shakubai after he drinks. Kajol is very pragmatic and strong about it. She just shrugs it off—can you believe it? She told me the other day, 'Didi, there's nothing I can do about it. I am going to get a nice job in an office, and I will buy a flat. Then I will keep my Aayi there. She does not ever have to be with my father then.'

Then there is Sanju. He is mischievous and isn't very good at his work. But he covers it up by cracking jokes in the class. He is the class clown. He makes everyone, including me, laugh. But Kanika never laughs in front of him. She says that will encourage him further. Sanju's mother died while giving birth to him. His father married again, and the stepmother, I think, doesn't much care for Sanju. She has her own child to look after. Sanju's father is an auto-driver. He had come to class yesterday to ask how Sanju is doing. His idea of making Sanju study is to hit him with a leather belt—can you believe it? Sanju came to class a few days ago with angry, red welts on his back. That day he did not crack any jokes and sat very quietly. When I asked him why, he just looked away. It was Kajol who told me what had happened.

I think Kajol has a crush on Sanju, but I am not sure. I could possibly just be imagining things.

Then there are Aishwarya and Shalini. These two girls are

inseparable. They both love art, and are amazing at it. You should see their work, Vidya. It is marvellous! Some of their designs have been chosen by a company that makes coffee mugs and other knick-knacks. These two girls earn a bit of income from their artwork. They are proud that they are earning, and all of it goes into fixed deposits in their name. They say that Sankalp has given them things they could only dream of. Both want a career in art, and after their Class 10, we will be helping them to get into a graphic design course.

Then there is Zinia. Her two older sisters got married at fourteen and sixteen respectively, and she was supposed to follow suit. But her parents moved to Pune from the village. She joined Sankalp and started excelling in studies. Kanika and a few others from Sankalp met her parents and convinced them to give her a chance to study. Her parents said that if she gets good marks and a job after Class 10, they will reconsider getting her married. Zinia is determined to excel in the exams. She has seen the kind of life her older sisters have (both are mothers already), and she does not want that for herself.

Every morning now, I get ready and eagerly look forward to the day. Interacting with these children brings me so much joy.

These classes happen before their regular school starts, and after the children leave (to attend regular school), I help Kanika with the study plans and class material. Then we have a batch of younger kids that comes in at noon, as their school gets over at that time. For this class, I am not assisting Kanika, but I work with another teacher called Srisha. This class is also a lot of fun. Since the children here are all in the age group of eight to eleven, we have to come up with different kinds of art and craft activities to keep them engaged. The classes for them go on till three in the afternoon. After that, I assist Srisha with the study plans, materials and activities for her class. I have also been given the responsibility of going through coursework and assignments that have been submitted by students.

We teachers sit in the classroom itself, after the students leave, due to a dearth of space. The admin occupies the cabin which the sponsor company has given, and there is no space for the teachers there. But I don't mind at all. The basement is bright and open on all sides. So it is quite airy and comfortable.

I leave home at 7 a.m., and I get back home only after 5.30 p.m. My MIL isn't at home then, as she goes to the temple, or she meets her friends. That suits me perfectly. She isn't happy about my volunteering at Sankalp at all. She brought it up the other day, when Bhuwan came back early from work. It is rare that he comes home early.

'So, for how long do you think you will continue this free work?' she asked me.

'Ma, let her do something useful with her time,' Bhuwan jumped in to my rescue. I was happy that he defended me. My mother-in-law then asked for details about who I was working with, what I was teaching and what Sankalp was all about. I explained it all to her. Bhuwan too pitched in, telling her about the artwork that their company had commissioned from the students there, and how Kanika had told him about the way in which Sankalp has made an impact in society. My MIL couldn't say much after that.

These days, I have got used to her snide remarks and comments. Before I leave for work, I have to assist her with breakfast and all the cooking. But I do it now with a smile on my face. I have many more important things to focus on, like what we will be discussing in class that day!

Have you decided what subjects you want to take for your degree? What is happening at your end? How are Vandu, Vaish and Ani?

I have enclosed a letter for Suraj. Please do give it to him. It has been a while since I wrote to him too.

Please convey my regards to Rudra kaka and Paro didi as well.

With love and hugs,

Your sister,

Veda

August 1996
Pune

Dear, dear Suraj,
Apologies for the long silence. I hate it when a letter begins with an apology. But an apology is due for such a long silence.

Sometimes life just engulfs you like a giant wave and sweeps you away, submerging you in itself before you realise what is happening.

That is exactly what has happened to me these past few weeks. But I will come to that soon.

I want to tell you that I am very happy about your decision to work in your father's company. When do you start? Are you looking forward to it? What will be your role? Are you comfortable with living on your own, in your flat, without your parents around? Won't the memories be too painful? (I can't even imagine what I would have done in your place, Suraj. You are a brave soul.)

How have you fared in the final exams? Are you happy with your marks?

As for me—I got a huge shock when the results came out. I failed my final year exams. I never got the time to study because of my MIL, but I had expected to clear them because I had paid attention in class. Evidently, I thought wrong.

After that setback, I joined this organisation called Sankalp. I am enclosing a brochure which will give you all the details. I just finished writing a long letter to Vidya telling her about my students there. (Yes, I have joined there as a teacher's assistant.) Since I am too lazy to write it all out again, and since I also now have a paucity of time, what I will do is photocopy the relevant pages from what I have written to her and enclose them with this letter. Please forgive me for not writing out the details again. You will understand what my work is like, and what my life is like these days, after you read the photocopied pages. (Please read the photocopied pages first before you read the rest of the letter.)

~~~

So, now that you have read the photocopied pages, you know what my students are like, and what my routine at Sankalp is. One of the good things about their system is that they group children according to 'levels'. So, though they are in the same age group, one child might be at level 1, and another might be at level 4. This is because their backgrounds are very different. They face such hardships and not all have the same learning opportunities. So we give them assignments according to their level and I prepare four
~~~

sets of assignments on the same topic. I think it is a brilliant way to learn, don't you agree? This way, nobody feels inferior to anyone else. I don't know why our mainstream educational institutions cannot adopt this method.

I must also tell you about a fun activity with which we start our classes every day. Every quarter, each centre of Sankalp receives a 'Thinking Questions' diary. These are some questions that encourage children to think. These questions stimulate creative thinking, problem solving and observation. On some days, we have easy questions and on some, we have difficult questions. We have to customise them to suit the needs of the class. We can use these thinking questions at any time we consider appropriate—at the class assembly, the language session or at the arts and crafts session. Kanika has made it a custom to start the day with the thinking questions for her batch, and she hands out candies to three students whose responses she likes best. I have to record the responses which the children come up with, and we have to submit this at the teachers' meeting, which we have every three months. To give you an example of some of the questions:

- If you had a choice, would you live in a village or a city? Why?
- Why do people say that fair people are more beautiful? Who is the most beautiful person in the world according to you?
- How would you spend your day, if your day had only six hours?
- Do you think there is a person who is only good or only bad?
- Why do birds build their nests on trees?
- Do you think it is important to tell the truth even if it means hurting someone's feelings?
- Do you think that with different varieties of fish in the sea, there is ever a traffic jam?
- Do you think trees have feelings?
- If we didn't have any paper, what would we write on?
- If you were given a chance to do some social service, what would you do?

So, as you can see, the questions are designed to inspire a discussion, as well as make them think, make them environmentally conscious (that's a mammoth task, if you know their backgrounds—they are from the poorest sections of society), make them empathetic, and also to understand how their minds work. I find these questions really interesting, and often, after class, Kanika and I talk about the responses that the children gave.

Sometimes, their answers are hilarious, sometimes pragmatic and sometimes sad.

But all the time, we are learning something new. No two days are the same.

For the question, 'Why do birds build their nests on trees?' Sanju said, 'Didi, birds make nests in office buildings now. Builders are chopping down all the trees. They should make tree-planting compulsory. Just like speaking in English here is compulsory.'

Everyone laughed at the way in which he said it, but I think he made a very valid point.

These children are resourceful, intelligent and smart. I am glad to be making a difference in their lives.

How is your grandmother? When are you shifting to Mumbai? What are you reading these days?

By the way, I never joined that library I had mentioned earlier. Bhuwan never took me there. But now, strangely, I do not feel bad about it, nor do I want to join it, as I hardly have time to read. My reading has suffered a lot, but I do read to my students! I choose the books carefully from the collection that we have at Sankalp.

So that is the news from my end, my friend.

Write back soon.

Eagerly waiting to hear from you.

Your friend,

Veda

Chapter 20

September 1996
Sankalp, Pune

'Unfortunately four of our volunteers had to leave Sankalp this quarter unexpectedly, due to personal problems, and now we are short-staffed. It is a serious issue that has to be addressed immediately. The urgency becomes magnified as this year, our very first "pilot batch" will be giving the Class 10 examinations. We *need* to get good results. Now Kanika here, and Veda, have been handling a few other batches, in addition to their own Class 10 batch. This places an undue burden on them.' Aparna was speaking at a meeting of all the staff of Sankalp. Two people from the head office were also present.

She held the stapled paper report which Kanika and Veda had given her earlier, and her brows knitted in concentration as she turned the pages, trying to find the data which Kanika had highlighted for her.

'Now, as I can see from the reports which Kanika submitted earlier, at least 54 per cent of the students in the batch are still at level 2. Unless they are brought to level 4—and this will require a lot of coaching—we cannot hope that they will clear the exams,' Aparna continued.

All the faces around the table wore grave expressions. Everyone nodded in agreement, the magnitude of the problem slowly dawning on them.

'So, we desperately need good volunteers who are willing to commit to the cause. Now where we find them is the challenge. The training part is not a problem as we have resources and I will be supervising it personally,' she said.

There were about sixteen people who had gathered for the meeting, which was taking place in one of the conference rooms of the sponsor company. They were seated around a large, oval-shaped conference table, which stretched from one end of the room to the other. Aparna stood at the head, in front of a whiteboard, and she was using a projector to convey the salient points of what she was presenting. The two people from the head office were seated at the head of the table, opposite each other. Veda, along with Kanika, Ron and a few volunteers, were seated next to each other at the end farthest from the whiteboard.

This was the first time in her life that Veda was inside a conference room, and when she walked in, she had gazed at the interiors in awe. It was a well-appointed room, sound-proof, with wood panelling, mikes for each seat and plush push-back chairs. Their names were printed on boards placed on the table, and Veda felt proud as she took her place. In front of her was a writing pad and a pen to take notes, and Veda found herself furiously scribbling, making diligent notes on everything that Aparna and the speakers from the head office said.

'Any suggestions?' asked Aparna.

'I think I can help out with the teaching.'

It was Ron who had spoken and everybody turned to look at him.

'Are you saying that you want to volunteer to teach?' asked Aparna.

'Yes, I am. And why not? I would like to. If you think I can do it, that is, and you don't think of me as a demented idiot who cannot handle tenth grade academics.' A collective low chuckle of amusement echoed through the conference room.

Aparna smiled and said, 'Of course not. You are more than welcome, Ron, but don't you have to head back to the UK?'

'I have an open ticket for my return. The Carman Foundation will certainly understand if I explain why I need more time in India. I am impressed with what I have seen so far at Sankalp, and I would love to help,' he said.

'That's great then, welcome aboard. You have already attended the training sessions and you know what to expect as you have spent time in the classrooms. So, that is taken care of,' said Aparna.

'I have a suggestion,' said a voice, and everyone turned to look at Himanshu from admin, who had spoken.

'Yes, let's hear it,' said Aparna.

'Why don't we tie up with youth clubs in colleges with part-time courses? I am sure there are many students who would love to teach. We can make posters and do presentations there. Once we explain our mission, I am certain we will get people to volunteer,' said Himanshu.

'Hmm, I think that is a workable solution,' said Aparna, as she considered it. 'What do you all think? Let's have a show of hands,' she said. Almost everyone in the room raised their hand in agreement.

Aparna looked around and nodded, mentally assessing all the people who had gathered there. Her eyes zeroed in on Veda and Kanika seated at the far end.

'I think we need some young people to go to the colleges and present what we do. Then we will have a better connect with the youth. Veda, do you think you can handle this? Ron and Kanika can be a part of it too,' she said.

Veda felt important to be asked. More than that, she felt proud that Aparna had chosen *her*. Aparna had confidence in her and felt she would connect with the students.

'Yes, yes, I would love to,' she said.

'Good, that is settled then. You can map out the colleges and chalk out a plan after this meeting. Please show it to me once you are done,' said Aparna.

The rest of the meeting was about their targets for growth, the impact that Sankalp had made in other cities, and a recap of their mission statement.

Aparna thanked them all for being a part of the journey, and reminded them how what they were doing was powerful work that had a deep impact on the lives of people. It was an inspiring talk. Aparna was a good speaker and a good leader, Veda thought. At the end of the meeting, everyone left the conference room feeling happy and satisfied.

When Veda returned home that evening, she let herself in. Bhuwan had insisted on her having a key to the house after he heard how she had been locked out. Padma Devi had been reluctant at first.

'Oh, if it's a problem, Veda can wait at Kanika's home till you return, Ma,' Bhuwan had said to his mother, when Veda had started volunteering.

Padma Devi had then immediately got a duplicate key made. She did not want Veda to waste any time at Kanika's home. She had shrewdly foreseen and calculated that, the earlier Veda got back home, the better it was for her, as she could get her daughter-in-law to cook dinner. Veda was happy to have her own key, as it meant she did not have to depend on her mother-in-law or Bhuwan to let her in.

When Veda entered the house, she heard a noise from the bedroom. She went in to investigate and discovered that Bhuwan was already home. A suitcase lay open across their bed, and several clothes were laid out beside it. It looked like he was packing for a trip.

'Are you off somewhere? You never mentioned it,' said Veda.

'Yes, so sorry, but this is last minute. It came up suddenly. My boss wants me to go to a conference in his place. He was supposed to go to Delhi, but his toddler son had an asthma attack. He was in hospital the whole night, as they had to give him nebulisation. He doesn't want to leave his wife all alone. So he suggested I go,' said Bhuwan, as he chose which clothes to put in the suitcase.

'Oh, I hope he recovers soon. Please convey my wishes,' said Veda.

'Uh? Ah, okay, I will,' replied Bhuwan, carefully placing back in the cupboard the shirts that he wouldn't be taking with him.

Veda asked him if he wanted some tea, and when he said he did, she went to the kitchen to make it for him. He followed her and waited for his tea in the drawing room. As Veda brewed the tea, she thought about all those movies she had seen where the man approaches the woman from behind her while she is cooking and surprises her with a hug. Bhuwan had never displayed any such behaviour in all the time that they had been married. He was polite, proper and kind towards her. She hardly shared anything with him, and he, too, didn't deem it necessary to share anything other than what was essential. Yet, when she had expressed a desire to work at Sankalp, he had conspired with Kanika and had gone out of his way to ensure that it happened. For that, Veda was grateful. She wished she could understand Bhuwan, and she wished he would make a small attempt at getting to know her. She consoled herself, saying that at least he was pleasant and kind. That was a lot more than what many women got. Her cousins who had got married before she had, had told her how controlling their husbands were, and how they did not bother about the needs of their wives.

'So, did you tell your mother that you are leaving?' asked Veda, as she served him the tea and sat beside him.

'Yes, I did. We talked for a while and then she left to go to the temple,' said Bhuwan.

'I think she is a little annoyed about my volunteering at Sankalp. But Bhuwan, it gives me so much joy. Do you know, I have been chosen to go to various colleges and explain our mission so we can get volunteers!' said Veda, her eyes shining.

'I am happy for you,' he said. His reply was polite and measured. Veda could never make out if he was genuinely happy or whether he was just saying the right things.

'I think I might get home a bit late the next few days,' she said. 'I hope your mother doesn't make a fuss about it.

'Don't be too afraid of my mother. Even if she says something to you, don't take it to heart,' said Bhuwan. 'I will speak to Ma and make her understand that you will be late. Don't worry too much about it,' he said, and left soon after for the airport.

Veda wasn't worried. She was in a tizzy thinking about the talks she would have to give, and how she would have to motivate the students to volunteer. She had never given a speech before.

When they were in school, it was Vidya who was adept at debates and public speaking. She always took part in competitions and had won many prizes too. Veda had shied away from them, but it was she who had written the speeches for Vidya. So Veda knew what to say. Though the thought of addressing a large gathering of students made her nervous, she wasn't too anxious, as she knew that Ron and Kanika would be with her to cover up in case she erred. Over the next few days, she began writing the speeches she would give, and each morning, she practised in front of the bathroom mirror.

When Bhuwan returned from his trip, he asked Veda whether his mother had made a fuss about her coming back home later than usual. He told her that he had spoken to her over the phone and had informed her about it.

'Oh, Bhuwan, that starts only next week. She did ask me details about it. She didn't seem too pleased, but she didn't specifically object,' said Veda. Bhuwan said that he was glad about that and told her to carry on with her Sankalp-related activities. Veda was happy with his reassurance.

The college visits started the following week and kept Veda busier than usual. She loved every minute of it. Kanika had called and made appointments at many of the colleges in Pune. Aparna liked the detailed plan that Veda, Kanika and Ron had drawn up, but categorically stated that they could go only after the classes at Sankalp were done.

Ron had started joining them in the classrooms. The students were fascinated with his accent and the way he taught. They loved him! They had never had a white person teaching them, and they sat quietly, trying to understand his accent. He was naturally good with children. He read them stories, and worked with all the level 1 and 2 students in small groups, so that they would get individual attention. They had a lot to catch up with, and it was English that was their weak subject. Ron was more than happy to help them learn.

Ron was also discovering many new things about Indian customs and traditions. They were completely alien to him.

The college visits went smoothly. Most colleges were receptive to the idea of their students volunteering at Sankalp. Since Kanika had lived in Pune all her life, she knew all the good places to eat near the colleges. After one such college visit, she took them to a popular joint on Fergusson College Road.

'What is *poori bhaji*?' asked Ron.

Veda smiled at how a very common Indian dish was exotic for Ron.

'What do you normally eat for lunch in the UK?' Veda asked.

She had gotten over her shyness around Ron, and she now conversed easily with him.

'Oh, usually a sandwich. I almost always have either a tuna sandwich or a chicken sandwich. Have you ever had those?' he asked.

'I am a vegetarian,' said Veda.

'Did you turn vegetarian for health reasons?' asked Ron.

'No, I have always been vegetarian. Nobody eats meat in my family,' said Veda.

'Not even fish?' he asked.

'No, Ron. In India, when people are vegetarian, they usually don't even eat eggs,' explained Kanika.

For Ron, it was new information, and he found it fascinating.

When the *poori bhaji* arrived, Kanika and Veda had to show him how to eat with his hands.

'You eat with your fingers and you don't get the food on your palms. See, like this,' said Veda, as she held her *poori* down with the three fingers of her right hand and tore off a piece with the thumb and forefinger.

Ron struggled to do it. After a few attempts, he gave up, rolled up the *poori*, and ate it like a roll. 'Maybe before I leave India, I will master this,' he said.

Kanika and Veda smiled at how hard it was for him.

'By the way, we have four volunteers already. Veda, you did a good job speaking,' Kanika said.

'Whatever I said came from the heart. I totally love working at Sankalp and I guess it shows when I speak. I had rehearsed what I wanted to say, and that helped. Also, you both supported me so well,' said Veda.

'Whatever it is, it is working. We might have more volunteer applications. Aparna will have to interview them and weed out the less suitable candidates,' Kanika said.

As they ate, they talked about the antics of the students that day and they laughed. Now that all three were working together, teaching the same sets of students, they had a lot of things to share. They knew that there was never a dull moment with Sanju around. That morning, he had sprinkled chalk powder over the mats, and all the children had got it on their backsides when they sat down. Sanju had laughed as they furiously tried to brush it off when they discovered it.

Veda, Ron and Kanika discussed how they could raise the levels of all the children to 4, so that they would do well in the upcoming exams.

'The only way we can do that is if we give them extra classes outside Sankalp hours. Though I am working with them in small groups, the progress is slow. The only thing that will help is more time, and more intensive coaching,' said Ron.

'But we will have to take permission from the sponsor company,' said Kanika.

'I'll speak to Aparna about it and get it done,' Ron replied.

The three of them knew that it would be a mammoth task. But they were so invested in the cause, that they were willing to put in the extra hours to make it happen.

Chapter 21

October 1996

Joshimath

My dearest Veda didi,

You have no idea how elated I felt after I read your letter. That's the way to go! Honestly, didi, your last few letters had me worried. It seemed to me that you had given up on life.

But now, I can make out that my old Veda didi has returned. I can see the enthusiasm you have from your letter and the way you described it all, didi. I badly want to come to Pune and see Sankalp for myself.

I want to meet Kajol, Sanju, Aishwarya, Zinia and all the others you talked about. It seems to be such a wonderful organisation to be a part of. I also want to meet Kanika. Please convey my greetings to her.

College has started off well. It is very different from school—but you already know that. I remember how you used to describe each day, when you first started college and I was still in school. It is exactly like that. Nothing much has changed from when you were here. Some of my classmates have gone to different cities to study, but many are from my class itself. So it feels like an extension of school, but where the teachers are not that strict. The best part about college is, no more uniforms. I love wearing different outfits each day. I mix and match the salwars. I have also secretly managed to buy jeans! Ma had given me money for college shopping. I went with Deepali, and we bought some smart clothes. I love the fit of the jeans, and we managed to bring the prices down by bargaining. I plan to change into jeans at college and then change back into a salwar kameez before I go home. That way, Papa will not know, and it is just easier. I can't understand why he has silly rules like girls should not wear jeans. I agree it is not very common—but why can't I be different from others if I wish to? One or two girls in my class do wear jeans.

Didi—I have already bunked college and gone for a movie in the neighbouring town. Don't be shocked! I know you may not approve as you were always a rule follower. But I think rules are meant to be broken, or at least bent a little. (Ha, ha—I can see you frowning, Veda didi. Don't worry, I do know my boundaries.)

I have become friendly with Kunal Saini. (You remember him from my class, right?) Didi—he drives his own Ambassador car to college. He invited me and Dipu for a ride, along with his friends, Bharat and Naveen. All five of us bunked college and went for a nice movie, and I got back home at the usual time. He drove safely didi, don't worry. We had a lot of fun. It was an English movie, but it was dubbed in Hindi, and we laughed at the dialogues! The translated version was ridiculous. I think that in college, it is important to have this kind of fun. This is the time we can enjoy.

Another important development—Suraj has moved to Mumbai. But fortunately, I managed to hand over the letter you sent before he left. So, from now on, didi, you will have to write to him directly, instead of sending letters through me. But do you know what I did? (You will thank me for this!) I handed him about fifty envelopes with your address neatly written on them. I sat down and wrote it all late into the night. I also put my name as the sender on the back of the envelope. I figured that, this way, he can still send you letters when he goes to Mumbai, and nobody will suspect anything, as all he has to do is use the envelopes I have given him. If you start getting letters from a new handwriting, you might be caught. Aren't you happy with what I did?

How is Bhuwan jiju reacting to your new job? Is he okay with it?

I am continuing this letter after six days, as I couldn't finish it the day I started it. That day, when I was writing the letter, Ma called out to me and I had to stop writing. She said that they have now started looking for a groom for me! I was so angry. I am only eighteen. They invited those same aunties home—the ones who brought the proposal for you. I had told Ma and Papa clearly that I don't want to be a part of it. Yet, they did not listen to me. So do you know what I did? When they told me to serve the aunties tea, I told them loudly that I am busy as I am going to talk to Kunal and that he was waiting for me around the corner. I marched out in front of them.

Of course, there was nobody waiting. I walked to the temple and sat there till such time as I knew that the aunties would have left. Then I went back home.

Didi—you should have seen how angry Papa was. I thought he would EXPLODE. He was stark raving mad. He slapped me as soon as I got home, didi. God—it hurt. The red mark of his palm on my cheek remained till the next day, and I couldn't go to college with that face. He would have continued to hit me, but Rudra kaka stopped him, saying that you cannot raise your hands on girls once they come of age. He stopped then.

But I don't care that he hit me. My little act of rebellion had the desired effect. All the aunties are now gossiping about how shameless I am, and that Kunal is my boyfriend.

Kunal heard about it that very day. You know how gossip travels in Joshimath. He got a shouting from his parents. And guess what—he is not talking to me now. He is angry with me for telling lies. He asked me how I could do that. I apologised to him, but he still hasn't forgiven me. He said, 'We only went out as a group, and that too because I thought we were all friends. If this is how you treat a friend, I have no words for you.' I said, 'So be it.'

I did not think that he would make a big issue of it, or that it was a big deal to him. I don't even know why I used his name. I just said it, as I had to use a boy's name to get them off my back. How could I know that he would react so badly? I did apologise to him and say that I did not mean to land him in trouble. But he is still mad at me.

But it is okay. True friends are those who stick around for you, in good times or bad, and not just when it is convenient for them. If he is a true friend, then he will come back. Else, it is best to move on. We don't need such people in our lives.

I told Ma not to look for a groom for me. She said that they did not have any face to show to the community now, and that news of my 'deeds' had travelled far and wide. Apparently, word has gone around that Rajinder's daughters are 'firebrands'. I laughed when I heard that term, didi.

If being termed a 'firebrand' means that you can do what you like, and you do not have to get married, then I am happy being a firebrand!

My studies are boring. It is so dull. I dislike my subjects this year—introduction to accounting 1, introduction to accounting 2, general studies, and everything else that we have in BCom first year. I think I have made a mistake in my choice of subject. But the problem is, I dislike all the subjects in BA too. I don't like sociology, literature or economics. Why can't they have some fun, interesting subjects? Next year, I have mercantile law and banking—those seem like good subjects.

Vandu, Vaish and Ani—all three send their love. You will be happy to know that Ani was selected for a debate and I have been coaching him. Vaish and Vandu have both got into the school basketball team. I am happy that the rascals are playing some sports. I read to them every night, and I am still reading all the books that you left behind here, and liking them.

Write back soon, didi.

With all my love,

Your rule bender sis,

Vidya

October 1996
Mumbai

Dear, dear Veda,

As you have guessed from the first line, I have moved here now. I am sorry I did not reply earlier. I had to get rid of a lot of stuff from this flat. It was painful for me to give away all of Mamma's sarees and my father's clothes. My uncle and his family came over and helped me do it. My uncle kept some of my father's clothes, like his jackets and suits. My aunt kept some of my mother's sarees. The rest went to a trust that distributes clothes to the needy. I kept one of my father's shirts and his glasses.

I can't tell you how painful it was. It felt like someone was skinning me alive. The pain was that intense, that physical. I never expected it to strike that way. I thought I had dealt with it by the time I went to live with my grandmother. But after coming back here, the wounds have opened up yet again. It is a searing pain. An acceptance of a finality that they will never come back. I cannot lie and say that I am fine. I try to cope. The sorrow is deep, engulfing, and there are days when I wonder why I came back to this flat.

My office is quite close to my home. That was one good thing that my father did—he bought this flat in Bandra itself, and the office is just a short drive away. I drive my dad's car. I think about how they would have felt if they could see me now—wearing formal clothes and going to work.

The people at work are very nice to me. My father knew so many people, and every day I get invited for dinner, or someone brings a home-cooked meal for me. I don't know how long it will continue. Obviously, they cannot keep it up forever. I do not want to accept these invitations as I do not want to talk about my father. But they think they are helping me, and they have seen me growing up. So it would be rude to refuse. I have to suppress everything I feel, and pretend things are fine, and listen to them recount memories of my father. It is so hard, Veda, so terribly hard. It tears me up from the inside.

Work, on the other hand, is interesting. I am working in the sales department, and I am a junior sales officer. The work environment is excellent and this company has emerged as the fourth-best company to work for, in a survey conducted recently by a reputed business magazine. The work culture is very participative. They take a lot of care to ensure that young officers feel proud and take ownership. And it works! I enjoy my job. There are programmes such as 'High Potential Future Leader' (HPFL), and if you get selected for that, which is essentially the fast track, the growth in your career is accelerated! Then there are things such as Youth Day celebrations, Friday team outings, etc. The training they provided has been excellent. I have some mentors here, and that helps too.

The building itself is large, with floor-to-ceiling windows, and is nicely done up. Computers have been introduced (we have the 486-Based systems, and for those who want to learn, there are free training courses). I find it very interesting, and I now work on my own computer. Many of the older officers and managers can't seem to get the hang of it, but it is one thing which I have quickly picked up.

I read your last letter at least thrice. I LOVED the photocopied pages you shared from your letter to Vidya, where you have described your students. I also read the brochure you enclosed. I am extremely happy that you are so enthused about your new job. The children sound delightful. I think I would like to meet them and interact with them. You are doing some excellent work, Veda. I liked the thinking questions—and I answered a few myself, in my head! I would love to have a conversation with you about them, and I want to know what your answers are.

I saw in a newspaper the other day that work has started on a six-lane expressway between Mumbai and Pune. The entire project costs Rs 16.3 billion!

Veda, when I read that, a thought occurred to me and it has been in my head for a while now. Have you realised that even without the expressway, we are only a few hours away from each other? I can easily come to Pune on a weekend and we can meet. I would like that. And it is perfectly okay if you say no, so please don't hesitate.

If you think our meeting will cause a problem at home, then I don't mind at all if you tell me we cannot meet.

Do let me know.

Your forever friend,

Suraj

Chapter 22

October 1996
Kailash Mandir Colony, Pune

Veda read Vidya's letter over and over, and she chuckled in delight over what her sister had done. How brave she was! Veda wished she had some of Vidya's courage. She would not have found herself in this position then—stuck with someone she had to share the rest of her life with, but with whom she had nothing much in common. They only shared a room and a home. She glanced at the clock. It was already 11.30 p.m., and she had an early start the next day. But she could not resist writing a quick reply to her sister.

Bhuwan was travelling on yet another work trip. Since he wasn't at home, she sprawled across the bed on her tummy. She felt wonderfully free, with the entire bedroom to herself. It was funny how such little things filled her with a sense of exhilaration, she thought. She did not miss him. Instead, it was a feeling of relief that had come over her. She had not realised how badly she needed this space in her marriage. She wondered what he was doing in Delhi at that very moment. Was he already asleep? Was he enjoying being away from her too? Did he feel the same way that she felt? Veda wasn't sure. Whatever it was, she was glad for this little break from him, even though he was far from being a tiresome or irksome husband; if anything, he was considerate towards her. Yet, this felt nice.

Veda propped herself up on her elbows, and lying on the bed, she wrote Vidya a letter.

October 1996
Pune

My dearest, darling, firebrand!

A hundred kisses to you. And a big hug. Well done! If I was in Joshimath right now, I would stand up and applaud you for what you did. But instead, here I am—sprawled across my bed (Bhuwan is travelling on work) and writing to you. Forgive my handwriting—it is untidy as I am not sitting at the desk, but instead lying down and scribbling away. It feels wonderful to have the entire bedroom to myself.

I am writing this quickly, because I have an early start tomorrow. I shall post this on the way to Sankalp. I was thinking that it's such a good thing you gave those envelopes with the address written in your handwriting to Suraj. My mother-in-law receives the letters as the postman delivers them when I am at Sankalp. I suspect that she cannot read English very well, but can recognise your handwriting by now, and so she doesn't bother much about it. The letter is there, waiting for me on the console table at the entrance, when I get home. I am always excited to get a letter and earlier, whenever a letter arrived from you, I knew I would usually get one from Suraj too. But now I have to open the envelope and see if it is from you or Suraj. That adds to the excitement.

You are right in what you say about true friends. Don't worry too much about Kunal. If he is a true friend, he will understand you and forgive you. I also don't think that boys get into as much trouble as we girls do. So I don't see why he should be that upset. The consequences are harsher for you than for him.

Vidya—I got a letter from Suraj. He is in so much pain about his parents' death. He wrote to me about being in the flat where he had lived with his parents, how painful the memories are and how he is struggling to cope. His work is going well, though. He wants to meet me, Vidya! He says that if I don't want to meet for some reason, he will understand. I am tempted. So very tempted. But I also feel like I am betraying Bhuwan. Bhuwan has been so kind to me. Sneaking off and meeting Suraj without telling him just doesn't seem right.

The news at Sankalp: we now have five more volunteers—thanks to the speeches I made at the colleges I visited. Do you know, I was a little nervous before we went to the colleges. But then, I just imitated you! I remembered how you used to practise your debates for hours and hours, and I remembered your mannerisms and expressions and the way you spoke. All I had to do was mimic them. It worked! Ron and Kanika both said I spoke well.

The trained volunteers are assisting the junior batches. Kanika, Ron and I are in charge of the most important batch in the centre, which is the Class 10 batch.

Aparna reviews our progress on a weekly basis. She goes through the work of each student personally. She is very keen that we get a 'cent per cent result' this year. Till now, not a single Sankalp centre anywhere in the country has had all their students clear the Class 10 exam. You can imagine why, as I have told you the very difficult backgrounds these children have. So, if we manage to accomplish this, it will mean a lot of recognition for us. Aparna seems to be certain that we will be able to make it. I too think we stand a good chance. So do Kanika and Ron. Most of the children in our batch are very smart and eager to learn. A few are keen to learn but are a bit slow. They are the ones we have to pay extra attention to.

Ron is also keen on achieving this goal. He says, if it happens, he can appeal to the Carman Foundation for a larger grant. Aparna is hoping that our Sankalp centre will be chosen as the model for others.

Ron is planning to stay back for eight to ten months in India, till these children finish their exams. He has got his visa extended. It came through easily because he intends to teach. He can stay for two years now, if he so desires.

My mother-in-law's snide remarks about my work continue. But you know what, Vidya, it doesn't bother me so much anymore. I am happy that I am able to do some good work at Sankalp.

I make dinner after I get back from work, and I help her make breakfast AND lunch before I leave. So it is not like I am neglecting any of the 'home duties' that she has assigned me. Yet, she is disgruntled!

But what has changed is my reaction to her. Earlier, I would be tense, worried and scared of her. Now I just humour her with a smile on my face. I just switch off from whatever she is saying, because I am usually thinking deeply about what happened in class, or what has to be done the next day. I am lost in my thoughts. Sankalp is like this alternate world that I escape to. My MIL just doesn't get it! I guess she must be wondering what has come over me. She tries her best to bully me, but now I have learnt to calmly side-step her. Also, I am out of the house most of the time, and I have to tolerate her behaviour only for a few hours; I guess that helps too.

I just looked at the time, and it is past midnight! I had intended to write only a short letter, but I had so much to say.

Write back soon, my firebrand.

I am so proud that you stood up for what you want.

Waiting to hear from you.

All my love,

Your sis,

Veda

Even though a couple of weeks had passed since Veda had received Suraj's letter, she had not replied to him yet. Each time Veda thought about his letter, her heart fluttered with excitement, and at the same time, plunged her into despair. She had never experienced anything like it before.

He was in Mumbai and he wanted to meet her! It was the best news she had heard since she got married, but it was also the worst. She was ecstatic about him being this close to her, in terms of distance. But she also foresaw the problems in what he was asking of her.

As soon as she had received his letter, her first instinct had been to ask him to come over, as at that time, Bhuwan had been out of town. She had the perfect excuse as well. She could have told her mother-in-law that she had to visit some colleges, and met Suraj instead.

But it just wasn't right. She told herself that she couldn't do this to Bhuwan. Writing letters was one thing. They didn't see each other, and they were miles apart. But meeting him secretly was taking it to the next level. Veda wasn't sure if she was ready for that.

Suraj had very tactfully told her that, if she didn't want to meet, he would understand. Oh, how she longed to see him! But each time she had started a letter to him, trying to explain what she felt, the words escaped her, and she crumpled up the paper. After several such attempts, she had given up trying to explain. Bhuwan had started travelling a lot these days and he was once again out of town. She decided that, when he returned from his trip, she would tell him about Suraj. If Suraj wanted to meet her, he could come home, and he would have to meet her mother-in-law as well as Bhuwan. Veda wasn't sure how her mother-in-law or her husband would react to a male friend of hers suddenly turning up. She instinctively knew that her mother-in-law would not be okay with it. That was only to be expected. But she wasn't sure about Bhuwan.

Bhuwan came back from his trip a couple of days later. Each time Veda thought about bringing up the topic of inviting Suraj home, she stopped herself. Why she did that, she herself did not know.

'How did it go?' Veda found herself asking Bhuwan instead.

'Eh? What?' Bhuwan looked puzzled.

'Your trip, Bhuwan. How did it go?' Veda asked.

'Oh, it went well. It was the usual work,' said Bhuwan.

'What exactly do you have to do on these work trips?' Veda asked.

'The usual, Veda. Client meetings, presentations—all of that,' said Bhuwan.

That night, as they lay in bed, Veda wondered why she did not want to bring up Suraj's letter. Why was she hiding it from Bhuwan? The answer troubled her. She had definitely started having feelings for Suraj. She longed to see him. She waited to hear from him. She loved reading his letters and she loved writing to him. She had so much to tell him. Though she had told Bhuwan about Sankalp, he hadn't asked too many questions, nor had he bothered to find out how much it meant to Veda. Veda got a distinct feeling that for Bhuwan, it was just something that his wife did to keep herself occupied.

But Suraj was keen to see the centre, meet the children and know more about what she did. He had answered the thinking questions and wanted to discuss them with her.

Suraj was *interested* in all she had to say. With Bhuwan, it seemed to come from a sense of duty, and then too, it was minimal. She knew she would have to reply to Suraj soon. She decided to do it over the weekend.

The next morning, when Veda reached Sankalp, one of the student volunteers from the junior classes told her that Aparna wanted to see her in her office. Veda frowned. This was not the norm at all. The students had just started arriving and the volunteer said that she would take charge of the class till Veda got back.

Veda took the elevator and went into Aparna's office. She found Ron and Kanika already there.

'Come in Veda, have a seat. We just have a few things to discuss,' said Aparna. Her tone seemed brusque and unfriendly. Both Kanika and Ron looked tense.

'See these assignments?' said Aparna, as she thrust a stack of papers in Veda's direction.

Veda took them from her as she sat down. They were the assignments that she had graded two days ago.

'Yes, I know these. I graded them,' said Veda.

'The standards are too low, Veda. Look at the errors that the children are making. Other than Kajol, there is not a single student in the class who can write without making grammatical mistakes. If this is how they write in the boards, not a single child other than Kajol will clear the exams. This is not what we expect,' said Aparna.

'But Aparna, these children have come a long way from when they—' Kanika began, but Aparna did not let her finish.

'Look at the prepositions they use, Kanika. Not a single thing is correct. They do not know the difference between "under" and "over", "on" and "in", and they make mistakes in so many basic things. And these are Class 10 students. Sure, they might have come a long way, but what we are concerned about is how much *more* there is to be done. And what is this? Did you see this?' she said, as she pulled out a paper from the stack.

Veda glanced at it and knew immediately that it was Sanju's. In a few pages of his assignments, instead of writing the answer, he had drawn elaborate drawings of planes and buildings. He had also written captions describing each illustration.

Veda had written a comment that read, 'Nice drawings. But for an English exam, we need to write, not draw.'

'Look Veda, I know you mean well, but this kind of remark will only encourage a kid like Sanju to do whatever he likes. We have to make him follow the rules. We don't need rule breakers here; we need conventional answers. So don't write such remarks from now on,' said Aparna.

Veda nodded.

'The next class test is two weeks from now. I hope to see better results than these,' said Aparna.

Ron and Kanika nodded. So did Veda.

'I also wanted to inform you about one other thing, Veda. Kanika has recommended that you be made a teacher. That means you are eligible for a salary. Congratulations,' said Aparna.

Veda was overjoyed to hear this. They would be paying her! She had a real job now.

'Oh! Thank you so much!' smiled Veda.

But Aparna was very business-like about it. She did not return her smile.

She continued to talk about raising the levels of the children's written English. She also said they could do better in maths, and added that all three of them would have to work harder.

When they were in the elevator on their way down, Veda said, 'Thank you so much, Kanika! You never told me about this recommendation you made.'

'You deserve it, Veda. You have worked so hard. I had sent the recommendation last month itself. But it got approved only now. Well done!' she said, as she patted Veda's shoulder.

'Congratulations,' said Ron, and Veda thanked him.

Kanika remarked that she was not too pleased about Aparna not recognising the progress they had made with the kids. 'I thought we were doing a good job. These children couldn't even speak a word of English when they joined. Look at the progress they have made.'

'I think Aparna may have a point though, Kanika. They aren't going to pass the exams if they write like this. Let's give them some additional coaching. Let's start today itself, or tomorrow, at the very latest,' said Ron.

'Yes, Kanika. I think we need to start the extra classes soon,' said Veda.

'Yes, just before you came, Aparna mentioned that she had managed to get permission from the sponsor company to use the premises in the evenings as well. So she has done her bit from her end; now we will have to work extra hard to do ours,' Kanika agreed.

The elevator reached the ground floor, and the three of them started walking down the stairs to get to the basement. They were a few minutes late for their daily classes.

'I have been looking at apartments to rent around here and I found one I liked. I plan to move in over the weekend. It is just a two-minute walk from here. It is in the new building behind this,' Ron declared, as he descended the stairs. Veda was just behind him, followed by Kanika.

'Oh, that's good! You can get here faster then!' said Veda.

'Yes, that's nice Ron,' Kanika said.

When they walked into the Sankalp classroom, they stopped short, staring in disbelief at the sight that greeted them.

Chapter 23

October 1996
Sankalp, Pune

'Blimey! What's happening!' exclaimed Ron.

'What the hell,' said Kanika.

Veda just gasped in shock.

Not a single student was on the mat for circle time, discussing the thinking questions, as they were meant to be doing. Instead, they were chasing each other around the pillars, screaming, laughing, shouting—and it was deafening. It was as though the entire classroom had turned into a playground.

The teacher's table lay overturned and the attendance register lay wide open with the pages fluttering. The pen holder that once stood proudly on the table lay like a fallen soldier in a battleground, with the pens and pencils lying scattered in all directions. A student stood on the teacher's chair, trying to reach the rope that stretched across from one pillar to another. The drawings made by the students were usually pinned to this rope, like colourful flags. Not a single drawing was on it. All of them had been pulled down and were fluttering about in the classroom. A few students had got hold of the aerosol spray that they used to make fake foam for special occasions such as parties, and were spraying it everywhere, tossing the can to each other and taking turns, screaming as they did so. The chessboard lay open. Some children were grabbing fistfuls of the chess pieces and throwing them at each other as missiles. Another set of students had grabbed the coins of the carom board, and the board itself had turned into a musical instrument, with one child holding it upright, and another using a ruler to drum on it.

The small bottles of poster paint lay overturned, the paints of various colours spilling out and staining the mats. Craft material that was stored in cardboard boxes lay strewn across the classroom. There were ice cream sticks, colourful confetti, glitter paints, glue, small shiny stars, crayons—all of it scattered everywhere, contributing to the wild spectacle that was unfolding before them.

Veda desperately looked around for the student volunteer to whom she had entrusted the class. At last, she spotted her amidst the chaos. She lay flat on the ground and there were two kids pinning her down. One was pulling her plait and the other was holding her legs down.

Kajol was trying to yell at everyone, asking them to behave. Sanju was laughing in delight as he tried to jump up and catch the bubbles that a kid was blowing with a bubble-maker.

Kanika went to the bell that was suspended from the roof and rang it loudly. Then she yelled, 'STOP IT IMMEDIATELY, ALL OF YOU. WHAT NONSENSE IS THIS?'

Her voice echoed and boomed in the open space. She succeeded in getting their attention. The children froze, pausing in mid-action, like a tableau.

'ENOUGH NOW. IS THIS HOW YOU BEHAVE? GO … SIT … DOWN!' she yelled, her face red with anger.

That was effective, and they obeyed.

The student volunteer leapt to her feet.

'I … I am so sorry. They just wouldn't listen to me,' she muttered, looking pale and visibly shaken.

In the weeks that Veda had been here, she had never seen the students behave this way, this out of control.

'It's okay. You can leave. We will take it from here,' said Kanika, and the student volunteer left hurriedly.

Kajol and Zinia straightened the mats. There was a deathly silence in the room, as the students took their places.

Kanika said absolutely nothing. She stood still, glaring at the students one by one. Veda and Ron stood on either side of her.

The children looked down guiltily; they wouldn't even glance up.

Still Kanika said nothing. She wanted the message to sink in loud and clear that this certainly was not appropriate behaviour. She wanted the children to apologise by themselves, without her prompting them to do so. They were old enough to know better than to behave this way.

The children kept quiet, and the silence lasted for more

than three minutes. The children were growing more and more uncomfortable by the second, and yet Kanika did not budge.

In the end, it was Zinia who spoke up. 'Didi—we are very sorry,' she said.

Kanika raised a hand, silencing her.

'What happened? Who started this nonsense?' she asked.

Everyone kept quiet. But a few children turned to look at Sanju.

'*Kya—mujhe kyon dekh rehe ho? Yahan picture hai kya?*' he asked, staring back defiantly at them.

'Sanju, could you please stand up and translate what you just said into English?' said Kanika.

Sanju stood up but kept his head down.

'Look at me, Sanju. What did you say? Say it in English, please,' Kanika repeated.

'Didi, he started it,' said Sanju, pointing to Sharan.

'I didn't ask you who started it; I asked you to say it in English,' Kanika insisted.

'Errr ... Why ... are you seeing ... at my face? Is ... there a picture here?' Sanju murmured in a low voice, hesitatingly.

'No. That's wrong. *Why are you all looking at me? Is there a movie going on?*' That's how you say it,' said Kanika softly, in better control of her anger now.

'Didi, Sharan said bad words about my father. I told him to keep quiet. But he repeated, didi. Then I got angry. I threw a carom coin at him. Sorry, didi,' he said.

'Who took out the party foam? And who took out the chess pieces?' Kanika asked.

Slowly, the story came out. Sanju had thrown a carom coin at Sharan but missed. It had hit one of the other kids. Two of them had grabbed chess pieces and had thrown them back at Sanju. Before anyone realised it, a fight had broken out. Then one of the children, in a bid to separate them, had sprayed foam at them. And soon, the whole class had got into a mad melee.

'The volunteer didi was helpless as nobody listened to her; they did not even listen to me,' Kajol added.

'You know, now we don't have colours to do our crafts and painting. You spilled everything,' said Kanika.

'Sorry, didi,' said the class in unison.

Kanika said that there was no excuse for bad behaviour.

'You know that Ron bhaiya here is from England. Do you want him to go back and tell the people there that this is how Sankalp kids behave? Like wild beasts?' she asked.

'No, didi,' they all said.

'Do you want him to think well of us and our country?' she asked.

'Yes, didi,' they replied.

'Then let's show him how fast we can get this classroom back in shape,' Kanika challenged them.

She said she would set the timer for eight minutes, and everybody had to get involved and restore the classroom to what it had been.

'Ready? Go,' said Kanika, as she took out the timer and pressed it. The children, eager to make amends, co-operated. They were genuinely ashamed of their behaviour. They knew Kanika was a no-nonsense person. She was firm, and yet compassionate, and the children loved that about her. They had also grown fond of Ron and Veda.

Before the timer rang, the children had restored order to the classroom. They knew where each item belonged. The only thing they couldn't fix, were the stains on the mats made by the poster paints.

'Good. See, when you co-operate and behave well, how much better it is?' asked Kanika.

She spoke to them about wastage and told them about how destructive behaviour led to no good. She said that she would pay for the cleaning of the mats.

'No didi—I will pay for it. I am sorry, it is my mistake,' said Sanju.

'How will you pay Sanju, you don't have a job,' Kanika reminded him.

'No, didi. I have a job now. I clean the vessels in a hotel, didi. I have money. I will pay,' said Sanju.

Kanika did not know that Sanju had taken up a job.

'When did you take up a job, Sanju? And why?' she asked.

'Didi—Sanju is now working for a *goonda*,' said Kajol.

'*Goonda*? What do you mean?' asked Kanika.

Kajol told Kanika that Sanju's stepmother had taunted him and refused to give him chicken pieces in the curry that she had cooked, saying that it was a 'waste of money' to feed him. Insulted, Sanju had not eaten the meal and had walked out. That very evening, he had gone to an eatery in the locality and taken up a job. The eatery was owned by a man who was known to be on the wrong side of the law.

'Didi, he pays me my salary on time. I work hard and I earn well,' said Sanju, jumping to the defence of his employer.

Veda felt bad for Sanju when she heard that. These children had to bear such a lot of hardship at a tender age, and yet they shrugged it off and just got on with life, without making a big deal of it. How stoic they were, she thought.

The rest of the class went off smoothly. The children, chastised by Kanika, behaved well. Ron and Veda worked with them in small groups, as they usually did. Veda could see why Aparna was worried. She was right about her concerns. The performance of many of the students was below par, and if things went on like this, there was no way this class was getting a cent per cent result.

Later, after the class was over and the children left, Kanika asked Veda and Ron if they wanted to grab a cup of coffee.

'Yes, after that session, I could definitely do with one,' Ron replied.

They went to a cafeteria that was basic, with practical, minimalistic decor. Ron got himself a *samosa* and bit into it.

'Mmmm, this is so delicious,' he said, as they all settled down. Kanika had got a coffee for herself and Veda.

'Listen, folks. We need an action-plan. Let's draw up a schedule,' said Kanika, as she took out a notebook and a pen from her bag.

Over the next fifteen minutes, they drew up a detailed plan that involved splitting the entire class into small batches. They divided them according to their levels. They decided that each of them could handle four children at a time, and they would have one-hour sessions. In two such sessions, between the three of them, each child in the class would receive an extra hour of coaching. That way, the three of them would have to put in two additional hours, and each child would have to spend only an extra hour at the centre.

Kanika said that it would be difficult for the children to spend anything more than an hour, as many of them had chores at home. Some of them, like Sanju, had taken up jobs to supplement their parents' income. At home, none of these children had an environment where they could study. The men of the house came home drunk, there would be fights in the family, televisions would be blaring, younger siblings would be noisy, and there would be many other things like festival celebrations, or brawls—common in these areas—that were an impediment to their studying at home. Hence, all the studies that the children did had to take place in these extra sessions that Ron, Veda and Kanika would start taking.

Once they had drawn up the plan, they decided to start the sessions in two days. The children would have to take permission from their parents and make a few adjustments to be able to come to class.

That night, when Veda was alone with Bhuwan in the privacy of their bedroom, she told him about the extra classes that she would have to take. She also told him about her promotion and how, from now on, she would be paid.

Bhuwan had got back from work at 9 p.m., which was early by his standards, and after dinner, they had retired to bed. It had taken Veda all her will-power not to blurt out the new development at the dining table. She didn't want to tell her mother-in-law. She knew that the old lady would be dismissive of it. But Bhuwan's reaction was not much better.

'Oh, that's nice,' Bhuwan said. 'Are you happy?' he asked.

Veda sighed. She wished he would show a little more enthusiasm.

'Of course I am, Bhuwan! I am elated. This is the first time in my life that I will be earning. It is my first job. But it does mean I will probably get back home well after 8 p.m. on some days and your mother will be annoyed,' she said.

'Don't worry. I will take care of it,' said Bhuwan.

'Thank you, Bhuwan. It means so much to me,' said Veda.

'It is the least I can do, Veda,' he said.

Veda tried to reach for his hand to squeeze it, but he had already turned towards the reading lamp and opened his book.

Veda turned on her side, wondering why there was such a massive disconnect between her and Bhuwan. Was it the lack of sex? Why was he not enthusiastic about anything she did? His behaviour puzzled her. It was not like he did not care. He very much did. Then why were his responses always so measured? Couldn't he be excited for her? Veda lay awake for a while, thinking about it, trying to see it from his point of view. She concluded that perhaps, for him, it was not such a big deal. After all, he earned ten times more than what she would be paid at this job. Still, not everything in life is about money, Veda thought, as she drifted off to sleep.

The next morning, over breakfast, Bhuwan calmly informed his mother that Veda would be home later than usual once the extra classes started.

'When is it starting, Veda?' he asked her.

'I think we start tomorrow,' replied Veda.

She was glad that he had brought up the topic with his mother instead of leaving it to her.

'Already you are out of the house from 7.30 a.m. Now you want to stay back further?' Padma Devi asked angrily.

'She has taken this up, Ma; she cannot quit now. The board exam results are important for these students. And besides, she is also getting paid for it now. She is no longer a volunteer. She has been absorbed as a teacher,' Bhuwan defended Veda.

Veda shot him a look of gratitude.

'Oh, when did that happen? And why didn't you tell me?' she asked Veda accusingly.

'It happened only yesterday, Ma. And we are telling you now, aren't we?' said Bhuwan.

It was the first time that he had used 'we' when talking to his mother. Veda noticed it and was happy. It made it sound like he was on her side.

'Okay, okay. I hope this will not continue forever. And now, does that mean I will have to cook dinner and wait for you?' asked Padma Devi.

'Ma, I think we should employ a cook. Veda is working now and is earning as well. It will be difficult for her to come back and cook. Also, I was thinking about how it will be unfair on you. You can get complete rest that way, and you don't have to enter the kitchen at all,' said Bhuwan.

Padma Devi considered this for a minute. She was pleased at the suggestion. She had not liked the idea of cooking for her son and her daughter-in-law and waiting for them to return from work. She liked going out with her friends to temples, for musical evenings and bhajan recitations from time to time. This arrangement was perfect for her.

'Hmm. We will have to find the right cook, someone who cooks well. Kanti behen was mentioning the other day that her neighbour's cook was looking for a job. I shall speak to her tomorrow,' said Padma Devi.

Veda could have kissed Bhuwan then. In a single stroke, he had solved the problem. She met his eyes and mouthed a 'thank you' to him.

Then she smiled as he smiled back, and they carried on with their meal.

Chapter 24

November 1996
Pune

Dear, dear Suraj,

How are you my friend? I hope you are doing fine. Your loss and what you are going through is so deep that anything I want to say to lessen the pain you feel seems inadequate. You are one brave person, Suraj. You have so much strength.

I was very happy to read about your work. You seem to have completely taken to it, like a duck to water. I know you must have heard this many times, especially from your father's colleagues, but your parents would be so proud of you right now. Their souls must be smiling at you.

I think it is only when you experience deep sorrow that you truly appreciate the power of kindness. I was overwhelmed to read that your father's colleagues are inviting you to their homes, and sending home-cooked meals for you. I can also understand what a strain it must be for you to pretend that things are fine. But, I guess, it is their way of coping with the loss too. They want to feel they did something to express their sorrow at the loss of their colleague, and that way, they can feel connected to someone who is no longer there, through their son. I once read a novel about a girl who loses her entire family in a famine. She is the only one who survives, and she is all alone. She longs for her family. The descriptions of the sorrow she experiences affected me deeply, and your situation now reminds me of that girl in the novel.

On a different note, the situation at home has improved a great deal. We have now employed a cook who comes twice a day. He makes breakfast and lunch in the morning, and in the evening, he cooks dinner. I don't have kitchen duties anymore. My MIL decides the menu and gives him elaborate instructions. The cook is a sweet chap by the name of Niranjan. He is only too happy to discuss the day's menu in detail with my MIL. It is an arrangement that suits me. It frees up a lot of my time in the morning.

Right now, as I write this letter, the delicious aroma of breakfast being made in the kitchen is wafting in. Bhuwan is on yet another work-related business trip, and since I have a bit of time on my hands before I leave for Sankalp, I am utilising it well in writing to you.

Right now, at Sankalp, I am neck-deep in work. We are giving extra coaching to all students who are going to appear for the Class 10 exams.

Kanika and Ron (my colleagues at Sankalp—I might have told you about them in my previous letter; we have now become friends) and I, are working hard. Ron is from the UK, and he has rented an apartment near the office complex where Sankalp is based.

Kanika and I helped Ron decorate his apartment. It was a wonderful experience to go with them to furniture workshops and help pick eclectic designs. Kanika is very good at it—her own house is done up beautifully. I picked up so many tips from her. I now know all the good places in Pune to get lovely, authentic furniture. Some of them are vintage pieces, some are antiques and some are replicas. Ron's apartment looks fabulous now. He's got air-conditioning installed all over the house. After we finished doing it up, he invited us to his place for dinner.

The three of us met there after we finished the extra classes for the children. The Sankalp centre (and Ron's home) are both within walking distance from my own place. Kanika and I walked back together, and since it was late at night, Ron escorted us, and then went back to his apartment.

Next weekend is my first wedding anniversary. One year has gone by so quickly—can you believe it? Kanika has invited all of us to her home for a meal. She is throwing a party for us. My mother-in-law was very pleased about it and I think it is very sweet of Kanika.

I took a while to reply to your letter because I wanted to think things over. My first instinct was to say yes, I do want to meet you. I long to see you, Suraj. It has been a while since we met. But I do not want to do it without telling Bhuwan.

I know I have told you in the past that Bhuwan does not own me, and that I can do what I want. That was how we began writing to each other in secret. I had to convince you to agree, as you felt this was wrong.

Now the tables seem to have turned! You want to meet me (and trust me, I very badly want to as well), and I am hesitating, as I haven't yet told Bhuwan. I do plan to tell him sometime, though. And once I tell him, we can perhaps meet the following weekend? The very thought of it fills me with excitement, my friend. It will be wonderful to see you. I would love to show you around Sankalp.

I hope you understand, Suraj.

Take good care of yourself, my friend. Remember, I am only a letter (and a few hours) away.

I hope we meet soon.

Your friend,

Veda

Veda read and re-read the letter she had composed. She had finally got the tone right on the fourth attempt. It was friendly, casual, and it did not betray how she really felt. It was strange, that she was thinking so much about this. Earlier, when writing to Suraj, she had never thought twice and had dashed off whatever was whirling in her head at the time. But now, she was measuring each word. She knew it was silly to do so. It was not that Suraj would sense what was going on inside her head. And yet, she couldn't bring herself to communicate as casually as before. It was as though, by admitting that she had feelings for Suraj that went deeper than mere friendship, something inside her had irrevocably changed. She had, up until now, convinced herself that they were just friends and nothing more.

But she knew that was not true anymore.

On the one hand, she had no *real* connection with Bhuwan. Yet he was so nice, kind and sweet towards her. She couldn't help but wish he had some of Suraj's qualities, though, and that she could connect with him the way she did with Suraj. She knew it was unfair to compare them—but she couldn't stop.

Guilt was slowly growing inside her, and she had no idea what to do about it. It wasn't something she could control. She solved the problem by focusing on Sankalp and throwing herself into work, so that she forgot about everything else.

When Veda got home that night, she found a letter waiting for her with her address neatly written in Vidya's writing. She rushed to the bedroom and opened it, as she wasn't sure if it was from Vidya or Suraj. It was from Vidya.

November 1996

Joshimath

Dearest Veda didi,

How are you? How are the students of Sankalp doing? How is Kanika?

I like how I write to you—like I know them personally! Strangely, even though I have never met them, I feel like I do. Please do convey my regards to them.

Happy first wedding anniversary, didi! Are you excited about it? Have you planned how you are going to celebrate it?

Didi, your firebrand is completely facing the heat here. Papa and Ma are so angry with me. They say that I have ruined their name and that everyone is talking about us. Papa shouted at Ma the other day, saying that it was her upbringing that had spoilt us girls. Ma started crying. Later, I heard Paro didi telling Ma, 'Just think about it. You raised all your girls the same way. Look at Veda. She is happily married and settled. So it is not your fault.'

Later, I thought about it. You are a role model because you obeyed them. You sacrificed your happiness and did what they wanted. That somehow makes you a person to emulate? Don't get me wrong, didi—I do admire you very much. But what I am reflecting on is how our parents and society in general view girls.

The girls who do not protest and who obey the rules are rewarded. The rule breakers like me are punished. Why? Only because we dare to have our own wishes? Only because we dare have our own dreams?

Who gives you a right to dream, didi? Who takes it away? Isn't it our right alone?

Kunal is still not talking to me. He invited Dipu for a drive in his car right in front of me, and ignored me, acting as if I did not exist. I did not even glance at him. And you know what—Dipu went with him. I thought she was *my* friend. I thought she would try and initiate a conversation between him and me, so we could clear the misunderstanding. Instead, she chose to walk away with him.

I have stopped talking to her as well. Life is better when you do not have false friends. Even if you are alone, it is better than having people who betray your friendship.

Do you remember the nerds of my class, Anita and Rajashree? I have started hanging out with them now. It was mostly because I couldn't find anyone else to hang out with. Kunal and his gang are the 'cool kids'. When Kunal ostracised me, all the others did too. I was like an outcast.

I think the company we keep in college is very important, didi. These two girls study all the time. I think I am influenced by them now, more than I care to admit. I have started finding the course interesting now—can you believe it?

It made me think about how we form opinions. When I was hanging out with Dipu and Kunal, I found the course boring, as they kept saying that it was boring—I was influenced by their thoughts. Now that I am with Anita and Rajashree, I am seeing the course through their eyes. They refer to so many books outside the syllabus. They write down case studies. For accounting, they work out many more problems after they are done solving those in the textbook! Now I take pride in being able to solve these problems.

I asked them both what they wanted to do after college. Anita says that she will apply for chartered accountancy, and that she has decided that she will do an apprenticeship in Delhi. Rajashree is determined to get into IIM. She has already started practising the questions they ask in the Common Admission Test. I had a glance at some of the past papers the other day. I liked the questions they asked! I especially liked the reasoning section. I told her that I want to study with her, and she said I am more than welcome.

As for Suraj, I don't think there is any need to take Bhuwan's approval as such. He is *your* friend. You knew him long before you knew Bhuwan. Let me ask you something—you said Bhuwan and Kanika are friends. Did Bhuwan ask your permission before he met Kanika, when they planned that little thing to outwit your mother-in-law? Let us now presume he was just meeting her to chat and to catch up because they are friends, and they were friends before you got married. Would he ask your permission then?

Didi—Suraj lives so close to you. It would mean a lot to both of you, if you met. It would mean so much to him, as he is coping with loss.

What kind of a friend would you be if you weren't there for him in his time of need?

Stop acting like you need anybody's permission to lead your life.

Just go do what gives you joy!

Write back soon, didi.

All my love,

Your nerdy firebrand,

Vidya

Chapter 25

December 1996
Pune

My dear nerdy firebrand,
I love that name! I was very happy to read your letter and find out the latest developments at your end. Ma called me up the other day to complain about you. She had to call twice to get me on the phone, as the first time she called, I was busy at Sankalp. My mother-in-law and she had a long chat. When I got back home, my MIL told me that Ma had called, and that she would call me back on Sunday, as that was the only day I was home. I think she was being sarcastic and it was a jibe at me. I am not sure, but I let it pass.

It is the truth, though. I am so busy these days that I don't have the time to think about anything other than the students at Sankalp. The progress we are making is painfully slow, but it is steady. Initially, the extra two hours that we spent at Sankalp to coach the students was not helping, as some of them could not turn up at that time. They have jobs and errands, and they keep odd hours. It is difficult for us to get access to the office basement at these times, as we have got permission to use it only for two hours in the evening.

So do you know what Ron said? He said we could meet at his apartment and the students can come there. Isn't that sweet of him? So now they tell us at what time they can come for extra class, and if it is outside the permitted hours, we simply meet at Ron's house. You should have seen the kids the first time they landed up there. They were in complete awe of the place. They behaved so well. Now they have quickly got used to it, and they love coming there.

We were having a class on prepositions the other day. We were trying to teach them 'below' and 'above'. I had made a chart on which I had drawn a large, multi-storied building with multiple windows. Kanika and I had painted the windows, and we had done it in such a manner that, when you opened the window of each house, you could see who lived inside. We did this by cutting out flaps like window panes, and sticking another chart paper behind that one, so that each window opens to reveal an occupant.

Each occupant has their name beneath the window. It looks very beautiful. Kanika and I spent many hours making it. The children loved this little prop. This is a good aid to teach them, as we can ask them questions like, 'Who lives above Mr Brown?' 'Who lives below Mrs Das?' or 'Where does Mr Brown live?'

We frame the questions in such a way that it will make them use the terms that we want them to get familiar with.

Using this chart, I asked Sanju: 'Who is below Miss Usha?' I opened the window below Miss Usha's window. The right answer was 'Mr Brown'.

But do you know what Sanju answered? He said, 'Didi, below Miss Usha is *khidkee.'* (He meant a window.)

Ron heard this, and said in his British accent, 'Blimey, who is *khidkee*?'

Kanika and I collapsed in laughter, as did the children. It was hilarious and I am chuckling as I narrate this to you.

So we have such funny moments in class too, which leave us in helpless fits of laughter. Even though we are working hard, classes are always so much fun!

I thought a lot about what you had so beautifully elucidated in your last letter, about the girls who are 'rule breakers'. You are so right, Vidya. I think society does expect women to conform to certain norms.

Take my mother-in-law, for instance. She has been educated only till Class 8. She wasn't keen on my working at all. If you think about it, it is because she has been conditioned to see life that way. She stayed at home all her life, and she doesn't see any need for women to work. She never broke any rules, and she conformed to societal expectations. She wants me to do so too.

If not for Bhuwan, I wouldn't have this job. I would still be at home, pressing her feet, making tea for her and cooking. I would have gone mad with frustration.

If I had dared break the 'rule', I would have probably been rewarded. But most women are so afraid to break out of the mould of societal acceptance. We have been taught to be obedient, sweet and kind. The thing is, breaking rules comes with a price. (In your case, it is facing the anger of Ma and Papa, being talked about, etc.) The reward for breaking the rules is not certain. Hence, most of us find it easier to not break rules and be 'good girls'.

I am happy that you have stepped outside it. I am with you, my dear sister. Though I did not have the courage to do it myself, I am delighted that you are able to live life according to your own terms. Well done!

I also did a fair bit of thinking on what you said, about whether Bhuwan asked for my permission to meet Kanika. You are so right. Why is it that I feel like I *have* to ask his permission?! I don't have to. Again, it is societal conditioning which makes us think so. We have been conditioned to please our husbands, please our children (if and when we have them) and to please everybody else, before pleasing ourselves. I think it is time I broke an unsaid rule too. I think you have convinced me, my dear sister.

I do *want* to meet Suraj. Yes, he is my friend, and you are absolutely right—I don't *need* Bhuwan's permission to meet him.

One part of me thinks that, when you are married, you owe it to your partner to tell them about what goes on in your life. With Bhuwan, it has been a year now, and I still barely know the person that he is! I do know his habits and routines, but I haven't been able to get beneath that surface, and truly get to know him. He never tells me about who he meets, who he sees and what he does. I do not know any of his colleagues' names or any of his friends other than Vikki.

Let me also confess one thing, my dear sister—I think I have started having feelings for Suraj. I know in my heart that he is more than just a friend to me. That is why I hesitate to meet him.

I am afraid. I am terrified to break the rules.

Where will it lead? What path will it take me on?

I do not know.

But something tells me I am about to find out. Thanks to you!

Write back to me, and study well! Convey my regards to your new friends, Anita and Rajashree.

I wish you a very happy birthday in advance. I shall call you up on your birthday and wish you too.

All my love,
Your rule-following sis,
Veda

January 1997

Pune

Dearest, dearest firebrand rule breaker,

I did it! I broke the rules. I met Suraj!

He came to Pune on Sunday morning. Bhuwan was out of town again. He had left on Friday and was slated to return only on Tuesday. So that gave me a long window. I knew this well in advance, and I wrote to Suraj saying that I could meet on Sunday, as I had classes with the Sankalp children the whole of Saturday.

On Sunday morning too, we had a few classes at Ron's apartment. But I finished at 8.30, after which I was free. Suraj came to the cafe at the office complex. It was just a short walk for me from Ron's apartment.

I did not tell Kanika or Ron that I was meeting a friend. I did not see any need to. Suraj was sitting in the cafe, his back towards me, and he kept looking around anxiously, to see if he could spot me. He kept glancing at his watch too. I could see him from a distance, but he did not see me as his back was turned towards me. I walked up to him and tapped him on the shoulder from behind.

He jumped up and hugged me so tight, I thought I would stop breathing. He was genuinely happy to see me. He looked so much older than he did in college. Maybe it is the stress of living by himself. He suddenly looks all grown up. He said I hadn't changed at all.

We had a cup of coffee and we chatted for a while. It was just like how it was when we were in college. There were no awkward pauses, no silences—we just kept chatting and chatting. It was as if no time had passed at all. He has always been very easy to talk to. Then, after about an hour, it seemed odd to keep sitting in the cafe, and he asked me if there was any place I would like to go. I hadn't thought about it or planned anything. I asked him what he would like to see, and he said that, if I did not mind, there was a historical place around, and he would like to see that. He said he had asked someone from his office who was from Pune about places to see, and they had recommended Shaniwar Wada.

So we took an auto-rickshaw and went there. It is a prominent historical landmark in Pune, and I remember Kanika once telling Ron about it. Even though I have lived in Pune for so many months, I haven't seen much of this city. I was more than happy to go wherever Suraj wanted.

It is a beautiful palace, right in the middle of the city! I can imagine how grand it must have been, when it was built in 1732. (It is that old!) It was the seat of the Peshwas, who ruled the Maratha Empire. Once upon a time, it was a magnificent seven-storied structure. The Peshwas, when they had commissioned the building, wanted the entire thing to be made of stone. However, after the construction of the first floor, the people of Satara complained to the king that only a king can sanction a stone monument, not the Peshwas. So they completed the rest of the building using bricks. The British took over this gorgeous building in 1818.

In 1828, a mysterious fire broke out here, and only the part made of stone, the base floor, survived. The rest of the floors were destroyed. Now, we only have descriptions of the rest of the floors. Suraj and I stood there staring at this wonderful building and imagined every scene that we had read about. It was a powerful experience. Together, we pictured the grandeur: the doorways with teak arches, the ornamental teardrop teak pillars, the numerous chandeliers, the rich Persian rugs, the paintings on the walls, the polished marble floors.... That palace truly came to life in our imaginations. We stood there, staring at it in awe. No words were needed. It felt like the rest of the world had faded away, and we were in a time capsule—just him and me. It was a magical moment.

We had lunch only at 3.30 p.m. or so. We walked to a local eatery and gobbled up *vada pavs*, and drank thick, milky, strong tea. It was the best meal ever! I got back home by 5.30, and Suraj left for Mumbai. He said he was elated that we had got some time together, and so was I. He hugged me again when he left. My heart was beating so fast, Vidya.

My mother-in-law was out. So I didn't have to explain anything to her.

I couldn't stop thinking of Suraj after that meeting. I was HIGH on him. I so enjoyed his company, and it was an out-of-the-world feeling, seeing the magnificent Shaniwar Wada with him.

The next day, I had my usual classes at Sankalp. Kanika remarked that I was glowing. She asked if I had used a face pack. She is a big fan of beauty masks. I just laughed.

'Come on—don't hide it from me! You have definitely used something new,' she said. She pestered me so much that I told her I had used a face pack made with besan. Remember how we both used to make it and religiously use it, when I was there? I told her all the ingredients and she wrote them down, saying she would try it on the weekend! It is a good mask, no doubt, but I know that the 'glow' came from meeting Suraj. I had no idea I could be *that* happy, Vidya! I am so very glad you nudged me in that direction. If you hadn't, I don't think I would have met him this way and spent time with him.

When Bhuwan came back on Tuesday, I told him that I had met a friend on Sunday.

'Oh good,' he said, absentmindedly. I cannot believe it, Vidya—*he did not ask who I had met!*

I cannot believe he can be that disinterested in what is going on in my life. I asked him how his trip was, and he just said, 'good'. He was very tight-lipped about that too.

Anyway—now my conscience is clear. I did mention to Bhuwan that I had met a friend. So I am not hiding anything from him. If he had asked me details, I would have told him about Suraj, and that he is a friend from college. But he didn't, and that's that.

Even though I haven't yet got a reply to my last letter from you, I couldn't wait to tell you all this, hence I wrote!

Your turn to write back now.

Write soon, my firebrand.

Your rule bender sis (not a rule breaker),

Veda

PS: Happy New Year!

Chapter 26

February 1997

Joshimath

Dearest, dearest rule breaker didi,

Hooray! As far as I am concerned, you did break the 'rules'. You managed to silence that inner voice in your head which was stopping you, and you went out and had fun. I am glad that whatever I told you helped you get a different perspective.

You also told jiju about your friend—now if he isn't even interested in knowing who it is, why should you bother? Don't even think about it, didi. It is not worth wasting time thinking about it. Just forget it and carry on.

You will not believe the turn of events that have taken place here. Those very same aunties just will not give up match-making even after what happened. They brought a marriage proposal for me from a widower who is based abroad. Apparently, he lost his wife last year and has a two-year-old daughter. He is very keen to get married, so there will be someone to take care of the child. How preposterous is that? Does he want a baby-sitter or a life-partner?

Ma told me, 'Now that you have this bad reputation, I think you should settle for this one. He is a good man. He is very religious and traditional. See, even though he lives abroad, he wants a girl from India, from our community.'

I told her that it was probably because he couldn't get any white girl to fall in love with him! Ma was angry with me and said that they had tried their best from their side, and now I deserved what I got!

You know what the strange thing is, didi? There are two other girls in Joshimath who are more than happy to marry him. Ma told me they are very keen and that he is coming to India with his daughter next month to meet them. She said that if I changed my mind, to let them know.

Ha! I am not going to change my mind.

But I am glad they didn't spring a surprise on me, and get him home without telling me. I guess they know now that if they had done that, there is no telling how I would have acted. I am pleased about that. It is a small triumph for me.

What I feel angry about is these 'threats' that Ma and Papa are making by telling me things like, 'We warned you...', 'You brought this upon yourself...', 'Look what you have done...', etc.

What have I done, didi? I have only expressed what I want. What is so wrong in that?

The other development that has taken place—Kunal Saini came to me (after all these weeks!) and said that I could get back into their 'gang' if I apologised to him publicly. I was enraged. I *had* apologised to him when all this had happened. Now I have moved on. I told him I simply wasn't interested anymore, and it did not matter to me whether I was in their 'gang' or not. He is acting like he is doing *me* a favour!

I have changed as a person, didi. I feel happy to be with Anita and Rajashree and hit the books. Yesterday, they were talking about the civil services exams. They said that it is an excellent career option as well. The preliminary exam has only two papers—general studies for 150 marks and an optional subject for 300 marks. For the optional subject, Anita says that if you take a less popular one like anthropology, your chances of success are higher.

She said that the UPSC wants creative, innovative people who are leaders and who do not just follow what is the popular opinion. So the more unusual your subject selection, the higher your reward. Rajashree said that, if that was right, then she would opt for animal husbandry. I did not know what that meant, so I kept quiet, and later I looked it up in the library, browsing through the newspapers in the archives section. I must say, didi, I am attracted to the challenge. Let's see! I have two more years to prepare.

What is happening at Sankalp? The final exams for Class 10 are next month! (And for me too, for my college first year.) Are your students well prepared?

Write back soon to me.

With lots of love,

Your firebrand.

February 1997
Mumbai

Dear Veda,
How are you? I am sorry I haven't written to you at all after we met in Pune. I enjoyed seeing you. I was so glad you said we could meet. It is always great to catch up with old friends.

It was nice to visit Shaniwar Wada and see all the history there.

After I got back, I was put in charge of Youth Day celebrations. I did not really want to be in the committee, but my boss insisted on it. He said it is mainly for the junior officers, and if young people like me did not participate in it, it would fall flat. The celebrations are on a rather grand scale. They last for ten whole days. Each day, after work, we are supposed to organise one event. It can be anything—like an Antakshari game, or a group dance, or we invite a well-known speaker to address the employees, etc. The main criteria is that it has to be 'fun as well as useful'. So the people in the committee have to meet, brainstorm and decide upon the events for each day. As the grand finale, we are getting a music troupe to perform exclusively for us. We have a big budget allocated for this, as the chairman of this company thinks celebrations like this are essential. It all feels like an extension of a college cultural festival to me. You would be surprised at how many people are enthusiastic about this kind of stuff. I must admit—though I was dragged in unwillingly, once I got into things, I am kind of liking it!

There is a girl in my office who is also on the committee. Her name is Priya. She is our age. She is extremely smart, funny and enthusiastic. She comes up with a hundred ideas a minute! Some of them are crazy, but some are doable.

It's the first time since my parents' deaths that I feel enthusiastic about something. Most likely we will be getting Colonial Cousins to play for us! They won the MTV Asia Viewer's Choice Award last year. Priya and I went and met them both. They are extremely approachable, humble and down-to-earth. Priya was very chatty with them too. It was like she had known them her entire life.

When we were getting back from meeting them, Priya asked me if I wanted to stop at her place for lunch. She lives in the same residential complex as I do, and I hadn't known, as she is from another department, which is on a different floor from mine. Priya lives with her parents. She has an older brother. He is married and is based in Australia.

I must admit I was a bit uncomfortable as there was nobody at home when we landed up there. Both her parents work. They have a cook, and he had made some delicious stuff. She said that her cook had mentioned that he was looking for additional work, and if I liked, he could start cooking for me.

So, now I have a cook! He makes breakfast for me before I leave for work, and he also packs lunch for me. I have left a key to my flat with my neighbour, and my cook (his name is Pawan) makes dinner for me as well.

My work is going well. I am able to manage my projects as well as these Youth Day celebrations, as the meetings for the latter typically happen outside work hours.

This weekend, Priya and I are going to see the Ajanta and Ellora caves. The moment she knew I was a history buff, she suggested it. I am so looking forward to it.

What is going on at your end? How are the exam preparations going? How is Bhuwan? Did you tell him about us meeting?

Write back when you can.

Your friend,

Suraj

When you have exchanged many letters with someone, there are subtle clues in the way they write that immediately tell you about what is going on in their lives—things that they aren't directly saying.

Veda read Suraj's letter and was instantly hit by a wave of jealousy. It was a feeling that started deep down in her tummy, and made its way up to her throat, and remained there, like something unpleasant that had stuck, which she could neither spit out nor swallow. Each time she read the letter, she grew more and more agitated. The jealousy had now grown into a gigantic wave and she was submerged in it. The more she thought about it, the more she drowned. He was definitely attracted to Priya. Three-fourths of the letter was about her. Priya this ... Priya that ...

She chastised herself, saying that it was not the right way to look at it. She tried to be rational. He had not said anything specifically. He *had* spoken about other things in his letter. As his friend, she ought to be happy that he was enjoying himself and having fun. She ought to be delighted that he had managed to put aside his deep sorrow, at least for a little while. But she realised that there was a huge gap between 'ought to' and 'is'.

She was not able to bridge that gap.

She felt let down. Then she felt silly for feeling let down. She herself had told Suraj several times that there could be nothing more than friendship between them. But she had felt some spark when they had gone to Shaniwar Wada. She now wondered if all of it was in her own head. Maybe he saw her as nothing more than a friend, after all?

She detested feeling like this. It was as though she had no control over her emotions. How was this even possible? Till she had read his letter, she had been over the moon every time she thought about him; and she was reasonably sure that he felt the same way about her too.

But now that he had mentioned another girl (Priya—how she hated the very name!), she was suddenly unsure of his feelings for her.

She knew that she was in love with him. There was no denying it. She also knew that this was a forbidden love that she was feeling. As a married woman, she had to connect that way with her husband, not with an old friend from college. But it was something that had to come from both sides.

She remembered a saying that her grandmother used to utter often: 'You need two hands to clap.'

But the thing is, you should want *to clap,* she thought.

Was she jumping to conclusions? Was Priya nothing more than a friend to Suraj? And even if she did declare her love for Suraj, what would they do? She was a married woman, after all.

The questions kept swirling around in Veda's head. As hard as she tried, she could not come up with any concrete answers.

All she knew was that when love was one-sided, it was the worst feeling in the world.

Chapter 27

February 1997
Sankalp, Pune

Veda did not feel like replying to Suraj's letter immediately. She first wanted to make sense of it all. She decided to cope with her jealousy by directing all her energy towards preparing the students of Sankalp for the mock board exams which would take place later in the month. These model exams would be conducted exactly in the manner in which the board exams would be. This way, the children would have adequate practice taking an examination, and the process would not be entirely new to them, when they gave their final board exams in March.

One morning, after class at Sankalp, Kajol approached Veda. Veda was with a group of junior children, teaching them the concept of fractions. These were the children who needed extra coaching, the ones whose standard in maths was abysmally low. Veda had been struggling to make them understand why they had to calculate something a particular way. They seemed to be memorising the formulas, and Veda wanted them to have a deeper understanding of it. After thinking hard, she had hit upon an idea. Kanika and she got two round vanilla sponge cakes from a nearby bakery. They sliced the cake into half. The children could now *see* what 'half' meant. Then they cut it further to demonstrate what one-fourth, one-third and one-eighth meant. By combining pieces from two cakes, they could demonstrate the addition of fractions easily. As a reward for getting the sums right, the children got to eat the cake. This motivated them to add faster. It was fun, and that made them learn quicker.

Veda had just finished giving away the last slice of cake, when she spotted Kajol hovering around.

'Yes, Kajol,' said Veda, as she dismissed the class and stood up, wiping her hands on a paper napkin, and putting away the box in which she had carried the cake.

'Didi, I want to talk to you in private,' said Kajol.

'Alright. Come with me,' said Veda, and she led her to the far end of the basement where they could be alone.

'What is it that you want to talk to me about, Kajol?' asked Veda, as soon as they were out of earshot of the other students. Veda could see that most of them were leaving.

'I have a wish, didi,' said Kajol.

'What is it?' asked Veda, amused.

'It's my birthday next week. I want to invite you, Ron bhaiya and Kanika didi to my house. Will you come, didi?' she asked, her eyes shining.

Veda hesitated.

'Ummm, I am not sure,' she said. She had been told in her training session that the children would get emotionally attached to them. Was this a warning sign of that?

'Why, didi? Why are you not sure? Is it because my house is not big?' asked Kajol, as her face fell.

'Oh, no, no! It's not like that at all,' Veda hastily assured her. She was horrified to think that that was what Kajol had presumed.

'Then why, didi? I have come to your house, no? Why can't you come to my house? Only for my birthday, didi. I am not calling everybody. Only special people,' said Kajol.

Veda did not want to hurt Kajol's feelings.

'I will check with Kanika didi, okay? I shall give you an answer tomorrow,' said Veda.

'You have to come, didi. I will feel very bad if you don't come,' said Kajol. She was emphatic, and she knew how to vocalise what she felt. 'I will be inviting Kanika didi and Ron bhaiya too. I didn't want to tell them in front of the other children, as I am not calling everybody.'

Veda nodded. 'I understand,' she said, as they walked back to where Ron and Kanika were standing. The other students had left by then. Kajol approached the two teachers and invited them.

'Sure, it's your birthday, I will be there,' Ron instantly agreed.

'Of course, we will come and help you celebrate,' Kanika said.

A million-watt smile lit up Kajol's face.

Veda now felt stupid for not agreeing instantly. Kanika and Ron had not thought twice about it. She wished she had agreed immediately too, like them, instead of telling Kajol that she would think about it.

'Thank you Kanika didi, thank you Ron bhaiya,' said Kajol.

As she left, she called out over her shoulder, 'Veda didi, you cannot say no. You have to come, okay?'

Veda, Ron and Kanika smiled as they watched Kajol skipping and humming a Bollywood number, as she left.

'What a cheerful, bright girl,' remarked Ron.

'Yes, she is definitely our best student. I am certain she will get a distinction in her board exams; her work is impeccable,' agreed Kanika.

Veda thought long and hard about what she could gift Kajol. She decided it would be best if she asked Shakubai. She got time only on Sundays now to chat with her, as most other days, she was absorbed in the activities that went on at Sankalp.

'What do you think Kajol would like for her birthday?' Veda asked Shakubai, as she swept her bedroom.

Shakubai looked up, startled. 'Oh, you remember her birthday, madam?' she asked.

'Errr … Kajol invited all of us,' said Veda.

Shakubai did not know about it at all. She was surprised to hear this.

'I don't know what that girl will do next. We … we don't have space … we don't have proper furniture. Our home—it's so small. *Hai Raam*,' she muttered to herself and continued sweeping.

'Don't worry, Shakubai. We are not coming to look at your house. We just want Kajol to have a great birthday party,' Veda said.

Shakubai wasn't comforted though, and kept muttering something incomprehensible.

'So shall I get her books? Storybooks?' asked Veda.

'No, madam. No place in our house for books.'

'What would she like then?'

Shakubai hesitated. 'Er um … she wanted…' she started

speaking and then stopped, unsure as to whether to go on or not.

Veda saw her hesitation and assured her, 'Don't worry, Shakubai. You can tell me freely what Kajol would like.'

'She would like a new salwar kurta, didi. She has very few, and expenses are always mounting. I am not able to buy her as many as she would like,' said Shakubai.

'It's a very good idea,' said Veda.

It was the best shopping spree that Veda had ever gone on. Kanika and she took an auto and went to Camp Area, the commercial centre of Pune. On Sundays, the main road was closed to traffic, and one could walk down MG Road and explore all the shops. Veda took great delight in selecting just the right salwar kameez sets for Kajol. She inspected the material, bargained with the shopkeeper, and ended up buying two of them. Kanika bought Kajol a trendy college bag and a salwar kurta. Ron had handed over some money, and had requested Kanika and Veda to pick up something on his behalf. With his money, Kanika bought a make-up kit and a wooden folding table that could easily be put away after use. Pleased with their purchases, they made their way back to the arch at the entrance of Sitawadi, where Ron had agreed to meet them.

When they reached the arch, they discovered Sanju standing there with Ron.

'Kajol told me to show you the way, didi. Come this way,' said Sanju, as he led them down a street.

The lanes grew narrower and narrower as they approached Kajol's home. This was not an area that Kanika was familiar with. Ron had become smarter when it came to navigating the puddles in his way, and he gingerly stepped over them, unlike the last time he was there. As they got closer to Kajol's home, they could see that it was lit up with multi-coloured fairy lights.

'This is like Christmas minus the tree,' Ron exclaimed.

The latest Bollywood numbers were blaring from a loudspeaker.

'I arranged didi, for Kajol's birthday,' said Sanju, his face beaming with pride.

There was a small rickety wooden table placed outside her

home, in the street. It was covered with patterned cloth, and it had the birthday cake on it. Kajol stood behind the table and a large smile broke out on her face as she greeted Kanika, Veda and Ron.

'Welcome didi, bhaiya!' she said, as she spun around, new long skirt twirling. Kanika and Veda smiled when they saw that.

'New skirt, Kajol? It looks so pretty,' said Kanika.

'Yes, Aayi got it for me. Thank you, didi,' Kajol beamed.

Shakubai hurried out of the house and greeted them.

'Go get chairs for the guests; why are you making them stand?' she said.

Sanju brought out three red plastic chairs that were nested within each other, from inside the house, and Ron helped him separate them.

'Please sit didi; bhaiya. Thank you for coming,' said Kajol.

'Happy birthday, Kajol,' said Veda, as she handed her gift to her.

Ron and Kanika did the same.

Kajol was overwhelmed.

'Can I open them, didi?' she asked.

'Of course,' said Kanika.

Kajol exclaimed in delight as she opened each box, slowly. She carefully folded the gift-wrapping paper and put it aside. She was overjoyed, and Veda could see how much she loved the gifts. She ran her hands over the salwar-kameezes and felt the soft fabric. She opened the bag and turned it around and looked at the insides. 'So nice, didi. So nice, bhaiya,' she kept repeating, over and over. Her eyes glistened with tears, and she said, 'Thank you so very much. This is my best birthday.'

There were just three other children from Sankalp, apart from Sanju. It seemed like it was indeed a special party where she had invited select guests.

Sanju said he would be back in a minute, and disappeared down the street.

'Where is he going?' asked Veda.

'To get cool drinks, didi,' said Kajol.

'Cool drinks?' Ron raised an eyebrow.

'It's not alcohol, Ron. In India, cool drink refers to an aerated drink,' Kanika smiled as she explained.

Shakubai had prepared hot *pooranpolis* and *vada pavs*. She brought them out and served it to them on paper plates.

'Let's cut the cake!' said Veda.

'No didi, first you eat. *Pooranpolis* and *vada pavs* are hot. If it becomes cold, it won't be so tasty,' said Kajol.

Ron had never seen anything like a *pooranpoli* before. Having eaten with Kanika and Veda in the cafeteria at the office complex, he was familiar with *vada pav*.

'This is scrumptious. You know, I should start a restaurant in Birmingham which serves this. There's nothing like that there,' he said.

'Shakubai, Ron is asking you if you want to start a hotel in Birmingham,' said Kanika.

Shakubai just laughed and covered her mouth with her saree *pallu*.

'*Mein idhar hi theek hoon*,' she said, waving her hands and shaking her head.

'What did she say?' asked Ron.

'She said she is fine here. She does not want to take you up on your offer, Ron,' laughed Kanika.

Suddenly, there was a commotion behind them.

'AYYYY,' shouted a male voice.

They turned to look. It was a very drunk man who was approaching them. He was swaying and could barely walk. He was dressed in a cleaner's uniform. It was Kajol's father, Rajaram.

'*Arey wah*! Party!' he said, as he came to the table.

Kajol's face stiffened in anger.

'Please go inside. We have guests,' said Shakubai, as she went to him and tried to steer him into their house. But he pushed her aside.

Then he saw the gifts that were piled up on the table and the cake.

He lunged towards the gifts and grabbed them.

'What is this? New clothes? Give them to me,' he said, as he grabbed the bottom of one of the new salwar-kameez sets.

'NO!' yelled Kajol, as she pulled it back from his hand.

Kajol's father lost his balance. He fell against the table on which the cake was placed. The table toppled and fell; the cake went crashing to the ground along with it.

'Oh, no!' said Ron.

Kanika and Veda stood horrified, watching the chaos.

Kajol's father lay sprawled on the ground with the overturned cake next to him, which was now mixed with the mud and dirt.

'Where did you get the money for all this from, EH?' he was yelling.

Then he saw Ron, Kanika and Veda. To him, they represented the 'upper class', the 'sahibs', the office workers he envied and detested.

'Why are they here?' he asked, pointing to them.

'They are here as our guests. Go inside,' said Shakubai, helping him up.

But Rajaram was not in a mood to listen to his wife. In his home, he was king. How dare these people turn up here, he thought, his drunken state exacerbating his feelings. He stood up, staggering, trying to find a balance, considering what he should do next. Anger was welling up inside him by the minute. And then suddenly, without any warning, he lunged at Ron.

'*ANGREZ. SAAALE!* WHAT ARE YOU DOING IN OUR BASTI? GET OUT! GO AWAY, WHOLE DAY I CLEAN YOUR SHIT. DO YOU HEAR ME?' he yelled, in Hindi.

The colour drained from Ron's face. He did not understand the words, but he knew he was not welcome there, and he stood staring. In that frozen second before he could react, Rajaram had swung at Ron.

Thwack.

The sound as the drunk man's balled fist collided with Ron's cheekbone rang loudly in his ear. Ron staggered back, reeling in pain.

Kajol was horrified and stood there in shock, her mouth open.

'*BHADWA ... SAAAAALA!*' Shakubai came charging from behind him, yelling at her husband, her eyes blazing. The years of violence that she had endured from this man had broken something inside her when she saw him hitting Ron. She had a piece of firewood in her hand, and before he could turn around, she hit him on the head with it.

THUMP. The blow landed on his skull.

She pushed him hard before he could recover from the sudden jolt of pain. Her action took him by complete surprise and he collapsed forward, losing consciousness as he mumbled a cry.

Sanju had arrived with the cool drinks and he stood there, shocked. He had witnessed the scene that had unfolded in front of him so quickly that it was over within a few seconds.

Kajol and Sanju rushed towards Ron, as did Kanika and Veda.

'Ron bhaiya. I am so sorry, sorry bhaiya,' repeated Kajol, over and over.

'Are you okay, Ron?' asked Kanika. She was in a state of shock too, as was Veda.

'Bhaiya, keep this cool drink against your cheek,' said Sanju, handing over one of the ice-cold bottles.

Ron held the bottle against his jaw, its coolness somewhat soothing the sharp sting.

'That was ... well ... unexpected,' he said, slowly recovering his composure.

'Shall we go to a doctor?' asked Veda.

'Oh, no, not at all. I will be fine. This is not as bad as some of the drunken brawls at a British pub. Thanks for saving me, Shakubai,' said Ron, and he managed a weak smile. Shakubai was looking at Ron in disbelief. It seemed as if she couldn't comprehend what had happened.

Ron was being a sport about it.

As the whole impact of what had happened sunk in, Kajol started crying softly.

'Hey—don't cry, Kajol. It's your birthday,' said Sanju, helplessly.

'Yes, he is right. You must not cry on your birthday,' Kanika wrapped her arm around Kajol's shoulders.

'Kajol. Keep those gifts inside and hide them before your

father wakes up. If he sees the new things, he will sell them and take the money for his alcohol,' said the pragmatic Sanju.

Kajol nodded and asked Sanju to keep them in his house, so that her father would not find them. Between them, they managed to quickly pack away the gifts.

'*Mein maafi maangti hoon sahib*,' said Shakubai, as she joined her palms and stood in front of Ron. Ron understood that she was apologising.

'It's not your fault at all, I am fine,' said Ron.

Kanika said that they should leave. Sanju escorted them back out of Sitawadi.

Once they were out of Kajol's street, Ron said, 'Just think about this. This is what poor Kajol endures on a daily basis.'

They walked out of Sitawadi in silence, each of them contemplating how tough life was for these children.

Chapter 28

February 1997
Pune

Dearest, dearest Vidya,

You have no idea how happy your letter made me. I might have said this before, but I want to say it again—I am very proud of you. I am especially happy that you are considering writing the civil services exams. Well done!

You inspire me. After reading your letter, I felt that I ought to give the exams a shot too. But I will probably have to do it after a couple of years. The reason is, I have to complete my graduation first. I have to apply to write the supplementary exams, and then take time off from Sankalp to study for them. Right now, though, I get immense satisfaction and joy teaching these children, and I want to focus on that.

I cannot believe those aunties tried to match-make again, after the way you behaved the last time. Will they ever give up? What joy do they get trying to match-make like this? It seems to me that they are trapped in unhappy marriages and now they want others to be trapped the same way too.

You did absolutely the right thing by refusing to marry that widower. He might be a nice person, but I don't think you are ready for the responsibility of a child. You have so much that you want to achieve. I think the girls who want to marry him just want a free ticket out of Joshimath. How naive they are! They have no idea what complications marriage brings.

Now for my Sankalp news—we are conducting the mock exams next week. Kanika, Ron and I meticulously went through the question papers of the last ten years. Then we formed a 'question bank' or a 'question pool'. We studied the patterns in the questions asked, wrote down the 'most likely to be asked' ones, and have prepared the children accordingly. Or at least we have tried to. We have also set the question paper for the mock board exam, and it's the closest we can get to the actual question paper. I have a feeling the paper we set will be pretty close to what will be asked, as I can see patterns in the questions asked each year.

I hope these children do well. For many, their futures depend on this. For Aishwarya and Shalini, the company that has bought some of their artwork has promised them a scholarship for higher studies, and after they finish that, a job, if they score above 65 per cent. Both are delighted at the prospect.

I think I am more nervous than the children themselves about the mock boards. Of course, these marks that they score here do not count at all, but it does give an indication of things to come. The fact is, Ron, Kanika and I have put our hearts into this and we have been working very hard.

The other thing I want to tell you about—I heard from Suraj. He wrote about this girl in his office, and I got the sense that he probably likes her. He hasn't given any indication that they are in a relationship and hasn't said anything remotely like that. Yet, it is a feeling I get.

I have told him over and over that there can be nothing more than friendship between us. But I think you might have guessed, after our last meeting, when we spent time together at Shaniwar Wada, I thought I had something special with him. Now I completely feel like a goose for even thinking that way. I think I read far too much than I should have into a simple hug. And Vidya, I hate to admit this—I am so, so jealous of the girl he mentioned.

He says she is fun, smart and great to be around. God—I burned with jealousy when I read that. I hate that she gets to be with him, and I can't. I know I shouldn't feel this way. I know I should focus on my work at Sankalp. Yet, I am unable to control my feelings. I thank my lucky stars that I didn't get carried away and hold his hand or kiss him or do any such thing. You know, Vidya, I *wanted* to. So badly. But I refrained.

I haven't written to him. It's an ostrich's way of dealing with the problem. It is not that a solution will come out of my *not* writing to him. But for now, this is the best I can do. This jealousy that I feel—I have never experienced anything like it before. I detest it. I do not want to think about that stupid girl, and I don't want my friendship with Suraj to be affected because of her. Yet, I am not able to get over it or brush it aside. I am not sure what I should do about this.

Give my love to Vandu, Vaish and Ani.

That's all from my side for now.
Study well for your exams. Do well.
All my love,
Your rule-bending regretter sis,
Veda

Veda posted the letter to Vidya and hurried towards Ron's apartment.

The children were already working with Kanika and Ron when she got there.

'Didi, can you tell me what questions you will ask in the mock exam?' Sanju asked cheekily.

'Come on, Sanju, you know you are not allowed to ask that and I am not permitted to disclose it,' said Kanika.

Kanika was seated at the dining table, going through some assignments that had been submitted earlier. Veda joined her. Ron was in the kitchen, rustling up sandwiches for everybody. If the children were at Ron's house close to a meal time, he usually offered them something to eat.

'Sanju, it would be better if you focus on your work, rather than trying to figure out the questions,' Kanika said.

But Sanju wouldn't give up.

'Come on, didi, please tell. Tell only one question,' he pestered.

'No!' said Kanika.

'Please, Veda didi—tell Kanika didi to tell us one question?' he now addressed Veda.

'What is this, Sanju, do you want to leak the question paper beforehand?' asked Veda.

'Yes didi, I want to leak the question paper. I will sell the questions, and I will make a lot of money. Many children will pay me money for questions,' Sanju said.

'Good luck with that!' Veda laughed and shook her head.

'Thank you, didi,' replied Sanju, missing the sarcasm.

'Sanju, please focus on your work. You can do your question paper-leaking business later,' Kanika reprimanded him, her tone sharp.

That made Sanju back off, and for the rest of the evening he managed to focus on his books.

When the mock exams were conducted at the Sankalp premises, Kanika coached them about what to expect in the actual board exams.

'Remember, your final board exams will NOT be in your own school. It will be in a completely different school. Veda didi, Ron bhaiya and I will accompany you to your exam centres a week earlier, so that you will know how to get there. The environment will be different, but don't get nervous because of that. Just focus on the questions. Now, please pretend that this is your actual board exam. Remember to write ONLY your roll numbers and not your names. DON'T write any religious symbols like "Om" or a draw a cross at the start of the paper. Such things are not allowed. And in the English paper, for the letter-writing question, remember, you should NOT write your real names,' Kanika's instructions were precise and detailed.

The children nodded. A few nervously licked their lips. Sanju looked petrified. All the playfulness and bravado of the previous evening were gone now.

'Sanju, take a deep breath and relax,' Kanika said, noticing his anxiety.

'The children here take these things very seriously, don't they?' Ron whispered to Veda. They were both standing on one side of the classroom, with stacks of paper in their hands to distribute as answer sheets when Kanika rang the bell.

'Yes, they do. Class 10 is considered an important exam in India,' Veda whispered back.

Ron nodded. 'Yes, I understand. Back home, we have the O levels,' he said. 'But there isn't much pressure on the kids who take it. They have it easier there,' he added.

Soon, the examination started. Veda and Ron distributed the answer sheets and allowed the children the time to write their roll number and the dummy centre number which Kanika had allotted.

Then she rang another bell. That was the cue for Ron and Veda to distribute the question papers.

For the next hour and a half, the children were hunched

over, scribbling furiously on their answer sheets. Kajol didn't look up even once, and she kept asking for supplementary answer sheets. Sharan, Aishwarya, Zinia and all the others seemed to be handling it well too, judging by their focused faces as they concentrated hard and wrote. The only person who looked a little lost and confused was Sanju.

'Sanju, write,' Kanika had to remind him quite a few times. Sanju had completely blanked out.

'I ... I don't know any answers, didi,' he whispered, his face pale and panic-stricken.

'Just be calm and it will all come to you. Just think of everything we learnt,' Veda told him.

She wasn't sure if that helped or not, but Sanju wrote in the answer sheet after that. The first subject was English. There was an essay to be written as well as a letter. The students were given a choice of three topics for the essay, from which they had to pick one. For the letter writing, they were again given a choice between an official letter and a personal letter. Veda, Kanika and Ron had made the children practise the format for letter writing over and over, when they were teaching them.

'Remember, even if you make grammatical errors in your writing, you will score marks if the format is right,' Kanika had repeatedly told them.

Most of the students asked for additional answer sheets and seemed to be writing a lot. Veda noticed that Sanju wasn't doing that.

When the final bell rang, Kanika asked the students to stop writing. Some had not yet finished and wanted a little extra time. But Kanika was strict.

'You have to learn how to manage your time. They aren't going to give you extra time in the real board exams,' she said.

Veda and Ron collected all the answer sheets.

This process continued for the next five days, as they conducted mock examinations for all the subjects.

'Phew, that was so stressful for me. I can't imagine what the children went through,' said Ron, when the mock exams for all the subjects were done.

'Well, we have our work cut out for the next five days. We

have to correct all these papers, and mark them according to the answer keys,' said Kanika.

'Only five days?' asked Ron.

'Less, if possible. The faster we do it, the more time we have to work with the children before the final board exams,' Kanika replied.

'Gosh—you are a hard taskmaster,' Ron threw up his hands in mock despair.

'Aren't you glad you are not a student in her class?' quipped Veda, and both Ron and Kanika laughed. It was a big relief that the mock exams were done.

Over the next four days, Kanika and Veda went over to Ron's apartment and all three graded the papers. They worked long hours, and were done by the end of the fourth day.

Almost all the students had done well, except for Sanju. Sanju had simply copied the question paper three times for his English exam. For his maths exam, he had left a lot of questions unanswered, although Veda was fairly certain that he knew the concepts. Among the ones he had attempted, he had got many wrong. As a result, he failed in maths as well as in English.

Aparna personally went through the answer sheets of all the students. She was pleased with the overall performance, but she was aghast when she saw Sanju's papers.

'What happened to Sanju? I thought he was doing well in class?' she asked Kanika.

'Yes, he seemed fine in class; even I am not sure what happened,' Kanika replied.

'I would like to talk to him and find out. Will you ask him to meet me?' Aparna requested.

Kanika said that she would pass on the message, and ask him to meet her soon.

Aparna met Sanju in her office, without Veda, Ron or Kanika. Aparna felt that, without the teachers, he would be able to speak freely. But Sanju completely clammed up. He did not like Aparna, as she wasn't as friendly to the children as his didis and bhaiya.

'Are you not able to understand what didi and bhaiya are teaching?' Aparna asked him.

Sanju shook his head and refused to meet her eye.

'Sanju, look at me. Talk to me. I want to help you,' she said.

But Sanju wouldn't co-operate.

After trying her best, Aparna gave up. No matter how much she tried, Sanju just wouldn't open up. Aparna stressed that he had to perform well in the boards and asked him to study hard. Sanju just sat still, glaring at her, refusing to talk. When Aparna said he could leave, he ran almost all the way home, to Sitawadi.

Kajol was drying clothes when he reached home.

'Oye, Kajol,' he called out, panting.

'What? What did Aparna didi say?' she asked. She knew that Sanju had been nervous about meeting her.

'I didn't answer anything. She wanted to know why I did badly,' he said.

'Why did you do badly? I want to know also. In the class you were doing well. What happened in the exam?' asked Kajol.

'I … I don't know. I am going to fail the exam,' Sanju said.

'Just study and calm down and write, Sanju. It will be fine,' Kajol consoled him.

'I have studied. But when I read the question paper, everything I studied disappears. I … I can't remember anything,' Sanju sighed.

'Maybe you should just practise all the important questions,' said Kajol.

Sanju thought for a while. Then he said, 'There is one way, Kajol.'

'What?' she asked.

'To get the question paper,' Sanju replied, smiling nervously.

Kajol shook her head. 'And how will you do that?' she asked.

'I have my ways,' said Sanju. He looked determined.

'How, Sanju? Whom are you going to ask?'

'How does that matter? I am telling you, I will get the question paper. If you want it, I will give it to you for free.'

Sanju's lips were pursed and his expression was grim. He was serious about this. Kajol's brain worked furiously, quickly thinking about what Sanju could do. Then it occurred to her. It was obvious, when she thought about it.

Of course, he would approach Agni, the mafia don of Sitawadi. The mere mention of his name sent shivers down the spines of the residents. There were many rumours floating around about him. It was said that he had connections with the underworld dons of Mumbai, and that he was wanted in twelve murder cases and eighteen cases of kidnapping and extortion. But the police had not arrested him so far. Nobody in Sitawadi dared testify against Agni and nobody had the courage to report him or file a complaint against him. It was said that, many years ago, someone called Prasad had dared to report him. The next day, Prasad's body, stripped naked and throat slit, was hanging from the tree under which the residents gathered to play cards. Prasad's daughters had disappeared overnight, and his wife had gone mad, unable to bear the grief. His wife still lived in Sitawadi, and she wandered around with vacant eyes, unkempt hair and a broken spirit. Some said that Prasad's daughters were kept as sex-slaves in Agni's mansion. Others said they had been sold to brothels at Kamathipura. Nobody knew the truth. All the shopkeepers, restaurant owners and anyone running a business in Sitawadi had to pay a percentage of their earnings to his gang members, when they came for collection each month. Agni also collected *hafta* from the local cemetery. Anybody who wanted to perform the last rites for someone had to pay him first. The members of his gang had very often beaten up people for the flimsiest of reasons. The best way to survive in Sitawadi was to stay away from Agni and his gang.

Every child in Sitawadi knew this, and yet, here was Sanju talking about going to Agni. Was he crazy?

'Sanju, don't be silly. Are you actually thinking of going to Agni?'

'How does it matter, Kajol? Do you want the question paper or not?' Sanju asked.

'No. I don't want it. Don't be stupid, Sanju. It is a dangerous thing you are trying. You don't want to be caught in his net,' Kajol tried dissuading him.

But she might as well have saved her breath.

Sanju had already made up his mind.

Chapter 29

March 1997
Ron's apartment, Pune

There were only five days left for the board exams to begin.

Over the last week, Kanika, Veda and Ron had taken the children to the designated exam centre in small batches and familiarised them with the place. Since they had to travel in autos, each group consisted of six children. Two children and one adult travelled in an auto, and they made many trips. All the children had now seen the centre where they would take the exam. It was a school in the neighbourhood, which was much bigger than the one they attended. They found their roll numbers on the noticeboard of the school, but the classroom and where they were to be seated would be allotted only on the day of the exam, and it would change for each exam, to safeguard against malpractices. The children weren't too bothered about any of those details, though. They treated this like a fun outing and were excited about it.

The last of the briefings for the exams had taken place the previous evening, and from now on, till the exams got over, there wouldn't be any more classes at Sankalp for the Class 10 batch.

Once the children were done with all the exams, Kanika had promised them a picnic to Sinhagad, which they were excited about.

'How will we go, didi?' Sanju asked.

'We will hire a bus,' replied Kanika.

'A/C bus, didi?' persisted Sanju.

'Oye, Sanju—at least we are going on a picnic, be happy,' Sharan said.

'How can I be happy? I am Sanju,' he replied, and the whole class laughed.

Sanju didn't seem too apprehensive about the board exams, even though he had done badly in the mock exams. Kanika, Veda and Ron had spent extra time with him, coaching him, making him practise the sums over and over again. When they sat with him, he knew and wrote all the answers, and he wasn't nervous. But what Kanika was worried about was how he would perform when he had to do it on his own. Veda was certain that he was putting on a front, and that deep down he was terrified of the exams.

But they had done all that they could; now they could only hope for the best.

At Ron's apartment, Veda and Kanika discussed the performances of the students in the mock boards. 'I am a little disappointed,' confessed Kanika. 'I would have thought that, with all the coaching we gave them, they would have performed better.'

'Most of the students passed, didn't they? Then why do you say you are disappointed?' Ron asked, as he served them steaming mugs of black coffee and sandwiches.

'Ron, these are delicious. You should stop spoiling us,' Veda said.

'Indian hospitality has rubbed off on me,' Ron said, as he shrugged.

'Yes, these are lovely. Thank you, Ron,' said Kanika. 'Coming back to your question, I would have thought that the average marks scored in the mock boards would be 65 per cent. But the average was just 45 per cent,' she said, as she looked at the sheet of paper in her hand, staring at the calculations she had been making meticulously.

'Let's take the median rather than the average. So we can see the bell curve and which students are deviating,' Ron said.

'Sanju is the deviant!' said Veda and Kanika together, and they laughed.

'Sanju failed all the papers. Incredible,' said Veda.

'Oh, yes. Of course, Sanju is one of the major culprits for our low average. Any idea why he gets into a panic? And what was all that—the conversation with Aparna?' Ron asked.

'I honestly think Aparna talking to him was the silliest idea ever! He is afraid of her—of course, he did not open up to her. She was frustrated. She called me into her room after that conversation with him and said she couldn't get any insights. As though I did not know that!' Kanika rolled her eyes.

'I am guessing that she felt she had to "contribute" in some way. Maybe this is her way of taking responsibility,' said Veda.

'Right, just intimidate the students, and get them to perform,' Kanika replied.

Veda looked at her watch. It was already 7 p.m. She hadn't told either her mother-in-law or Bhuwan that there were no more classes at Sankalp till the exams got over. She didn't see any need to. She left home at the usual time each day, and went to Kanika's house. They would then go to a cafe or an eatery which Veda and Ron had never been to. Over the past few days, Veda and Ron had explored all the nice eating places that Pune had to offer—Cafe Goodluck, Subhadra, Kamath, Roopali, Vaishali, Marz-O-Rin, Savera, Deewar, Amrapali, the list ran on and on. It had become a daily routine for them. Today, for a change, they had decided to meet at Ron's apartment.

'I think I had better leave,' said Veda, as she lazily stretched out.

'Yes, me too; I told my mother that I would help her with something,' Kanika said.

Suddenly, there was a loud knock on the door.

THUMP. THUMP. THUMP.

Ron frowned, wondering who it was. Then the doorbell rang as well. It appeared that someone was leaning on the doorbell and holding it down. It rang continuously, the shrill urgent chime echoing through the apartment.

'One minute!' called out Ron, as he hurried to the door.

Ron gaped in astonishment at the sight that greeted him when he opened the door. Veda and Kanika could not see who it was, as Ron was blocking their view.

'Oh, good lord! What happened?' they heard him ask, as he stepped aside.

Standing before them, her face contorted in pain, a bruise on her forehead, dirt on her clothes and her face, her hair dishevelled, and her right arm bleeding, stood Kajol with tears in her eyes.

She was breathing hard and she couldn't speak.

'Oh my God. Come inside, Kajol. Come, sit,' said Veda, as she rushed to her.

Kajol walked in holding her right arm up. She grimaced in pain as her left arm supported her right and she took one hesitant step after the other. Her lips trembled as she struggled to control her emotions. She hobbled to the sofa and sat down.

Ron rushed to the kitchen to get the first aid box. Kanika poured out a glass of water and gave it to Kajol. Kajol tried to extend her right arm to hold the glass, but her face contorted with the effort.

'What happened, Kajol? Are you okay? Here, drink,' said Kanika, as she held the glass to the girl's mouth. Kajol drank, taking in large gulps.

'Didi, Sanju ... didi ... Agni ... stop him...' Kajol managed to say once she finished drinking the water, the words tumbling out in disjointed fragments. Kanika saw that Kajol was so perturbed that she couldn't speak coherently. She was making no sense whatsoever.

'Listen Kajol, please take deep breaths, and calm down. You have to tell us what happened so we can understand,' said Kanika.

'Didi, Sanju said he is getting the question paper from Agni.'

'Who is Agni?'

'Bad man, didi ... He is very bad man. The hotel Sanju works in, it is owned by Venkat Rao. He is from Agni's gang, didi. They are *goondas*,' Kajol grimaced as she said the words. Her arm had begun to hurt again. The pain was intense.

Kanika, Veda and Ron looked puzzled. Who was this Agni, and why would he have the question paper? And what had happened to Kajol's arm? These questions raced through their minds and it was Ron who spoke.

'Kajol—what happened to your arm? You seem to be badly hurt,' he said.

'Paining, bhaiya. Very bad pain. I tried to stop Sanju, but he pushed me. He fought with me,' Kajol said.

The story was emerging in bits and pieces now. Kanika, Ron and Veda were putting it together like a jigsaw puzzle.

'Did you fall down and hurt your arm?' Veda asked.

'I fell, and there was a cycle parked on the side. My leg hit the cycle, and the cycle fell on my arm,' said Kajol.

'But Kajol, why will this Agni have the question paper? And why will he give it to Sanju?' Ron asked.

'He sells it, bhaiya. Question paper leaking. It's a business for him, and Sanju went to buy it.'

Ron did not understand what 'question paper leaking' meant. He looked at Kanika for an explanation.

'It means you can buy the question paper that's been set for an exam through illegal methods, for a huge sum. This is a racket, where some unscrupulous people make money; so some of the children taking the exam know the questions in advance, and hence, have an unfair advantage,' Kanika explained.

'Didi. Stop Sanju fast. Agni—he is not a good man,' said Kajol, slumping into the sofa in pain. Her head had begun to hurt and her arm was throbbing.

'Let's first get some first aid for you. We need to take you to the hospital. Your arm—it looks pretty bad,' said Ron.

Ron called the security personnel in his building and got a taxi organised. When it arrived, Ron sat in the front seat, and Kajol sat between Veda and Kanika.

In the cab, Kajol told them the whole story. She said that Sanju had been very worried about the examinations. He had confided in her that he would try and get the question papers. She told them about Agni, and how everybody in Sitawadi had to pay him money, and how the very mention of his name frightened people. She said it was a terrible idea to get involved with him, and that she was extremely worried for Sanju. Sanju had just scoffed and said that he was heading to meet Agni right then, and that he wasn't scared of anybody.

All this had taken place in front of Sanju's house. Kajol had physically blocked his path and told him that she would not let him go. Sanju had warned her to step out of the way, but Kajol had not listened. She stood in the doorway and said she wouldn't let him go. But Sanju had pushed her and run out. Kajol had fallen and her leg had hit the neighbour's cycle which was leaning against the wall, sending it crashing on her arm. Her hair had got caught in the handlebars.

'Why didn't you go home and tell your mother?' asked Kanika.

'My mother was not at home, didi. Also, what is the use? If I tell her, she will tell me not to get involved with Sanju's business, especially if I mention Agni's name,' said Kajol.

Her arm had swollen up by then, and it looked strangely out of shape. Kajol was still holding it up with her left hand. That the pain was increasing was obvious.

Kanika was worried. So were Ron and Veda. As soon as they reached Jehangir Hospital, they took Kajol to the emergency Out Patient Department. The people at the reception said that one of them could take Kajol inside while the others filled the forms. She was asked to sit on one of the beds in the OPD and Veda stood by her side. Ron waited outside with Kanika while she filled the forms.

A nurse came and took Kajol's temperature and checked her blood pressure. She recorded the readings on a sheet of paper, which went into a file. After about ten minutes, the doctor on duty came and examined Kajol.

She looked young and she was friendly. She listened carefully to what had happened and wrote down the details on a chart. She said that she suspected a fracture and that they would have to go to the orthopaedic department and take x-rays.

Veda and Kanika accompanied Kajol for the x-rays. By then, Kajol was in excruciating pain.

The orthopaedic doctor came by and looked at the x-rays.

'I'm afraid it's a type of Monteggia fracture,' he said.

He showed them the x-rays and explained how the bone was dislocated and broken. 'The good thing is, we can manage this without surgery. She is still not an adult, and it will heal very fast,' he said.

He added that Kajol would need a cast.

'Oh no, doctor! She has her board exams in five days!' Kanika said in dismay. 'Will she be able to write them?'

'Five days? No, no. Her arm will be in a cast. She will need about six to eight weeks at least, for this to completely heal. I am afraid she will not be able to use this arm,' she said.

Kajol looked at Kanika helplessly, her eyes welling up with tears.

'Didi—board exam...' she said.

'It's ... it's okay, Kajol. We will do something,' said Kanika.

'What, didi? What can we do?' asked Kajol.

Kanika didn't have any answers.

Ron and Veda did not know what to say either. They looked at Kajol helplessly, as her shoulders slumped in defeat. The hospital attendant wheeled her away to have a cast put on her arm.

Chapter 30

March 1997
Jehangir Hospital, Pune

When Kajol came out of the orthopaedic department, her right arm was in a cast. There was a sling around her neck and the encased arm rested in it. She was crying silently.

Kanika rushed towards her as soon as she saw her, and gave her a half-hug. Even though Kajol could walk, the hospital attendant said that they had to take the patient around in a wheelchair till they were ready to leave the hospital. Kanika took care of the final formalities. The doctor had prescribed a few painkillers and Veda and Ron picked these up from the hospital pharmacy.

On their way back, Kajol was still sniffling, using the arm of her kurta to wipe her nose. The tears just wouldn't stop.

'Didi—I will not be able to give the exams,' she said.

'We will see,' said Kanika. A plan was forming in her head, but it was too early to talk about it. Also, she did not want to give Kajol false hope.

'How, didi?' asked Kajol, between sobs.

'Have patience dear, and a little faith,' said Kanika.

'Didi—the money for hospital. Thank you for paying. I will pay you back, didi,' said Kajol. She remembered that Kanika and Veda had paid for everything.

'Kajol, don't even worry about it,' said Veda, and Kanika agreed with her.

'What do we do about Sanju?' Kajol asked.

'If Sanju has gone to see this—what's his name—already, I don't think we can do anything, can we?' asked Ron.

'Yes, you are right, Ron. Agni—his name is Agni,' said Kanika.

'Ag-knee. What does that mean?' asked Ron. He pronounced the 'Ag' so that it rhymed with 'Bag'.

Kanika corrected the way he pronounced it. 'It means fire,' she said.

'Is he a dangerous criminal? Is that why you are worried, Kajol?' Ron asked.

'He is very bad, Ron bhaiya. He has murdered people. He is a *goonda*. Everybody is scared of him,' Kajol said.

'Why doesn't anyone complain to the police?' Ron was baffled. He had no idea what a '*goonda*' meant.

'He pays all the policemen. Policemen will not arrest him. If you complain against him, they will make out a false report against you and put you in jail,' Kajol explained.

Ron was only now beginning to comprehend the gravity of the situation. But Kanika and Veda understood it all too well.

'He is the local don. He kind of rules the area and everyone has to listen to him,' Kanika elaborated for Ron.

'So does he rule over your area too? Don't I stay in the same area? Then how is it that I haven't heard of this Ag-nee?' Ron was trying to grasp the intricacies of the situation.

'Let's just say there is a huge class divide in India. He typically rules over the lower economic strata, as they are powerless. People like us live in residential complexes, which are insulated from things like this,' Kanika explained.

'That is just so unfair then,' Ron said in anger.

'It is, and more than unfair, it is sad,' Veda replied.

'What do we do, didi—about Sanju?' Kajol asked again.

'I think the best we can do is to inform his father,' Kanika said.

'No, didi. His father hits him with a belt. And one more thing, didi,' Kajol hesitated, unsure as to whether she should say it or not.

'Yes, Kajol. Go on. Tell us,' Kanika coaxed her.

'Didi—please don't tell anyone. Sanju—he stole money,' Kajol blurted out.

'Stole money? From whom? And for what?' Kanika was taken aback. Veda and Ron looked stunned as well.

'He stole from his father, didi. His father was going to buy new seat cover for his auto-rickshaw. So he had the money at home. Sanju stole it. He told me, didi, and showed me the notes. He said he would get the question paper. Then he would make photocopies, sell them, and earn back the money. His plan was to replace the money.'

'Good lord!' exclaimed Ron.

'So why did he show it to you, if he stole it? I would have thought that he would hide it,' Veda asked.

'Didi, I said I did not believe him when he told me he had money. I told him he was lying. That was when he showed me the money. He ... he had hid it, didi. In his underwear,' Kajol said, a little shyly.

'Oh, I see! And that was when you tried to stop him?' Kanika asked.

'Yes, didi. That's when I knew for sure that he was serious. I said I will not let him go,' Kajol confirmed.

Kanika took a minute to absorb this information. She wasn't sure what to do about Sanju. She decided she would focus on Kajol first.

'Listen, Kajol—I am going to see what can be done about your exam, okay? We have all put in such a lot of effort, and we can't let it go to waste. I am not sure yet, but please come and meet me at Ron bhaiya's house tomorrow evening, and we will let you know what can be done, alright?' said Kanika.

The car had reached the arch at Sitawadi, and Kajol said she would make her way home from there.

'Kajol, about Sanju. Let's wait and see. For all you know, he might have changed his mind, or he might not have been able to meet Agni. Anything could have happened, right? You go home safely now and take care of yourself. Here are your medicines and here's your prescription,' Kanika said, as she handed them over to Kajol.

Kajol took it with her left hand. Her eyes were red from all the crying, and she looked miserable.

Veda was distressed at the turn of events and so were Ron and Kanika.

'So, what can we do about it? What is your plan?' asked Ron, as they emerged from the taxi and walked back to the intersection of the road. From here, Kanika and Veda had to go in the opposite direction as that was where Kailash Mandir Colony was situated. Ron's apartment was across the road.

'I have heard of this system, where if a student is indisposed, or if they suddenly fall ill, they can still take the examination with the help of a scribe. The school education system is sensitive to the needs of students with disabilities. So, usually, blind children give the exams with a scribe. Another person can write the exam for them, and they dictate the answers. I am wondering why the same can't be applicable to Kajol as she is handicapped temporarily. I think we should try and approach the school education department to see what can be done,' said Kanika.

'Oh, that's wonderful, if it can be done! I can be her scribe,' said Ron.

'Well, let me inform Aparna. Once she gives us the go-ahead, we could try and meet the deputy director of education tomorrow. I don't see any other way out of this,' said Kanika.

'I will go with you,' Veda volunteered.

'Oh, me too,' said Ron.

'So let's meet here. Tomorrow at 8.30 in the morning?' asked Kanika.

'That sounds like a plan,' said Ron.

By the time Veda got back home, it was well past 9.30. Bhuwan was not yet home, but Padma Devi was waiting for her. The door was left open and she was sitting in the living room, looking up every now and then to see if Veda was back.

The moment Veda entered, Padma Devi said, 'Give a camel an inch, and it will take the whole tent. Is this any time for you to get back home?'

'Maaji, I have told Bhuwan that we have to be there for the students for the exams, and that I would be coming late. I had informed you too,' said Veda, as she walked in, removed her slippers, and placed her handbag on the sofa. She was exhausted from the day's events, and the last thing she wanted was to give a long explanation to her mother-in-law.

'I hope you have eaten, Maaji? What is for dinner? I have had a long, tiring day, and I am hungry,' said Veda, as she walked towards the dining table.

'I have eaten. You can go help yourself. The food is on the dining table,' Padma Devi said gruffly.

Veda washed her hands and sat down to eat. She did not even think about how she was no longer as scared of her mother-in-law as she used to be. Her mind was preoccupied, worrying about whether Kajol would be able to get a scribe.

Kanika knew where the Department of Education offices were located. In the course of setting up this Sankalp centre, she had met the deputy director, Mr Palekar, a few times with Aparna, to let them know about the organisation's activities. Mr Palekar was a pleasant man, and he had always been helpful.

Veda and Kanika met Ron at the intersection as agreed.

'I called Aparna this morning and she was aghast. Kajol is our star student. She was in complete agreement with our plan,' Kanika informed them.

'I do hope we succeed in getting her a scribe,' said Veda.

They took an auto to Bhabha Saheb Ambedkar Road, where the offices were located.

'Shikshan Upasanchalak Karyalaya,' Kanika read the board in Marathi, and directed the auto-driver to take them to the education offices. It was a pale yellow, one-storey building. The peon made them wait for about forty-five minutes, saying, 'Sahib is busy.'

'Do you think he wants a bribe?' Veda whispered to Kanika.

'No, this is how it is here. We have to wait,' sighed Kanika.

After another fifteen minutes, they were shown inside. Mr Palekar recognised Kanika immediately.

'Welcome, welcome, Kanikaji. Please take a seat. How are things?' he asked.

'Thank you, Palekar *sahib*. Things are going very well. These are my colleagues. This is Veda and this is Ronald. Both of them teach at Sankalp too,' Kanika said.

'Which country are you from?' asked Mr Palekar, as he shook Ron's hand.

'I'm from England,' said Ron.

'How are you liking India?' asked Mr Palekar.

'It is such a wonderful country. I love it,' said Ron. Then he explained how he had stayed back to help coach Sankalp students.

'Very nice to know,' said Mr Palekar.

Kanika then explained the reason for their visit. She said that Kajol was one of their brightest students. She had brought along Kajol's answers sheets from the mock board exams and she now handed them to Mr Palekar.

'See sir, see for yourself how well this girl writes. She definitely does not deserve to lose a year because of her fracture. Could she please have a scribe and write the exams?' Kanika asked.

'I volunteer to be her scribe,' Ron piped up, before Mr Palekar could answer.

'You?' Mr Palekar looked surprised.

'Yes. I would love to,' Ron said.

'See—that's very kind of you. But these things are not so simple. We have rules for taking a scribe. The rules specify that the scribe has to be two classes lower than the student, so you do not qualify, Mr Ronald,' Mr Palekar said firmly.

'Oh, I see. But how will a Class 8 student write the exam for a Class 10 student?' Ron asked.

'I do not make these rules. We have to follow them. The Class 8 student has to only write what is dictated. They don't have to understand. So what is the problem?' Mr Palekar looked a little annoyed.

Kanika indicated to Ron with her eyes that she would handle it.

Ron did not miss the cue.

'Yes, right, sorry!' Ron said.

'Also, in case of a sudden accident, like that of your student, you will need to produce a medical certificate by a medical officer of a rank not less than an assistant surgeon from a government hospital. Then there are other formalities, like registering the name of the scribe. We have to also arrange for a separate room and a separate invigilator. It's not so simple,' Mr Palekar explained.

'Sir, we would be extremely grateful to you. You hold the future of a girl child in your hands, sir,' Kanika said. Her tone, her body language—all of it had changed to become as ingratiating as possible.

Ron and Veda did not miss it. They followed suit.

'We would be highly obliged, Mr Palekar. I know it is complicated, but could you please help us out?' said Ron.

'Sir, we will get all the necessary paperwork done. Please sir, help us,' said Veda.

Mr Palekar sat up a bit straighter in his chair and leaned back.

'Normally, the application has to be submitted many days in advance. We have to get permission from concerned officials.'

'But the fracture happened just yesterday evening. And we have come as soon as we could, sir,' Kanika said.

Mr Palekar scratched his chin and thought for a minute.

'Hmm ... Since this is a deserving case, I will see what I can do. Get the papers and submit them here, today itself. The board exams start in four days. We don't have any time to waste,' he said.

'Thank you so much, we will do the needful,' Kanika said.

'Much obliged,' said Ron.

Veda too thanked him.

Once they were out of earshot, Kanika said, 'You are a fast learner, Ron. I noticed how quickly you changed your tone.'

'Ha! I was only following your lead. How did you learn to speak like that?' asked Ron, and he imitated Kanika, exaggerating her pose and adopting a subservient tone. 'Please sir ... help us,' he mimicked.

'Well, we got our work done!' said Kanika, as she joined in the laughter.

'Now, who do we get as a scribe? We need someone from Class 8, according to the rules,' Veda said, as they got into an auto to head back.

'Do you have any suggestions? You work with the junior classes, don't you? Any bright kids out there?' Ron asked.

Veda thought about all the junior students she had worked with. One name stood out. 'Preksha. She is smart and hardworking. She also has good handwriting. Let's ask her if she will be Kajol's scribe,' said Veda.

When they reached Sitawadi, Kanika and Veda decided to go to Kajol's house and take her to the government hospital to get a medical certificate. Ron offered to come along, but Kanika and Veda said they would manage.

'We don't want Kajol's father to punch you once again,' said Kanika.

'God no, I don't want that either,' said Ron.

Veda and Kanika went to Kajol's home and gave her the news. She was happy to see them and to hear about the possibility of getting a scribe. She said she knew where Preksha lived, and all of them made their way to Preksha's home.

Seeing the didis in her home, unexpectedly, was a big moment for Preksha.

'Ma, come here. See—these are my didis,' she proudly introduced Veda and Kanika to her mother.

Preksha's mother insisted on serving them tea. She was happy that her daughter was chosen to be the scribe, and she told Preksha that she should accept.

Getting the medical certificate from the government hospital took another two hours. Except for the fact that they had to wait in queue, it wasn't very hard. After that, they went back to the deputy director's office.

By six in the evening, all the paperwork was ready. Mr Palekar handed over the necessary documents to them.

'Thank you so much, sir, this means a lot,' said Kanika.

'It is our duty to help. That is what we are here for. All the best to Kajol,' he said.

Veda and Kanika were overjoyed. They couldn't wait to get back and tell Ron.

Kajol would be able to give the exams. At last, she had a scribe.

Chapter 31

March 1997
Kailash Mandir Colony, Pune

Ever since Bhuwan had hired a cook, Padma Devi had stopped asking Veda to make tea. She would sit in the drawing room on the sofa and call out to the cook, 'Niranjan—one cup masala tea please', and Niranjan would happily oblige.

Padma Devi had never had a cook before. When her husband was alive, and she broached the subject with him, he would dismiss it as wasteful expenditure. 'Now, if you were working, I could understand; but why employ a cook when you are at home all the time?' he would say. Over the years, Padma Devi had accepted that he would never agree to it, and she had become resigned to being chained to the kitchen all the time. When Bhuwan had got married and Veda had come into the house, Padma Devi had derived great pleasure in having someone to 'order around'. Now she had transferred what she had designated as 'Veda's job' to Niranjan.

Veda was not completely off the hook, though. Whenever Padma Devi caught her sitting in her room, her aches and pains would suddenly start, and Veda had to press her feet.

But, of late, Veda had been so busy with Sankalp that she hardly spent time at home. On the rare occasions that she was at home, and Padma Devi asked, Veda did it uncomplainingly, even though she did not feel any great affection for the old lady. She did it out of a sense of duty. The most important thing was that Padma Devi's demands had stopped bothering Veda the way they used to.

That morning, Shakubai was late as usual, and that set Padma Devi off on her usual rant. 'I think I should start looking for another maid. She takes me for granted,' she grumbled, as she sat on the sofa, drinking her tea.

'I think you should stick with her. She is honest and reliable. Even if she is a bit late, how does it matter?' said Bhuwan, looking up from his newspaper.

Veda sat opposite him, going through the class plans for the junior classes. Sankalp had wanted to start summer workshops for the children this year, during their two months of vacation. Veda and the other teachers had been asked to submit reports of the activities they thought could be feasible. Since she was free in the morning and did not have kitchen duties anymore, Veda had taken to doing her work on the balcony, where she sat with Bhuwan.

The doorbell rang, and even though Padma Devi was seated on the sofa right next to the door, she called out to Niranjan.

'See who it is, Niranjan,' she said, knowing well that it had to be Shakubai.

Niranjan wiped his hands on a kitchen towel and opened the door.

It was Shakubai, but with her was Kajol.

As she walked in, Padma Devi said, 'You can't keep walking in here at any time you choose,' she said. Then she spotted Kajol with her arm in a cast.

'What happened to her?' she asked.

'I fell down, madam. Can I please speak to Veda didi?' Kajol answered Padma Devi, while Shakubai hurried into the kitchen.

Veda heard her and called her out to the balcony. But Kajol hesitated. Veda could see that Kajol was not comfortable speaking in front of Padma Devi and Bhuwan. So she stood up and motioned for Kajol to follow her to her bedroom.

'What happened, Kajol? How is your arm?' Veda asked.

'The pain is slightly better today, didi. But it's very uncomfortable. Didi—Sanju did not come home last night. I am worried, didi.'

'What? How do you know?'

'I went to his house at around 10.30 p.m. yesterday. His stepmother was there. His father was not around. I asked her where he was and she said she did not know. This morning, I went again. His father was there and he was angry because he knew that his money was missing. He asked me if I knew where Sanju was. I did not tell them anything, didi.'

'Oh, God!' said Veda. She wondered what to do about this.

'Didi, please don't tell Sanju's father that Sanju took the money.'

'I won't, but doesn't his father suspect it already?'

'I don't know, didi. He is very angry. But he does not care about Sanju. He only cares about the money. Please didi, we have to find Sanju,' Kajol pleaded.

'Let's go and tell Kanika. We will figure out what to do,' said Veda.

She told Bhuwan that she had to go to Sankalp as there were some formalities that needed to be completed so Kajol could use a scribe.

Bhuwan looked up, surprised. 'Aren't you having your breakfast?' he asked.

Veda had completely forgotten about it.

'Eat and then leave, madam. Hot *pooris* and *bhaji* is ready,' said Niranjan, as he placed two containers on the table, one full of *pooris* and the other with potato curry.

'Please eat, didi. I will wait,' said Kajol.

'What about you, Kajol? Would you like to have some breakfast?' Veda asked.

'No didi—I finished eating,' said Kajol.

'Are you joining me?' Veda asked Bhuwan, but he said he would have breakfast later.

'Maaji, what about you?' asked Veda.

'Let the working people eat first. We don't have any urgency. We old folk can always eat later,' said Padma Devi.

Veda wasn't sure if that was intended as a jibe. But she was in too much of a hurry to get to Kanika. She wolfed down two *pooris* with potato *bhaji*, and drank a glass of water.

'Didi, tea?' asked Niranjan.

'No, Niranjan, I have to go,' said Veda, as she picked up her bag and rushed out with Kajol.

They rang Kanika's doorbell, and it was she who answered the door.

'Oh!' she said, as she hadn't expected to see either Veda or Kajol. 'Come inside.'

Once they were seated, Veda repeated what Kajol had just told her.

'What do we do?' asked Veda.

'I think we have to tell Sanju's father the truth,' said Kanika.

'No, didi. Please don't do that. Sanju's father is UNREASONABLE. He will hit Sanju with his belt. His stepmother also treats him badly. That was the reason he started working at the hotel,' Kajol said, in tears.

'Good lord—what a terrible fiasco. And honestly, all Sanju had to do was to study instead doing all this,' Kanika shook her head.

'He studies a lot, didi. But he blanks out when he sees a question paper,' said Kajol.

'I wish we had talked to him and helped him get over his fears,' said Veda.

Kanika nodded.

'How about we go and ask that hotel owner, Venkat Rao, where Sanju is? We can say he was supposed to come to Sankalp for extra coaching, and then see what he says? We won't tell him anything else,' said Kanika.

'Okay, didi, let's do that,' said Kajol.

'Do you think we should let Ron know?' asked Veda.

'Yes, Ron can come along, if he is not too intimidated,' Kanika said.

'My father is not there, didi. He has gone to work,' Kajol said, immediately understanding what Kanika was implying. She still felt very sorry about the whole incident.

'Alright, let's go. Give me a few minutes,' said Kanika.

'Where's Shanta aunty?' Veda said.

'Oh, she is visiting her sister in Kerala,' called out Kanika, from her bedroom, as she changed her clothes.

'I hear it is a beautiful place,' said Veda.

'It is. It is lovely. Some day you must visit,' said Kanika, emerging from her bedroom. She had combed her hair and changed into a smart salwar kurta.

'Come, let's go,' she said, as she led the way.

They went to Ron's apartment and told him what had happened.

'I think we have to investigate. We have to go and speak to this Venkat Rao,' agreed Ron.

A little later, a mini procession consisting of Veda, Ron and Kanika, with Kajol leading them, made their way through the main street of Sitawadi. People paused to stare at Kajol. Some asked, 'Hey Kajol, what happened?'

'I fell down. Have you seen Sanju?' she asked each one who greeted her. She must have asked at least eleven people the question.

But they shook their heads. Nobody had seen Sanju.

They reached Venkat Rao's hotel. The hotel was a tiny, nondescript hall, about 20' x 15' which opened out into the street. In front of it was a collapsible signboard that jutted out onto the street, which said 'Balaji Hotel'. It was a small place, dark inside, with fading light-yellow paint on the walls. The plaster was peeling off in many places, and there were cracks on the wall. At one end of the room stood a low wooden table with large aluminium vessels that were covered with aluminium plates.

Outside the building, to one side of the hotel, a thin man wearing a green vest, a red towel thrown on a shoulder, stood next to a large, flat pan. He was scrambling eggs on it. The iron ladle that he held in his hand made a rat-at-a-tat-a-tat sound as he scrambled them deftly at top speed, like a machine.

Inside the hotel, cheap plastic chairs were arranged neatly around Formica-topped tables. Though the hotel was tiny and dark, it was surprisingly clean.

The man in the green vest looked up as Veda, Ron and Kanika approached him. He recognised that these were not his usual customers and he stared curiously at them. Then he spotted Kajol.

'*Oye—kya hua, Kajol?*' he asked, pointing at her arm.

To Kajol, it seemed like she was answering this question for the millionth time.

'Fell down, Vijay bhaiya. Where is Sanju?' she asked, speaking in Marathi.

'He didn't turn up for work. I don't know where he is,' he said, a bit too quickly, as he shiftily looked to the left and right. He was afraid of being seen talking to them.

It was obvious to Kajol as well as to the others that he was withholding information.

He definitely knew something about Sanju.

'When did you last see him?' asked Kajol.

'I don't remember,' Vijay said, and continued scrambling the eggs.

Kanika knew that there was only one way to make him talk. She took out two one hundred-rupee notes and quietly extended them to him, lowering her hand, so that the large pan he was cooking on blocked the view.

'Vijay bhaiya, please tell us anything you know. His exams are in three days,' Kanika pleaded.

Vijay furtively glanced around, and in a second, he pocketed the money.

They looked at him expectantly.

'Meet me at 11.30 a.m., near the arch. Today I get off duty then. I can't talk here,' said Vijay. 'And go inside and order something now,' he said.

Kanika and Veda looked at each other and nodded.

'Come Ron, this is one hotel in Pune you haven't tried out,' Kanika said.

Ron smiled. 'Yes, I've always wanted to try this one out, but haven't had a chance to,' he said, shaking his head.

They went inside, sat down and ordered four cups of tea.

The other diners looked at them curiously.

'We are from Sankalp. We came to campaign for children to join,' Kanika addressed them.

'What is this Sankalp?' asked one of the men, who was digging into a *misal pav.*

'It's like a free tuition, Bhavu—but only better,' Kajol replied.

'Free tuition?' he asked, disbelievingly.

'Yes,' said Kanika, and she explained Sankalp's mission and objectives in Marathi. She then handed out some brochures, printed in Marathi. Vijay too turned to look inside, to listen to Kanika. She had a small audience, and she managed to convince many of the diners to bring their children to Sankalp. She did all this even before they finished their tea.

'I am very impressed, Kanika. Do you always walk around with those brochures in your bag?' asked Ron.

'Always. You never know when you might meet the parent of a potential student,' said Kanika, shrugging.

After they finished their tea, they headed to Ron's apartment, where they waited till 11.30. Then they made their way to the arch. They wondered what Vijay knew about Sanju, and whether he would have any useful information. But it was mere speculation. They wouldn't know till they spoke to him.

'Didi, I am so nervous,' said Kajol.

'It's okay. We will find out soon. It seems like he has some information,' said Kanika.

'Do you think he will turn up? After all, we have already given him the money,' said Ron.

'Oh yes, he will turn up,' replied Kanika.

'How do you know?' asked Ron.

'You just know, Ron. People are honest here, that way,' Kanika assured him.

Ron was puzzled. Here was a man who was taking money for divulging information that they needed. And yet, Kanika trusted that he would show up. India worked in strange, mysterious ways that he did not understand.

They waited near the arch for Vijay, their eyes squinting in the hot sun, hoping he would turn up soon. Ten minutes later, Vijay arrived. He walked with a limp. He had changed out of his earlier attire, which Veda guessed were his working clothes. He was wearing a shirt and trousers now.

'Where can we talk?' he asked, glancing around. He spoke the Mumbaiya dialect of Hindi. Veda thought that he sounded exactly like the people they depicted in Bollywood gangster movies.

'Let's go to a restaurant and sit inside?' suggested Kanika. She did not want to take Vijay to Ron's apartment, as she was not sure about the kind of person Vijay was.

They went to their regular coffee shop and ordered fresh lime sodas for everyone.

'I can give you all the information, but it will cost more money,' said Vijay shrewdly. He had taken in the surroundings and thought he would hike up his price.

'What? How do we know that what you have to say is useful?' Kanika asked.

Vijay said, 'Madam—whatever I tell you is right. He came

yesterday, asking about question papers. I know everything about it, as I used to run the operation for Agni dada. I was a driver, madam.'

Vijay hitched up his trousers to show them a scar running from the back of his left knee, right down to his ankle. 'See this? Last year, I was injured, and I am unable to use this leg. That's why Agni dada got Venkat Rao to employ me. Your boy Sanju—I know where he is likely to have gone. I told you—he turned up yesterday, asking about the question papers. Now you decide whether this information is worth it or not,' said Vijay, as he leaned back in the chair and sipped the cold lemonade.

Kanika, Veda and Ron exchanged looks. There was no doubt in anyone's mind. Ron reached into his wallet and took out ten hundred-rupee notes, holding them like a fan and waving them in front of Vijay.

'Will this do?' Ron asked.

It was impossible not to miss the gleam in Vijay's eyes as he looked at the notes.

He nodded.

'Talk,' said Ron, as Vijay pocketed the money.

Chapter 32

March 1997
Cafe near Sitawadi, Pune

'Look, I have some conditions. The first is that nobody should know about this. If the police ask me anything, I will deny that I met you. The second is, you cannot ask for proof of anything that I am going to tell you. You can either believe me or not believe me. The third is that you listen to me without interruptions,' Vijay said.

Ron concentrated, trying hard to understand what Vijay was saying.

'I will translate for you later, Ron,' Veda whispered to him.

'What did you say?' Vijay turned towards Veda and asked sharply.

'Just that I would translate for him later,' said Veda.

'Hmmm, okay,' Vijay frowned.

'Vijay bhaiya. We believe you and we will not interrupt,' Kanika said, eager to get the information. She gestured to Veda and Ron to be quiet. Kajol sat as still as a rock, listening to every word.

'See, I know all about this question paper-leaking business,' said Vijay.

Kanika nodded encouragingly, hiding her impatience. She thought he was showing off.

'The question papers are set in Pune, the headquarters of the education board, two months before the board exams. Strict confidentiality is maintained. The people who set the paper—they discuss, debate, revise and agree. A month before the exam, they are sent to a printing press. Now, the location of this printing press is not revealed to anyone, except to the education officers. After it gets printed, the question papers and the answer sheets are dispatched in batches to various divisions in cities such as Mumbai, Pune, Nashik, Nagpur, Kolhapur, etc. Just a few days before the exams start, the boards of these cities send these bundles to "custody centres". The custody centre will allot spare rooms to store the papers. There will be one policeman, one board official and two peons, who will accompany each truck to the custody centre. The policeman is fully armed, mind you. The policeman and the education officer will keep vigil the whole time at the custody centre. About four hours before the exam begins, the question papers are taken from the custody centre to the exam centre. The seal is opened only when the exam begins. Do you understand the process?' Vijay asked.

Kanika took a deep breath. 'Wow—I had no idea. Yes. I understand,' she said. Vijay indeed knew the process in detail.

'Can you now see at which points it can leak, and how easy it is for someone with Agni dada's reach to get hold of a copy?' Vijay asked.

'Yes,' Kanika nodded.

'I was one of the drivers that Agni dada "placed". I was the one who was driving the van from Pune to Nashik till last year.'

'Oh, I see,' said Kanika.

'It was a well-planned operation. We have our regular people for making a copy. All I had to do was stop at a designated point for a tea break and leave the back of the truck unlatched. In fifteen minutes, once I finished my tea and toilet break, I would leave. Agni dada would have got the question paper in two hours.'

'What a well-oiled operation,' said Kanika. Veda, Ron and Kajol just listened with rapt attention.

'Yes, but last year I was attacked. It was one of Agni dada's rivals. His men stopped me, and they wanted me to open the door of the van, as they wanted a share in the question paper business. Have you heard of Muthanna?'

Kanika shook her head.

'It was Muthanna's men. I had a narrow escape. I managed to deliver the question papers, but business was badly hit, as Muthanna too had got copies. So, this year, instead of making copies in a centre in proper Pune, the copies are being made in an isolated shed behind Maldhakka goods yard. And that is probably where you will find your boy—what is his name? Sanju?'

'Yes, Sanju,' said Kanika.

'Now, why I went into this much detail—it is because I wanted you to know that it is a serious business, and I know what I am talking about. This boy Sanju came yesterday and insisted on seeing Agni dada. I told him to go away, but he wouldn't listen. Then he pestered Venkat Rao so much, and also showed him some money. He said he could pay. Venkat Rao told one of his guys to take Sanju to Maldhakka. I am not sure what happened after that. But that was where he was last headed,' said Vijay.

'Will you tell us how to get to the shed?' Kanika asked. Her heart was beating rapidly, having heard all this information.

'It's not hard to find. You can go to the railway yard. You will see it about a thousand metres away from where they load the trains. It is a large godown-like structure, grey in colour, no windows. It is a massive shed, fully secured.'

'But Sanju—he could have left after getting the question paper,' Kanika said.

Vijay looked at her. Was she daft? He couldn't believe what she was saying.

'Why did I explain to you so much in detail? Why?' he asked.

'Eh…?' Kanika was puzzled.

'Your boy—did he come back?'

'No—of course, not. That's why we are asking you.'

'So, understand what might have taken place. I can only tell you this much. I have to leave now. Thank you for the juice,' he said, and he stood up, pushing back the chair.

Kanika, Veda, Ron and Kajol stared at him wordlessly as he limped his way out of the coffee shop.

'Didi, did you understand what he was trying to say? I am so frightened, didi. Anything, just anything could have happened. That's what he was saying, didi,' Kajol gripped Kanika's hand with worry writ large in her eyes.

'Shhh … Kajol. I suggest you go home now. We will go to this Maldhakka yard and find out,' Kanika tried to calm her. But Kajol didn't want to stay back.

'Please didi, let me go with you. I am so worried,' she pleaded.

But Kanika wouldn't hear of it.

'No, Kajol. You must go back home. Veda didi, Ron bhaiya and I will take care of this. You have to trust us,' Kanika was firm.

'Also, four of us won't fit into an auto. We will have to hire a car then. Kajol, please remember, we have very little time left for the exams. You should go and revise. And rest your arm,' Veda advised her.

Reluctantly, Kajol agreed.

They all walked towards the Sitawadi arch. Kajol walked home from there, while Kanika hailed an auto.

'You know, I am terrified to go there and look. I don't know what is worse—finding him there or not finding him there,' said Veda, over the din of the auto. She was squished between Kanika and Ron, and she brushed her hair away from her face. Kanika's hair was fluttering in the wind too.

'Yes, but since that's the only lead we have, we have no choice but to follow it,' Ron raised his voice to be heard.

It was a bumpy forty-minute ride, and by the time they reached the Maldhakka yard, Veda's throat was parched. She looked around to see if there were any shops nearby. There was nothing. It was an isolated place, just as Vijay had described.

Kanika took one look at the place, and she turned to the auto-driver.

'Bhaiya—we need to go back too. Will you wait?' she asked him.

'How long would you need me to wait?' he asked.

'We have come to find out something. About an hour? Will you wait?' she asked.

'Extra charges,' he said.

'No problem,' Ron quickly agreed. It was evident to them that there was no way they would be able to get an auto back from this lonely place.

A barren ground, only sparsely populated with some shrubs, which were more brown than green, stretched endlessly in front of them. To their right was a railway platform, which was more or less deserted. A lone bench stood on the platform, and they could make out a human figure asleep on it. There were a few wagons parked on one of the tracks. There was not a single person anywhere near them. On a second track stood another train of closed wagons. At the end of the railway tracks, stood large railway sheds.

'Do you think that could be the shed Vijay talked about?' asked Ron, pointing to them.

'No way—those belong to the railway; let's walk ahead,' said Kanika.

'I wish I had brought some water. I am so thirsty,' Veda said.

'Here,' said Kanika, as she reached into her bag and pulled out a bottle of water.

'Wow! You carry water too! Thanks,' said Veda, as she gratefully took a few sips.

They continued to walk on the barren land, which sloped upwards. When they reached the top of the slope, they could see what lay ahead, and there it stood—the building that Vijay had described. It was like a large shed, just as he had said.

'Let's go. I think that's the one,' said Veda, as soon as she saw it.

They walked a few metres and reached the building. The large, rusted, faded red iron doors in the front were padlocked. The lock was bigger than Kanika's palms.

She rattled it.

'Nobody here,' she said, as she walked around the godown.

'I don't even know what I expected to find, but certainly not a locked building,' confessed Ron.

'What do we do now?' Veda asked, and they looked at each other.

Ron pushed at the doors of the godown, trying hard to part the iron doors a teeny-weeny bit, to see if he could peep inside. But the doors were tightly shut, and he could not get them to budge even a little bit.

They walked around the godown, trying to see if they could look inside. But there were no windows at all, just like Vijay had said.

When they got to the back of the godown, they noticed

a small structure, like a little kennel, about four feet high, right at the centre. An asbestos sheet served as a 'roof' for this tiny structure. Damp gunny sacks hung from the 'roof', forming curtains, closing off the inside of the structure from view. Veda spotted a pair of feet protruding out from under the gunny sacks.

'Hey—look, there is somebody there,' she said, clutching Kanika's arm.

'Oh yes, you are right!' said Kanika.

Kanika, Veda and Ron edged forward cautiously. As they approached the structure, they saw a bamboo stick lying by it.

Ron lifted the gunny sacks. An old man in the uniform of a security guard was sleeping with his back turned towards them.

Kanika took the bamboo stick and hit the ground next to his ear hard, making a noise, so that it would wake him.

'Bhaiya, BHAIYA!' she said loudly, near his ear.

If they weren't so tense, they would have found the way he jumped up amusing. But instead, all three looked at him in sheer relief.

The old man rubbed his eyes, unsure if he was dreaming.

Then it seemed like he had remembered something. He stood up immediately.

'Eh? Sorry, *sahib. Aaankh lag gayi.* Good morning, sir,' he said, when he saw Ron.

Then he looked at Veda and Kanika. 'Good morning, madam,' he said. The old man wasn't sure who these people were, but he didn't want to be berated for dozing off on the job.

'Bhaiya, we came to ask about a young boy. He was here yesterday?' Kanika said.

The old man's expression changed. He instantly looked alert.

'Please, bhaiya, helps us. That boy did not come home yesterday, and his mother is very worried. She sent us here to look. He had told her he was coming here,' Veda lied, improvising on the spot.

'Ummm...' The old man hesitated, weighing his options, unsure as to who these people were and what they wanted. All he wanted was to keep his job. He had created a natural air-conditioning system with the damp gunny sacks, and hardly any people came here. It was a cushy job and he did not want to risk losing it. He had to ensure that whoever these people were, they did not report back to Ganga *sahib*, who employed him, that they had caught him snoozing on the job.

'Bhaiya—the boy is missing. If you have any information, please tell us. Else we will have to make a police report and the police will come to search this place,' Kanika spoke firmly.

At the mention of the police, the old man made up his mind. If these people who looked like educated folk brought the police here, Ganga *sahib* would be furious and would throw him out. If he gave these people the information that they wanted, his job would be safe. It was evident that Ganga *sahib* did not much care for the young boy these people were enquiring about.

'The young boy was thrashed. And rightfully so. He tried to steal,' said the old man.

'Steal? Why would he do that? What did he try to steal?' asked Kanika, shocked.

'You know—the papers,' said the old man, pointing to the godown.

He was so casual and matter-of-fact about it, that it sent a chill down Kanika's spine.

'But, I don't understand. Why would he do that? He … had money!' said Kanika.

The old man shrugged. 'I think he lied to them about the amount of money he had. They chased him with sticks. He took off like a plane—zzzzzzzoooooom—and he ran all the way over there. They told me to catch him as he ran out. I could only make it to the top of the hill. But they pursued him. I stood here and watched as they caught him there,' said the old man, pointing in the direction of the railway platforms.

'Did … did you see them beating him?' Kanika asked, not wanting to hear the answer.

'You should know who you take *pangas* with. Foolish boy. He walks into a lion's den and hopes to get away by offering the lion stale meat? Will the lion spare him?' he asked.

Kanika thanked him, thinking hard. Veda and Ron were doing the same. They all reached the same conclusion independently.

There was only one place that Sanju could be. The railway platforms.

They hurriedly climbed down the slope and headed for the platforms to search for Sanju.

Chapter 33

March 1997
Railway yard, Pune

Veda, Ron and Kanika almost broke into a run to reach the deserted platforms of the railway station.

Ron ran towards the man on the bench whom they had seen from a distance. He wondered if that was Sanju. But when he got closer, he saw that it was a homeless person, probably a beggar. Sanju was nowhere to be seen.

They looked around carefully, combing every inch of the platform. The sun beat down relentlessly, and sweat trickled down Veda's forehead. They were frustrated and anxious. Where was Sanju?

'More water?' asked Kanika, as she took a sip and offered her bottle to Veda.

'No, thanks. I am okay,' said Veda.

'I will take some,' said Ron, as he took the bottle and sipped some water.

'God—that old man said that Sanju was thrashed. How could he be so foolish? Whatever was he thinking! And did you see the size of that godown?' asked Veda.

'Yes. But that does not mean the whole thing is full of papers, but this is probably where they have a photostat machine or a xerox machine, who knows,' said Kanika.

'Yes. Do you think yelling for Sanju will help so that he knows we are here?' asked Ron.

Kanika looked around. Apart from the beggar on the bench, the platforms were deserted. What would they lose in trying?

'I think that's a good idea. If he is somewhere around, hopefully he will recognise our voices,' agreed Veda.

'SANJU ... SAAAAANJUUUUUUUUUUU ... SANJUUUUU...' they shouted, walking along the length of the platform. Their voices echoed back at them, cutting through the oppressive heat. Not a leaf stirred.

Ron walked right up to the end of the freight train. Then

he looked at the other platform, where the covered wagons lay. He crossed the railway tracks and walked towards them.

'SANJUUUUUU ... SANJU ... IT'S RON,' he yelled, feeling a little foolish. This was like looking for a needle in a haystack. Suddenly, a piece of wood landed behind him. The sound made him stop in his tracks, and he turned to look. It had come from one of the covered wagon cars. He rushed towards it and peeped inside. For a few seconds he couldn't see anything as it was dark inside the wagon car. Then he heard a feeble sound.

'Ron bhaiya!' It was a hoarse whisper.

Ron blinked a few times. Was he imagining it? Then his eyes adjusted to the dark, and the silhouette of a young boy came into view.

It was Sanju. Unable to speak, he had hurled the piece of wood to attract Ron's attention.

Ron had found him.

'OH MY GOD! SANJU!' he exclaimed, as he climbed on to the wagon. Sanju lay huddled in a dark corner, a gaping wound on his forehead. He was shivering. There was a pool of blood beneath his head. One of his eyes was swollen and he could barely open it. A trail of blood from his nostril had caked up. His left cheek had swollen up like a balloon. There were bruises on his arms and shoulders. There were angry red and purplish bruises on his legs too. It seemed as though there was no part of his body that was not hurt.

Ron stood gaping, his heart pounding in his ears. What should he do? Should he move Sanju? How long had he been lying like this? How much blood had he lost? It took him only a second to decide. He had taken enough health and safety classes in England to know that in such cases, it was best not to move the victim, but to get qualified medical professionals instead.

'Sanju, Sanju, we have found you now. Don't be scared. We are here now, okay? Just wait, we will go get help,' said Ron.

He waited to see if Sanju had understood. Sanju nodded slowly. Ron shot out of the wagon like a bullet.

'KANIKA, VEDA, HURRY ... I FOUND SANJU,' he yelled, as he jumped out of the wagon and gestured frantically to them.

'Oh, thank God! Where?' asked Veda, as she and Kanika hurried towards Ron.

'He is inside,' said Ron, pointing to the wagon.

Veda and Kanika climbed into the wagon to look at Sanju. They gasped as they spotted him, their eyes taking a little while to adjust to the darkness.

'Sanju, we are here. Don't worry, we will take care of you,' said Veda.

She couldn't believe her eyes. Sanju's face was an unrecognisable mess of blood and dirt. The men who had beaten him up had been merciless. What in the world was Sanju thinking, to have got into this situation?

'He is in pretty bad shape. He is badly beaten up. We need to get medical help immediately. I think one of us should stay here with him while the other two get help,' said Ron.

'Veda and Ron, you both stay. I will go and get help. We don't need two people to do that,' said Kanika.

She took out her water bottle and handed it to Veda.

'Give him water, I will be as fast as I can,' she said. She jumped out of the wagon and ran towards where the auto was waiting.

Veda removed the *chunni* of the salwar kameez she was wearing and tried to make a pillow for Sanju to rest his head. But he could barely move his neck. He was whimpering in pain.

'Don't move him, Veda. You might make it worse,' said Ron.

So Veda just poured water into the cap of the bottle and held it to Sanju's lips. His lips were swollen very badly. Veda could only tilt the cap little by little, so tiny droplets of water dribbled down his parched tongue.

Ron and Veda sat in the wagon, waiting. Veda looked around and saw that this was some kind of a wagon used for transporting machine parts. At least that's what the stacked-up crates indicated.

'Sanju, why did you do this?' Veda asked him gently, the sorrow evident on her face.

Sanju did not reply. He had a glazed look in his eyes. He stared at her with his mouth open. He was breathing through his mouth, as his nose was swollen.

They heard the siren of an ambulance in about forty minutes. Kanika had managed to get help. The men spilled out of the ambulance along with Kanika and hurried to the wagon with a stretcher.

'Over there. Inside the wagon,' Kanika directed them.

Veda peeped out and waved, so that they could locate it easily. Ron sat with Sanju, speaking to him softly, reassuring him, giving him tiny sips of water from the bottle cap.

The men moved Sanju expertly. The stretcher they had brought was not entirely flat, and when they put Sanju on it, he was in a sitting position, at about a 140-degree angle, with his spine stretched back. They strapped him, and then carried him quickly out of the wagon and into the ambulance, which they had driven onto the platform.

Kanika rode in the ambulance. Veda and Ron followed them in the auto.

The hospital was close to the railway station and they were there in less than ten minutes. It was a small hospital, but Veda could see that they were very efficient. Sanju was admitted to the emergency OPD immediately, without too much paperwork.

Kanika filled up the forms.

'Madam, we need his father or mother or relative to sign. Are you related to him?' the receptionist asked.

How can you define a relationship that goes deeper than sharing a common genetic pool? This was a boy Kanika *cared* for. But medical science and law were professions not interested in emotions like caring and love. They just wanted the biological facts and legal standing of all relationships.

'I shall get his father to come in the evening. He is yet to be informed. This is an emergency,' said Kanika.

'You will also have to fill up the forms to be submitted at the police station, as this is a medico legal case,' said the receptionist.

'Oh, alright, I shall do that,' said Kanika. 'Er ... so will there be a police investigation?' she asked.

'Don't worry, madam. Mostly these things are just a formality. Unless someone has initiated a complaint, these just go into the police file. If the police investigate each and every case like this, they won't have time for anything else,' the receptionist said.

That reassured Kanika somewhat.

They waited for the doctor to arrive. He came almost instantly. He took one look at Sanju, turned towards Kanika and asked, 'Street fight?'

Kanika did not want to go into a long-winded explanation.

'Yes … something like that,' she said.

The doctor nodded, his suspicions confirmed.

He examined Sanju thoroughly. Two junior doctors stood next to him, taking notes, and a nurse stood in the background.

'We have to take him to the ICU immediately. There seem to be many injuries. There are some fractures of the ribs. We will also have to do an MRI scan to rule out internal bleeding inside the skull as there appears to be head trauma; and we have to run all the tests to rule out possibilities of other complications. He needs a blood transfusion as well. It looks like he has lost a lot of blood,' he said.

'Will … will he be okay, doctor?' Kanika asked.

'At this stage, it is very difficult to give you an assurance. He is badly hurt. We will have to see. He might require surgery. We can't say anything,' said the doctor.

Kanika's heart sank on hearing this.

'Bloody hell,' muttered Ron.

Veda just stood there, wishing the doctor had at least given them some hope.

The attendants came immediately and wheeled Sanju into the ICU.

The junior doctor asked Kanika, 'Are you his mother?'

'No—no. I am his teacher.'

'We will need a parent or a guardian for the signatures,' he said.

'Please go ahead, doctor, and do whatever needs to be done. We will get his parents,' said Kanika.

'One of you will have to stay here. We might need you to get the prescribed medicines. Just wait outside the ICU, we will let you know,' said the junior doctor.

'Veda, I can stay back here. Do you think you and Ron can go to Sanju's house and bring his father here? Do you know the way?' Kanika asked. Her fingers picked at the edge of her handbag, shredding away pieces of flaked leather. Her voice betrayed her anxiety.

Ron looked grim and pursed his lips as he nodded.

Veda nodded too. She was nervous about this. She had never gone into Sitawadi without Kanika. But this was an emergency, and she could see how distraught Kanika was.

'Let's go,' said Ron, as he and Veda made their way out of the hospital.

They took an auto and reached the entrance arch of Sitawadi.

'Are you sure you know the way?' Ron asked.

'I think I do. If we get lost, we can ask someone where Sanju's house is, and I'm sure they will point us in the right direction.'

Ron was a little worried about bumping into Kajol's father. But Veda told him that most likely, he was at work.

As they made their way to Sanju's house, they spotted Kajol at a tiny shop that sold *paan,* cigarettes, and a few other things. She was buying bananas.

'Veda didi! Ron bhaiya!' she called out.

'Oh, hello Kajol. I'm glad we met you here. Could you take us to Sanju's house?' asked Ron.

'What happened, didi? Bhaiya—did you find Sanju? What happened?' Kajol asked. The expression on Veda's and Ron's faces told her that something was amiss.

'Yes, Kajol. We found him. He is in hospital. We need to get his father urgently,' Veda said.

'Didi. Is he okay? Did ... Agni's men—?' Kajol asked. She had guessed the truth.

'Yes,' Veda interrupted her before she could complete the sentence.

'Come, didi—I know where exactly Sanju's father is. I saw his auto just a little while ago,' Kajol said, as she led them through the lanes.

Then she remembered the stolen amount.

'Didi, what will you say if he talks about Sanju taking the money? Please didi—he will get so angry,' Kajol said.

Veda and Ron had forgotten about that. They looked at each other, and in that instant, the same thought crossed their mind.

'I'll take care of it,' said Ron.

'We will cover that,' said Veda, speaking at the same time.

'Listen, let's split all these costs, including the hospital expenses. It isn't fair otherwise. Kanika paid for the hospital,' said Veda.

'I am happy to take care of this,' Ron insisted.

'No, let's split everything three ways,' Veda said firmly.

Sanju's father had parked his auto at the end of their lane and was having a cup of tea at the bakery, which was opposite where his auto was parked. Kajol knew his routine, as he always took a break at this time if he happened to be in the area.

Ron and Kanika, led by Kajol, approached him.

'Namaste. I am Veda. Sanju's teacher at Sankalp. And this is my colleague, Ron. I am afraid we have some bad news. Your son, Sanju—he is admitted in hospital,' Veda said.

'What? How? Which hospital? Is he fine?' he asked.

'We need you to come with us. He is in Vinayaka Hospital and he is in the ICU. He ... is hurt,' said Veda, speaking in Hindi. She did not want to tell him that he had been beaten up.

'He is becoming too big for his boots. Useless fellow—he deserves a good thrashing, if you ask me. Now I must go to the hospital to see my stupid son. And he has spoilt my duty for the day. Who does he think will earn?' Sanju's father began an angry tirade in Hindi.

'Well, we need an auto to go to the hospital. Will you take us there? We will pay you,' said Veda.

'*Arey* madamji—you can come in my auto. I haven't been reduced to that level where I have to take money to go and see my son. Sit,' he gestured, as he walked to the auto and climbed into the driver's seat, pulling the lever to start it.

Ron and Veda got in and sat in the passenger seat. Kajol wanted to go along with them, but Veda was insistent that she stay back.

'Do you know he stole my money? I had five thousand rupees. All gone!' Sanju's father turned back to exclaim, as he drove away.

'I have your money. Don't worry. It is safe,' said Veda.

'How? How do you have the money?' he asked.

'Er ... Sanju—he told us to keep it safe. I will give it back to you,' said Veda.

That pacified him somewhat.

When they reached the hospital, Ron pulled out a bundle of ten five hundred-rupee notes and gave it to Sanju's father.

'Here's the money. Sanju is very sorry about it. So, please don't be upset with him,' said Ron. Veda translated what Ron had said.

Sanju's father hesitated for second, and then took the money.

Then they all went inside.

Once they were in, Sanju's father had to fill out and sign the consent forms. That was when Veda learnt that he couldn't write or read. He seemed to be very ashamed of it.

Veda filled up the forms for him, first writing out his name neatly.

'Jadhav,' he said, and Veda wrote it down.

For his signature, he put his thumb impression.

'The blood transfusion is done. We got blood from the blood bank,' said Kanika, when she saw them.

She brought her palms together and greeted Jadhav, tears brimming in her eyes.

'I am so sorry to see Sanju like this,' she said.

Jadhav looked away, refusing to meet any of their eyes.

None of them were allowed to meet Sanju, but they could peep though the little glass window in the door of the ICU.

When Jadhav saw Sanju in the ICU through the window, he was shaken. So were Veda and Ron. When they had left, he was just being wheeled in. But now, he lay without a shirt, looking frail and helpless. It was a frightening sight. There were tubes coming out from all over his body. An oxygen mask was helping him breathe. Two more tubes were attached to his chest and were connected to some complicated-looking apparatus. There was an IV line with a needle pierced into his hand, for the saline drip. A monitor at the head of the bed continually recorded his heartbeats. He was hooked to several frightening-looking machines.

They waited outside for hours. There were several other people there too, waiting for some news of their loved ones. One of them was having a cup of coffee and the aroma assaulted Veda's senses. She inhaled appreciatively, and that was when she remembered that none of them had eaten anything since morning.

'Kanika—you go with Ron and grab something to eat. I will wait here. And once you return, I shall go,' Veda said.

Kanika thought that was a good idea. She was beginning to feel the pangs of hunger, and so was Ron.

'Yes, I'll do that. I will also call my mother from the pay phone and let her know we will be late. Shall I tell her to inform Padma aunty as well?' Kanika asked Veda.

'Yes, please. You know, I had forgotten about informing them,' Veda confessed.

'We might as well, because we don't know how long all this is going to take,' Kanika said.

'Would you like some coffee?' Veda asked Jadhav. But he shook his head.

Kanika and Ron left for the cafeteria, saying that they would return soon.

Veda continued to wait with Jadhav. His expression was grim and unfriendly, so she did not attempt to make conversation with him. In any case, what could she say?

'Sister, Sister. I am that boy's father. Can I go inside and see him?' Jadhav asked a nurse, pointing to Sanju in the ICU.

'I will have to check with the doctor. I don't know if the patient is allowed visitors,' she said.

'Just two minutes, Sister. I just want him to know that I am here,' Jadhav pleaded.

'I will see what I can do,' said the nurse.

Jadhav paced up and down the corridor outside the ICU. He wished Sanju had not got involved in this mess. Why did the boy always get into trouble? He shook his head disapprovingly. Then he turned to Veda.

'The reason I am so strict with Sanju is that I want him to study well. I don't want him to be an *angoota-chaap* like me. And now see what this useless boy has done. How will he write the exams?' he asked Veda.

'I am as helpless as you, and I feel bad,' she replied.

'Bad? Why will you feel bad? What do you know about feeling bad? Eh? What kind of teachers are you, if you can't even guide him properly? And also—why did you take money from a kid?' Jadhav bombarded Veda with questions. He was growing angrier by the minute. He was upset about Sanju being in the ICU, and he was also irritated about losing his earnings for the day. He had to pay a daily rent to the owner of the auto, and all this time that he was waiting in the hospital, he was losing money.

Jadhav glared at Veda, expecting her to say something.

Veda had no answers for him.

Fortunately for her, a nurse came and asked who Sanju's father was.

When Jadhav said that he was the father, she said that Sanju was now awake. She said he could come inside and speak to his son for two minutes.

Jadhav nodded.

'Normally we don't allow anyone in the ICU. But since you requested, we are letting you in. Two minutes only, okay?' the nurse warned him as he went inside.

Chapter 34

March 1997
Vinayaka Hospital, Pune

Sanju opened his eyes. His head throbbed with pain. He struggled to focus. All he could hear were the sounds of the machines around him, whirring softly. He was confused about where he was. He looked at his hand and saw the saline drip. Though one part of his brain told him he could be in a hospital, another part grappled with how he had got there and who had brought him here. He didn't remember anything. He recalled the sharp blows that he had received. He grimaced as he remembered the pain. It felt as if someone was sawing off bits of his body. Bolts of dull pain came and went in waves. Every part of his body was affected. He had felt himself drifting in and out of consciousness, but now he was hearing a voice.

'Sanju ... Sanju beta,' he felt a palm on his hand.

Could it be his father? Sanju felt a cold, clammy sensation grip his heart.

Indeed, it was his father. How had he got here?

Sanju shivered in fright as he remembered the money he had stolen, and now lost. The sequence of events came back to him. Agni's men had said that the cost of one question paper was ten thousand rupees. Sanju had shown them the money he had. He had then claimed that he had more money, and he would pay when they gave him the question papers for all the subjects. They had taken him to the godown. Once he was inside they had shown him all the question papers. He had attempted to grab the papers and run, when they had chased him and caught up with him. They had beaten him with hockey sticks and an iron bar. There were three of them. 'This will teach you a lesson,' they had said as they rained blows on him. They had hit him till he lost consciousness. When he opened his eyes, he realised they had taken the money as well. Sanju had crawled into the wagon and taken shelter there till Ron had found him. And now he wondered how his father was here.

Even in its dazed state, one part of Sanju's brain worked hard. He had to come up with an explanation for the missing money before his father asked.

'Sanju. Why ... why did you...? his father was asking.

'Veda didi ... she told me to ... she told me ... question paper, we can buy. I wanted to ... do business...' Sanju interrupted his father, the words coming out slowly.

'What? They told you to buy it?' Jadhav asked, shocked.

The effect of seeing his father and recollecting the chain of events caused Sanju's blood pressure and his heartbeats to rise, immediately setting off the monitor.

The nurse rushed in, hearing the sound.

'Enough, sir. Visiting time is over. Three minutes are up. Please wait inside. The patient needs to rest,' she shooed Jadhav out.

Sanju closed his eyes and lay back.

But Jadhav had heard Sanju clearly. The implication of what Sanju had said dawned on him. The vein in his forehead throbbed. He took short shallow breaths as what he had just heard sank in.

He came out of the ICU and spotted Veda, Kanika and Ron.

'How is he?' asked Kanika.

Fury built up inside Jadhav as he slowly worked out in his head what must have happened. He thought about it as he walked out of the ICU. Rage simmered in him, he was ready to explode.

'How is he?' asked Kanika, as soon as she saw him.

Jadhav took one look at her face and his anger erupted.

'WHAT KIND OF TEACHERS ARE YOU?' he yelled, losing control of his emotions.

'SHHHH ... silence.... This is a hospital,' a nurse passing by told him.

But Jadhav did not keep quiet.

'You are doing a question paper business?' he demanded angrily, gesturing for them to step outside the corridor.

'What—of course not,' said Veda, shocked at the preposterous suggestion.

'What, madam? You are acting all innocent now because

my son got beaten up. Didn't you tell him to go and buy the question paper?' Jadhav's eyes were blazing as he spat out the words. 'You come outside, we will talk,' he said.

They followed him and stood just outside the corridor of the ICU room, near the waiting area.

'Look here, you are mistaken. I did no such thing,' Veda said firmly.

'Why are you pretending, madam? I might be uneducated, but I am not a fool,' Jadhav said.

'Listen, bhaiya. We would never do such a thing. Why will we ask our students to buy question papers? WE are the ones teaching them, coaching them and we will be the happiest to see them succeed. Do you see Ron here? He has come all the way from England, and he is spending time with children like Sanju to *teach*. Do you understand? Why in the world would we ever do something so repulsive?' Kanika explained in a calm voice.

But Jadhav was in no mood to listen. He was belligerent.

He shook his fist at Veda and said, 'So you think I should believe that you do it out of the goodness of your heart? You think I am such an *ULLOO*, EH? You don't get anything out of it? Then why did HE return the money to me? EH? EXPLAIN.' He was pointing at Ron now. Ron looked a little frightened. He took a step back. Though he could not understand what Jadhav was saying, he knew he was being accused of something.

'Good lord,' said Veda. How could she explain the whole story to Jadhav without implicating Sanju?

'And Sanju told me HIMSELF. Just now, he told me,' Jadhav continued.

'What? What did Sanju tell you?' Veda asked, shocked.

'That you told him to buy the question papers.'

'I am telling you, I did no such thing. Don't you understand?' Veda said.

This was getting bizarre.

But before they could argue any further, there was a flurry of activity. A nurse ran out of the ICU, saying, 'Call the doctor ... call the doctor! It's an emergency.'

Next, they saw three physicians running towards the ICU.

They rushed to the ICU, and peeped in through the window.

The three doctors as well as the nurse who had called out for them were standing around Sanju's bed. The back of one of the doctors was turned towards them. They all seemed to be frantically doing something.

It was like watching a silent movie, where you saw the actions but did not hear any sounds. The whole process lasted only a few minutes, but the minutes were slow and painful.

Veda clenched her fists and involuntarily held her breath. Jadhav closed his eyes and muttered a prayer. Kanika looked at the tiles on the hospital floor and paced up and down. Ron just stood very still, leaning against the wall.

It was Veda who knew it was over before the others did. She saw the doctors moving away from Sanju and the nurse removing the oxygen mask, as well as the other tubes that had been attached to his body. Veda stood silently, in shock, as the doctors came out. She knew what they would say.

She watched Kanika, Ron and Jadhav rush to the doctors, their eyes hopeful.

'We couldn't save him. The internal lacerations were too many. His lungs failed.... So sorry,' said the senior doctor.

Jadhav stood and stared, not entirely understanding the doctor. He could not believe what he was hearing.

'Doctor. Please, please save him. He ... he is only fifteen. His exams, doctor. He is a good boy, doctor,' he was rambling on, meaninglessly.

The doctor patted his hand, shook his head, and walked away, followed by the junior doctors.

It was only then that Jadhav understood.

He sat down on the floor, his head in his hands. The wail he let out echoed through the corridors of the hospital.

His Sanju was gone.

Veda could not speak. There was a lump in her throat. She put her hands to her lips and stood silently, leaning against the wall.

An attendant went into the ICU and wheeled the body out. Sanju's face was distorted, but his eyes were shut now. There was a stillness about him which only death can bring.

Jadhav held Sanju's lifeless hand and wept, saying over and over, '*Mera beta … Mera beta…*'

'There are some formalities before you can take the body. Please complete them,' said the nurse to Kanika. Kanika nodded.

Slowly, Jadhav and Kanika walked towards the administration department to clear the dues and claim the body.

Sanju's body was taken to his home in an ambulance. The funeral was to take place by 11 the next morning. As was the custom, the body was wrapped in a white cloth. They laid him outside in the same spot where, a few weeks earlier, Kajol's birthday celebrations had taken place.

Almost the whole of Sitawadi turned up to pay their final respects.

Ron, Kanika and Veda stood to one side, silently watching people as they came, walked around the body, and said their prayers.

Kanika had her arms around Kajol, who was inconsolable.

'I tried, didi. How much I tried,' she said, over and over. Her eyes were swollen into slits from crying.

The only person who was stoic and pragmatic was Sanju's stepmother. His father sat completely immobilised, but his stepmother took charge of the proceedings. She greeted the people who came. She had arranged for the pandit, and she gently coaxed Jadhav to perform the rituals that were necessary. Sanju's stepsister, who was only two, pranced about playfully, not understanding what was happening around her. Shakubai kept watch over her.

'It's better to die than to perform the last rites of your son,' said Jadhav, as he did everything he was asked to do.

All the things that Sanju had said in class, the way his eyes twinkled, the way he made everyone laugh—all of it played like a movie in Veda's mind. His death felt surreal, and it seemed as though Sanju would jump up at any moment and tell them that this was all an elaborate prank. But Veda knew that this was just a part of the denial of the truth. She just wasn't willing to accept that Sanju was dead.

Neither Bhuwan nor Padma Devi attended the funeral. Veda had told both of them about it, but Bhuwan had said that he had an important presentation, which he could not miss. Padma Devi had been irked at Veda coming back home late the previous night. When a distraught Veda had said that Sanju had passed away, Padma Devi had remarked that, every single day, Veda had new excuses for coming late. Veda was too beaten down to even explain things to her and had let it go.

Kanika's mother had come over, paid her last respects, and gone back. Aparna and all the other staff at Sankalp, as well as the student volunteers, had turned up. They joined Veda, Kanika and Ron, and stood respectfully, their heads bowed till the body was taken away for cremation. All of Jadhav's relatives from the neighbouring town had turned up and paid their last respects as well.

The worst thing about Sanju's death was the timing. The board exams were to start the next day, and Kanika had called all the students to Sankalp for a final briefing at 4 p.m.

After the body was taken away, there was nothing left to do and people started leaving in groups. The Sankalp staff too left, with Veda, Ron and Kanika.

'Do you think I should cancel today's briefing?' Kanika asked Aparna, as they walked out.

For Kanika, each step she took needed a supreme effort. One part of her just wanted to curl up into a ball and stay in the comfort of her home. She wasn't ready to face the world. Yet another part of her reminded her of her duties towards the other children who would be taking the board exams.

'I think you should *definitely* address them today. It is especially important after what has happened. They are already in complete shock. WE have to help them cope and deal with it. They need motivation and advice. So please do not cancel it,' Aparna said.

Kanika nodded. Aparna was right. She needed to motivate the other children.

It was the most difficult speech she had ever given.

Ron and Veda stood next to her, as she addressed all the students who were to give the exams the next day.

'Children, let's observe a two-minute silence for Sanju. Please remember him in your prayers,' she said. Everyone stood with their heads bowed.

Kanika went on to say that it was a big tragedy that they had lost Sanju. She said that in life sometimes unexpected things happened.

'We don't have any control over what happens and some outcomes are not in our hands. All we can do is put in our best efforts. After that, we have to just leave it. Have all of you prepared well?' she asked.

'Yes,' they replied collectively.

'Good—you must remember that you have worked hard the whole year. That should not go to waste. No matter what happens, we must go on. We feel bad, no doubt. But do not let sadness affect your work. When you focus on the exam, you should forget about everything else, and everybody else. Just look at what is in front of you, take a deep breath and write. Will you all do that?' she asked.

'Yes, didi, we will,' they said.

Kanika told them that anytime they needed help, the three of them—Ron bhaiya, Veda didi as well as herself—would be available at Sankalp at the usual hours, as the summer camp for the younger children would begin the next day. She told them they could come anytime if they needed clarifications on anything that they had learnt so far.

'All the best then,' said Kanika.

Ron and Veda too wished the children the very best.

Then they stood by and watched the children leave, all charged up to take the exams the next day.

'That was a powerful talk you gave,' said Ron.

'There's only one problem with it,' said Kanika.

'What?' Ron asked.

'I am not able to follow my own advice,' Kanika sighed and said.

Part Four

THE RULE BREAKERS

You are remembered for the rules you break.

– Douglas MacArthur

Chapter 35

March 1997
Sankalp, Pune

No matter what they did, the shadow of Sanju's death hung over them like a black cloud. Veda, Kanika and Ron dealt with the burden of sorrow in their own ways—and this involved throwing themselves completely into the various activities for the summer camp with the younger children. There were brief pockets of time in which Veda would forget about the tragedy that had struck. In those moments, she even managed to chuckle and laugh at something one of the younger kids did or said. But the very next moment, the enormity of the sorrow and the irreversible finality of death would strike her as a hard blow, and she would reel under the impact of it, finding it hard to breathe. Ron and Kanika reported feeling the same way and they empathised with each other.

They discussed that fateful day's events over and over.

'Could we have saved Sanju if we had acted immediately and not waited till the next day?'

'But how could we have gone that day? Kajol had broken her arm.'

'We went looking for him as fast and as soon as we could.'

'Sanju should not done that. Did we put undue pressure on him?'

'Could we have helped with his exam anxiety?'

'Were we too harsh on him?'

'Should we have told his father that he stole from him?'

They discussed these over and over, as though talking about it would help them make sense of it all. They found little solace in knowing that they had done everything they could, and with the best of intentions. There wasn't anything they could have changed.

'Life must go on. These children deserve a great summer camp, and we are going to give it to them,' Kanika reminded Veda and Ron, when they took their coffee breaks.

Aparna had said that she wanted innovative ideas from them for the summer camp.

'Let's give them an experience which they will never get in their schools. It has to be educative, informal, hands-on, as well as a lot of fun. Let's see what you come up with,' she had said.

They had suggested many ideas and Aparna had loved most of them. More importantly, they were a hit with the children.

Ron and Veda got the children to start a little garden patch just outside the basement. They removed the tall, reed-like plants that were growing there. Then, Veda showed them how to loosen the soil by digging it.

'Careful now, we don't want anyone to get hurt,' she instructed, as she watched the enthusiastic twelve-year-olds get completely immersed in gardening. It reminded Veda of the times in Joshimath when she and her siblings used to plant seeds and wait for them to sprout.

Ron showed them how spinach had to be sown in rows. They got powdered cow dung and scattered it in the soil. They made borders with bricks. They watched in excitement as tiny shoots of spinach sprouted on the fifth day.

'Gardening requires a lot of patience. Just because we want something, doesn't mean we will get it immediately. We have to be patient,' Ron said. They were dispensing little life lessons to the children.

Kanika made the children create puppets from ordinary everyday objects like a paper cup and some wool. She got clay and taught them to make little figurines of Lord Ganesha. She read storybooks to them, and afterwards, the children enacted what they had read. Their summer camp was an absolute hit with the children.

Aparna came to see what was going on and she was pleased by the level of engagement and activities. She was also pleased to see contented, happy and productive children. She began coming almost every day towards the time that the children were getting ready to leave.

The children would then proudly tell her what they had done that day—be it a puppet or a story or a craft activity. If they had made models, Aparna would look at them and appreciate their efforts. Kanika told Veda that Aparna was probably coming every day just to check on whether they were working or not.

'How does it matter? We are enjoying ourselves and so are the children. She can come and check all she wants,' Veda said, shrugging.

It was on the eleventh day of the summer camp, when Aparna was listening to one of the children narrate what they had learnt that day, that they heard an unusual noise. It sounded like an army was marching on the floor upstairs. Aparna looked at Kanika puzzled, wondering what was going on.

Ron and Veda were in the garden patch with the kids, and did not hear anything.

Kanika and Aparna glanced at each other in surprise as they saw many pairs of feet emerging into view, descending the stairs.

They stood gaping when they saw that it was a mob of at least forty people, men and women, led by Kajol's father, Rajaram, and Sanju's father, Jadhav, that had marched into Sankalp. They were angry and were speaking in raised voices.

Ron and Veda looked up from the garden patch and knew at once that something was amiss. They gathered the children and herded them into a corner with the other kids. The children were confused, seeing many of their parents there, and they huddled together.

Veda and Ron walked to the front and faced the mob, with Kanika and Aparna.

'WE DEMAND TO SEE THE HEAD OF THIS PLACE. WE WANT TO COMPLAIN,' yelled Jadhav in Hindi.

'I head this centre. What is the problem?' asked Aparna.

'THROW OUT THE TEACHERS. SHUT THIS PLACE DOWN!' one of the people in the crowd shouted. The others chanted it like a slogan.

'SHUT IT DOWN, SHUT IT DOWN,' the person said again.

'SHUT IT DOWN, SHUT IT DOWN,' the crowd repeated.

Veda felt sick to the pit of her stomach, seeing the angry

mob yelling loudly. Her hands shook. She knew she had a problem when people got angry, but she thought that she had managed to control it. She discovered now, as her hands shook, that she hadn't quite managed to overcome it. This was a big mob of angry people, and it threw her into a panic. It was her worst nightmare coming true. She felt a tightness in her chest as she stood petrified.

Ron, too, had gone pale.

Kanika seemed calm, but it was Aparna who was in total control.

'Whatever the problem is, we can sit down and have a discussion; what is the issue?' she asked.

All of them started speaking at once. 'Cheaters—not teachers', 'Making use of poor people', 'Fooling us'—these were some of the things that Aparna could decipher. Their faces were contorted with rage and hatred as they yelled. It looked like they were being incited by Rajaram and Jadhav.

Ron had read reports of mob violence in India. He instinctively stretched out his arms and extended them, forming a little 'fence' to keep the children safe. He didn't want any of the kids to be hurt, in case things turned nasty.

'See, if you all speak together, nothing will be achieved. I will listen to all of you. But please, have a thought for these children. They are your own kids. They are getting scared of you. May I please request that you choose a representative, and we can have a discussion in my office?' Aparna spoke confidently and assertively.

Rajaram and Jadhav looked at each other and nodded.

'Alright. I am the representative, and I am ready to speak to you. But I don't want these teachers to be present when we speak,' Jadhav said, pointing to Veda, Ron and Kanika, darting murderous looks at them. He clenched his fists tightly, as if he wanted to hit them—his fury was apparent. Veda shuddered when he looked at her.

'Alright, let's go up to the office. Will you tell your people to wait outside?' Aparna asked.

'We are going to take our children home,' someone in the crowd said. 'Mahesh ... come here,' she called out to her child. Mahesh refused to go to her and stood behind Kanika.

'Look, this is just frightening the children. Let them continue their class. I will send them home at the usual time, and tomorrow you can decide whether you want to send them or not. Okay?' Aparna mollified the angry parents.

But they did not budge till Jadhav raised his hands and told them that he would update them after the meeting.

The mob led by Rajaram slowly dispersed and made its way out of the office building.

'Come with me,' Aparna told Jadhav. They took the elevator to the floor where the Sankalp office was.

Ron, Kanika and Veda heaved a collective sigh of relief when they left.

'Good lord, what was that about?' said Ron.

'I guess we will soon find out,' Kanika replied.

'Settle down, children. I will read you a story,' said Veda, trying to restore the balance that had been disturbed.

But the children did not settle down so quickly and were full of questions.

'Why are they angry, Ron bhaiya?' they asked him.

'Er … I don't know. They must be upset about something. We will soon get to know,' Ron said the only thing he could think of.

'Why are they asking you to shut this place down?' asked another child.

'We don't know, but we will soon find out. Don't you want to hear the story?' Veda said, trying to distract them. One part of her was fighting with her own anxiety. But she had to be calm for the sake of the children. She forced herself to take long, deep breaths, and she managed to quell her agitation. She pretended everything was okay. She waved a book with beautiful illustrations in front of the children.

'Who wants to know what happens in this story?' she asked.

It took a while for the children to calm down. By then it was time for them to leave for the day.

Aparna hadn't yet returned from her meeting with Jadhav.

'That was quite disturbing. My hands were shaking when that mob descended on us,' confessed Veda.

'You did better than me, I think. I was frightened, and I

did not even understand what they were saying,' Ron admitted.

'It seemed to me that Rajaram masterminded the whole thing, and Jadhav was just following his directions. It is easy to incite a grieving person when emotions are running high,' Kanika observed. 'Whatever it is, I'm sure it can be resolved by properly communicating with the parents. It's probably a huge misunderstanding,' she added confidently.

'We faced a lot of resistance when we were setting up Sankalp. Then, all it took was for one person to say that they thought it was a good idea. Immediately, the others followed suit. This, too, is like that. Rajaram, it is clear, dislikes white-collared workers. He must have filled their heads with some distorted information. I am sure we can sort it out; I am not too worried,' she continued.

But she could not have been more wrong.

When Aparna came down, her face was grim, her lips were pursed tightly together, and she shook her head as she approached them.

'Will you please come up to my office? This is a serious issue,' she said.

They followed her to her office and sat down.

'Look—they are making some grave allegations here. They say that Veda took money from Sanju, and it was on her instructions that he set out to get the question papers. He followed her directions and got beaten up. Then, she got frightened and returned the money. Is that true?' Aparna asked, looking at Veda.

Veda was stupefied. In her grief, she had forgotten the altercation she had had at the hospital with Jadhav just before Sanju passed away.

'That is simply not true, Aparna,' Ron spoke up before Veda could.

'Did you hand over money to Jadhav? Is that true?' she asked Ron.

'Yes, but that was because—' Ron began, but Aparna did not let him finish.

'Enough! I don't want to hear anything more. So there *is* a grain of truth in what they are saying. These are not entirely baseless allegations then,' Aparna said.

'Look, Aparna, I can tell you the whole sequence of events,' Veda said.

But Aparna was not in a mood to listen.

'Is it true that you have been inviting the children to your home, and that you also went to their house to attend a birthday party?' Aparna asked Ron.

'Yes. It is true,' admitted Ron.

'Oh, God. So they were right then. I did not believe them when they said that,' Aparna clutched her head.

'Well, we had to coach them at all odd hours, and the Sankalp premises was not available,' Kanika said.

'Can't you, of all people, see the problem here, Kanika? At least Ron and Veda can be excused, as they are new and they may not be aware of the guidelines and rules. But an experienced person like you knows very well about Sankalp rules. You cannot visit them in their homes, and you cannot have them over at your home. You have violated our guidelines, our basic rules. The rules have been put in place for a reason, are there for a reason. How could you do such a thing?' Aparna asked.

'Aparna—the kids, they needed that extra time. And the birthday party—it meant so much to Kajol.' Veda surprised herself by speaking up, defending what they had done. She couldn't remain silent on this. This was unfair. They had put their hearts and souls into their work.

Aparna was having none of it. She shook her head. 'Sorry—I cannot excuse such flagrant flouting of the rules. I will have to report this to the head office and there will be an inquiry commission. They will investigate and submit a report. This is mandatory.'

'Aparna, we did it because we wanted good results. We have been working day and night for that. How is it that you don't see what we have achieved?' Kanika tried to reason with her. She was angry with the way Aparna was quoting the rules.

'What have you achieved, Kanika? The death of an innocent boy?' Aparna's voice was as cold as steel.

That sentence hit them hard. They couldn't believe what they were hearing.

'And yes, all three of you are suspended from duty. We cannot have you as teachers till the commission finishes the inquiry and submits their finding. You don't have to come to Sankalp from tomorrow onwards,' Aparna added calmly.

'What?! How can you dismiss us like that?' Kanika asked.

'I don't owe you an explanation for my actions, Kanika. I am not the ones the parents have a problem with. They don't want you near their kids,' Aparna said. Her tone was curt. As far as she was concerned, the conversation was over.

Veda and Ron were dumbfounded at what they heard. They sat there, staring at her, not knowing what to do.

'You can leave. That's it,' said Aparna, indicating the door. She shook her head disapprovingly, her eyes narrowed to crinkled slits.

Kanika stood up without a word. Veda and Ron followed suit.

They walked out of Aparna's office in silence, completely flabbergasted by the unexpected turn of events, not knowing what had hit them.

Chapter 36

April 1997
Kailash Mandir Colony, Pune

Not being able to work with the children at Sankalp affected Veda. She found that she had a lot of time on her hands. She went to college one morning, to find out about the paperwork to be completed to retake an exam that one had failed in. She got all the necessary forms, filled them up and submitted them. She found out that she would be able to retake the exams in a few months.

Now that they had employed a cook whom she could order around, her mother-in-law did not involve Veda too much in the housework. As a result, Veda had a lot of time to spare, and she did not know what to do. She asked Bhuwan about the library, and he directed her to it. She took a membership there, carried books home, and began reading. She also started a vegetable garden on their balcony, which her mother-in-law, to her surprise, approved of. She went with her mother-in-law to a nearby nursery and got soil, fertiliser and seeds. Together they planted coriander, mint, ginger and green chillies. When the tiny chilli saplings sprouted, her mother-in-law was delighted and eager, like a happy child.

Veda had never thought that it would be possible to enjoy doing something with her mother-in-law. A few months ago, she had seen her as a torturer and a sadist whose only purpose in life was to trouble her. But now, here she was, planting seeds and watering the garden with her mother-in-law. She had started the garden just so she would have something to do, and to preserve her own sanity. She was surprised to see how proud Padma Devi was of it.

Padma Devi invited Shanta and Kanti behen over to show off the little garden. 'See, look at this mint. How fresh it is,' she gushed.

'These are so wonderful, Padma,' exclaimed Shanta. 'You must teach me how to do this,' she said. She had a lot of questions about how to plant seeds, what soil mixture to use, how long it would take to grow and many such things.

'My daughter-in-law is very good at all this gardening. You can ask her the details. But for her, we wouldn't have fresh greens,' Padma Devi boasted.

Veda was happy to answer all of Shanta's questions and even offered to set up a garden for her.

'That would be very nice, Veda. Come over. It is nice having Kanika around these days,' said Shanta.

Kanika had not told her mother about them being suspended. Neither had Veda told Padma Devi. They had decided not to. They both stuck with the story that there was construction activity going on in the office buildings, and therefore, Sankalp was closed temporarily.

Once a week, Ron, Veda and Kanika met at the coffee shop near Ron's house.

'Ron, don't you want to go back to the UK? Now that you are not teaching?' Kanika asked him.

'Yes, I have been considering it. But since I signed on to be a teacher, and since there is an inquiry pending against our names, I cannot leave till the final report is submitted and our names are cleared. Also, I am waiting to see the results of the exams. I do want to be around when they are announced,' Ron said.

'I miss seeing Kajol and the others,' said Veda.

'Oh, me too. But in the present circumstances, there's no way we can enter Sitawadi,' said Kanika, ruefully.

Until now, since Veda had been so immersed in Sankalp activities, she had not thought about Suraj at all. But over the past few days, she had increasingly felt she needed to respond to his last letter. There was so much that had happened in her life since then. And she had put off replying to him long enough. However, since a lot had happened, and she still did not know what to say about his friendship with 'that girl' (she couldn't bring herself to say her name), she continued to postpone writing to him.

One morning, just as she and her mother-in-law finished their morning round of gardening, a letter arrived. She expected it to be from Vidya, but the moment she opened it in her bedroom and saw the familiar writing, her heartbeat increased.

April 1997
Mumbai

Dear, dear Veda,
How are you? It has been a while since we wrote to each other. What is going on? Hope everything is fine at your end?

I am sorry I haven't been in touch earlier. There is such a lot going on in my life.

The Youth Day celebrations went off well. Everyone loved the programmes that we managed to put together. They enjoyed the contests, the dance, the fashion show—all of it. The senior managers appreciated it immensely as we had added events keeping them in mind. We managed to get a renowned motivational speaker, and they loved his talk. Oh, the logistics involved in organising this kind of thing is mind-boggling. There are hundreds of details to be taken care of, so many egos to manage, and a lot of things can go wrong. There were a few tiny emergencies, but we had a good team in place. Priya and I were heading the team and directing everyone, giving them instructions about everything. The crowd went crazy when Colonial Cousins performed. The performers were happy with the arrangements too.

Later, the chairman of the company himself called Priya and me to his cabin, and told us how much he appreciated our work on the programme. It feels great to get recognition for your efforts from the senior management team.

A few weeks back I went to the Ajanta and Ellora caves with Priya. (Her parents were very okay with her travelling with me. I have met them a few times now and they like me.) It was a fantabulous (fantastic + fabulous) experience. We took a train from Mumbai to Aurangabad, and stayed two nights at Aurangabad, as the journey takes about six hours. I wanted to explore the caves leisurely, and since we stayed for two nights, we had ample time to wander around.

You know how history excites me. Visiting a historical site is like visiting a fairy tale that happened in the past, with proof to show for it. The cave shrines were all cut from rock, by hand, and they rank amongst some of the most outstanding specimens of our ancient Indian architectural heritage. The thirty-four caves at Ellora and the twenty-nine caves at Ajanta remained shrouded in obscurity for over a millennium, till John Smith, a British Army officer, accidentally stumbled upon them while on a hunting expedition in 1819. The point from where John Smith first glimpsed the caves provides a magnificent view of the u-shaped gorge and its scenic surroundings.

A visitor said that he was so overwhelmed when he first entered it, that it took him a few moments to compose himself. He was speechless with awe. I can imagine why.

They are simply breath-taking, astonishing and awe-inspiring. I was so excited that I clicked at least three film rolls (thirty-six photos per roll!) of pictures.

There are a few places in the world that one MUST DEFINITELY visit. Ajanta–Ellora is one of them.

The other news from my side—I have been nominated to go for a team-building activity which is happening in two weeks. Priya has been nominated for the same as well. It is a three-day event and the company has booked a beautiful resort for this, on the outskirts of Delhi. After the team-building exercise, I wanted a few days off to visit my grandmother. I took permission from my boss to do so. He readily agreed.

When I mentioned it to Priya, she said she has never been to Joshimath and she would love to come with me. I asked her what her parents would think. She laughed and said that her parents completely trust her judgement and that they trust me. So I will be taking her to Joshimath.

I will definitely try to meet Vidya and I shall introduce Priya to her as well. How is Vidya? How is college going for her?

How did the children of Sankalp fare in the board examinations? How are Sanju, Kajol and all the others?

Write back when time permits.

Your friend,

Suraj

Veda read the letter, and with each word, her jealousy returned and coiled itself around her heart. She could already foresee where all this was heading. There was no doubt in her mind now that Priya was in love with Suraj. She re-read the bit about them spending two nights at Aurangabad. Had they stayed in separate rooms? Or had they shared a room? He had not mentioned that detail at all.

She was his friend before Priya was, and yet, he had never taken her to meet his grandmother. Would Priya stay with him at his grandmother's house? She pictured both of them walking in *her* hometown, breathing *her* mountain air. Priya had no right to be there. She was not from Joshimath. How *could* Suraj take her there?

She knew she was being irrational, but she could not help feeling this way. She felt like going to Mumbai and telling Priya to back the hell off, and that Suraj was her friend and hers alone. The next moment she chided herself for being jealous and silly. She should be pleased for him. She was a married woman. There could never be anything between her and Suraj, she reminded herself. She *tried* to feel happy about it. She said to herself that Suraj deserved to be happy and that Priya was making him happy. But she could not.

She wanted so badly to have been with Suraj when he went to the Ajanta and Ellora caves. She wanted to be with him when he went to Joshimath. She knew it was wishful thinking on her part, and yet she *longed* for it. It mattered so much to her. She had no right to feel this way, yet she did. But more than anything else, what she could not understand was why she felt betrayed and oh, so hurt.

Each sentence in Suraj's letter felt like a blow to her insides. She was so upset that she crumpled the letter in frustration. Then she smoothened it out and read it again, feeling fresh waves of jealousy and pain. It made her feel helpless, to be caught in the grip of something she could do nothing about. She had to do something, or else she would go mad. To distract herself, she tried reading a novel that she had got from the library. But she could not focus on even a page of it. No matter how many times she tried to read a paragraph, she lost focus and did not know what the author was talking about. She had a sinking feeling in the pit of her stomach, and it stayed there like an unwelcome guest. She couldn't get rid of it.

She asked herself what she had been hoping for when she had started exchanging letters with him in secret. She did not know. All she knew was, hearing from him, talking to him, made her happy. 'But you are still hearing from him, aren't you?' the logical side of her brain asked. 'Yes, but I don't want to hear about his time with that girl in his life. I hate her,' the emotional side of her brain answered.

Who knew love could hurt this much?

That evening, Bhuwan returned home early from work. Her mother-in-law had gone to meet her friends and Veda was alone at home.

'Veda, I have some good news. I will soon be getting a promotion at work. I am also getting a raise,' he said, his eyes shining.

Veda was happy to hear it.

'We should celebrate, Bhuwan. That is wonderful!' she said.

'I am very happy that my efforts have been recognised. It just motivates you to work harder, knowing that someone cares,' he said, as he removed his shoes and put them away.

'I know. It is sad when it doesn't get recognised,' she said.

'What do you mean?' he asked.

'It's a long story, Bhuwan,' she said.

'Tell me, Veda. I want to know. And as a special treat for you, I shall make tea. Please go and relax on the balcony. I will join you there,' he smiled and said.

Veda did as she was told. Bhuwan was being sweet and caring, as always. She chided herself for having feelings for Suraj. Here she was, a married woman, with a husband who was kind, thoughtful and considerate. Why was she carrying on writing to Suraj? She was suddenly filled with shame for what she had been feeling all this while towards Suraj. She should have, instead, focused on making her marriage stronger, and she should have made a bit more of an effort in her relationship with Bhuwan.

It was true that Bhuwan was immersed in his work most

of the time. But it was also true that she had been immersed in her Sankalp activities as well, up till now. Initially she had been busy 'adjusting' to the marriage, and then had got completely involved with Sankalp. She had not even paused to think about their marriage. Now it occurred to her, and she could see it clearly for what it was—their marriage was in a state of limbo. It wasn't great, but it wasn't bad either. Veda saw with accuracy how emotionally involved she was with Suraj. She hated herself for getting carried away. How could she have allowed that? Bhuwan was not a monster, and he deserved a lot more love than what she was giving him. She made up her mind to make an effort to communicate with him a bit more openly from now on.

Bhuwan joined her on the balcony with the tea he had made. He had also arranged some biscuits, as well as two delicious-looking chocolate pastries, on a plate.

'Oh, nice! Where did you get the pastries from?' asked Veda, in surprise.

'It is from a lady who bakes at home. The moment Vikki heard about the promotion, he called her and she had it delivered to me,' said Bhuwan.

'That is so sweet of him!' said Veda.

'Indeed. He was the first person I called this morning, when I heard of the promotion. He immediately placed this order, so that I would have it before I left for home.'

'Do thank him for me, Bhuwan.'

'I will. He wants to treat us to dinner over the weekend. He wants to try out a new restaurant in Koregaon Park. Want to go?'

'Of course, that would be nice,' said Veda.

'So, when will you be starting work again at Sankalp? When will the renovation be done?' asked Bhuwan.

Veda then narrated the entire story of why she wasn't at work, and what had transpired over the last few days.

'Oh no, Veda! That is just terrible!' said Bhuwan.

'Yes, and the worst thing is, we can do nothing about it,' she said.

'You know, it struck me that you were looking sad the last

few days. But you never said anything, and I thought I was just imagining things,' Bhuwan remarked.

'Yes, Bhuwan. I am actually *very* upset about it. It is just that I didn't get the chance to tell you before.'

'I am sorry about that, Veda. I know I have been a workaholic, of late. I know I have been travelling a lot and keeping late hours.'

'It's okay! You have now been rewarded for it, haven't you?' she said, as she smiled at him.

'Yes, I most certainly have been. Thank you for putting up with me,' he said, as he smiled back at her.

Talking to Bhuwan was like a balm to Veda's aching heart. She was happy that he was home early. She decided that, no matter how late he came home, she would take a few minutes from her day to have a conversation with him.

When Padma Devi came back from her walk, Bhuwan told her about his promotion. She was happy to hear about it.

Veda noticed that he did not invite his mother to the celebratory dinner that Vikki had planned for them. Later, when they went to bed, she asked Bhuwan about it.

'Don't you want to call your mother for the dinner? Won't she feel bad?' Veda asked.

'She has planned to go for a music concert that day! Why do you think Vikki chose that date?' he grinned.

'Clever!' said Veda.

'Oh, yes. It's not that my mother will ruin the fun. It's just that the place he has selected is a lovely bar and she won't enjoy it at all. It's not a place where I can take her,' said Bhuwan.

'Yes, I understand,' said Veda.

Over the next few days, Veda made an extra effort to talk to Bhuwan. She started waiting up for him, making conversation with him about his day. She discovered that she enjoyed this.

That weekend, Veda and Bhuwan went out with Vikki. It was a nightclub which played peppy dance numbers. Veda had never been to a place like it before.

'Bhuwan, everyone here is wearing Western clothes. I am

wearing these traditional clothes. I think I stick out like a sore thumb,' Veda whispered to him.

'Veda, you look beautiful!' shouted Bhuwan, over the din of the loud music.

Bhuwan did not want to dance, but Veda saw that Vikki was dancing and enjoying himself. When the song ended, he came towards them and pulled them both onto the dance floor.

'Come on, you two! Just copy me. I will show you the moves,' he said.

Bhuwan started copying his steps and Veda joined in, laughing. Soon she was enjoying herself. This was the most fun she had had in ages. Bhuwan did transform into a fun-loving guy in Vikki's presence.

When the night ended, Veda thanked Vikki.

'Don't thank me. I had fun too. We should do this more often. Get this husband of yours to step out like today, and I will take care of the fun bit,' said Vikki.

A few days later, Veda decided to visit Kanika. It had been a while since they had met, and Veda wanted to catch up with her. She thought she would go over to Kanika's house for a cup of tea and have a chat with her to find out how she was coping.

Kanika was happy to see her.

'Come in, come in,' Kanika said, smiling.

'Where's Shanta aunty? I don't see her around?' Veda asked.

'Oh, mum has gone to the local store. After that, she is meeting your MIL for their usual gupshup,' Kanika replied.

She said that she was sewing something, and asked if Veda would mind waiting while she finished it. Veda did not mind at all.

'I didn't know you sew,' she said.

'Oh, I like making little wall hangings, purses, quilted bed covers and such. Now that Sankalp isn't taking up our time, I have to keep myself occupied,' she said, and shrugged. 'Come and sit with me in the bedroom while I finish it,' Kanika said. Veda followed her into her room.

She gasped softly in surprise at the beauty of the bedroom. It was done up in soft pastel shades. The wooden bed was painted white and had a cushioned, upholstered, pale emerald-green headboard. The bed had a comforter with a white lace edge. Scented candles stood in a wooden tray at one corner. There was a window seat covered with the same pale emerald-green material, and large cream-and-white cushions placed on it neatly. The floral design on the curtains matched the pattern on the fluffy, soft rug on the floor, which her feet sank into. The look was dreamy, gentle and comforting.

At one end of the room was the sewing machine, which could be folded away and put inside a cupboard.

'Kanika, this bedroom is so beautiful!' Veda said admiringly.

'Oh, thanks! You should have seen how much clutter there was before I redecorated. Clutter is negative energy. We hold on to it, and it is bad because it does not allow new things to come into our lives. Only if we let go of the old, can we make place for the new,' said Kanika.

Her words were like an epiphany for Veda. Kanika was so right. She would try to do just that. She had to let go of Suraj. Veda had not forgotten his letter—each time she was alone, she thought about it. She still felt hurt, and then she felt foolish for feeling that way. Being here with Kanika was a good distraction.

Just as Kanika finished her sewing and put away the machine, her phone rang. 'One minute,' Kanika said, as she went to the hall to answer it.

When she came back, she looked grim.

'Aparna wants to see us in the office tomorrow. Apparently, the inquiry commission has submitted their report and folks from the head office have arrived. They told me to convey this to you. They have already informed Ron. We have to be there at 10.30 tomorrow morning to hear the "verdict",' she said, and made a face.

Veda shrugged. '*Que sera sera*,' she replied.

Veda returned home, and her mother-in-law left for her usual evening stroll with her friends. Veda was alone with her thoughts once again.

She did not want to think about Suraj. She had to deal

with this and get a grip on her mind, which seemed to have a will of its own. She looked around for something to do, and inspired by Kanika's decorating skills, Veda struck upon an idea. She would revamp her entire bedroom. She would get rid of the clutter, re-organise everything, re-arrange the furniture, and make it a delight to enter. That would keep her busy and distracted. It was a great idea, she decided. She would surprise Bhuwan when he got back from work.

She studied the room carefully and took stock of the furniture. There was a bed, two bedside cabinets, a chest of drawers, a mirror and a mismatched rug. The chest of drawers was stuffed to the brim with old newspapers and files. The bedside drawers too were full of unwanted clutter—old tapes, medicines that were long past their expiry date, a tool kit, a torch, hundreds of old bills, brochures, paper napkins, a nail cutter, some electrical wires, and many other odd bits and ends.

She began by clearing out the junk. By the end of an hour, she had completely cleaned out one of the bedside cabinets. She felt a sense of accomplishment. It took her mind off everything, and she felt better, getting rid of stuff. It made her feel lighter. Enthused, she began going through the other drawer, when the bell rang. It was Niranjan, the cook, who promptly made her a cup of tea.

Refreshed and recharged, Veda attacked the other drawer and got it in order as well.

'This is therapeutic,' Veda thought, as she headed to the chest of drawers. She discovered that there was a tonne of stuff there as well. It was bursting with old curtains, tablecloths and all kinds of knick-knacks, like an old statue, a clock that was not working, and many other things that were no longer being used. Veda decided to make a big pile of it and ask her mother-in-law if she could get rid of them.

It was when she was clearing out the last drawer that she came across a slightly heavy bundle which felt like a stack of books, tied up neatly in a cloth bag. The bundle was hidden in the middle of a pile of old newspapers that were pushed right to the back.

Curious, Veda opened up the bag.

She froze in utter shock when she saw what it contained.

Chapter 37

April 1997
Kailash Mandir Colony, Pune

Stacked up neatly, one beneath the other, were several copies of *Bombay Dost,* a magazine for gay people. Veda had read an article about it once, when she was in college. The article talked about this taboo magazine, which was started in 1990, and how it was a lifeline for many homosexuals, and how hard it was to procure a copy, as distribution was tricky. It had to be bought discreetly, and only a couple of vendors dared stock it. It could not be displayed openly, either. The buyer had to ask for it. The vendor would disappear inside and come out with the magazine in a brown paper bag.

Veda could not believe that she was looking at copies of this magazine. Then, the implication of finding it, hidden away, sank in slowly.

Oh my God. Is this what I think it is? This cannot be, she thought, as her heart started beating faster. Her brain had figured out what this meant. She was thrown into a tizzy.

Her mind raced and she found herself drowning in a sea of emotions. One part of her did not want it to be true. She was in denial. And yet, here was proof, staring at her in the face. Was she jumping to conclusions? Could there be an innocent explanation as to why these magazines were here? Was she over-reacting? Perhaps they were here merely because he wanted to read them. Surely, that did not mean he was gay. Or, was he?

It slowly dawned on Veda that she had no idea at all about the man she had been married to for so many months. They had lived under the same roof, eaten together, slept together and lived together physically, but there had never been any real connection between them. What did she feel for him? Affection? Surely, she felt affection? She was fond of him. He was nice to her. Over the past few days, they had been spending a little time together, talking. She was beginning to grow fond of him. But other than that, there was nothing.

There had never been anything.

The realisation hit her with the force of a ten-tonne truck ramming into her. How could she not have *known* all these months?

Her pulse raced. A thin film of sweat appeared on her forehead. She was suddenly aware of every movement of the seconds hand of the clock in their bedroom. Time was mocking her—or so she felt.

Calm down, she told herself. Maybe Bhuwan would walk in and he would tell her that he was holding on to it for a friend? The explanation sounded farfetched in her own head. Maybe there was another explanation.

Then she spotted an envelope in the pile. She opened it, her fingers trembling. She bit her lower lip as she took out its contents. There was a card with an ornately embossed border, and a photograph. She stared at the photograph. She recognised the people in it instantly. It was a picture of a younger-looking Bhuwan with Vikki, probably clicked in their college days. They were wearing the ridiculous acid wash jeans and printed T-shirts that had been a rage back then. It was an innocuous photograph, and Bhuwan had his right arm around Vikki's shoulders. In his left hand he held a cola bottle. Both were grinning straight into the camera. Had she come across this photograph without the pile of magazines, she would not have thought twice about it. Then she looked at the card. She felt she was falling from the top of a cliff when she read the words written with a blue ballpoint pen:

Happy birthday, my darling. Hope you enjoy your present. Can't wait to see your reaction when you open it.

All my love,

V

There was no doubt in her mind now. All those improbable explanations she had conjured up in utter desperation sounded ridiculous and her theories crumbled to dust. *Bhuwan and Vikki were in love with each other.* There were no two ways about it.

Her mind raced back to the time when she had gone out with them to Sinhagad Fort and when they had gone dancing. The way they smiled at each other, their inside jokes, how happy they were around each other—it all made sense now. Whenever Bhuwan talked about Vikki, he was *happy.* It was only in retrospect that she realised it. There was an unmistakable twinkle in his eyes. She had never been able to elicit that kind of smile and joy from him, when *she* was with him.

She thought back to that one time that they had had sex. It was when he was drunk. No wonder he wasn't interested in sleeping with her. She, in her naivety, had thought that it was simply because he was too immersed in his work and too busy. She thought about all the times when he had come home late, only after she went to sleep.

He had never been attracted to her in the first place. Why did he even get married to her? Why did he deceive her? How long had he known?

She felt like a complete idiot. What a fool she was not to have realised this. Was there anyone more stupid than her? All these months of marriage and she had not even known. It occurred to her that it was partially her fault too, for not realising that there was something very wrong with their marriage. This wasn't how marriages were supposed to be. Or perhaps she had been too busy waiting for letters from Suraj to even notice that something was amiss here. She felt she was the biggest moron in the world, the prize-idiot.

She wondered if Bhuwan and Vikki laughed at her behind her back. What did they think about her? What should she do now?

Her mind was in a whirlwind. She placed the bundle of magazines and all the other stuff that she had pulled out back into the chest of drawers, crawled to the bed and lay down. She did not know what to do.

The cook called out from the kitchen saying that he had finished his work and he was leaving.

'Okay, bhaiya,' she called out, surprised at how normal her voice sounded.

Veda felt as if she was drowning. A few days ago, it was Suraj's letter. And now it was discovering this huge truth about her husband. She did not know what to do. She lay on the bed, replaying in her head all the events of her life that had occurred ever since she had met Bhuwan.

Then it became apparent to her why he had been so nice to her. He *pitied* her, and he felt guilty. That was it! No wonder he had found a way for her to work at Sankalp. No wonder he had stood up for her when his mother was nasty to her. It all arose from guilt.

Suddenly, all those out-of-town trips, the long meetings, the slightly evasive answers whenever she asked about his travel—it fell into place. She felt as if she been living in a dark room all this while, and someone had turned on the lights.

She thought about what she should do. Should she call him up at work? What purpose would that serve? She decided she would wait for him to get home. She would stay up late and would not sleep till he arrived.

The minutes ticked by slowly. Her mother-in-law came back from her meeting with her friends. Veda was dying inside, but she made herself sound cheerful and tried to act normal.

'Yes, Maaji. Hmm ... Maaji. That's nice, Maaji,' she went on brightly, barely listening to what her mother-in-law was talking about. She was relieved when dinner was over and she could flee to the safety of her bedroom. She placed the envelope and the card that she had found in the packet beneath her pillow on the bed. She lay back and stared at the rotating fan, waiting for Bhuwan to return from work. She did not know for how many hours she lay there. She saw the moon rising and gazed at the stars from her bedroom window.

Eventually, she heard Bhuwan turn the lock in the door and walk in. She heard the splash of water as he washed his hands and face in the dining room wash basin. She heard him draw out a chair at the dining table and heard him sit down. She heard him hum a tune as he helped himself to the food that was waiting for him on the table.

At last, he entered the bedroom.

Veda was sitting up straight. The reading light was on.

'Oh! You are up so late today? What a surprise,' he smiled, as he walked towards the chest of drawers to place his office bag there.

Veda felt a tightness in her chest and a knot in her stomach.

Blissfully unaware of what had happened, Bhuwan changed into his nightclothes.

'How come you are not asleep today?' he asked, as he got into his side of the bed.

'Long day, Bhuwan?' Veda asked.

Something in her tone made him freeze.

'Umm, yes. The usual,' he replied, as he pulled the sheet over himself and turned to the other side, his back towards her.

She stared at his back. He felt her gaze and turned around to look.

'What?' he asked, a little perturbed now. There was something strange in Veda's behaviour today.

'Bhuwan—I know,' she said softly, in a low, aggrieved voice.

'What? What do you know?' Bhuwan's tone was cautious.

'About you and Vikki. The truth.' Her expression was deadpan, betraying none of the turmoil that was whirling within her.

'What do you mean, Veda?' he suddenly sat up bolt upright.

'This,' she said, as she handed him the envelope from under her pillow.

He took it. She watched his expression change from confusion to recognition to panic.

'Errr … Uh … well …' he stammered.

'No need to hide, Bhuwan,' she said.

Then the dam inside her burst open. She couldn't contain the tears anymore.

She sobbed. Gut-wrenching, large sobs.

It was the sound of heartbreak.

Veda did not know if she was crying because of Suraj's letter or because of what she had discovered. But she could not stop the tears. Her nose ran and she wiped it with the back of her hand.

Bhuwan clenched his fists and unclenched them. He looked helpless. Then he took Veda's hands in his.

'I am so, so … sorry, Veda … I truly am,' he said, struggling to speak. His face was full of regret and pain. He was remorseful. He hated himself at that moment and wished he could disappear.

She stopped sobbing then.

'No ... don't be sorry. I ... I am such an idiot for not even realising it. How ... how long have you known, Bhuwan?' she asked gently, sniffling.

'I am sorry Veda, I am sorry,' he said, over and over.

And then he broke down.

Veda had never seen him cry and she didn't know what to say.

He turned away, got out of the bed and stood near the window, staring out.

Veda sat in silence, waiting till he composed himself. She was filled with a wave of sympathy for Bhuwan, for herself, and for all the people in the world who desperately sought love. How fragile human beings were.

She said gently, 'Come and sit here beside me, Bhuwan. I am not angry with you at all. I think there wasn't any marriage between us. I did not even realise it, Bhuwan. It is not like I made an effort to get to know you, except for these last few days.' Her voice was full of compassion. She knew why she had made that effort too. It was because of Suraj's letter. But she did not tell him that.

Bhuwan turned away from the window and came back to the bed. His eyes were red.

'Nor did I, Veda. I too did not make an effort to know you. But what makes it worse is that I cheated you. I cheated *on* you. I felt guilty about it, Veda. Trust me, I did. But ... but honestly, I cannot live without Vikki. And he feels the same way about me,' Bhuwan confessed.

'True love. I know how hard it is to find. And when you do find it, it is worth holding on to, at any cost,' Veda said.

'At any cost? Even at the cost of cheating someone?' asked Bhuwan.

'I haven't been entirely honest with you either. Remember when you asked me if I had a boyfriend?'

'Yes. You lied? Have you been cheating on me too? Ha!' Bhuwan's voice rose a little.

'No, Bhuwan. I haven't been cheating on you.'

'Then?'

'Well, I don't know how to explain it to you. I kind of like him. I kept telling myself that it was as a friend that I liked him. But now I know I was always in love with him. I was in denial. He is with someone else now. And it is only now that it is clear to me. Do you remember the time you went to Delhi?'

'Ummm ... yes.'

'I met him then. He came out here, and we went to Shaniwar Wada and spent the day together. I did try to tell you about it; I said I had met a friend. You didn't even ask who it was.'

'I remember that day, Veda. Do you know, I kind of suspected it? But I kept quiet because I wanted you to have a good time with your friend. You see, I was not in Delhi at all that whole time. I was with Vikki, in Matheran. We can only get stolen moments like those, Veda. I am so sorry for everything. I feel terrible.'

Veda was silent as she considered what Bhuwan had said. Neither of them had been honest with the other.

She asked him how it had all started, when had they known, what was it like to hide it from the world. She was curious. She wanted to know.

Bhuwan talked. He told her that it had started in college, when they had gone on a hiking trip organised by their college. He had always known that he had felt that way about Vikki. But he had not known whether Vikki was straight or gay. They had been camping in the foothills of the Himalayas, and Vikki had asked him if he wanted to go for a smoke. They had sneaked away from where the tents were pitched and had gone to the woods. Suddenly, they heard a sound. Bhuwan was terrified, as he was convinced it was a bear. He had clutched Vikki's hand in fright. It was a false alarm. It hadn't been a bear, but a fox, which had slunk away. When Bhuwan let go of his hand, Vikki had grabbed him and kissed him on the lips. Bhuwan had been blown away.

'You know, that was such a risk he took. What if I had been straight?' he asked. His eyes took on a dreamy look, as he recalled the incident. Veda could see how much Vikki meant to Bhuwan.

They talked almost till the wee hours of the morning. Strangely, being honest with each other had removed a giant invisible wall between them, breaking the barriers which they themselves had constructed.

'You know, Veda—that one time ... er ... that one time we did it—I am so sorry about it. It was after a fight with Vikki. I was drunk and it was to prove a point to him. I didn't mean to hurt you. I regretted it and I didn't know how to talk about it. So I pretended it did not happen,' Bhuwan looked ashamed as he admitted it.

Veda did not know what to say. It seemed to her like it was a long time ago. Bhuwan had been a perfect gentleman, but for that one incident.

'It's okay, Bhuwan,' she said.

'You—you did not mind?'

'It's in the past. And I knew no better. It's okay,' Veda replied.

'People have so many misconceptions about gay men,' Bhuwan said.

'Such as?' Veda asked.

'Like any other group of people, we homosexual men are attracted only to certain types of men who spark our interest. Everyone thinks that just because we are gay, we will have sexual desire for *all* men. That is absurd! Straight men think they should be afraid of us as we may hit on them, which is ridiculous. Gay men are NOT predatory, and it's not like we cannot control our desires and that we lust after every man,' Bhuwan was earnest in his explanation.

Now that Veda had shown interest in what it was like for him, he wanted to explain it to her. It mattered to him that she understood.

Veda completely understood what he was trying to tell her. 'Yes, it's not as though a straight guy is going to hit on every woman, just because he is a man,' she said.

'Precisely!' said Bhuwan.

Veda nodded.

'Then there's another misconception. People think that gay men are promiscuous and have multiple partners. That's simply not true. Sexual promiscuity is a *human* phenomenon. It's not restricted to men alone—whether straight or gay. We gays are a misunderstood lot,' he said.

'I know. I honestly did not even think about all this. You see, I haven't known anyone who is gay. Then there's the whole law thing. I guess that hurts too,' Veda said.

'Yes—I don't know how what two consenting adults do in the bedroom is anybody's business but theirs. What antiquated laws we have! Vikki and I have discussed this ad nauseam,' Bhuwan admitted.

'I can only imagine what a life of secrecy you must have to lead,' said Veda.

'Oh, you have no idea, Veda. It is always in fear and in secret, hiding from the world. And can I confess something?' he asked.

'Oh! More to confess?' Veda teased him.

Bhuwan smiled. 'You know, to be honest, it is such a relief to speak to you so openly. That's what I wanted to confess—that this is a big thing for me, to be able to speak openly like this,' he said.

Veda looked at him and saw the relief on his face. She thought of all the kind things he had done for her. She thought of how he must have felt growing up with this knowledge. She thought of how he must have hidden it from his parents. She felt another massive wave of understanding and sympathy for him.

'Bhuwan, it is strange—but it is only now that I feel connected to you; you had never let me in all this while.'

'Thank you, Veda, for being this understanding. And I am sorry. I ruined your life,' Bhuwan said emotionally. He placed his hand on Veda's shoulder as he said it.

Veda was quiet again, as she thought about her marriage, the turn of events and where she was at this moment in her life.

Then she said, 'No, Bhuwan. You have not ruined my life. I have my whole life ahead of me.'

Bhuwan told her about his childhood, about how strict Padma Devi had been, and how she meant well. He told her about his connection with his father, and how lost he had felt when he had died, and what a big anchor Vikki was in his life. Veda told him about her own strict father, about how Sankalp meant everything to her, and how depressed she felt about Sanju's death. He listened carefully.

'I hope things get resolved soon. Don't worry, they will,' he assured her.

Veda said that they had to go to Sankalp the next day, for the final decision.

Bhuwan glanced at the clock. It was almost 3 a.m.

'Look at the time!' he exclaimed.

She was surprised. They had been talking for hours now!

She felt no anger towards this man who was her husband. She could empathise with what he had been through.

'Let's go to bed,' he said.

And for the first time since they got married, he put his arms around her.

She rested her head on his chest, and they slept.

Chapter 38

April 1997
Sankalp, Pune

At 5.30 a.m., Veda's alarm buzzed loudly in her ears, jolting her awake. She could barely open her eyes.

She struggled to sit up and nudged Bhuwan.

'Bhuwan, Bhuwan. Could you please tell your mother that I just cannot wake up today to do the pooja? I need to sleep for a bit more,' she mumbled.

'Yes. Please sleep,' said Bhuwan.

She was pleasantly surprised when Bhuwan woke her up at 8 a.m. with a cup of tea.

'Oh, thank you!' She smiled, as she sat up. 'How is it that you decided to let me sleep?' she asked.

Bhuwan smiled at her. 'Well, after last night,' he said, and shrugged, not completing the sentence.

Veda understood. She smiled back at him.

'It is your big day today, isn't it? You said you had to be at Sankalp for the inquiry commission meeting?' he asked.

'Yes. Yes,' said Veda, as she hurriedly got dressed. Kanika rang her doorbell soon after, and they left Kailash Mandir Colony together and walked towards Sankalp. They met Ron at the lobby. He had been waiting for them. Together, they took the elevator and went to Aparna's office.

'There you are. Go wait in the conference room. They will be here shortly,' said Aparna. She was curt and terse in her greeting and she wouldn't meet their eyes. There was something very different about her manner today.

The three of them took their seats in the Sankalp conference room. They did not talk about the meeting that was to take place. Instead, they talked about what they had been doing with their days. Ron had been going around Pune, and he had been filming a lot. Kanika had been sewing and making many things—something she had never otherwise found the time for. Veda just sat quietly, listening to them, trying to focus.

Veda was sleep-deprived, and she had developed a slight headache. She was still in turmoil from the discovery of Bhuwan's sexuality. One part of her was hurting over Suraj's last letter as well. She had not yet recovered or come to terms with either. But she did appreciate Bhuwan's honesty. He had been completely open with her, and that had made all the difference. She could see why he had agreed to marry her—to satisfy his mother's incessant demands. She could see how he too must have been feeling stuck in the marriage, as much as she was. Their fault was that they hadn't spoken up about how they felt.

The door to the conference room opened and Aparna walked in, followed by the three-member inquiry committee. Aparna introduced Ron, Veda and Kanika to them, as they took their seats. She also introduced the members, one by one.

There was Gopal Krishnan, who took his place at the head of the conference table. He was a former education officer and had served as the head of many educational institutions. He looked to be in his late sixties. He was tall, thin, and had sparse grey hair. He wore brown-rimmed thick glasses.

To his left sat Shamshad Begum, who was short and was dressed in a starched cotton saree. It looked like she did not have a neck, and her head was fitted straight to her body. Her hair was pulled back in a thin, tight plait. She had been an advisor to the government education board, and was very senior.

Then there was Khuswant Pandey. He was portly, and the buttons of his shirt stretched tightly across his belly. He was middle-aged, had a shock of black hair, and his moustache stood out on his face like the bristles of a toothbrush. He had been the dean of a college and now oversaw educational content at Sankalp. He took his place at Gopal Krishnan's right.

Aparna sat down next to Shamshad Begum, fiddling with the ballpoint pen in her hand, her brows knitted together, her posture upright and alert.

They looked serious and grim, like they were judges of the supreme court. 'We have already made our report, but we need to officially record your responses on this issue. Hence, please let us know what you have to say,' Gopal Krishnan told them.

If you have already made the report, what is the point of this discussion, Kanika thought. She wanted to say it to him, but held her tongue. There was no point antagonising these people—it was best if she just played along.

'So shall we begin?' asked Gopal Krishnan, speaking as if he was addressing a group of students in a classroom.

Everyone nodded.

'Can you tell me the exact words you said to the deceased, when you were at Ronald's house, with regards to getting the question paper?' Gopal Krishnan asked Veda.

'What?' asked Veda, puzzled. What was this gentleman asking her?

'You heard me, Ms Veda. Our reports say that you encouraged the deceased to obtain the question paper by illegal means. Do you recall the exact words you said?' he asked, looking over the rim of his glasses, reading out from the paper in his hands.

'I did not tell Sanju to get any question paper,' Veda denied the allegation indignantly.

'Please think back, Ms Veda. That is not what the children we spoke to said. We have recorded their responses. There are at least six children saying that you did. Are they lying?' Shamshad Begum took over from Gopal Krishnan.

'How can they say something like that? It's not true,' Veda said. She could not believe what she was hearing.

Shamshad Begum looked through her notes and turned a few pages.

'Many children said that the deceased had mentioned his intention of leaking a question paper, and you wished him luck. Is that true?' asked Shamshad Begum.

Veda struggled to remember. But when Shamshad Begum said that, Kanika recalled it.

'Oh, goodness! I now remember that conversation. That was not how it happened,' she clarified. Then she narrated it as she remembered it. 'Sanju was pestering us to tell him the questions that would be asked in the mock exam. Veda jokingly asked him if he wanted to leak the question paper beforehand.'

'And when the deceased said that he would start a business, Ms Veda wished him luck, and Ms Kanika said he could start a business later, is that accurate?' Shamshad Begum asked.

Veda went pale as she remembered the conversation. This was not how she had meant it, at all. The way Shamshad Begum said it made it sound sinister. It made it sound like she and Kanika had deliberately encouraged Sanju.

'Yes. But we were being sarcastic,' said Veda.

'Veda, haven't I warned you once before too, not to encourage children like Sanju? Do you remember?' Aparna asked.

Veda remembered only too well. It was when Sanju had made drawings in his English test and Aparna had reprimanded her for the remarks she had made.

'Yes, I do,' she admitted, tremulous at the sudden reminder of an incident she hadn't thought would be brought up again.

'Look, ma'am—we were only trying to help these children. We have worked hard with them. You should see the effort we have put in, rather than going into a single inconsequential detail,' Ron spoke up, defending Veda and Kanika.

'This single *inconsequential* detail, as you put it, has cost a life, sir. It has created a black mark on the reputation of Sankalp. Don't you know the value of a life? Just because they come from the poorest sections of society, do you think their lives do not matter?' It was Khuswant Pandey who had spoken.

'I beg your pardon. That was not what I said at all. We *care for* these children. Their dreams, their hopes, their aspirations—all of it matters to us. Very much,' Ron asserted.

'So much so that you kept inviting them to your house,' Shamshad Begum responded. 'Do you have anything to say to that, or are you going to deny that as well?' Her tone was derisive, condescending.

'We did conduct classes at my home. I mentioned it to Aparna when she asked,' Ron said.

'It was *after* the mob of parents came, and I asked you, that you admitted it. Did you take permission *before* you started coaching the children at your home?' Aparna asked.

'No, we did not think that was needed, as we were acting in the best interests of the children,' Ron said.

'How can you decide their best interests, Mr Ronald? If this had happened in your country, do you think it would not have mattered?' Gopal Krishnan's voice rang loud and clear.

Ron was taken aback at what Gopal Krishnan had just said and explicitly implied. He had never looked at it that way. He was as deeply aggrieved by Sanju's death as Veda and Kanika were. He was shocked at the accusation being made—that he didn't care as much because he was from another country.

Veda had controlled herself up to this point. She had silently heard all the allegations that the committee was making. They were so wrong! Could they not see it? Why were they being so thick-headed about it? The sequence of events of the last few days, the mob of angry parents, Sanju's death—everything had affected her deeply. She had endured it with all the strength that she had. Now the committee sitting here, passing judgement on them for no fault of theirs, was too much for her to take. Sanju's beaten up, bruised face, helpless as he lay in the ICU in the hospital, the anguished wail that rang in the hospital corridor when the doctor pronounced him dead, the look on Kanika's and Ron's faces when they heard the news, Sanju's body lying covered in a white sheet—it came to her in clear images. They had worked so hard with these children, going beyond the call of duty. They had put in so many hours of work, because the children *mattered* to them. Couldn't these people *see* that? She had to set the record straight, once and for all. They had to understand what had happened. They couldn't just sit here, quoting the notes that they had made in their reports. How could they not see their side of the story? Nothing that they said was making a difference to them. It seemed that they had already drawn their conclusions and were now looking to fit Ron, Kanika and Veda's narrative into their report and weave it in, in order to just wrap it up. Something in her snapped, and she made a decision that very instant. She *had* to speak up.

'Look Mr Gopal Krishnan, Ms Begum and Mr Whatever-your-name-is. I cannot listen to this anymore. For you, this is just a CASE. An INVESTIGATION which you have to close, REPORTS you have to submit. DO YOU REALISE THAT FOR RON HERE, FOR KANIKA AND FOR ME, THIS IS OUR WHOLE LIFE?' Veda's voice had risen and now boomed across the conference room. The anger and agony in her voice took everybody by surprise.

'Ron could have made his film on Sankalp and gone back to England where a happy, EASY life awaits him. Instead, he CHOSE to STAY. Kanika went BEYOND the call of duty. She was there day and night, always available for the kids, for whatever they needed help with. I was there for them THROUGHOUT. What they thought, what they did, where they worked—all of it MATTERED to US. Do you know—the "deceased", as you keep referring to him, Sanju, had a job at a restaurant run by the henchman of a local goon? Do you know Sanju had exam anxiety? Do you know how Sanju would score good marks in assignments, but when he saw a question paper, he blanked out? DO YOU EVEN UNDERSTAND what that *FEELS* LIKE? Do you know his father used to WHACK him with a belt and he would come to Sankalp with red welts on his back? Do you know he felt UNLOVED by his stepmother? Do you know that his father did not even BOTHER when he was missing! It was Kajol who came to us, PLEADED with us to look for Sanju. She BEGGED us not to reveal that Sanju had stolen money from his father to buy the question paper, which HE DECIDED ON HIS OWN—do you hear me—*ON HIS OWN*. Sanju was beaten up, the money was taken from him. Ron here did not want Sanju's father to lose that money. So he GAVE IT TO HIM—FROM HIS OWN POCKET. DO YOU UNDERSTAND? And you accuse HIM and me and Kanika of not caring? WE CARED TOO MUCH, that was what our fault was! And yes, we broke the rules. We did attend Kajol's birthday party. You should have seen the joy on her face when we gave her the gifts. We did invite the kids to Ron's home and we coached them. Ron made sandwiches for them. The kids LOVED coming there. YOU CAN WRITE ALL THIS IN YOUR REPORT. GO AHEAD. As for me, I am DISGUSTED by this whole committee and the investigation and the rules that you are quoting, trying to make it out that it is our fault. I QUIT. DO YOU HEAR ME? I QUIT!' shrieked Veda.

Everyone in the room sat back in stunned silence at what Veda had just said. It was the absolute truth.

'I quit as well. I don't want to be a teacher at Sankalp anymore,' said Ron, as he pushed his chair back and stood up. He had had enough too.

'Oh, me too. I quit. You can write whatever you want in your precious report,' said Kanika, as she stood up.

Then the three of them, led by Veda, marched out of the conference room together.

Chapter 39

May 1997
Kailash Mandir Colony, Pune

'Look, Bhuwan, you do realise that there is no future in this for us and staying together would only be a meaningless charade to please society, don't you?' asked Veda, as she took a sip of the lime juice they had ordered.

It had been three weeks since Veda had walked out of Sankalp with Kanika and Ron. Every single day since then, when Bhuwan came back from work, Veda and he had sat late into the night talking about this. Today, they had decided to meet at a restaurant near Bhuwan's office.

'Yes, Veda. We have discussed this so many times over the past three weeks. We have talked about it every single day. I do realise it. I know I have to. But this is not easy for me. I don't know how to,' he sighed.

These days, he came back home early. It was as if he was trying to compensate for the past few months. Now that there was no pretence between them anymore, they had become friends, and Veda discovered that Bhuwan was scared.

'Then better to do it soon, isn't it? You are not making it easier by putting this off,' Veda reasoned with him.

'Vikki also tells me the same thing. He says it's best to get it over with.'

'Bhuwan, it's like peeling off a band-aid. It will hurt, but that does not mean you keep the band-aid on forever.'

'Ha! Bad analogy, Veda! But yes, I get your point, I will do it soon.'

'Really?'

'Yes,' said Bhuwan, and took a deep breath.

Ever since Veda had quit Sankalp, Bhuwan could see a change in her. He sensed a fire raging within her, a kind of steely determination, an inner strength that he had never seen before. He had felt in awe of her, when he heard how she had told off the inquiry committee and how she had walked out.

Veda, Kanika and Ron had met almost every day, since that day. They met in the evenings at Ron's apartment. They did not feel like going to restaurants like they used to earlier. Ron was clear about one thing. He would write to the Carman Foundation and tell them exactly what had happened.

'Do you think they will believe your report? Aparna too will be writing to them, won't she?' Kanika asked.

'Yes, but I think I am a bit more closely connected to them than Aparna is,' said Ron.

They had been talking almost daily about starting their own school. They discussed their ideal school, what they would teach, what was lacking in the education system, how they could bridge those gaps and how they could make learning more fun. It was their favourite topic, apart from cribbing about how unfairly they had been treated.

'The more I think about it, the more I am convinced we should,' said Kanika.

'I agree. There's nothing like being in charge of your own place,' Ron said.

'You know, I have a friend who is a real estate agent. I casually mentioned to him that I might start a school and he showed me the perfect place to start one, can you believe it?' Kanika said.

'What? What do you mean the perfect place? And have you been secretly going and looking at spaces without telling us?' Veda asked, smiling.

'Yes! I have,' Kanika smiled back. 'It is an old family home. It is a beautiful, old, two-storey structure, not far from here. I have been secretly dreaming of it. But I don't know how you two will feel about it. I mean—it's an old building. It has a large compound, though. It belongs to a banker's family but no one lives there now. The entire family has settled abroad. Since it is an ancestral property, it just stands there unoccupied, and they don't know what to do with it. My real estate agent friend said that if we are very keen, he can easily get it for us, as he knows the current owners well. He apparently went to the same school as them. I just have to say the word, and it is done.'

'And you tell us now! Why haven't we looked at it already?' asked Ron.

The doorbell rang just then. When Ron answered it, he was surprised to see Kajol. Jadhav was standing next to her.

'Bhaiya, good evening. He wanted to see you,' said Kajol.

'Oh! Come in, please,' said Ron, a bit stiffly.

He did not know what Jadhav wanted. He had not seen him since the day he had led the mob to Sankalp. Did he want money now? Why had Kajol brought him here? When Veda and Kanika saw who it was, these questions immediately ran through their heads as well, and they were instantly on guard. This man had caused enough trouble for them, and now he had turned up at Ron's house. What in the world was Kajol doing, bringing him here?

Jadhav carefully removed his shoes and walked in behind Kajol.

'Namaste, sirji. Namaste, madamji,' he greeted them, bringing his palms together.

'Please sit down,' said Ron.

Jadhav sat on the edge of the sofa. He looked uncomfortable, as if he would get up and run in an instant. He sat with his head bowed.

'Namaste Jadhav, what brings you here?' Kanika asked in Hindi.

'Madamji, I came to apologise. I am extremely sorry. Please forgive me,' he said. He sat there looking down, refusing to look up.

'Why? What happened?' asked Ron, genuinely puzzled. He understood that Jadhav was apologetic.

'Please tell sir that I will return the money,' said Jadhav.

'What money, Jadhav? I don't understand,' Kanika said.

'Madamji. Sirji is so kind-hearted. I was wrong in what I had presumed. When I heard Sanju that day in the hospital, I jumped to conclusions. I ... I also believed everything Rajaram said. I got carried away,' he said. 'Kajol here... Well, Kajol told me the truth about Sanju. I know now that you paid the money out of your pocket so that I should not suffer a loss. And in return, I led those people there and complained against you all. Please, you can punish me any way you like. I am ready to do anything you say. I am sorry.' His voice was full of remorse.

Ron, Veda and Kanika stared at him in surprise. They hadn't expected this. Sanju's father had come to apologise to them, despite his tragic loss. This fact slowly sank in, and they sat there, not knowing what to say. It was Kanika who recovered her composure first.

'Jadhav—what has happened, has happened. It is okay. We have now quit,' Kanika told him.

'Sorry, madamji. Can't you please tell Aparna madam to take you back? Our children—they want to start the classes with you. They miss Sankalp. They keep asking when Sankalp will start, and when the classes will resume. I have come here to request you. My Sanju will never get to attend these classes, but at least the other children of Sitawadi can. You were all doing a good job, madamji. The children miss the summer camp very much. I can talk to Aparna madam, if you like,' he said.

'The important thing here is that you know the truth now. That is what matters. I am glad you don't believe that ridiculous story about us asking Sanju to buy question papers so we could make money off it,' Veda said.

'Yes, madamji. Please forgive me for even thinking like that,' Jadhav said. He was genuinely remorseful.

'It wasn't your fault at all,' Ron assured him.

Kajol had a triumphant look on her face.

'Didi, I gathered the courage to tell Sanju's father the truth,' she said.

'Yes, you did! We are all very proud of you, Kajol,' Ron said.

'Yes, Kajol. You know, it is so important to speak up for what you believe in,' Veda said. It was a lesson she had learnt the hard way.

Kajol revelled in the praise.

In the last week of May, the results of the board exams were declared. Ron, Kanika, Veda and Kajol had been waiting with bated breath ever since they got to know the date on which the results would be announced. On the day, Kanika, Veda and Ron went to the school, as they couldn't bear the thought of waiting at home. They wanted to be there when the results were announced. The school was a single-storey building with just a few classrooms, one next to the other. It was a school with very basic amenities.

Kajol, Sharan and all the other students of Sankalp who had given the examinations were present there.

As soon as they saw Kanika, Veda and Ron, they rushed towards them.

'When can we come to Sankalp, bhaiya?' they asked Ron.

'I don't know. I don't have an answer to that,' replied Ron.

'Please didi ... please bhaiya, start Sankalp again,' they pleaded.

'We will see,' Kanika said.

'Didi—we will go and talk to Aparna didi,' Sharan said.

Kanika and Veda simply nodded at their enthusiasm. Veda's heart was heavy. She missed Sanju. She knew Ron and Kanika were remembering Sanju too. It was what they had talked about on the way to the school.

Just then, an old man, a peon, walked out of the office room of the school with sheets of papers in his hand. He walked to the noticeboard and pinned up the results.

'*Accha result haaaaaai,*' he said loudly and grinned. His front tooth was missing and he waved his hands in the air as he slowly walked away.

A roar of excitement went through the crowd of children who had been waiting. They rushed to the noticeboard and craned their necks to see the results that had been pinned up.

Veda was reminded of her own college results. A few months ago, it was she who had been standing like this at her college noticeboard. It seemed like aeons ago. There was such a lot that had changed since then.

As each child came to see their marks, they shouted in glee, and rushed to Kanika to tell her how much they had scored. Kanika made a note of each child's aggregate percentage in her diary.

At last she got the names and the marks of all the children.

'I don't believe this,' she said.

'What?' asked Ron, his forehead crinkling with worry. What not to believe?

'We have achieved cent per cent results! Hooray!' Kanika said.

'YAY!' shouted Veda.

'Oh, good lord! You had me worried for a moment,' said Ron.

Kanika and Veda hugged each other.

'We did it, Veda, we did it,' said Kanika.

'Come here, let me give you both a hug,' said Ron, as he hugged both of them at the same time.

Later, when they were walking back, Veda said sadly, 'You know what the irony is here? If Sanju was alive, we would probably not have got cent per cent results. He would have not cleared the exams.'

Kanika and Ron nodded.

They knew it was true.

As the days passed, living with Bhuwan and pretending things were fine was becoming increasingly hard for Veda. Bhuwan still had not told Padma Devi the truth.

Veda declared that if he didn't tell her, she would.

'Also, I have to tell my parents, Bhuwan. I think I should make a trip to Joshimath soon. Do you know, I have not gone back there after marriage?'

'I know Veda—and that was my fault. Your parents invited us for the first Diwali after marriage, and for so many other occasions. But I kept making excuses. And now … now I can't even face them,' said Bhuwan.

'I'll tell you what, Bhuwan—let me make a trip back home. I will speak to my parents, and you tell your mother, okay?'

Bhuwan thought about this and finally nodded. That was the best way to do it. If Veda was not around, it would make it less awkward, he thought. Vikki had said that he would be present with Bhuwan when he spoke to his mother, if he wished. He wanted Bhuwan to be with him when he told his parents.

'Yes, Veda. I shall book your flight tickets for you. You know, Vikki said he would be with me when I tell my mother. And he intends telling his parents too,' Bhuwan told her.

'That's good, Bhuwan. And I think I shall surprise my parents. Don't tell them I am coming,' said Veda.

Padma Devi was surprised when she heard that Veda was going home alone. Bhuwan told her that Veda's father had wanted her to come over for a few days as it had been more than a year since she had gone home. He said he couldn't take time off from work, and hence he was sending Veda on her own.

'For how many days will you be gone, beti?' Padma Devi asked Veda.

'Let's see. Bhuwan will let you know,' Veda replied, as she smiled at Bhuwan.

Bhuwan gave her a squeamish, uncomfortable look in return.

Veda was excited to be going back to Joshimath. What a big surprise it would be for everyone back home. On the way to the airport, Veda thought about Suraj. In comparison to the problem of discovering Bhuwan's sexuality, and the aftermath of the showdown with the inquiry committee, Suraj—and her relationship with him—now seemed trivial to Veda. She thought about how the problems we face are only relative in nature, to one another. When we have a problem, it seems big and important. But when we face a bigger problem, the one we faced earlier seems so silly. That was how she felt. Things had changed such a lot in the last few weeks.

It was dusk when Veda arrived at her home in Joshimath in a taxi. The brilliant crimson of the sunset filled the sky. The cedar, deodar and the pines swayed in the cool mountain breeze. Veda felt they were dancing to welcome her. She was elated to be back home. She stepped out of the taxi, took a deep breath and looked up at the sky. She spotted a lone eagle soaring high.

Her arrival caused an excited commotion in her home. It was Ani who first saw her.

'Veda didi?' he asked, unsure for a moment.

She smiled.

The next moment, he yelled, 'VEDA DIDI IS HERE. VEDA DIDI IS HERE!' and he rushed to her to give her a hug. Veda stumbled when Ani threw himself at her, hugging her tight. Ani had grown stronger and taller.

One by one, everyone in her family came out of the house to welcome her—her mother, Vidya, Rudra kaka, Paro didi, Vaish, Vandu and, lastly, her father.

Vidya ran towards her and hugged her so tightly that Veda could barely breathe.

'Oh, didi—so suddenly, how come?' she asked, overjoyed to see her sister.

Then they all hugged her one by one, exclaiming in happiness, asking many questions all at once.

Her father stood in the background and he patted her on the shoulder as she walked in with her suitcase.

'Bhuwan hasn't come. Is everything okay?' he asked, frowning.

Her father was a sharp man, and he had known almost immediately that there was something amiss.

'Umm, let's talk inside, Papa,' she said.

'What happened, beti?' asked her mother.

'I think we need to talk—just you, Papa, Vidya, and me. I have something to say. I don't want to talk in front of the others. It's not a suitable topic for them,' said Veda.

They sat in their parents' bedroom, and Veda talked. She talked about everything that had taken place ever since she had left home. She talked and talked, and her parents and Vidya listened. She told them about how her mother-in-law had treated her, how she thought her world had ended when she had failed in her exams, how she had met Kanika, about Sankalp, about Sanju, Kajol and Ron, Aparna, the inquiry committee. They nodded, listening in rapt attention. She left out the bits about Suraj. She did not want to tell them that.

'Vidya knew some of this. But what I am going to tell you now, even Vidya does not know,' Veda continued.

Then she told them about how she had discovered the magazines, the photograph and the card.

Her father sat in shocked silence. Her mother gasped. 'Hai Ram!' she said, as she hit her forehead with her palm.

Vidya's jaw dropped in surprise.

'Look, Papa, there are no two ways about this. Bhuwan and I have decided that this marriage cannot go on. He will be telling his mother about it.'

Rajinder's face was grim. He could not believe what he was hearing. How was this even possible!

'You should have tried harder to keep him happy,' Rajinder said finally.

Veda could not believe what she had just heard.

'How is it my fault, Papa?' she asked.

'If you had taken enough care of him and kept him satisfied, I don't think any of this would have happened. You should have had a child and everything would have been okay. We wouldn't have had to face this situation then,' Rajinder pursed his lips as he looked away.

'Papa, he was like this long before he met me. And you are wrong—having a child wouldn't have solved anything. In any case, we could never have had a child,' Veda said. She did not know how else to explain her non-existent sex life to her father.

'Oh, beti! If you leave him, where will you go? Will you come back here?' asked her mother.

'I don't know yet, Ma. I don't have an action-plan as of now. Bhuwan is not a bad person. And it is not like I cannot stay there. I will figure it out eventually,' she said.

Then she turned towards her father. 'Papa, I know you mean well and you want the best for your daughters. But with your other daughters, please do not make the mistake you made with me. When it came to my marriage, it was you who insisted and I did not have the courage to refuse you or Ma. Please do not force Vidya to get married. Do not force Vaish or Vandu. I had a dream not a long time ago, Papa. I wanted to be a college lecturer. I wanted to study in Delhi. You never let me go. You clipped my wings. If there is one thing that you can do for your daughters, it is to give them a strong education and make them independent. That is the only way you will be doing what is best for them. Teach them to fly, Papa. Please don't do to them what you did to me. This is a request.' Her voice was full of anguish and sincerity. It was a heartfelt plea from her.

Rajinder looked away. He had no idea of the amount of pain she had been through. He had never seen it from her perspective. Deep down, he knew he was being silly when he blamed her for her failed marriage. He had only seen it his way—the way that his father and grandfather had seen it. Now, listening to Veda speak, he thought about the one-sided view he had held until now. Veda speaking up and begging him like this struck a deep chord in him.

There was a lump in his throat as he heard his eldest daughter's words. They rang true and clear. His eyes filled. He turned to look out of the window and blinked the tears away.

He put a hand on Veda's head and said, 'God bless you, beti.' He stood up and walked out, leaving the others staring after him.

It was the closest he would come to admitting that he was wrong and that his daughter deserved better.

Chapter 40

September 1997
The Rocket School, Pune

Dearest, darling Vidya,

How are you, my darling sister? I am sorry I took such a long while to write you this letter. It has been almost four months since I visited you in Joshimath. Thank you for waiting for me to write to you and giving me the space that I needed. You are the bestest sister anyone can ask for!

First, the BIG, big news. This is not going to come as a huge shocker to you, as we had talked so much about it when I was in Joshimath.

I am separating from Bhuwan and we will be filing for a divorce soon. It is a decision we made jointly, and you can't imagine what a relief it is, to be making your own decisions about whether you want to stay in a marriage or not.

Vidya, the strange thing is, even though we are parting, we have become such good friends. He helped me *understand* him. You know how, over the last few months, I have faced such a lot. Life has thrown all kinds of things at me and I have grown as a person. I feel I have so much more compassion now—more than I did when I got married and moved to Pune.

Over the last few months, I have seen for myself how people who are homosexual are completely misunderstood. Bhuwan is such a sweet, nice and kind guy. He *deserves* to be with Vikki. You should see them together, Vidya. They are so happy. Their relationship is so strong, and a part of me envies that, as I too want that in my life.

Over the course of the last few months, I have met Vikki with Bhuwan many times. The three of us have gone out for meals together. We have been talking a lot and discussing what we should do. Vikki is a very mature, kind and understanding guy, just like Bhuwan is. I had been trying to convince Bhuwan for many weeks, and we agreed that he should tell his mother the truth. While I was with you guys, Bhuwan managed to tell his mother about it. Vikki was with him.

Vikki told me, 'You should have seen her, Veda. She was like a deflated balloon. It was as if she did not know her son anymore.'

When I got back to Pune, my MIL started talking to me and telling me what she wanted to convey to Bhuwan, not addressing him directly at all. It was the strangest thing.

'Maaji, he is the same person. Nothing has changed just because you now know his sexual preferences. Who he is as a person remains the same,' I told her.

Can you believe I said that to her? This alone will show you how much I have changed, and how I am no longer a timid little mouse, though I know you don't need any convincing about that.

My MIL continued behaving in a bizarre way for a few weeks. She wouldn't even look at Bhuwan and would only communicate with him through me. When I saw that it was continuing, I knew I had to do something. I told her that if she had to tell him something, she would have to say it to him to his face. Bhuwan and I had to 'train' her to talk to him.

The second BIG news. I am not living with Bhuwan anymore. It was a mutual decision. I moved out two weeks ago. To make you understand where I am living, let me give you the whole story, even though you know parts of it.

You know how after Ron, Kanika and I walked out of Sankalp we kept meeting every day. We were each other's support system. For a few days, we wallowed in self-pity and the unfairness of it all. Here we were, giving our all to Sankalp. It was bad enough that we got absolutely no recognition for anything we had done so far. What made it worse was that we would have been unceremoniously asked to leave. I am glad I told them off and we quit before they asked us to leave. It was obvious that the inquiry committee was setting us up for that.

Ron seethes with anger whenever he talks about it. You should see him—he physically changes colour when he is angry! He becomes a deep shade of crimson. He wrote a long report to the Carman Foundation about the truth of the matter. They believed his report, rather than anything Aparna might have sent them. They were pleased that he was so involved in Sankalp and had been teaching the children. They value that kind of thing over there. He said that when he was done with his report, he was certain that the Carman Foundation would not support Sankalp anymore. A few days after he sent the report, Ron wrote another detailed proposal to the Carman Foundation, with copies of the mark sheets of the children. He proposed that he would personally head this new school that we were planning to start. Between the three of us, we have enough experience, and we are all capable of making meaningful contributions to change the lives of hundreds of children.

And so, my dear Vidya—drum rolls and trumpets please—**THE ROCKET SCHOOL** was born!

We thought of many other Indian names—like Samarthan, Asha, Umeed—but found out that there are already NGOs with similar sounding or the same names. So we came up with a unique name. Just like a rocket launches into outer space and soars, we hope to give our children a launch pad which will help them 'take off' in their lives.

Ron requested that the Carman Foundation give aid to The Rocket School.

I had told you about Kanika's friend who is a real estate agent, right? He spoke to the family members who own the old house I had told you about. It is an old, two-storey house, with a large compound and many rooms. They did not know what to do with it, and when they heard we wanted to rent it for this cause, they were more than happy. They are delighted that it is being used, as otherwise, it would be neglected and become dilapidated. They offered it to us at a nominal rent. The Carman Foundation is footing the bill for this. Getting it at a nominal cost means that we have extra funds for other activities.

And now—the big surprise—I have moved into this house! We converted one of the rooms on the first floor into a lovely one-bedroom apartment. It has an adjoining study. Kanika helped me do it up. The classrooms are downstairs and I live by myself, upstairs. I must admit it felt rather strange for the first few days. But now, I have gotten used to it. The house has many rooms and Ron loved how Kanika has done up my 'quarters', as he calls it. He said that, when his rental lease expires, he too is going to move in here. Kanika, he and I are converting another set of rooms upstairs into an apartment for him.

The 'classrooms' downstairs are spacious, sunny and cosy. Oh, you should see them, Vidya. Kanika has worked magic here.

We have employed a watchman for the premises and he acts as the gardener as well. We have named our herb garden after Sanju, and have planted a tree in the centre of it, in his name. I sit here at my desk, in my home, and I am gazing out of the window as I write you this letter. The Sanju tree is swaying gently in the breeze. It is a small bush as of now, but with care, it will grow to be a large, shady tree. The contentment I feel is unexplainable.

The children absolutely LOVE coming here. Instead of just being a support facility, we are now applying for permission and getting all the paperwork done to turn it into a full-fledged school. We met the director of education, and he was all for it.

When you come to Pune (and I think you should make a trip soon), you will be staying with me in MY HOUSE. You have no idea how satisfying it feels to say this.

Bhuwan has been very supportive. He and Vikki have started volunteering here on weekends. The kids love them!

As regards Suraj, I am glad I met you and we talked and talked about it. I am more or less sure that he and Priya are a couple now. I can tell from the tone of his letters, and it is only a matter of time before he tells me himself. I think I have lost him forever now. As far as I am concerned, that is a closed chapter, Vidya. Yes, I was in love with him at one point of time. But my circumstances were very different then.

We all change, Vidya. Things happen to us and we change as people. Our relationships change. And as long as this growth makes you a stronger person, a more compassionate person and a kinder person, then that is all that matters.

So, after I finish this letter, I will just write him a short note, wishing them both well. I will tell him that I am happy that he has found a good friend in Priya. If he gets back to me, and wants to know more details, or asks why I wrote such a short letter, then I will tell him over the phone of all the changes that have taken place in my life.

When I think about it, I have lost Suraj and I have also lost Bhuwan. But I have found myself. That is priceless. If there is one thing I have learnt from my experiences, it is this—speak your mind. Have the courage to go for what you want and stand up for it.

Bhuwan did not speak up, I did not speak up and we were thrown together in a mockery of a marriage. Had we spoken up, who knows, I might have been on a different path. I am very proud of myself for speaking up at Sankalp that day, in front of that inquiry committee.

Anyway, much has happened, and we have all grown.

For that, I am grateful.

You know, Vidya, I am very sure that with all the preparations you are doing, you will sail through your civil services exams.

Write back soon.

All my love,

Your ultimate rule breaker,

Veda

Acknowledgements

To my daughter, Purvi Shenoy—with whom I discussed the book at length, and whose inputs helped shape the story.

To my father, K.V.J. Kamath, and my mother, Priya Kamath. Also Satish and Atul Shenoy.

To my early readers, whose inputs were invaluable.

To Madhav Kini (for the tour of the printing press) and Suresh Sanyasi (for the inputs on Maharashtra).

To Dr. Oliver (for the medical inputs).

To hundreds of my readers who shared their mother-in-law stories anonymously.

To my friends in Pune, who provided me with details of the city in the '90s.

To my wonderful editors, Sandhya Sridhar and Deepthi Talwar, who made the book so much better.

To the HarperCollins India team—a pleasure to work with.

To Saurav Kumar for the cover design.

To Manjula Venkatswamy, who takes care of everything behind the scenes, so I can work in peace.

To Lostris, for the exercise and the madness she brings into my life.

About the Author

Preeti Shenoy, among the highest selling authors in India, is on the Forbes longlist of the most influential celebrities in India. Her books include *When Love Came Calling, Wake Up Life Is Calling, Life Is What You Make It, The Rule Breakers, A Hundred Little Flames, It's All in the Planets, Why We Love the Way We Do, The Secret Wish List, The One You Cannot Have* and many others. Her work has been translated into many Indian languages. Preeti is also a motivational speaker, and has given talks at many premier educational institutions and corporate organizations like KPMG, ISRO, Infosys and Accenture, among others. An avid fitness enthusiast, she is also an artist specializing in portraiture and illustrated journalling.